THE WISE CHILDREN

BOOKS BY CHRISTINE WESTON

THE WISE CHILDREN

THE WORLD IS A BRIDGE

THERE AND THEN

THE DARK WOOD

INDIGO

THE DEVIL'S FOOT

BE THOU THE BRIDE

* * *

Juvenile

BHIMSA, THE DANCING BEAR

THE
WISE
CHILDREN

BY CHRISTINE WESTON

CHARLES SCRIBNER'S SONS

NEW YORK

PRINTED IN THE UNITED STATES OF AMERICA

Library of Congress Catalog Card Number 57-11666

CHAPTER

I

A NEON light in the pink ceiling of Mr. Ramond's salon de coiffeur shone on his bald head and sun-lamp tan, giving him a puce-colored tinge, and as she caught his eye in the mirror Delia Dalton smiled faintly. "Not such a tight set this time, please, Mr. Ramond. I prefer a softer curl, so I won't look quite like a terrier when I get home!"

"It will shake out nicely by tomorrow," Mr. Ramond assured her with his flashing smile. He was a handsome Italian with the supercilious air of one who knows he has his clientele eating out of his hand. "By tomorrow you will see, it will be parfect."

Delia wanted to retort that she would like it to be parfect for this evening, but refrained. Really, she thought, I'm a fool. Why don't I insist that he do as I ask, instead of supinely deferring to his idea of what's becoming and what isn't? Invariably, on her visits to Ramond's establishment he and she would engage in a duel of wills, he to exploit to the utmost her quite remarkable good looks, she to try to preserve those small characteristics—imperfections, in his eyes—which she considered essential to individuality. She sometimes asked herself, impatiently, why feeling about it as she did she continued to patronize him to the tune of ten to twenty dollars a visit. Well, the answer was obvious enough: she was beautiful but no longer young, just one of the millions of women who hoped that Mr. Ramond's brand of first aid might preserve them for a brief spell from a fate worse than death: a balding, fading, moustachioed old age.

"So what are we doing for mischief this evening?" Mr. Ramond inquired, intimately. "The t'eater, the Stork Club, movies? Or just home sweet home for a change?"

Delia said that she was spending the evening at home, whereupon he gave it as his opinion that there was no place *like*. Deftly, he fixed the last curling pin in her hair, enfolded her head in a magenta hairnet, adjusted the drier, and after placing a beaten-up copy of *Harper's Bazaar* in her lap, glided away to a neighboring cubicle where Delia heard him engage in an immediate, animated discussion of somebody's aunt's arthritis and his own long-overdue vacation at Miami Beach.

Delia reflected that he was after all a friendly soul and there was no reason why she shouldn't have mentioned that today was her own and her twin sister Frances' fiftieth birthday, that Fran was coming on from California to help celebrate it, and that she, Delia, was giving a small family party in honor of the dual event. "My daughter Veronica and her young man . . . but unfortunately Nicholas, my fourteen year old son, is away at boarding school, so, poor dear, he is going to miss all the fun."

Delia could imagine Ramond's practised response: "And there will be 'ow many candles on the cake? Fifty for you and fifty for your sister? That will make one 'ondred. Impossible! I have not 'ad the honor of meeting your sister, but for you I would say thirty candles at the most. Thirty!" She could feel his rich baritone laugh flowing over her like oil.

Sighing, Delia thought about Fran, whose train was due at Penn Station later in the afternoon. Fran had characteristically neglected to specify the time of her arrival and had merely telegraphed to say she was breaking journey with her friends the Jacksons in Baltimore, and would show up at Delia's some time before nightfall. I hope to God, thought Delia, that Veronica or Katie remembers to hide the liquor in case she gets there before

I do. I should have done it myself, but a year is a long time and one gets out of practice . . . and anyway, why not hope for the best? For the past six months Fran had made a point, in her letters, of mentioning that she was on the wagon and determined to stick to it.

"Not a drop, Delia, darling! Not even sherry in my soup."

It had been a year since the sisters had been together, and Fran's letters, the long-distance calls at New Year's, Easter, Veronica's twenty-first birthday—all these had been normal, loving, gay, and Katie had said hopefully: "Might as well give Mrs. Hight the benefit of the doubt. People *do* reform." But Katie didn't know about the bills, or about those brief, apologetic postscripts: "Darling, I've let Hearn's go for months and they're being very nasty. Could you possibly . . . I'll be careful from now on, I promise!" Or: "The damn bank tells me I'm overdrawn and I haven't got a red cent until Herbert's next quarter . . . could you possibly?" Or: "I feel like hell, asking you again . . . had an awful session with my teeth and the goddam dentist must have used platinum for the fillings. I simply can't face him . . . literally . . . until I've squared his last account and all I've got is seventy bucks to tide me through this month."

Mr. Ramond materialized suddenly in the mirror before Delia.

"Uh uh uh!" he barked richly, and raised two fingers in the V for victory sign. "That frown is not to be worn between such beautiful brows. Remove it . . . ah! That is better."

He vanished and Delia smiled sardonically at her image in the mirror. After all he was paid to help her stay beautiful, and she had been beautiful a long time. She'd miss it when it was gone, and so would a lot of other people. "Lovely Delia Dalton! Do you remember her at thirty—at forty—at fifty, even? You'd hardly know her now."

"Well, she had *that* at all events! And it was something while it lasted, believe me!"

"Can't blame a good-looking woman for hanging on to all she's got left, can you?"

Yes, but would Katie remember to hide the gin, or would Veronica? Careless Veronica, always indifferent to the immediate situation, would she obligingly produce the bottle the moment Fran asked for it? But perhaps there is nothing really to worry about. Perhaps I'll get back to the house in time. Fran was always more apt to arrive late than early, and after all, she *had* been at some pains to state that she was on the wagon. I could do with a cure myself, Delia reflected, grimly. The faith cure. She winced. The ignominy of the thing, the scurrying around shoving liquor bottles out of sight, making excuses for being out of whisky or trying the old dodge of pouring the drinks herself. As though anyone could hope to deceive an old hand like Fran! She never came unprepared, and you could usually bet that there was a flask tucked away in her suitcase. On her last visit Delia had unearthed a pint carefully concealed in a shoe bag. In the old days she used to secrete half pints in boxes of Kotex, and on one occasion a rubber hot-water bag had leaked its tell-tale contents all over her bed.

Trying not to think about her sister, then trying to think about her constructively, with detachment, Delia found herself caught in a familiar treadmill of remembrance and disquiet. It wasn't only the drinking, the debts, the aimless drifting through life waiting for something to happen that never did happen—for the kind understanding man to come along and take Fran off her hands, and off her mind; for some miracle of resuscitation which would restore the Fran of their youth, gay, handsome, vital Fran, always the more tireless and energetic of the two, so that people were in the habit of saying: "Delia is the better looking, but Franny has the *stuff!*" Fran swimming in the icy waters of Lake Umbagog. Fran hiking, gardening, dancing, acting. She'd loved to act and had had great promise in those days. But nothing had come of it except stacks of books relegated, now, to the attic of her house in San Francisco, and a few ancient programs in which she figured in school plays, and later and more briefly in stock companies here and there—New Haven, Lakewood, Ogunquit, and last but not least, wistful memories of having won the praise of George Pierce Baker of Harvard, when she had just turned nineteen.

Fran had started drinking when she was sixteen and she'd been very clever about hiding the fact from her parents, from every one in fact, except Delia. She'd been especially clever about hiding it from Herbert Hight, and it did seem at that time as if the nice understanding man of Delia's later dreams had really come along and taken poor Franny off everybody's hands, and their minds. After her divorce from Herbert in 1936 she'd returned to her acting career in a kind of desperate impulse to clutch at the one positive thing she'd ever known, but the mood was short-lived like all the other odd jobs which she took on between bouts of drinking, sleeping around with any man who'd have her, and nerve racking disappearances designed to punish the people who still cared for her, presumably for daring to care for her at all.

The twins' parents had died before Fran's divorce; her old friends had cooled off, and she was careful nowadays to stick around only with the new, the shoddy, or the unwise. Could a miracle really overtake a woman like Fran? And at fifty? Gazing at herself in the mirror Delia repeated her stricture of a moment before: What I need is a faith cure. Depression, faithful harbinger of her sister's reappearance, threatened to engulf her and she made an effort to throw it off. It isn't, she reminded herself, as if there was anything new in this picture. It isn't as if this thing that is between us hasn't been there long enough for me to have learned to take it. I have taken it. I continue to take it, and it's all right, more or less, as long as Fran isn't around. You can live with a thing like this for years and years and it becomes part of your existence like a physical fact and the sense of crisis wears off, as it must, and you can even persuade yourself that God's in His heaven and all's well with the world. Tell yourself something often enough and you end by believing it. It's what I've tried to do, and most of the time it works. I can keep a secret as long as I am its sole custodian, but to know oneself an accomplice is something else again.

The word brought its all-too-familiar reflex and Delia admonished herself in the mirror: None of that! The drinking was bad enough, the slowly going to pieces—it had to be slowly, Fran's constitution giving points to an ox, but worse than either was the abuse of talent. Delia suffered from an uncreative person's diffidence towards everything that was artistically creative. She believed that the word *gift* was exactly right when applied to the talents of people like Fran and Veronica, and Fran's neglect of her own was, in her sister's eyes, nothing short of criminal. If it were not for Veronica, already at twenty-one well on the way to becoming a writer, the family might as well have been stevedores for all the difference it would have made to the world at large.

But there *was* Veronica . . . and at this point Mr. Ramond returned to Delia's cubicle, removed the drier, and began taking the pins out of her hair. It was a peculiar moonlit blonde which contrasted strikingly with her dark eyes, and as Mr. Ramond drew his comb through its shining length he murmured with feeling: "It is a privilege, always, to fix your hair, Mrs. Dalton. And by tomorrow it will have shaken itself out in those soft waves which you like. Nice, h'm? Mr. Dalton will approve." He had always taken it for granted that she was married, and she had never found any good reason to enlighten him on her widowed state.

Outdoors at last, the air felt fresh and vigorous after the stuffy fragrance she'd breathed for the past hour, and she walked with a sense of lithe well-being intensified by an occasional glimpse of herself in a shop window. Passing a florist she hesitated, wondering whether she should buy herself and Fran a corsage apiece, then passed up the idea as being silly. Maybe Nick would have thought of it, or Veronica? Suddenly, unexpectedly, she had a vision of her daughter's face, young, brooding, and heard the chilling sound of Veronica's voice: "Not reduced to buying orchids for yourself *yet*, are you, Mother?"

Delia walked on quickly. That's unfair of me, she chided herself, ashamed. I've never heard Nonny say that, even if she has said other things almost as bad, often worse. But not that particular thing. This is all because of Fran. The thought of her putting me on edge, stirring up all the sleeping dogs and cats, setting them to bark and mew. Habit. The habit of anxiety, of bracing oneself against God alone knows what. One's own sister, one's own daughter, oneself.

She strolled up the avenue with the October air cold against her face, taking it easy, trying to rid herself of her depression as one tries to free oneself of quicksand. It had not been so difficult when she was younger and her problems still green—too green for the picking. She'd had youth to buoy her up, youth and the temper of youth, and youth's heroic impulse, that great maker of mistakes. She'd believed that all that was involved in any decision was the deciding. Life was a gesture, a succession of gestures perhaps, self-sacrificing, generous, brave, and she'd been equal to the stance expected of her. It had taken her a long time to find out that the trouble with any decision is that one has to live with the consequences. *None of that.*

The traffic lights changed and Delia crossed the street to the west side. Again she paused before a shop window, this one filled with an assortment of horsey paraphernalia. Charles' store, as she had always thought of it, for it was here that her husband bought his riding whips, his cravats, cuff-buttons, Tattersall vests; his books on hunting, his information on hounds, foxes, spavin, bridles, martingales. She'd always imagined the last to be a species of misbegotten calf until Charles uproariously set her right.

Queer how the sight of this window brought him back. His death had seemed to her to be almost as preposterous as everything he did. In the age of automobiles and airplanes, to be thrown off a horse and have one's neck broken in Central Park! Would it have been easier in the long run if he'd gone on living? Could he, for all his vices, still have made life simpler for the rest of us, for the children especially . . . and yes, particularly for Veronica? Well, Charles had not gone on living, and all she could find it in her heart to say to his shade at this moment, was: "Damn it, Charles Dalton, if you're dead, stay dead!"

Veronica would hate her for these thoughts, but Veronica would never know she had them. Veronica had her own thoughts about Charles, and as heaven is my witness, Delia assured herself, I have never, neither by word nor deed, tried to tamper with Veronica's thoughts, or with that grief which she hoards as she does other reminders of him—his old typewriter, his ashtray shaped like a horseshoe, the tiepin he was wearing when he died.

Most of us have to come to terms with grief sooner or later, but Veronica had never come to terms with hers. In the troubled privacy of her own mind Delia sometimes perceived Charles as a sentinel between Veronica and herself, and the fancy lent him a significance he'd never enjoyed in life. Imagine Charles a sentinel! Imagine him significant! She turned from the shop window, reddening at the uninvited memory of his bruises on her arms and thighs, of his savagery in bed. No Casanova nevertheless, nothing subtle about him, least of all in his love-making. The morals of a tomcat, that was about all. And how can I tell Veronica *that*?

It was not as a ghost that Delia saw Charles now, ten years after his death, but rather as an incongruous and inconvenient memory, the hero-sentry of her daughter's being, helping her hold at bay a universe which she would accept on her own terms, or on none. And yet what were Veronica's terms? Perhaps her teachers had known, and her classmates in school and college; perhaps her brother Nick had some idea of those terms—they were fond of each other, he and she. Perhaps her new friend Chris Wallingford had too. Attractive Chris, badly in love. Only her mother had no idea.

And that's because she doesn't want me to have any idea, thought Delia as she walked away from the store with its shiny spurs, its models of men on horseback trailed by microscopic hounds. Veronica doesn't want me to have any idea. She doesn't want *me*, and that's the plain truth of it. Fran can't do without me, but Veronica doesn't want me on any terms at all. And I asked for it long ago and I got it and I'm stuck with it, and one of them is bad enough, but two of them . . .

Her thought veered like a creature trained to servitude, as, exquisite, elegant, she continued up the avenue in the fading light, catching what pleasure she might from the suddenly arrested glances of passers by. Admiration, envy? Even her smile as she registered it all concealed a braced and naked nerve.

CHAPTER

I I

THE Daltons lived in a brownstone house on East 68th Street, a house which Charles had inherited from his mother and to which he had always been sentimentally attached. After his death Delia had wanted to sell it and move to their summer place in Connecticut, or even to California, where Fran begged her to come and stay for a year or two or at any rate until she and the children adjusted themselves to the drastically altered situation. Money was no particular consideration since Charles had attended to that, nor did the little boy, Nick, present any great problem. But Veronica was another story. At the first hint that she might be taken away from the house where she'd spent all her life, the child became hysterical, lapsing into such profound, brooding despair that Delia was frightened and dropped the whole project. Her friends the Bowers—old friends, too, of Charles—had warned her that this might turn out to be pure emotional blackmail, and advised her to use the whip hand while she still had it.

"Let the kid get away with her act now, and you'll have a whole succession of them ever after," Freddy Bowers declared with emphasis, being the old-fashioned type and without children himself.

But it was one of Delia's tenets that any one who uses the whip hand deserves to have it cut off at the elbow, and Veronica, she knew, had been hurt enough—seriously hurt. Consultations with a psychiatrist who used terrifying words like trauma, schizoid tendencies and basic insecurity confirmed her in her decision not to sell the house or even to move out of it, for the time being anyway. With the crisis past, Veronica seemed to recover her equanimity more or less and it seemed simpler thereafter just to go on living where they were.

The evening was dark and a mean little wind whipped down the street as Delia approached her door and saw lights behind the drawn shades of the parlor downstairs. She let herself in just as Katie emerged from the parlor door. "Mrs. Hight is here," Katie told her, adding with quick assurance of voice and glance: "She asked for *tea*. I set a cup for you too, Mrs. Dalton."

Delia thanked her. They had been in cahoots for many years.

Fran called from the parlor: "That you, Delia?"

Delia went into the room and Fran rose from her chair. The sisters embraced, clinging for a moment in the embarrassed affection which overtook them at such moments. If only, Delia thought, we could always meet only to part! Hating herself, she held Fran away and smiled at her. "Dearest, how are you?"

"All right. And you? What a question!" Her hair, always much darker than Delia's, was rimed with gray, like dirty frost. She'd been the first from their mother's womb, but those ten minutes had swollen painfully into ten years at the least. There were pleats under her eyes, and a beauty which once had matched her twin's hung on her now like an old dressing gown.

"How do you manage it, Dele—love, glands, vitamins—what?"

Her voice was still exciting, thrilling even and she seemed somehow or other—probably from not eating enough—to have retained her figure. Delia inventoried these initial facts by a kind of osmosis, without really looking.

"Glands, probably," she said gaily. "The Cranshaw system, of which you have your fair share, don't forget. When did you arrive? I'd have stayed home if I'd only known. Have you seen Nonny . . . No, that's right, she said she was going to Miriam

Werth's for a little while this afternoon. How were the Jacksons?"

Well, what did one say to one's sister after a separation of a whole year and the Lord only knew what obstacles to perfect communion between them? Parlor chat was invented to get one over the bumps. Nothing else would serve. How to say: "My God, Fran, what have you done to yourself since I last saw you?" One knew without even looking at her what she'd done to herself. She, and no one else.

While speaking, Delia removed her cape and hat and tossed them with her pocketbook on a corner of the sofa. She had a sudden feeling of tears. That well-remembered face, dark where hers was fair, darkened now like an old shoe, the beautiful eyes exactly like her own veined with red, and uncertainly moving, as though they'd come loose in their sockets. Worse than last year . . . or does it only appear so to me, vulnerable as I am until habit exerts its muscle and I teach myself in one simple lesson, not to mind?

Fran was gay about her journey and about the Jacksons. Delia came back to the tea tray and poured herself a cup of tea. Fran's cup, half empty, stood on the table beside her chair, a cigarette burning itself out in the saucer. She never smoked one more than half through, and somehow just that one little thing seemed to sum her up all over again. Everything half done, half finished, half thought through, half loved, half lived.

"They were fun in a way, the Jacksons, though I never can be sure of my old pals, and it did strike me as if Lee and Marie are a bit on the stuffy side these days."

"Stuffy?"

"Success, probably. You know what it does to people, sometimes."

"I can imagine. More tea, dear?"

"No, thanks. I can't get over how you look, Delia. You don't seem to have changed a bit since last year, unless it is to grow younger." Her smile was genuine. Delia felt her love like something wistful, reaching out.

"It's all due to my Mr. Ramond," she said, deprecatingly. "Comes out of a bottle." Then, hastily: "You know—hair rinse, contour lift, lotions and so on."

"And no love, m'm?"

Delia had herself in hand now and could smile without strain. "Silly. Love at fifty, and with two grown children?"

The words brought a shock of recollection and they embraced again. "Happy birthday! Imagine forgetting it."

Fran released her and said: "Remember when we were sixteen and the dresses Mother bought us? Blue for you and pink for me, with white rickrack trimming, and those cute straw hats?"

"And Father gave us wrist-watches. I've still got mine somewhere."

"I ruined mine swimming with it on in Umbagog."

"I think the birthday I enjoyed best was when Mother and Dad brought us to New York to see *Rose Marie*. Remember? A matinee, with lunch at the Plaza first, and afterwards a drive through the park in that old carriage with the Irish coachman and the parents sentimentalizing over their courtship when Father took Mother driving in *his* father's buggy along lonely country roads."

"And he was embarrassed because the horse kept breaking wind!"

Delia laughed. "Oh God! I can even remember that evening in the park. It snowed."

It was getting easier. With every minute that passed, with every triviality uttered, it was getting easier. At least Fran had gone to the trouble of buying herself a good-looking new suit and some decent shoes. And she had never, even at her worst, lacked a kind of elegance. I'll get after her about it, Delia told herself with reviving optimism. I'll make her go to Ramond's and do something about that hair and that skin . . . bring back her self respect, feed that numbed vanity of hers so she'll begin to care again.

"And now," Fran said with elaborate casualness, "I've got a bit of news for you." She finished quickly: "I've rented my house!"

"How come?" *No*, cried her heart, panicking. *No, not that! Not indefinitely, without a period, no exit, no . . . no promise of an end!*

"People I know in San Francisco, and since I was coming east to see you, it seemed like a good idea to stay on a while and make a profit out of the house at the same time."

Fran went on to speak enthusiastically of her tenants, the trustworthy kind who appreciated a good thing when they saw it. "I wish now that I'd made it two hundred a month instead of one-fifty, but they were so nice, I didn't feel like gouging them."

"Of course not. You were lucky to get the kind of people you can trust. It's such a lovely place. And now you're here . . . darling, I'm so glad to have you!"

Say it and perhaps you'll mean it. Your own sister, your twin. And you're all she's got, remember that. Not that you're likely to forget it. Nor is she.

Fran smiled. "I'll stay with you a few days, if you'll have me. Later, I shall move to the old Leonard, as usual."

"You certainly will not. Your room's been ready for you for ages."

Fran looked at her quietly, then shook her head. "Thank you, darling, but you know me. I like my independence, such as it is. Besides, I want to scout around and find something to do."

"Fran."

"Anything wrong with that idea?" Fran laughed. "I had a job back home. Book store and rental library, but they paid nothing, and anyway I'd have had to give it up when I came east."

"Well, don't let's discuss it now. Where's your suitcase?"

"Katie took it up, I guess. Heavens, I almost forgot! I have a present for you."

"And I have one for you, but I was going to save it for tonight."

"I can't wait to give you mine. I got it at Bonniers this afternoon while waiting for you."

Fran went into the hall and reappeared with a white pasteboard box tied with ribbon. Stooping, she kissed Delia lightly on the cheek.

"How did it happen Veronica's young man didn't fall for you?"

"Chris?"

"He sounds promising, I must say, through your letters. And how opportune for Veronica that his father should be in the publishing business!"

"Chris is coming for dinner tonight, so you'll meet him." Delia sat with the box on her knees and looked at Fran. "You missed Nonny, I guess."

"I had a glimpse of her just before she left the house to see Miriam. She condescended to stop and talk awhile. Will you tell me why she scorns lipstick and gives the impression of having just sawed off her hair with a bread knife?"

"She's hardly the vain type, is she?"

"Pure literary affectation if you ask me, though I'm glad to see she doesn't go in for the Greenwich Village style—those god-awful flat shoes and the Arab gelding hairdo."

Delia began undoing the elaborately-tied ribbon and said: "You'll like her young man. He's twenty-three, but very mature in a civilised way that's rather unusual in the young nowadays."

"Not a pantywaist, I trust?"

"Certainly not. And very much in love with Veronica."

"And she with him?"

"You've seen her. What'd be your guess?"

"I had no time to judge. She had that date with her friend, the anthropologist, Miriam. Somehow Nonny didn't give the impression of being in any great state of euphoria, if you know what I mean."

"It's her book," Delia said, picking at a knot. "I've written you how hard she's worked all year. It's bothered me a bit because she's seemed to exclude so much . . . even Chris, at times. It's probably going to be all right, though. One can't judge her as one might other girls."

She moved aside a caressing mass of tissue and lifted out a crystal bowl steeped in light and shadow, sensuous to the touch, lovely, and without question expensive. "Fran!"

"I had to buy it," Fran said, looking pleased. "I felt it ought to belong to you."

"It's beautiful, but I hate to think what you must have paid."

"So do I. Let's skip it."

Delia set the bowl on the table and carried the box and wrappings away to deposit in a waste basket beside her desk. It was like Fran to have bought something fine and expensive to give her; it was part of her recklessness, her generosity in everything, the good things and the bad, the right and the wrong. And I'm the one person who matters to her and to whom she matters. All this show of independence, this living in hotels, this parade of friends, visits here and there—and not always the welcome guest.

"Tell me about Nick," Fran said as Delia came back to her chair. "You know, I believe I miss him more than I do any of you."

"Nick called last night to wish us many happy returns. He sent you his special love."

"The pet! What's his latest gambit? Last time I was here it was a convict haircut, bebop and baseball."

"This year it's trout fishing and Marilyn Monroe."

Katie came to remove the tray and Delia asked her whether Veronica had come home. The maid looked surprised. "Veronica came through the kitchen not five minutes ago, and went up to her room."

When she'd gone Delia met her sister's gaze and shrugged. "Funny Veronica didn't come in to see us."

"She was nice enough to me," Fran said, lighting a cigarette. "In her way, which is never any one else's. What's the novel about, have you any idea?"

Delia laughed. "You know perfectly well she never speaks about her work to me, and of course I wouldn't dream of asking questions."

"Isn't it time you put your foot down?" Fran said, frowning.

"Put my foot down on what? She's always been like that, about everything." She added thoughtfully: "It does seem, though, as if she'd been rather more so than ever during this past year. Touchy, nervous, keeping me more than ever at arm's length."

There was a brief silence, then Fran said: "You wrote me that you'd talked to a psychiatrist, but you didn't mention what came of it."

"Nothing, specially," returned Delia, sighing. "He couldn't give me any worth-while opinion without talking to Veronica, and she has already flatly refused to go near a psychiatrist. I've hinted that it might help both of us, but that merely inspires her to sarcasm, so I've let it drop."

Fran glanced away. "You were frank with him, I suppose? I mean, absolutely?"

"Absolutely? No, how could I be? And even if I had been it wouldn't help much if Veronica was not prepared to cooperate."

Fran said slowly: "I was thinking of you, not of Veronica."

"It sounds almost simple-minded, doesn't it, for me to say that all I really want is for the child to be happy?"

There was a further pause, then Fran said: "Perhaps now she's finished her book and got herself a lover, she'll straighten out."

Delia felt the surprise of this like a small chilling heat in her breast. "Finished her book? Since when?"

"Friday. She told me so herself this afternoon."

Delia stared at the crystal bowl which although empty seemed to be filled with a mysterious element, mauve and mercurial, to its very brim. "This is news to me," she said at last, on a meditative note. "I rarely see her except at meals, and she hasn't said a word about finishing the book."

"I took it for granted that you knew!"

"One would, wouldn't one?"

Fran stared at her intently. "Delia, does it matter so much? I mean, after twenty years?"

Delia smiled absently. "Twenty-one, are you forgetting?"

She continued to study the bowl, suffused now with a saturated darkness whose outer rim floated like phosphor in the darkening room. She rose suddenly, dropping her cigarette into the ashtray at her side. "It's six o'clock, Fran. Time we dressed for dinner. Chris Wallingford should be here any minute."

Fran rose too and put her arm through her sister's, saying with a touch of harshness: "Veronica has hurt your feelings—I can see she has! Damn her guts . . . I wish . . ."

Delia pressed her arm quietingly. "Not my feelings . . . not really. I'm just puzzled, that's all. She acts as though she were trying to hide something, and what in the wide world can *she* have to hide?"

Without waiting for Fran to answer she stooped and picked up the bowl. "My dear, it's so beautiful! Look, I can turn it upside down and it loses nothing of its light! I better warn you I haven't got anything nearly so nice for you."

For a moment it seemed that Fran was on the verge of an emotional outburst, but she controlled herself, and they left the room together, talking lightly of other things.

CHAPTER

III

"Coffee?" asked Miriam Werth, and poised a battered enamel coffee pot over Veronica's cup, one of those enormous objects with a floral design and the pronoun HE in Gothic gold script. Miriam's own cup was its twin in size and shape, marked SHE, also in Gothic gold.

"Thanks," said Veronica. "God, this should make my hair curl. How long's it been brewing, Mim?"

"Since morning. There's no point in drinking coffee unless you want it to do something for you."

"There's no point in doing anything unless you want it to do something for you!"

"Live dangerously."

"Always do what you are afraid to do."

"Go West, young man, go West, and let who will be clever."

They laughed, and Veronica, holding the cup in both hands, wriggled her behind into the cushions of Miriam's dilapidated sofa, drawing her dungareed legs under her. Leaving her mother's house after greeting her aunt, she'd taken the subway to Fourteenth Street and walked over to Miriam's apartment which comprised a room, a bath, and a kitchenette—each, including the bathroom, crammed with bookcases, African masks, strips of batik, and odds and ends of Mayan sculpture, for Miriam was studying for her doctorate in anthropology and seemed to have little space in her home, or her thoughts, for much else. She was a tall finely built girl a year or two older than Veronica, with magnificent eyes behind her spectacles, and an air of such total relaxation as to give the impression, at times, of being a somnambulist. She and Veronica had been friends at college and it was through Miriam's brother Jerry, a senior at Harvard, that Miriam had met Chris Wallingford and, several months later, introduced him to Veronica. Miriam had been regretting this, silently, proudly, ever since.

"So you've finished it," she said, shovelling three spoonfuls of sugar into the cup marked SHE. "Almost a year, h'm? How's it feel, sort of like having a baby?"

"Oh God!" screamed Veronica. "Must you? It's what Fran asked me this afternoon. Why will people bracket books and babies in the same breath? You wouldn't ask a man a question like that, would you?"

"There are some men I'd like to ask a question like that," Miriam said with a grin. She glanced at her friend. "And now what?"

"I'm not sure. A publisher, I suppose."

"Chris's pop?"

Veronica looked uncomfortable. "That's Chris's idea."

"Sounds logical. Might as well keep it in the family."

Veronica took a long noisy sip from her cup. "I don't know about that. I'm all mixed up about it, as I told you."

"Why not let Chris see the manuscript? He'd give you the straight dope, you know he would."

Veronica stared hauntedly into space. "I have this thing about letting people see what I've written. You are the only person I'd trust. I've told you so."

"I should be flattered, but you haven't let me see it either. Listen, don't think I don't understand how you feel about it, Nonny. The wrong word; the wrong reaction and poof! It can have horrible consequences. But after all, Chris!"

"He might hate it and get off one of his nasty cracks, and then I'd probably tear the whole thing up."

Miriam spooned some of the sludge off the bottom of her cup and ate it thoughtfully. "Well," she said presently, "I take it you mean that if the publishers should turn it down no one else is going to have a look-see. Right?"

"I suppose so."

"You're being awful arty-party about the whole business, if you ask me. Unprofessional. And I'm surprised, really. I've read other things you've written and I wouldn't have told you they were darned good if I hadn't thought so. Harper's thought so when they took that story of yours. Why this sudden accentuation of coyness over the novel?"

Veronica reddened. "How often have I got to tell you that it's just this feeling I have, that when a thing is *out*, I mean published, then it's out and beyond one's control. One can't undo it, unwrite it, even if one should want to."

"If it's good, and knowing you I'd bet that anything you wrote would be good, why should you want to unwrite it?"

"I might, that's all."

It isn't all, Miriam thought as she drank her coffee. It isn't all by a long shot. She stared across the cluttered room at a mirror on the further wall. She and Veronica were grouped in it, crouched on the tumble-down sofa, looking like a pair of waifs. Veronica was still wearing her trench coat with its alpaca lining, Miriam's apartment being on the cool side and the tiny cannel coal fire in the grate giving out about as much heat as a lighted cigarette. Cold and coffee had flushed Veronica's cheeks and given a brilliance to her eyes, a clear brown, matching the brown of her hair. Cropped short, this hung shiningly against her cheeks like two softly-folded wings. Except for her coloring, thought Miriam, her likeness to Delia was very marked. Veronica glowed against the drab cushions like a youthful odalisque and the older girl, lowering her eyes over her cup, thought falteringly: She doesn't even have to bother to make the best of herself. She's got the family looks, and she could be a knock-out. No wonder Chris . . . that, and her talent, and all that latent wildness. She keeps him stirred up and wondering, like a woman out of a Yeats poem, and he's almost as arty-party as she is, and I'm too damned sensible for my own good—or for his.

Veronica said abruptly: "I don't know. I might not even take it to Donald Wallingford. I might just destroy it."

Miriam dredged more coagulated sugar from the bottom of her cup.

"Have you ever," she asked slowly, "thought it might be worth while to go somewhere and have yourself analysed?"

Veronica laughed. "You and Mother! She's been after me to do that ever since I was old enough to crawl. Can't one have honest doubts about oneself without being considered manic-depressive or something?"

"Depends."

"The world is full of people who think they can write."

"Well, if I felt that way about it," Miriam said, shrugging.

"If you felt that way what would you do?"

"Wouldn't write."

They were silent, listening to the sound of traffic on the street, to a woman forlornly calling a cat. Veronica said: "You get a kind of protective feeling about your work. When you've done something like writing a book, it suddenly has its own life, its own independence, no matter what the impulse that made you write it. You even forget about the impulse, or the inspiration, or whatever, in the job of creating." The color had deepened in her cheeks.

"One shouldn't," she said, "have to apologize for anything one creates. One shouldn't even have to explain."

Miriam waited, sensing a confidence, perhaps a confession. After five years of friendship Veronica could still mystify her, shift the ambivalence of her feeling one way and the next. There were occasions when she told herself she wouldn't care if she never saw Veronica again, yet she knew that she could not bring

herself to call it a day, for without Veronica when would she ever
see Chris? And there were days and nights—nights especially—
when she damned them both for her dependency upon them, for
their utilization of her as an audience of one, a convenient aphrodisiac for their love.

As Veronica remained unaccountably silent, Miriam said
coolly:

"I'll tell you something. You sound to me a bit as if you had
reservations about this novel of yours. I don't mean aesthetic
reservations. I'm sure you'd take care of those. I mean something
else, quite different."

Veronica turned slowly to look at her. "What do you mean,
then?"

"You sound as if you were on the defensive about something.
I'd even say that you were ashamed. And not because you fear the
book is no good, either. Perhaps because it might turn out to be
too good."

Veronica's gaze had a deceptive steadiness. "Is that the way I
sound, honest?"

"It's the way you sound to me. I could, of course, be wrong."

Veronica continued to look at her. "Would you read it if I. . . .
if I brought it to you?"

Miriam laughed impatiently. "If you wanted me to, yes, of
course. But I'm not sure that I'd take the responsibility."
She hesitated, then finished: "You've made me self-conscious
about it, and I hate mysteries. If I read it now I'd still tell you
my honest opinion of it, but I'd be scared to death of the consequences."

Veronica put down her cup and sat for a minute with her
hands dug into the pockets of her coat. "You make me feel like
a fool," she said at last in a low voice. "I don't mean to be one.
My reaction to whatever you had to say about the book would
depend on your reasons for liking it or not liking it." She added
as an afterthought: "Naturally."

"Naturally nothing! You'd have *your* reasons for rejecting anything that I might have to say."

They stared at each other, then Miriam smiled. "Look, why don't you let your mother read it? She's no constipated intellectual like the rest of us. I think I'd rely on her judgement every time."

Veronica gave a wild laugh. "*Mother* read it? She doesn't even understand me—do you imagine she'd understand my book?"

She rose violently to her feet. "Mother's a dope! Oh, I know you like her, but to suggest that I depend on her judgment!"

Miriam continued to sit, staring up at her friend. "I do like Delia. Why shouldn't I? She's always been swell to me. And I wouldn't hesitate to ask her opinion on anything."

Veronica took her beret from a neighboring chair, where she'd flung it when she came in. "Just because she brought you a baked custard when you were sick?"

Suddenly amused, Miriam rose. "It was a damned good baked custard too! If your book's as good . . ." She broke off and put her arm round Veronica's shoulder. "What's come over you, Nonny? You used to have a sense of humor!"

"I feel awful," Veronica muttered abjectly, and leaned her head against her friend. "Awful. Maybe I worked too hard or something. Maybe just finishing a book always makes you feel like this . . . as though all of a sudden it was hardly worth while."

"Nuts," Miriam said, and held her awkwardly, wishing for the old days of sincerity, when she would have known how to give the comfort and the reassurance Veronica seemed always so chronically to need. Well, she had Chris. Let Chris give it to her. Let Chris hold her in his arms and tell her how wonderful she was, how little she had to fear for her art and the opinion of the world. He could be good at that when he felt like being. A born lover, which he always felt like being though not always with the same girl. How long before Veronica found that out?

They moved apart and towards the door and Veronica smiled shamefacedly. "Won't you change your mind and come, Miriam?

There's lots of food. And it would leaven the boredom for me."

"You expect to be bored with Chris?"

"No, but I expect he'll be bored with Mother and Fran. Family stuff, you know."

"I can't," Miriam said, opening the door on to a dark passage and precipitous stairs. "I've got to work. It goes on and on and I sometimes ask myself whether it'll ever get done. Not like a novel, you know. One has to do so darned much research."

Veronica laughed queerly. "Not so much unlike a novel, at that."

She started down the stairs. "Chris'll miss you. I told him you'd be having dinner with us."

"Bring him around, then."

"He has to go back to Cambridge Sunday."

"Then come yourself. We'll have pastrami on rye, and beer. O.K.?"

Riding uptown in the subway Veronica felt the rock and sway of the train like hands wrenching her apart and putting her together again in an unfamiliar mould growing more familiar by the minute. For a whole year she'd lived in a separate world, more real to her than the real. Now she was back once more in the real or what passes for reality, and this gave her a near-sighted feeling, a peering feeling, a sense of estrangement from both. It was like coming back to a place from which one has been a long time absent, finding the old landmarks, the old belongings untouched and unchanged, cloddishly unaware that magic has transfigured them, briefly, set its seal in their dull substance, and passed on.

Across the seat from her a row of figures lurched and strained as though they, too, were being torn asunder, yet all remained chained to their seats. Above their heads in the advertising fresco a blonde with a fondant complexion, her breasts packed like marshmallows into Perfection Plus bras, smiled with faithful realism at a bottle-fed nurseling chewing gum as a substitute for the real thing. Veronica's gaze slanted downward, following the uncoiling descent of a laddered nylon stocking as it sagged away from a fat bruised knee. Directly across from her a blind man sat leaning on his white cane and at him she gazed for a long time, wondering at his thoughts, seeing him as one of an elite for his uncommonness, a kind of aristocrat in the midst of these other blind.

Arrived home, she let herself in the front door and went quietly upstairs to her room. It was dark, and as she switched on the light the whole place sprang golden around her, and she suffered a momentary loss of balance, a faint shock as of finding herself where she somehow least expected to be. For the past twelve months she'd scarcely left this room and its familiar contents—the bed that used to be her mother's when she was a girl, the maple bureau and chairs which had come from the Cranshaw farm in New Hampshire, the desk and typewriter belonging, once, to Charles. One wall was lined with bookshelves filled with his books and her own—more of hers than of his. They made a weird company between them: *The Brothers Karamazov* and *Mr. Jorrocks,* John Masefield and Stendhal, Camus cheek by jowl with Ellery Queen. On the mantel a photograph of Charles gazed supervisingly into space, and the last present he had given Veronica trooped from one end of the mantel to the other—a complete hunt in miniature, with huntsmen, horses, hounds, and the fox, which last had fallen into the fire and had been retrieved in the nick of time, its brush a stub of shining lead.

Veronica went to the desk and unlocking the top drawer, took out her manuscript in its new pasteboard binder. She opened it at random and immediately a fearful excitement made her blood race. Sentences she scarcely remembered having written rose out of the neatly typed pages; entire scenes recurred with the suavity of long rehearsal, phrase following phrase, chapter following chapter—fitting, fitted, planed down to a right and essential whole, she asked herself with new amazement, was this thing really hers? I shall close my eyes, she said, like the blind man with his white cane, back there in the subway, and see it with my private genius in my personal darkness, tapping with the white cane that knows the edges of things, not needing to ask the way of anyone barging proud-eyed and know-it-all, knowing nothing, blinder than the blind.

"All's fair in love and war!" Charles reminded her jovially, over her shoulder, from his picture on the mantelpiece. His ipse dixit in a nutshell. Once when his horse Pedro kicked him on the shin and she'd cried with fright, thinking his leg broken, he'd laughed and admonished her: "All's fair in love and war!"

Meaningless like most of his gems and under the circumstances, but at least he lived in no fear of plagiarists. "An attractive woman is like a well-bred horse," or "You've got to give a young thing it's head once in a while . . . ride it with an easy rein!"

The room seemed to shrink round Veronica, its walls to crowd upon her. Love and war, the long silent war of listening, hearing, seeing, finding; the war of shock and discovery, of loving and being loved and not being loved and not loving, and above all the war of hyprocrisy, that dulcet poison on which Charles had fed, unknowing, to the end.

"He sounds," Miriam had remarked once after listening a long time to what Veronica said, "he sounds—your father, I mean— like such an improbable sort of man!"

"Why improbable?" Veronica demanded, hostile at once in her immediate defense of him.

"*Improbable*," Miriam repeated, laughing with some embarrassment. "To be your father, I mean. To have been Delia's husband. He doesn't seem somehow to belong in the picture at all. You know, *horsey*. Cigars. Walking around in riding boots in Delia's house!"

"It wasn't Delia's house. It was his. Everything we have was his."

Miriam had stuck, though politely, to her guns. "I still think he sounds improbable to be anybody's father. But of course you should know. He was yours, after all."

That was two years ago and coming home from Miriam's

Veronica had locked herself in her room and cried, as she had not cried for a very long time. Was she then his only friend?

"It's a wise child that knows its own father," Fran had volunteered years and years ago, as, somewhat drunk, she looked from the photograph of Charles to Veronica, and, taking the latter's small pointed chin in her hand, repeated besottedly: "A wise child, all right. More than he was, poor old Charles. You do look like him though I must say, in your own funny way. Aping, probably. That 'counts for most likenesses, so I'm told. If there's any accounting for anything, anywhere, any time."

The damned parables in which grown-ups talked, drunk or sober, as though, at eleven, you were still an embryo in its caul. There is a book on a certain type of mental disturbance, postulating a theory that children, before birth, might be aware whether they are *wanted*, or not wanted. This book had its place in Veronica's bookcase next to Otto Rank and Theodor Reik, on a shelf just below the poetry, the old school text books, the collected stories of Salinger and the novels of Turgenev and Virginia Woolf. Charles frequently offered the information to his friends, and not without complacence, that his daughter had learned to read before she could walk and that she'd ruin her goddam eyes, but that was long before she discovered Rosen, Rank, and Reik. Charles would have thrown *those* out of the window at the pigeons if he'd caught her reading them, but he died before she graduated from the *Wizard of Oz*, via Saki, to À *La Recherche du Temps Perdu*. He died without having read more than a baker's dozen books in his life. Reading, he said, always made him nervous. It was apparently the only thing that did. And like his son Nick he held that unless a book were good for a laugh it was good for nothing. Would he have laughed at this one under Veronica's hand, this with its sardonic title: "Who is Silvia?" Would he have guessed, and, laughing, ruffled her hair and given out for the uncounted time that all was fair in love and war?

Abruptly, her cheeks blazing, Veronica picked up the manuscript and carried it to the fireplace. She lifted the clayball from its Cape Cod lighter on the hearth and set it under the stacked kindling and at that moment heard Delia's voice outside the door: "Veronica!"

Veronica crouched before the grate, her heart pounding.

"Veronica dear, are you almost ready?"

"I'm getting dressed, Mother. Be right down."

She waited until she heard Delia's footsteps pass on down the hall, then rose and went back to the desk, replaced the manuscript in its drawer, locked it, and hid the key. Undressing quickly she went into the bathroom to take a shower.

CHAPTER

IV

DRAGGING the comb through her short damp hair, Veronica thought: "I was a fool to tell Fran I'd finished the book. She's sure to have told Mother, and there'll be talk about it tonight in front of Chris. Why can't I make up my mind about things . . . if I don't want to tell something, don't tell. 'If you think there are too many lousy writers in the world and you might be one of them, quit writing,' says Miriam. 'If you want to go to bed with Chris, go to bed with him.' Just like that. Just as easy as that."

If . . . if . . . if! But there were no ifs in Miriam's bright lexicon, or if there were she kept them under her hat. Did Miriam have a case on Chris? Veronica frowned, tossing back her hair. I'd almost bet on it. He was seeing her pretty regularly before I came along, and she somehow managed to arrange it that his visits never coincided with mine until that afternoon by the purest accident, and then you'd never have guessed, not from either of them you'd never have guessed.

She thought earnestly about Chris. Chris loves me. He's said so, and I can feel it in him. He loves me and he resents me. My talent especially, what he calls my precocity. He can be damned patronizing and why not admit that I'm a bit afraid of him? He's clever and he can say sharp, hurting things without apparently meaning to. And at his most generous he holds something back.

Urging me to send my manuscript to his father, he still didn't succeed in making it sound quite sincere! I can recognize my own fears in him, the fears one is ashamed to acknowledge even to oneself, the fears of someone else's good luck which for some reason seems always to pose a kind of threat to one's own. Intellectual honesty . . . my God!

The doorbell rang downstairs and she heard Katie's voice greeting Chris, and Chris's voice, which could give her this crawly sensation in her thighs. Damn him. Should she put on lipstick? He'd notice if she didn't. He always noticed things like that, he noticed everything about a woman, about any woman. There was no doubt that he had a thing about women. You didn't have to be with him ten minutes to become wise to it. It wouldn't surprise me if even about Mother. Even! Veronica caught her breath and tossed the lipstick on the bureau, gave herself a desolate glare in the mirror, and went downstairs.

They were all in the parlor, her mother, Fran, Chris, and Katie. Delia was wearing a white orchid on the shoulder of her dress, and Fran wore another, identical, on hers. Veronica noticed at once that Fran had been at some pains over her appearance—she looked fresher, her hair had a sheen, her eyes were alert, and her clothes were new.

"I'm overcome," Fran exclaimed as Veronica entered the room. "I can understand your thinking of Delia, Mr. Wallingford, but you don't even know *me*. That's the trouble with being twins—it puts such a burden on one's friends!"

So Chris had brought them both orchids, and I, thought Veronica with sudden realization, I never even thought to get either of them a single thing.

Chris was smiling, looking pleased with himself. He possessed, to perfection, that combination of strength and sensitivity which many women find devastating, nor did he ever pretend to be unaware of the fact.

Delia was thanking Katie for her present. "I love the little pin. Thank you!"

Is there anything Delia doesn't love? Veronica questioned the air as she advanced into the room in her two-year old navy blue dress, unpressed, her hair still wet from the shower and sticking to her cheeks, her manner elaborately disengaged.

"You've got to have a drink with us, Katie," Delia insisted, gaily. "This is Fran's and my fiftieth. I don't propose to celebrate any others after this."

Chris turned to see Veronica, his blue eyes taking her in with that intense, appropriating glance which she had learned to know well.

"Hi," he said softly, and went to meet her with his long, languid stride. "Where you been, kid?"

She turned to her mother. "Happy birthday again. You too, Fran. Do you know that I completely forgot to buy either of you a present?"

Delia smiled at the girl, a smile full of tenderness. "Darling, you've given us the best present of all. You've finished your book."

"Bitch for not telling me," Chris said, and slipped his hand inside her arm, drawing her against him. "What's the idea?"

"I was going to call you, but decided it could wait until you came to town."

"Doesn't cost that much to call Cambridge!"

"You know me!"

"Do I? Does any one? Do *you*?"

Delia raised her glass. "A toast to Veronica and her book!"

"Veronica and her book!" Yet they all looked at Delia, at the soft radiance of her hair, her bare throat, her arms. There were moments when she seemed able to increase her effectiveness, like one of those three-speed lamps, and she had it on full, now.

Veronica had flushed. "Mother! It's your birthday and Fran's we're supposed to be celebrating, not my book."

Fran looked at her curiously. "Don't you want us to be excited about it? Aren't you?"

Chris came in tactfully: "How does it feel to be through at last?"

"*Not* like having a baby," she replied with an attempt at lightness. "Actually it doesn't feel like anything. Relief, I guess. But don't let's talk about it. This is Fran's and Mother's party, and we haven't seen Fran for ages. Let's eat, drink, and be merry."

She trailed off into a laugh, forced and ungracious, hating herself, and turning to Katie inquired abruptly what had happened to the flowers that Nick had sent earlier in the day. Katie, smiling, sipping her champagne, said that Nick's flowers were on the dining room table, where Delia had put them. "White stock, he sent. Masses of it, smelling up the whole place."

"And he sent me a tortoise-shell comb and Fran a silk scarf!" Delia laughed. "It wouldn't surprise me if he'd blown his whole month's allowance on us." Then with a quick glance at Veronica: "What happened to Miriam?"

"She was busy, and anyway you know she hates parties."

"Miriam Werth hate parties?" exclaimed Chris. "Since when?"

"Oh well, family parties."

Katie finished her drink, thanked Delia, and left the room, and Fran turned to Chris. "Veronica has her novel, Miriam has her thesis, and you, Mr. Wallingford? What's your specialty?"

He turned, giving her his whole attention in the flattering way he had. "Looks as if I will be going for a soldier, come fall. After that, I'm not sure."

"When you were here last you were all excited about writing a book, yourself," Delia reminded him, smiling.

"I'm still excited about it, but I have to get my ideas straightened out first." And he talked for a little while on the subject which had interested him all through his junior year and which hoped to "get straightened out" before he graduated in June. A study of the psychological differences and similarities of the novelists Herman Melville and Joseph Conrad, both of whom he found fascinating. He talked simply, even diffidently to the two older women, seeming in a curious way to exclude Veronica who in her turn appeared to be thinking of something else. When he'd finished Fran said with a laugh: "Delia, how in the world are we going to compete with these children?" And Delia replied in her gayest voice: "I wouldn't dream of trying."

She sat on the sofa with Chris beside her, and Veronica took a chair beside Fran. Sipping her champagne, Veronica noticed that her aunt left her own glass untouched. "What's the matter?" Veronica asked her. "Would you prefer a martini?"

"No thanks. I'm on the wagon."

They were always on easy terms, unemotional except on the rare occasions when Fran took it into her head to be disapproving or critical of her niece. "I like your young man," she remarked, and nodded at Chris, deep in conversation with Delia. "Intelligent but modest. A rare combination."

"Sure you wouldn't like something instead of champagne?"

"Are you hinting for mine? You can have it. I just took a swallow."

Veronica looked at her appraisingly. "Must have been quite a binge, the last one, for you to be so abstemious."

Fran made a face. "It was. But tell me, honey, are you going to marry him?"

"He hasn't suggested it."

"Go on, Nonny. You're twenty-one, and now that you're launched as an author you ought to think of more personal things."

Veronica smiled slightly. She was content to be talking to her aunt, whose virtues and vices were none of her concern, and to whom in a queer way she felt closer in age than she did to many of her own generation, except perhaps, to Miriam Werth. And she sensed, too, that Fran's affection for her was of the same detached variety as hers for Fran, which made it easier to be friends. She said presently: "One can think of personal things without thinking of marriage, can't one?"

"One can, but I'm not sure it's such a good idea."

"Don't be a prude."

Fran laughed. "That's one thing I haven't tried!" Then she added soberly: "No, I mean it. Get married anyway, and choose a nice guy like that one over there. If it doesn't work, well then, it doesn't. But at least you will know what it's all about."

Veronica watched the bubbles breaking in her glass. "I must say you sound horribly old-fashioned. I'm surprised at you."

"Why should you be?" Fran frowned. "As for being old-fashioned, there's nothing more *dated*, my dear, than a certain brand of bohemianism which I sometimes think I detect in your generation. Better get wise that there's nothing for free in the world nowadays, not even love."

Veronica lifted her glass and took a sip. Fran watched her.

"Besides," she said, with a touch of sarcasm, "now you've got your first book out from under, you'll be needing material for the next. I should think that marriage would be about as good a subject as any?"

Veronica's nostrils whitened a little, her eyes narrowed above the glass which she still held to her lips, feeling the breaking bubbles cool, crisp on her mouth. Before she could speak Chris hailed her from the sofa: "Won't you at least tell us the title of the damned book, Veronica? Or is even that asking too much?"

Veronica felt the champagne beginning to work up a new kind of excitement in her, and she stared at Chris where he sat beside her mother, his black trousered knee touching Delia's dress. Chris's air of maturity and Delia's appearance of youth seemed to make them for a moment almost contemporaries, and the thought brought a sharp pang to Veronica's heart. "I haven't decided on a title," she said, lying. "I thought of one, but I'm not sure I care for it."

"Tell us," Delia urged. "No, don't if you'd rather not."

Veronica said abruptly: "I might as well. 'Who is Silvia?' That's the title. I mean I think it's one I might decide to use."

Chris gazed at her speculatively. "Who is Silvia, what is she, that all our swains commend her? Sounds all right, if it applies. Does it apply?"

"Titles don't necessarily have to, do they?"

"But they should," Fran declared, and reached for the glass

on the table at her side. She held it in her hand, not attempting to drink from it, and Veronica caught the sudden look of strain in her aunt's face. For the first time the thought crossed her mind that it must cost Fran something to pass up a drink. It seemed almost as though she were praying—praying for strength! Meeting Veronica's eyes she said with an effort: "Anyway I think your title sounds O.K. I can hardly wait to find out who Silvia is, though, or what she is."

"Probably turn out to be a dog," Chris observed slily. He had an almost feminine type of mouth which gave his smile, when it was not sweet, that peculiar slyness, as of some inner sense of mischief.

"You know what I mean—like Flush, or Bob Son of Battle. Dad's always getting manuscripts about dogs, cats, horses, even mice. Sure your novel isn't about a dog, Veronica?"

He was needling her, mad probably because she hadn't told him about finishing the book, but now she didn't mind because the champagne felt wonderful, changing the chemistry of her emotions from depression to elation. Chris went on: "Now it's really finished, shall I tell Dad that he can expect to see the manuscript—when, tomorrow?"

She gave him a proud glance. "Tomorrow and tomorrow and tomorrow!"

"Well, I've laid the ground for you anyway." He turned to Delia. "This silly girl won't even let me take her to call on my father and Mr. Watts! Thinks it would be taking advantage of our friendship, and that she wouldn't know what to talk to him about. Just like a little wallflower at a party."

"Wallflowers went out of fashion with high button boots," Fran said, twirling her glass. "Though of course I can't speak for literary wallflowers."

"*They* went out with blue-stockings!" Chris said. "All before my time. Yours too, Veronica. Dad rather regrets it, I think. He has a theory that mass education has loosed a sort of mass competence on its own intellectual level and that, like Gresham's law on money, it's well on the way to pushing out the first rate for the third. I'm inclined to agree with him."

"Only because it's in line with one of your favorite gripes," Veronica told him, her cheeks very flushed. "You insist that trash pays, and so it does, but you can still buy *War and Peace*, or *Sense and Sensibility* in paperbacks, don't forget!"

"Granted. But who's writing the kind of thing Tolstoy wrote, or Jane Austen?"

"Who wants to write what they wrote? We're not living in the nineteenth century. Don't be such a snob!"

Chris gave a long, low laugh. In the six months that she had known him Veronica had never succeeded in making him lose his temper, though he often made her lose hers. "I have authority on my side," he told her blandly. "In *Man and Superman*, Shaw makes the comment that people get the kind of government they deserve, and I don't think it's going too far to say that they also get the kind of art they deserve. And I'm not talking, now, of trash. I'm talking of the mediocrity of competence, or, if you prefer, the competence of mediocrity."

"I don't prefer." Her eyes were glowing and she had a sudden wild loveliness, for all her damp hair and uninspiring dress. Under his pleasant civilised manner Chris could launch barbs, and despite her scornful exterior, she could feel them. This, Veronica was sure, was his way of letting her know that he had his doubts about the quality of her book, as, a month or two before, he had voiced his doubts about her capacity—at this stage—for writing one. When suggesting his father's firm as a possible publisher for her he had done so with the air of giving her a pat on the head, and a condescending: "There there, little girl! We'll see what we can do for you."

Delia moved in to ward off a clash between them. "I think you're being altogether too pessimistic, Chris. Gresham, I believe, spoke only of a tendency, didn't he? Not of an established fact."

Katie came back with another tray of cocktails, which she

offered first to Fran, who shook her head. "Still on my first, thanks."

Chris helped himself and turned to Delia with his most considerate air. "I used Gresham merely as a useful analogy. Good artists have always been in the minority. The point I'm trying to make is that they have never been in greater danger of being swamped by the majority as they are now. Miriam Werth has an even more depressing theory." He smiled exclusively at Delia. "Like to hear it?"

"I'm not sure that I do."

"Miriam's idea is that there may be an anthropological reason for the decline in creative genius during the past fifty years. She suggests that, like any species which comes into existence and then perishes, certain elements in society do the same thing, and of these elements the artist, and likewise the priest, might have served their turn and had their day, and so—kaput."

"But you've just reminded us that mass education has unleashed mass talent!" Veronica protested. "What's going to happen to all that talent?"

"You can see for yourself what's happening to it. It's becoming an aphis herd, milked by big business ants for *their* purposes, and their main purpose is conformity, and conformity, for the true artist, is death." He lifted his glass to Veronica. "Get me?"

"All this doesn't prevent your wanting to write your own book," Veronica said with a shrug. "And what's more, it doesn't discourage me either."

"That's because we function in the only way we know how. You do, anyway. I'm not sure about myself. I wouldn't, for instance, want to end as a *slight* literary success."

"Cheer up," she glowered. "You might not even be that."

"Nonny," Delia murmured, and Fran gave a sudden laugh. "Nothing like frankness between friends," she exclaimed, and handed her scarcely touched glass of champagne to her niece. "Finish this for me, will you, honey? I don't want to waste it."

Chris looked urbanely from one to the other. Being with

women always made him feel wonderful, full of sex, and a kind of indiscriminate desire. "You mustn't mind Veronica and me," he said, with firmness. "This is what goes whenever we get together. It's good for us."

Katie came to announce dinner, and as Chris stood aside to let Delia and Fran pass into the dining room, he put out his hand and held Veronica back. "Nonny, when am I going to see you alone? I've got to beat it back to Cambridge tomorrow, and I do want to see you alone."

"Doesn't leave us with much time, does it? But you'll be back for Thanksgiving."

He frowned. "You sure sound beside yourself with enthusiasm. What's the matter?"

"You weren't being too nice, yourself."

"Mad?"

"I don't like you in that mood."

"Prefer this?" He kissed her suddenly, with great knowledge and skill, murmuring against her ear: "You're not acting right, either. Is it because of the book?"

She sighed a little, relaxing in his arms, and for the first time this evening met his eyes with honesty. "Chris, I wish we could talk without needling each other the way we do. I want to talk to you. There's something special I'd like to ask you . . . a problem."

"What problem?" He drew her back into the room. "Just a sec. I want to know what problem."

"Oh God, everything!" She gave a small laugh that was stifled again under his swift, hard kiss. They tasted each other's lips, the sweet, scented harshness of wine on their tongues. Chris murmured:

"I could fix one of your damned problems fast, if you'd let me. Veronica, I'm crazy for you. And you are for me. Do you think I don't know it?"

"It isn't that."

"It is that. Everything was fine in the beginning, and now

you're acting like that goddam girl in Gide's *Strait is the Gate*—what's her name, Alissa. Cut it out. Let me read your book, let me go to bed with you. Let's share things."

"I feel so queer," she whispered. "I feel as if I'd done something really . . . you know, worth while. And now all of a sudden there's this empty feeling."

"That has nothing to do with the book. Oh Veronica, darling."

They clung together, straining breast to breast, groin to groin, then he let her go, his eyes blazing. "Not here, not now . . . ye gods! Tomorrow. Listen, I'll send old Greer a telegram saying I've come down with the mumps."

"Not *mumps*! Can't you think of something less—awkward?"

They laughed, caught together again, then heard Delia calling them from the dining room. Hand in hand, they went in.

CHAPTER

V

LATE that night before going to bed Deila knocked on her sister's door. "Sleepy, Fran, or may I come in for a minute?"

"Come in, of course," said Fran. She was in bed with the light on, a book on her knees. Delia closed the door and drew a chair near the bed. She had undressed and now wore a blue brocaded wrapper and carried a hairbrush with which she began to brush out the wave put in her hair earlier that day by Mr. Ramond. "We've hardly had a chance to talk," she said, "and there's so much, I don't quite know where to begin."

"We don't have to begin with me," Fran smiled. "I could tell you everything that's happened in my life in a few words, if I thought it worth while. Let's talk about you and the kids."

"Well, for a starter—what do you think of Chris?"

Fran reached for her cigarettes. "I'd say he has altogether too pretty ears for a man, but I like him."

"I do, too. I wish I could be sure that Veronica did."

Fran watched the smoke from her cigarette rise into the quiet air. "Can one ever be sure of anything Veronica does?" She turned her head a little to look at Delia. "I think you take that child too seriously, Delia. You always have, you know."

Delia replied with peculiar evasion: "I wish I believed she took Chris seriously. I thought, in the beginning, that she did.

Now all they do is spar with one another, as you saw tonight. It could of course be their idea of making love."

Fran laughed. "I can't help feeling a bit out of step with them, myself. They seem to live in a world so much their own, and it makes one feel excluded, a little. Perhaps that's just me. I noticed he paid you rather special attention—not that that's surprising!"

Delia was silent for a moment, then she said: "I don't think they want to exclude us—not deliberately at any rate. They probably feel that the world is uniquely their own, and not always in the happiest sense."

"In what sense then?"

"In the sense of being excluded themselves. Pushed out in front and expected to bear the brunt of whatever comes along."

"Baloney," Fran said, and squirmed her shoulders on the pillows. She looked handsome in bed, her hair sleek and loose against the peach-colored linen, her features more tranquil than they had been earlier. She looks more like me when she's in bed, Delia mused, and felt a wryness at the thought, which she kept to herself.

"Doesn't every generation have to bear the brunt of whatever comes along?" Fran asked after a minute. "Ours did. So did our parents."

"It's never quite the same, though, is it? I'd say that the future looked a good deal more dangerous for Chris and Veronica than any we can remember."

Fran disagreed. "Pity is wasted on the young. At least all their mistakes are ahead of them. But ours!"

None of that! warned Delia's mentor, and she waited, letting Fran's remark founder in the silence. It was a trick she'd learned a long time ago, a studied refusal to recognize the implied or to let Fran lure her, at any unexpected juncture, to take it up. It was the only way she knew to deal with Fran, and with the threadbare drama which Fran would occasionally have loved to dredge up out of that silence and hold to the light. Between the two of them, of course. Each the other's claque—it was what Fran would, once in a while, have liked. But Delia had the trick of silence. Simply by extending it she deepened it and made the crossing—for Fran—a dangerous game to play.

She went back now to Chris and his remarks during dinner. They had been discussing the future of his college class, the gifted and the not so gifted, alike destined for two years military service in the atomic age. On this subject too he was not without ideas.

"We are expected," he'd said, "to respond with the psychological reflexes of 1914 and 1940 to a situation which has already made those reflexes obsolete. So I do my two years' hitch, and come home to find my family and my friends vaporized in their own backyards. So what then? So we do what's demanded of us, and try not to think."

"How can one not have pity?" Delia asked Fran, smoking her cigarette sceptically among the peach-colored pillows. "I think of Nick, and of four years from now, or maybe a little longer, and I feel something worse than pity. I feel sick."

"In other words," Fran said after a pause, "your reflexes and mine date back to 1914 and 1940!"

"I feel sometimes that mine must date back to the Battle of Waterloo!" Delia laughed, brushing her hair to a sheen. They listened to the parlor clock downstairs distantly chime one, and to the sound of late traffic grinding through cold streets. From Veronica's room music, muted, spilled into the quietness.

"Oh well," sighed Delia, "it went off nicely. This evening, I mean. Even Veronica seemed to enjoy it eventually." She gave her sister an affectionate look. "You know, I had the loveliest, foolishest feeling at one time. The feeling I used to have when we were kids at our birthday parties, the feeling that everything was beginning, new, exciting, fresh."

"You always were an optimist," Fran told her with a faint smile. "God knows why, considering."

"Well, tonight there was the feeling of pride in Veronica's

having written her book and of her life really beginning. That, and of course your being here." She meant it. She'd meant it all evening, in a dawning gratitude for this companionship denied her by absence and estrangement and mess. She stared at a thick strand of hair caught in the brush. Fran said in a low voice: "Coming back here to you is like touching wood. If you're an optimist, I'm plain superstitious. Sounds horribly sentimental, but I ask myself what in the devil Veronica and I would do without you, Delia."

Delia went back to brushing her hair. "I love Veronica, you know. I want her to be happy. There was a time when she was little, when she seemed happy enough. All that fire and high spirits, do you remember? And she loved me then. I know she did."

Fran said meditatively: "That was the time, perhaps, when you didn't especially love her."

Delia took it without flinching. "I wasn't very good in the beginning, I know. But I can't believe that she'd have remembered that. It didn't last. Bad enough that she should remember what she does remember."

She flung back her head, the heavy hair raining back from it in a great wave shadowed in the lamplight. "I've tried to make it up to her . . . if she'd only let me."

"You're forgetting Charles," Fran said drily. "He's always come between you and Veronica. That insane loyalty of hers."

"And believing me disloyal," Delia nodded, peculiarly without bitterness, since she'd been over this ground before, often enough, alone and with Fran. "Which of course I was."

"Which of course you had every excuse to be."

Delia spoke at a tangent: "Do you think she will ever care for another man as she did for Charles?"

"If she were ever to know the truth about Charles, she might."

No, thought Delia, this won't do. She went back to brushing her hair. Around them the city slept or moved restlessly in its honeycombs under October stars shining through the bare branches of the park where Charles had died. Then by unspoken consent the sisters changed the subject and began to talk about Fran's life in California. It was a journey over a well-known road, the wonder all spent, the ohing and ahing done with, and no point in rushing from window to window in extemporaneous joy. At fifty there's no place to go except backwards, but they pretended, at fifty there being nothing else to do.

Fran spoke of various jobs, some more fun than others. Of an affair or two ditto. Of the eucalyptus trees in her garden, and the idea she'd had recently that she might take up book-binding and perhaps even make it pay when she got to be good at it.

Delia said diffidently: "You've definitely given up all interest in the stage, then?"

"Good God, yes. Look at me!"

"Well, at any rate you've got enough to get along on. That's something."

Fran looked across the room at the wallpaper on the wall. "It's something, yes."

But not enough, Delia thought, recognizingly. Well, I'll hear about that soon enough. She asked after certain friends of theirs in San Francisco, but it seemed Fran didn't see as much of the Bretts as she used to. "You know how people are. Busy with their own lives. I see the Wicks occasionally, and Lorna Edwards, but Lorna's become something of a bore since Eddie died, and I don't especially care for cloying female friendships. Bad enough to be lonely oneself, but to have to share some one else's loneliness . . . ugh!"

Yes, two lonely women, Delia reflected with vision. And both with nothing to pool but their weakness. She'd been in on some of their sessions when, far gone in liquor, they searched through closets for the heel ends of old bottles, sopped up the cooking sherry, and the maudlin bout of sympathy erupted at last in the confessional, the I've always wanted to tell you what I think of you and now I'm going to, and the telling, and the expedience of next day, pretending you must have been so potted you can't remember what you said, and knowing yourself far too dependent to dare recall what *she* said. And hating each other. Under it all, that female hating which passeth the hatred of men by a long, long shot.

Fran looked at her. "You don't have the ordinary problems, do you, dear? You've managed to keep clear of them. You've kept your friends. Dull, but nice. And you have the children, and this house, and the place in Connecticut, and the rummage shop with Nadine Bower, and your work at the Red Cross. You keep busy. That's the ticket I guess—keeping busy."

The ordinary problems, Delia thought, incredulously. How dare Fran? She said with a laugh: "You make it sound dull enough, and of course it is. But what does one do? I have no talents except as a housewife, and for me to take a regular job would be to deprive someone who probably needs it more than I do. I'm not the adventurous type anyway, as you know."

"There's marriage. Not for me, but for you. Why not?"

This too was a well worn road, the hurrahing petered out, but Fran was always coming back to it, one of her queer little vulgarities.

Delia replied lightly: "I'm not pregnant and I don't need a man to support me, so we don't need to go into that question again, do we?" Fran was silent and Delia said: "Besides, I'm reconciled to my life, more or less, as it is. I enjoy it after a fashion. There are odd moments of rediscovery, even."

Fran rolled on to her elbow and stared at her sister. "Rediscovery of what?"

"Silly, simple things. Things I've always known were around, but which I've never stopped to notice, particularly, until recently. The way voices sound out on the street in the early morning. The way leaves move in a storm, so you see their undersides as you never do when it's calm. A lion roaring in the zoo. You know."

"Do I?" The note of self-pity, imminent, inevitable. Delia waited resignedly. "Maybe I did once, but not any more. People bore the hell out of me. Politics, jobs, world crises . . . you can't get away from the fact that it's all run by people, the same kind of people you see around you everywhere, all the time. Remember how idealistic we used to be when we were young? Remember losing sleep over Sacco and Vanzetti? My God, we actually believed that losing sleep over a cause must somehow affect it! Now I take a slug of booze and a seconal and *everybody* can go to the electric chair for all of me."

Delia put down her brush and looked at Fran steadily. "Bad as that?" she murmured. "Darling, not really. It can't be?"

"Why the hell not? Try letting down your guard for a bit and you'll soon find how bad it can be."

Delia drew the heavy coil of her hair over one shoulder and began slowly to braid it. "Look, Fran, I'm not letting down my guard. Not now. Not ever. And I wasn't going to mention this, but I guess I will after all. You were wonderful this evening. Brave, strong. No, don't make a face—you were fine and I know what it cost you. Don't think I missed it. Don't think that I didn't understand, that I wasn't grateful."

"Grateful because I didn't get potted and disgrace you before your prospective son-in-law?" Fran rolled back on the pillow and blew a long plume of smoke towards the ceiling. "Veronica was the one who really got the picture straight. She knew that the reason I didn't drink tonight was because I'd done such a good job at the Jacksons two nights ago, and I was still hung-over."

"Did you tell Veronica that?"

"Didn't have to. I could see from the way she looked at me. You know that indifferent compassion of the young, thanking their stars *they* aren't old and washed up. She even offered me a martini."

She lighted another cigarette from the stub in her fingers.

"That night at the Jacksons was worse than a binge." She gave a sudden laugh. "Whew!"

Delia asked reluctantly: "And the Jacksons?"

"Well, it was intimated to me that the most comfortable train out of Baltimore was the one which left immediately after breakfast. So of course I took it." She looked suddenly amused. "The whole thing was as much Lee Jackson's fault as it was mine. Want to hear?"

"Not especially." The depression which had hovered over Delia all afternoon and which had lifted briefly during the evening, closed in on her dankly, and she knew that whether she wanted to or not she was going to have to listen to Fran's story. Better to get it over with now when she was sober than put it off for the unavoidable occasion of tears and maudlin pleas and protestations of a drunken confessional. "All right," she said, sighing. "But oh Fran . . . why do you? Why must you?"

"This was a lulu," Fran declared, with an enthusiasm designed to sugar-coat the pill. "It began innocently enough, God knows. I felt good to be with people after being alone as I am most of the time. Don't have to be especially fond of them—just to be with them. And the Jacksons have always been able to take it. Me, I mean. Urging me on, though they've always known what was apt to happen. But after all why expect my friends to change their habits and act like governesses or policemen just because I never know when to stop?"

Why indeed, thought Delia, saying nothing.

Fran laid her cigarette ash carefully in the ashtray beside her bed. Sober, she had this careful deliberation as though rehearsing for less studious occasions. Delia thought of nights when she'd awaken to the smell of burning and had rushed to find Fran's bed on fire or a waste basket smouldering and Fran in a stupor with the light on, an empty glass beside her, an unread book lying on the floor—she made a point of carrying books to bed though she never read them—the air dense with fumes of whisky, face powder, cigarettes, burning linen. But sober she was meticulous, as though committing a lesson to heart so it would serve at some later date.

"I hadn't seen the Jacksons for two years," Fran began matter-of-factly. "They'd always been rather nicer to me than some of my other old friends. Glad to see me, or anyway, never giving me reason to suppose they weren't. Easy going, you remember? I know you alway thought them light-weights, but they're hospitable, and have the dough to afford it. Visiting firemen coming and going all hours, liquor on tap, marvelous food, and a colored houseboy to wait on you hand and foot. Anyway it was fun stopping in on them last week. Lee met me in his Jaguar and we sat in the greenhouse and the colored butler brought us martinis, and more martinis. You know I've always been a sucker for luxury. It was one reason I married Herbert. He liked his fleshpots, too." She diverged into a realm always close at hand.

"Herbert liked his tosspots up to a point. But he had that prissy streak which made him always want to call it a day just about the time the rest of us were getting warmed up. Remember how mad it used to make me after we'd had a couple of drinks and he'd suddenly pick up the bottle and say in his precise way: 'Guess that'll be all you need for tonight, Fran!' And off he'd go and lock it up."

Delia thought: Must we go back to poor Herbert? Apparently they must, for a moment anyway, for Fran murmured thoughtfully: "You know I often think that if Herbert hadn't been such a stick about my drinking, I might not have gotten so bad. It was the fighting to get it that made it so important. Don't you think so?"

"You'd been at it since you were sixteen," Delia reminded her, feeling temper suddenly, the sharp edge of outrage at Fran's inimitable ability to pass the buck. To pass it to Herbert, even at this late date! "All during Prohibition, if I remember rightly. And ever since."

Fran gave her a sidelong glance, then went back to the Jacksons.

"The first evening with them was swell and none of us got more than passing high, and there was so much to talk about. I told them about my life in California, gilding the lily some because otherwise it'd have sounded dull compared to their life in Baltimore. Then on the second night Marie came down with a toothache and Lee filled her full of gin and gave her a sleeping pill, and she went to bed, leaving the world to darkness and to me . . . and Lee."

Delia looked at her. "Don't, Fran."

"I got plastered, and so did Lee. And I mean plastered. I suppose we ate dinner, though I can't remember anything about it. I do remember shutting all the doors and Lee turning on the Hi-Fi, and the two of us dancing in the parlor till all hours. It was fun, and I hadn't had a chance to dance for ages."

Delia could picture that middle-aged romp, Fran a head taller than paunchy Lee Jackson, both unerringly headed for the next day's ennui.

"We called it a day finally, and I went up to bed in their guest room, and who should appear in the door but Lee in his pyjamas—God-awful looking things in two tones of gray and his moustache waxed into points so you could have stuck an olive on each one. He looked like something out of a Mack Sennett comedy, and just about as dated! I couldn't help but laugh, and there was poor Marie in the next room, groaning with her tooth so I could hear her through the walls, and then I got mad at Lee's trying to exploit the situation."

"Did he succeed?"

"Hell no. We had quite an argument, though, all in whispers because of Marie, and you'd be suprised how complicated it is to repulse a man in whispers. It was funny in a way—really funny. The conceit of the guy in that outfit, playing the wolf! But I was scared to death Marie would come out of her seconal and wander in and catch us, though there was nothing, of course. Lee just tighter than usual—tighter even than I was . . ."

She petered out, biting her lip, her face and neck suffused in sudden crimson, and for several minutes neither spoke. In the parlor downstairs the clock struck again, and left the silence rounded and whole until a taxi in the street slammed on its brakes and the sound smashed the silence like a fist smashing glass.

Delia threw the braid of hair over her shoulder and rose. She stood for a moment staring down at Fran. "And Marie came into your room and found her husband there with you?"

"For heaven's sake, Delia! It was bad luck and stupid, but there was nothing. I mean honestly there wasn't. Lee was a fool and so was I to have gotten so noisy, but aside from that I give you my word . . ."

"Did you give Marie Jackson your word, or wouldn't she take it?"

"Dele!"

Delia said slowly: "Another friend gone. And why, I wonder, do you have to tell *me* these things? Why me?"

"But I've always told you things!"

"Yes," Delia said, shrugging. "Yes, you always have."

Fran sat up in bed. "Delia, listen. I didn't mean . . ."

Delia turned at the door. When she spoke, it was in a normal voice: "It's late, Fran. Better get some sleep."

She went out, shutting the door quietly after her.

CHAPTER

V I

VERONICA'S manuscript lay for several days in the locked drawer of her desk while she tried to make up her mind what to do about it. Every so often she took it out and read a little, trying to achieve detachment by fancying herself as Donald Wallingford or his partner Mr. Watts, or, more often and with considerably less detachment, as Miriam Werth or Chris. Her moods veered sharply from confidence to revulsion, yet she was unable to leave the thing alone, to send it away or to dismiss it from her mind. In a desperate attempt to attain some sort of perspective she re-read, at random, the writers she admired—Mary McCarthy, John O'Conner, Scott Fritzgerald, going as far as Proust, Sartre, and Colette. All this did was to sharpen the tangent of her indecision. At one moment she was convinced that she was as good as any of them, in spots at all events; the next she was sure she was no good at all, and that her book stank. Then in an access of common sense she reminded herself that she had after all *written a book*, which was more than Chris had been able to do for all his lofty aspirations. She had at least proved to herself that she was equal to the stern discipline demanded of an artist, and that that could not, should not, be allowed to go for naught.

Alternately exulting and exhausted by this interior soliloquy, Veronica tried to escape from herself by taking long walks in the Park, stirring the fallen leaves with her feet, watching old men feeding pigeons, and anonymous figures huddled in winter over-coats sitting on benches, and strollers sucking the November air into their sooty lungs.

In the coldest weather these city dwellers turned to this tame substitute for the countryside, in search of heaven knows what primitive memories of a lost innocence and greensward grown to asphalt and concrete. There was not much surcease for Veronica here, on her own stamping ground, its habitués transplanted lock stock and barrel to the pages of her book. Walking, she recognized them with a sense of wonder that they should, after all, be real. Sometimes it was the face of a slight, dark man who every summer lay on a little grassy eminence above the zoo, his jacket for a pillow, his bare feet pointing to the sky, his eyes fixed unblinkingly at its hot and empty blue. And the woman with knotted bare legs harsh as the branches of a tree, a handkerchief tied round her head, and a pinched angry face frozen in its hatred of everything that moved. Passing her one day where she crouched on a bench, Veronica heard her apostrophizing the pigeons which waddled round her feet: "I don't stick around to bother you, you sons of bitches! Why must you stick around bothering me? Get the hell out of here!"

Veronica laughed, but the woman gave her such a glare of hatred that thereafter, whenever they chanced to meet, the girl passed by with head averted, half fearful of having a spell put on her by the old witch, who looked as though she could do it, too. Then there was a pair of elderly lovers whom she often encountered walking in step, their bodies close together, hands tightly clasped, and from the peculiar nature of their silence and their unseeing gaze she had learned to measure the desire which seemed to fill and drain in them, their expressions as revealing as the pressure in a barometric gauge. It gave Veronica a peculiar feeling to meet these characters walking about as it were loose, instead of being safely embalmed where she had put them, between the pages of her book.

Dropping in for a cup of coffee with Miriam one afternoon

when the weather was too nasty to walk in the Park, Veronica conjectured aloud whether perhaps writing a book were not somewhat like living in sin, with its private excitements, its estrangement from the dull diurnal round.

"I wouldn't know," Miriam said, sipping coffee out of the cup marked HE. "I've never written a book."

"But you've lived in sin?"

"Have I? I wouldn't know that either."

She was clever at deflection and Veronica let it go. They listened to the sound of sleet pattering against the windows. The radio gave forth the final strains of *Cosi fan Tutte*, and Miriam hummed the last verse of the chorus in a rich contralto which always took her friend by surprise. It's like her coffee, Veronica thought—thick and dark and sweet, and for some reason disturbing.

> "Fortunato l'uom che prende
> Ogni cosa pel buon verso!
> E tra i casi e le vicende
> Da ragion guidar si fa!"

"There's a practical moral for you," Miriam remarked, turning to Veronica. " 'To find peace in the midst of the world's tumult!' Not a bad idea."

"Not especially exciting either—like most of Mozart's ideas when he was not writing music."

She sat as usual in a corner of the sofa, among the hard cushions and the crumbs of Miriam's last meal. Things were always getting lost in that sofa—spectacles, pencils, even books, for it was capacious and one could fish for hours and fetch up unexpected trove. Whenever Miriam mislaid some article she made for the sofa and plunged into its recesses up to her elbows, coming up flushed and heated, but triumphant, once with a doughnut which she calculated must have been there for at least three months.

Still humming, she went to the stove to replenish her cup and came back with a plate piled high with Danish pastry which she bought from a shop around the corner, and which with pastrami and sour pickles seemed to constitute her main dietary standby.

"How did the birthday party go off?" she asked, sitting down in her corner of the sofa with the cup marked HE.

"Mothers and Fran's? Oh, as usual."

"How did Chris get along with your aunt? There was some question, wasn't there, of her getting tight and perhaps shocking him?" She laughed. "Shocking *Chris*!"

"It's one of Mother's nightmares whenever Fran's around. It went off all right though, the other night. Fran was on the wagon, and it was all very proper and dull. You didn't miss anything, except, of course, seeing Chris."

"He left next day, didn't he?"

Veronica nodded. The remembrance of her last telephone conversation with Chris made her heart sink. He had called her the morning after Delia's birthday party to say that he was leaving shortly for Cambridge, and would she come over to his father's apartment and join him for a late breakfast? "Dad's out of town and we'll have the place to ourselves. Come on, Nonny."

"I can't."

"You said last night we'd see each other before I left town."

"I can't, with you alone there."

"Oh for God's sake!"

"I'll see you when you get back for Thanksgiving."

"Will you?" He'd laughed grimly. "I'm not so sure you will."

"Chris, listen."

But he'd hung up, leaving her chilled and at a loss. That night she tried to call him at his rooms in Cambridge but his phone didn't answer, and then, disgusted by her own vacillation, she made no further attempt to get in touch with him. Nevertheless, no sooner was he out of her reach than she was beset with fear and longing, haunted by the memory of his eyes, the sensitive line of his mouth, the particular cadence of his voice. She felt herself to be powerless against her own contradictory impulses, against this difficult and dangerous balancing act—wanting him and repulsing him, attracting him to her, and sending him away. There was, as she knew, a name for this sort of thing, and Chris hadn't hesitated to call her by that name, but while she suffered because of it, it also brought her a sneaking pleasure. In her clear-eyed moments she was ready to admit that she feared giving herself unreservedly to love. She had given herself once, given the unquestioning, defenceless self of her childhood, and the gift, and the loss which followed, had left her in a condition of emotional penury from which she often wondered whether she would ever emerge. "The trouble with you," Chris had told her once, brutally, "is that you're making some sort of a drama out of this love for your father. And I do think that the time for all that is past, don't you honestly?"

She knew she'd surprised him by the meekness of her reply: "I think it is too, but what does one do?"

"Coffee?" Miriam asked, at her elbow. "Pastry?"

"Thanks," said Veronica. She tore one of the pastries apart and dipped it in her cup and ate it. It tasted like wet pasteboard, yet she always got a curious comforting satisfaction from eating these unwholesome snacks in Miriam's apartment with its assorted smells, its Mayan artifacts, its atmosphere of independence and privacy. When she was twenty-five she'd come into the patrimony left her by Charles and then, she decided, she'd have an apartment like this one and be entirely on her own. True, Delia had offered to set her up before that. The psychiatrist whom she'd consulted had suggested it, but Veronica stalled at the notion—unacknowledged panic seizing her at the prospect of being, for the first time in her life, completely alone. But perhaps it wouldn't be so bad after all. Miriam thrived on it, so did other girls she knew. Why wait for her patrimony? *Her patrimony!* Charles, who had kept her free while he lived, who had cherished and protected her, would once more set her free with the money he had made from his own muscle, guts, and brain. But should she take it, had she the right to take it? Would he, knowing everything, have wanted her to take it?

"What's the matter with you?" Miriam asked suddenly. "Got a cramp?"

Veronica said slowly: "I was just thinking about this business of money. Of accepting money—you know—from one's family."

"What's happened? Somebody died and left you a pack?"

"I shall be independent one of these days, you know, according to my father's will."

"So you told me before. Lucky you." Miriam looked at her curiously. "You don't act as if you thought yourself especially lucky. How long did you say you had to wait?"

"Three years. I don't have to wait that long, though. Mother's quite agreeable to my having an apartment and being on my own any time I want."

"I've often wondered why you didn't want," Miriam told her after a pause. "I mean, now you've finished the book you could get yourself a job until you felt like writing another, especially as you and Delia don't seem to get along too well."

"I hate taking the money. I feel that neither Delia nor I have any real right to it."

"Why in heaven's name not?"

"I hate being in the same class as Mother and Fran. A parasite, like them."

Miriam shrugged. "You're getting dopier and dopier. I've noticed it all this past year, ever since you got started writing the novel. It really seems to have done something to you, made you self-conscious, full of ifs ands and buts."

Veronica flushed. "At least I can feel that the book has been some sort of justification, and that I've put father's money to good use, and that's more than Mother could say, or Fran either, living off alimony all these years and not lifting a finger to do a damned thing."

She spoke with such passion that Miriam stared at her in silence. Then she sighed. "Look, I don't get this. So far as your aunt Fran is concerned I agree that it's wrong for her, an able-bodied childless woman to take dough from a man she's divorced. But Delia's another matter. Your father died, leaving her with two young kids to bring up, and from what I can gather it was no great fortune he left, either. What would you have had her do—

give it all to the Salvation Army and send you and Nick to an orphanage while she took in washing?"

"It would probably have been the most honest thing she ever did," Veronica murmured with a strange air of recklessness, and it was Miriam's turn to flush. Both realized suddenly that they were on the verge of a scene whose real cause was very far from the one under discussion. Miriam was the first to get herself under control. She said quietly: "I've known Delia for years and I like her. I know you have this complex about her and I've never been able to understand it, except that I realize people do have complexes about their parents. Mine are dead, so that lets me out. Still, you seem to have it worse than any one I've ever met."

Her gust of emotion evaporated, she was able to smile. "Poor Delia! What's the use of my trying to say anything in her favor when it'll only make you madder?"

Veronica was trembling. "Your parents are dead," she said slowly. "But when your mother was alive, did she, when she gave you a bath, ever sink her nails into your flesh so it made you scream?"

Miriam stirred the coffee cooling in her cup. "No," she said, expressionlessly. "No, she never did."

"Or look at you sometimes with a look as though she hated you, even when you were only six or seven years old and didn't know what it was all about—what anything was all about?"

Miriam made a gesture of distaste. "*Delia?*"

"Until I was ten, until after Father's death, it used to be like that. Oh, not all the time. Only when she couldn't hold it in, the feeling she had about me. I don't believe Father ever noticed it. But she was careful when he was around, that he shouldn't notice it. I noticed it, though. I lived with it. Seeing her face at night when I'd been put to bed, her face all knotted up like a fist with the hatred clutched inside it."

They were silent, and Miriam's heavy lashes moved uncertainly behind her glasses.

"Until you were ten, you said." Her eyes turned as though

unwillingly to the other. "What happened when you were ten?"

"Father was killed. You know all about that. In the Park. And she became quite nice to me. Apologetic, as though she wanted to make up for the past. For what she'd felt about me. Perhaps for what she hadn't felt about Father."

Miriam gave a little shudder. "But why should she have been unkind to you before he died, then changed so suddenly after? I don't get it." She set the cup marked HE violently on the table before them. "I don't get any of it!"

Veronica said with a pondering air: "I suppose because by then she knew that I'd got her number, and it scared her to know that I had."

"Oh Veronica!" Then, savagely: "What do you mean, her number?"

"Why she didn't like me, couldn't bear the sight of me. That's all."

Miriam rose and carried both cups into the kitchen and rinsed them, setting them upside down with their saucers on the drain board. She seemed to find it necessary to do something and to do it with noise. Coming back to the living room she looked gently at Veronica. "Doesn't one get over these childhood things? You've got a lot of psychological insight—doesn't that help?" When Veronica remained silent, Miriam said: "You were jealous of each other because of him, weren't you? Because of Charles. I've always suspected it. But Nonny, for heaven's sake! He's been dead ten years, and she couldn't have had it so easy since!"

Veronica said abruptly: "Let's skip it. I didn't mean to bore you with all this talk about family. It's just that sometimes it helps."

"I wish I could help you about Delia," Miriam said impulsively. "I can't help being fond of her. Do you know what Chris said about her, once? That of all the women he'd ever known she had the greatest tenderness. And it's true, Nonny. I guess it sort of puts you and me in the shade—but it's true."

A gust of wind struck the window, leaking in cold air, and

as Miriam went to make it fast Veronica, shifting among the sofa cushions, felt something hard under her buttocks. Her fingers closed on a smooth oblong—a silver cigarette lighter with the initials C.W. For a second, she hesitated, then slipped it into her pocketbook and rose.

When Miriam turned from the window it was to see her friend standing faintly smiling and composed, her sudden passion a thing of the past. "I've got to scram, Mim. Promised Fran I'd go to the movies with her tonight."

Miriam said with relief: "You O.K. kid? I mean, not depressed or anything, now?"

"I'm O.K. Don't mind if I let off steam, do you? Maybe you're right and I've been sort of dopey working on the book. I shall now begin to mend my ways."

Miriam accompanied her to the door as usual. She rarely pressed people to stay, and one pictured her when they'd gone, returning to her corner of the shabby sofa with a book or to her typewriter, the cup marked HE or SHE on the table beside her, the radio seeping music. She would not be long alone. Other friends would drop in and she'd brew more coffee, rinse out the cups, dive into the refrigerator for whatever indigestible snack might be lurking there.

Meantime, out on Greenwich Street Veronica paused to watch two cops load a drunken bum into a police van. There was something easy-going and practised in the way they did it and in the bum's philosophical acceptance of his fate. She thought of her Aunt Fran, who, two years before, had taken just such a journey to a downtown police station, and Delia and Katie, notified by the sergeant in charge, had hastened thither in a taxi to bail her out. Afterwards there had been a row in Delia's bedroom and Veronica had heard Delia's voice, harsh with desperation: "Does it ever occur to you to think what this must do to the children?"

And Fran, abjectly contrite: "It must have been a Mickey Finn. I swear I only had two drinks."

"When in your life have you only had two drinks?"

Tenderness, thought Veronica, and laughed. Sleet cut her face and froze in her hair, her whole being pulsed with a violent almost erotic excitement. Seated in the bus she stared through the darkened window at streets slashed with orange light, and the hand in her pocket clutched the cigarette lighter she'd found in Miriam's sofa. She had no doubt that it must belong to Chris— the initials were enough to convince her, and she'd seen it often, the last time at Delia's party three nights ago. So he hadn't gone back to Cambridge that day as he'd told her he was going! After hanging up on her he'd rushed off to Miriam's apartment and spent the day with her, and perhaps the night. They'd discussed Delia and her *tenderness*, drunk Miriam's coffee, eaten salami and knockwurst with beer, then turned out the lights and listened to music from the radio, there on that sofa with the lumpy cushions among which, after lighting a cigarette for her and one for himself, he'd dropped the lighter. Easy to imagine what had followed. Chris was not one to turn down a good chance, and Miriam looked as though she could use a man. She could keep a secret too . . . that airy question this afternoon: "Chris left next day, didn't he?" Oh, she was a deep one. Perverse too, probably. Getting a thrill out of knowing she shared him with her best friend. Oh God!

Veronica felt hear heart beating in long-drawn hammer strokes which she tried to control by taking deep, steady breaths as though she were swimming. It was frightening how her heart could beat sometimes, as though trying to spring out from her breast. Whenever she got excited or angry or scared, like that afternoon long ago when she'd run all the way from the bridle path in the Park and down the avenue towards home, running, gasping, her throat and chest pulled tight with a dry tightness as though she'd been crammed into a box, and at every step her heart thudding as it was now, thudding, drawing its fearful inspiration from the vision of her father, his neck broken when the big brown horse fell on him, lying on the grass, his suffused eyes searching the faces of strangers who'd gathered round him, trying to catch his last whispered words: "Delia! Fetch Delia."

Delia? "Who is Delia?" What is she, that all our friends commend her? Is she kind and is she fair, for beauty lives with kindness . . . Love doth to her eyes repair . . . to help him of his blindness . . .

Veronica rubbed the cigarette lighter in her pocket as though it were Aladdin's lamp, and drew a terrible intoxication from the feel of it against her flesh. Delia's tenderness in another man's arms, Chris's tenderness in another woman's! Hypocrisy as a way of life, suave, ingrained, triumphant—an end in itself. And innocence paying the price, Charles' innocence, mine! Well, there was her theme all right, perfect in its way, par with another kind of perfection which had commended the precept that all was fair in love and war, and another kind of innocence which died in merciful oblivion of itself under the eyes of strangers, while a frightened child ran gasping through the streets, coming to an enforced stop and waiting as Charles had taught her to do, his loving, restraining hand holding hers, his gay voice in her ears, waiting for the lights to change. And all the time her heart swelling, swelling till she thought it must burst in her chest before she could reach Delia to tell her that he was hurt and dying and that she must come to him at once.

"Then to Silvia let us sing, That Silvia is excelling . . . She excels each mortal thing . . . Upon the dull earth dwelling!"

And there was Delia in the parlor with her arms locked round the head of a young man, the two of them twined so close together that the child standing in the door behind them fancied they must in some nightmarish way in this nightmarish moment have lost their separate identities and become one.

"Then to Silvia let us sing!"

A woman sharing the seat beside Veronica turned to her with a smile. "I always liked that song." she confided, comfortably. "Last time I heard it, Lawrence Tibbett sang it when he came to my home town of Bangor, Maine to give a recital. Long time ago. Must be all of twenty years."

CHAPTER

VII

"Sure you won't change your mind and come?" Delia asked. "I called Nadine and she said of course to bring you. I know you don't care for bridge, but you could leave after dinner if you were bored."

"I don't think I could face Fred and Nadine after that business last year!" Fran laughed as she spoke, but looked as though she meant it. "Doubt whether they'd care to face me either."

"Don't be silly. They've forgotten all about it. They're not the sort of people who bear a grudge."

It was a year ago during her last visit to New York that Fran had gone to dine with Delia's friends the Bowers, and an amicable enough argument over politics had ended nastily, with name calling on Fran's side, and, on theirs, a final exasperated suggestion that she take herself home. Later she'd apologized, and the Bowers, who as Delia pointed out were not the sort to bear a grudge, had good-naturedly laughed it off. But Fran, who had certain not-too-vague recollections of having called Fred Bowers shifty and his wife a moth-eaten liberal, recoiled from the prospect of meeting them again with no ameliorating memory between.

"I'd really rather go to the movies with Veronica," she said cheerfully to Delia. "Besides, I told her I would."

Delia hesitated. Her fortnightly dinner and bridge game with her friends was a time-honored custom which she hated to pass

63

up, but at the same time she felt guilty at deserting Fran. Both sisters had been under something of a strain since their conversation in Fran's room on the night of the birthday party, a strain heightened by Fran's visibly desperate struggle to stay off the bottle. The ensuing tensions set up a vibration in Delia's nerves, reviving an old ache of anxiety, a contagion as though poison were seeping from Fran's arteries into hers. Both tried to ignore it, and there had been some happy, even carefree hours together— at the theater, the picture galleries, walking in the Park, shopping, a dinner or two with friends who by some fluke Fran had not succeeded at one time or another in insulting. Each in a wistful moment thought to herself: If it could always be like this!

Standing in the parlor before a gold framed mirror above the sofa, Delia rearranged the tortoise-shell comb in her hair and said over her shoulder to Fran: "It's Katie's evening off, but there's cold turkey in the refrigerator unless you and Veronica would rather eat out."

"We'll manage," Fran replied, lightly. The evening paper in her lap and a cup of tea beside her, she watched the sapphires in Delia's ring burn blue in the lamplight.

"How do you like the Spanish effect?" Delia asked, turning. "I'm not so sure myself. But it's Nick's birthday present and I've got to get used to wearing it."

"The comb? Swell. You look swell. Isn't it all rather thrown away on Fred and Nadine? They're such sticks."

Without the least desire to spend the evening with the Bowers herself, Fran still suffered a prick of resentment at being left with only her niece for company. And the long, interminable haul without a drink, and no sleep, probably, unless she took a pill.

Delia picked up her coat and pocketbook. She had, all at once, that gaiety to which she could give way like a child going to a party. "Well, darling, I shan't be late. We usually break up around midnight."

"It's foul out. Got an umbrella?"

"Yes, and I'll take a cab. It's no distance anyway."

"Have fun," Fran said, smiling rather fixedly. "Give Fred and Nadine my salaams."

Delia turned at the door. "Franny?"

Fran looked up. "What?"

"If you and Nonny should want a drink, there's a bottle in the liquor closet, and Katie put soda on the ice. Got your latch key?"

"Of course. Don't worry about us. We'll probably be home about the time you are, anyway."

When the door had closed on her sister, Fran sat for a minute staring at the newspaper on her knee. Fury spiralled up in her and she stammered her thoughts aloud to the empty room:

"Why did she have to say it? As though I didn't know where she kept the liquor! As though even if she'd locked it up and buried the key I couldn't call Murray's and have them deliver a quart. This damned pretense of trusting me when she knows and I know I'm not to be trusted, and haven't been since I was sixteen. This game of faith healing, this sisterly crap . . ."

Trembling, she rose and went to the window which overlooked the street. Pulling aside the curtain she stared into molasses-colored gloom spiked with sleet that glittered in the passing beam of automobile lights and tapped like claws against the panes. "Urging me to go to the Bowers, knowing they'd serve drinks and that I couldn't pass it up with all of them drinking under my nose, but trusting me just the same, or pretending to. 'See, I trust you. You're a big girl now and you wouldn't abuse that trust, would you, Fran dear?' Trying to make me see, feel, know what I see feel and know is a goddam lie. My lie. Her lie. Charles' lie. The universal lie. Lie of a strength that doesn't exist and never did. Lie of faith, loyalty, love that doesn't exist. Even the Bowers know it's a lie and connive in it. Friends of the family, with their fingers in every pie, superior, patronizingly indispensable!"

Turning from the window Fran began to walk round the big, beautiful room, mellow in the lamplight, the last of Nick's birthday bouquet in the crystal bowl she'd given Delia, sending puffs of fragrance into the air. The scent was a kind of reproach, making her ashamed of her unreasoning bitterness. She felt Delia's touch in the absence of a single jarring note. It had not been so during Charles' lifetime, when his obstreperous personality invaded every nook and corner in a species of perpetual fox hunt or gymkhana, and, hating solitude, he involved every member of the family in it. After his death Delia had dispersed the paraphernalia of Charles' consuming passion—or at any rate one of them. The silver cups and shields he'd won at racing and polo were transferred from the dining room sideboard to Nick's room in the house at Connecticut, Charles' hunting books and sporting prints to Veronica. Delia removed a mouldering fox mask and brush from its place of honor above the parlor mantel and in their place hung her favorite Waldo Peirce still-life of water-lilies which Fran had given her at her wedding. "I'd like to remember Charles," Delia had explained to the interested, "with a little less violence, without the view-halloo, if you know what I mean!" And those of their friends who had known Charles knew what she meant, all right.

The parlor was by all odds the loveliest room in Fran's recollection of all the lovely rooms she had known. During her frequent protracted absences from it the memory of its special quality of stillness, its inviting peace undisturbed by the ghostly echoes which trouble too many of our memories of places and things, always had power to move her to gratitude that it should exist whether she were in it or not, and this notwithstanding all the things that she knew had happened beween its four walls—all the things she wished had never happened.

But tonight the charm seemed to have grown strangely threadbare, a crooked nail seemed to be clawing at her insides where she couldn't reach it, and she could feel sweat beginning to bead out on her forehead and upper lip. Passing the bowl of flowers she bent to smell them, but they'd spent their last breath of sweetness, and all she got now was a rank whiff from the water which Katie had forgotten to change. In her craving for activity of any kind, for any distraction, this at least offered itself, and picking up the bowl Fran carried it to the pantry and dumped the flowers into the trash can. She washed the bowl and dried it, and heard the French travelling clock on Delia's desk chime six, the rounded, luminous notes dangling in the silence like lanterns imagined under closed lids, a radiance strung through the years, going back and back through the night-blackened branches of space until they faded out against a treeless landscape which might have been a field or some windless waste of the sea on whose deserted shore she stood alone, waiting. Waiting for what, or for whom? There was nothing, no one, to wait for. She'd seen to that. This was where her exuberance had landed her, with craving for company, defeat to cheer her on. Whatever it was that stretched before her stretched behind her and on either side, above, and under her feet. She'd always known it even if Delia always hadn't. Both were caught in a trap—the trap of middle-age, a trap filled with echoes. Why pretend otherwise? Delia and her appearances! Wait till she was sixty and the pleats in the sagging skin became permanent and the obscene vanity of an old woman made the rouge more reckless, the dye denser, covering less, and *then* pretend.

The liquor closet was in the wall beside the pantry sink. Fran opened it and took out the first bottle that came to hand. It was a pathetic little game that Delia and Katie played between them. When Fran was on a drunk there was never liquor to be found; when sober, they left it open, determined, apparently, to make her feel that they had no qualms whatsoever about her dependability. And this mind you after a life-time of experience!

Fran opened a bottle of soda and got out the ice cubes. They floated in the bright liquid in Fran's glass and the soda whispered intimately round the edges as she stood smiling laconically, her mind steadying in its remembered, its always unexpected, always surprising resolution. For several minutes she stood thus with the glass of whisky in her hand, a febrile sense of drama inclosing her like a shell, then abruptly she emptied the glass down the sink, rinsed it, replaced the whisky bottle in the closet, and went into the hall in answer to Veronica's ring on the door bell.

A blast of wind followed the girl into the house. "Gosh! Am I late, Fran? Forgot my key. And it's so slippery out the bus simply crawled. Sorry if I held you up."

It was out of character for Veronica to apologize or to explain anything, and Fran gave her an appraising glance, noticing her high color and the extraordinary animation in her eyes.

"What's the matter, Nonny? And look at your hair—it's frozen! Go in the bathroom and dry it before you get cold."

"I'm O.K." Veronica replied impatiently. She ran her hands through her hair, baring a beautiful brow too often lost under her untidy bangs. Fran's eyes followed the lovely clean line of youth from chin to throat, and she felt a catch in her breath.

"You look so excited, Nonny. What is it?"

"The weather, and the look of New York on a winter night!"

Fran helped her off with her coat and felt the young body charged with passion. "I wish you'd tell me," she said, frowning. "You seem beside yourself."

"Well, if you must know, I've made a decision. Know how it feels to have made a decision?"

Fran smiled. "Guess I do. What's yours—to marry Chris Wallingford?"

"God no." Standing on one foot, supporting herself with a hand on Fran's shoulder, Veronica pulled off her rubbers and tossed them in a corner. "Nothing to do with Chris."

They went into the parlor. "Mother gone to the Bowers, I suppose?"

"You just missed her," Fran said. She continued to study the girl. "All right, now. No stalling. Tell me."

Veronica turned to her, smiling. "I've just suddenly made up my mind to send the book off to Watts and Wallingford first thing tomorrow morning."

"Is that all? I thought you decided that the minute you'd finished."

"I had and I hadn't." She helped herself to a cigarette from the silver box on the coffee table, and lighted it with Chris's lighter which she took from her pocket. "It's a great relief to have gotten it off my chest, Fran. You've no idea."

"Perhaps I can guess," Fran said, looking at her with increased curiosity. There was something odd in the girl's voice and manner, a suggestion of defiance, of bravado even. Fran added after a minute: "It's been so long since anything of the sort happened to me that I find it a little hard to understand right off how someone else might feel under the circumstances. But maybe you'll be more normal yourself, now."

Veronica frowned. "Normal? Have I been acting abnormal?"

"Obnoxious would be nearer the truth, cranky, suspicious, uncommunicative."

"Just my usual self, in other words." Veronica laughed, and the ice, thawing in her hair, ran in trickles down her cheeks.

"How come Mother didn't pressure you into going to the Bowers with her?"

"She tried, but you know I don't especially care for the Bowers, and I loathe bridge. Besides, you and I had a date, remember?"

"Then let's go out some place and celebrate my decision."

"We could eat here. There's cold turkey."

"I feel about cold turkey the way you feel about the Bowers. No, let's go to your pal George's and order a thick red steak and a bottle of wine."

"I'm going to get a towel and dry that hair before you get pneumonia," Fran said. She went to the bathroom in the hall and returned with a towel. Veronica submitted to her ministrations with unaccustomed meekness. She smiled at her aunt. "Thanks." Then, with an air of detachment: "Do you think Mother goes to the Bowers because of her old friendship with Nadine, or to see Fred?"

Fran gave the short, shining hair a final rub, then stood back. "What do you mean, to see Fred?"

"He's always had a bit of a case on her, hasn't he?" Veronica asked, coolly. "Haven't you noticed the way he looks at her sometimes, sort of the way I look at one of George's steaks?"

This was something new, in keeping with the sudden, uncharacteristic expansiveness about her book. Fran hesitated, then said coldly: "They're old friends. Fred was your father's best man at their wedding, and Charles liked him well enough to make him trustee for his estate. Cut it out, Veronica."

"There's no reason why he shouldn't have a case on her, is there? Or she on him. It's done in the best circles, and she's been pretty circumspect these last few years—or so I'd say."

Fran felt a sudden onset of wariness. "Why won't you learn to accept the fact that Delia is a beautiful and charming woman, that people have always been attracted to her, and probably always will be?"

"Oh, I accept the fact," Veronica replied with an easy laugh. She gave her head a shake, the hair falling softly, like a child's. "I accept the fact, you accept the fact, Delia accepts the fact, the boys accept the fact."

"The boys?"

"The guys, then. When she gets into a taxi or out of it, into a bus or out of it, when she steps out of a revolving door or down the subway entrance and the wind catches her skirts and blows them around . . . and have you noticed that she always wears the kind of skirt the wind can catch?"

Fran stared at her fixedly. "You've never talked like this before. What's got into you?" Then, angrily: "You know how you sound, Veronica? You sound just plain jealous."

Veronica's eyes were wonderfully clear, the flush in her cheeks two bright flags of youth and health. Staring at her in perplexity Fran remembered her own musings of a little while ago, her unjustifiable resentment against Delia, and her heart contracted. Veronica returned her scrutiny without flinching. "Wouldn't . . . not to sound jealous mean just not to sound anything at all? Actually you're wrong. I'm not in the least jealous. Is there any reason why I shouldn't speculate about my own mother? I'm sure lots of her friends do. They must wonder what in the world she does with her life. Her sex life I mean, of course."

"Of course," Fran repeated, thin-lipped. "You would."

"Well, don't you? She's beautiful and attractive, as you say. Is there any harm in my wondering, for instance, why she never married again?"

Fran folded the damp towel neatly over her arm and gave the girl a slow, measuring glance. "Why don't you ask her sometime?" she suggested drily. "I'm sure she'd tell you."

"I'm sure she would, too. It would be, naturally, because of Nick and me. Fear of hurting or upsetting us. Mother love, or something of the sort."

Fran gasped. "You really are turning into a little bitch, you know."

Veronica took a comb from her pocket and began energetically to comb her hair. She looked utterly unconcerned, as though, having brought off the effect, whatever it was, she had intended, she could now relax. Fran watched for a moment, then said somberly: "Whenever I come back here after I've been away, I hope—if I were the prayerful type I'd pray—that you will have come to your senses about your mother. God knows I'm not so hot as a sister, but for you . . . I don't understand it. You seem wise beyond your years in so many things, one would suppose you'd be above this—pettiness."

Veronica finished combing her hair and put the comb back in her pocket with the cigarette lighter. "Must we be so solemn?" she asked, lightly. "Because if we're going to make that movie . . ."

"I think I'd like a drink," Fran said dully. "I shouldn't, but I think I'd like one."

Veronica took the towel from her and kissed her on the cheek. "I don't mean to sound like a bitch and I'm not, really. It's just that I don't happen to be as sentimental about Delia as everyone else seems to be." She smiled into her aunt's eyes. Her own were like the bed of a brook in spring—amber colored, pellucid.

"Make us both a martini, Fran. Just one apiece, while I go up and wash."

Fran watched her leave the room, then went to the pantry and got out Charles Dalton's silver cocktail shaker, ice cubes, gin, vermouth. She thought grimly: Who am I to talk? I waged my battle and won it. Losing it now won't be so hard. I've never won a lasting victory yet, and even losing has its compensations.

She watched the tremor go out of her hands as she measured the liquor and set two glasses on a round silver tray. "Veronica talked to me the way she did simply because she doesn't give a damn about me—less of a damn than she gives about Delia. She's never taken me seriously, as even Nick has. No protest about my having a drink! And yet if she'd said a word? But it matters nothing to her. It matters to Delia, it matters horribly to Delia. But to Veronica obviously nothing matters except Veronica. It's why we get along, she and I. It's why, even over Delia, we can't quarrel too seriously. And who am I to talk . . . who in hell am I to talk!"

Veronica came into the pantry with her hair slicked down, giving her face a demure, madonna look belied by the expression in her eyes. She took the martini which Fran had poured for her and raised it in salute. "Chairs, as the English say. I haven't had one of these things for ages." She sipped. "Glug! Strong."

"Not really, I made them mild on purpose, and just one apiece as you said. You know I shouldn't even be taking this."

"You've done very well so far, Fran. This can't hurt."

"Anyway I'm glad I'm not spending the evening alone," Fran confessed suddenly as she felt the warmth of the liquor filter into her veins. The memory of her earlier self-denial was still sweet in her mind, and it endued this lapse with a taste of pure luxury, like the knowledge of an unexpectedly large balance at the bank. She could even smile at the analogy, thinking of Delia's birthday present of a few days before, in the shape of a generous check to pay off the more pressing of her debts. "Cheers to you, Nonny, and to the book. It was nice of you to stay home and entertain your old aunt."

"Silly!"

They finished their cocktails, and with coat collars muffling their ears, let themselves into the street. The sleet had stopped but the air was charged with ice, a black gleam of it everywhere, and they clung, giggling, to each other's arms as they made their way to Madison Avenue to catch a bus downtown.

CHAPTER

VIII

GEORGE's restaurant was in the mid-Fifties—small, unpretentious and expensive. The floors were covered with sawdust and the walls with crude murals of cows trustingly chewing their cud in vegetarian splendor. Tonight, probably because of the weather, the place was less crowded than usual at this hour, and the proprietor, George himself, recognizing Fran, came to meet her with the smile, at once deferential and intimate, which the proprietors of restaurants keep for their favorite customers. "Ah madam! Long time no see!"

"A year, George."

"And California?"

"It's still there, George. And your wife?"

"Still there, Mrs. Hight!"

Both laughed happily, and when he'd gone to hang up their coats Fran seated herself in a booth facing Veronica, and said:

"Nice to be remembered, I must say. Last time I came here was with you and Nick, wasn't it?"

Veronica was faintly surprised that she should have remembered. It had been one of Fran's especially bad occasions, with George and a colleague practically having to carry her to the door, and Nick going in frantic search of a taxi while aunt and niece argued vehemently the merits and demerits of Fran's returning to the bar for a quick one while they waited. Nick had providentially reappeared in a cab and there had been further protracted argument between Fran and him, ending rather abruptly when Fran collapsed on the sidewalk and had to be half lifted and half dragged into the cab by both children. Funny, mused Veronica, how we always seem to be doing the same thing, going to the same places, saying the same things. Weeks, months, years pass, and you'd scarcely know it. In the larger, wider patterns of action people tend to repeat themselves, like birds that fly across continents from one pinpoint of rest to another, never losing their way, or like the nomadic beasts which moved from water hole to water hole in time of drought.

She gave a sudden laugh, and Fran, deep in conversation with George, raised her brows. "What's so funny, dear?"

"I was thinking about water holes. No one ever thought of naming a bar that, did they?" She turned to George. "I think I'd like a beer. What about you, Fran? And we might as well order."

George gave her a faint understanding smile. He, too, probably remembered their last visit, for it had been quite a feat to get Fran through the revolving door into the street. It had had its funny side all right, though Nick had been scared and Fran had made them promise not to tell Delia.

George turned to Fran. "Martini," he murmured. "Martini, double, very dry, with onion. Right?"

"Right," Fran said, genially. "I shouldn't, but I'm going to."

When he'd gone she said to Veronica: "He never forgets about the onion. You'd think that after a whole year and all the people he sees every day, he'd slip up, but he never does."

"Not as long as you don't slip up on the size of your tip," Veronica remarked, examining the menu which George had put before her. It was rather exclusive, and there was nothing under five dollars. She hoped that Fran had brought enough cash, because she knew she hadn't. No point in worrying about that, though, at this stage.

Fran said reminiscently: "It comes back to me, though vaguely to be sure, that when you and I were here last I overdid rather, didn't I?"

"Some."

"Delia was sick with a cold and I took you and Nick out to dinner, and Nick and I quarrelled. What was it about?"

"Nick was feeling very responsible. He was trying to look after you, and you didn't appreciate it."

"He was fourteen, the poor duck. But what did we quarrel about?"

"He decided in his manly little way that you'd had enough to drink for one night, and tried to put his foot down, and you didn't like it." Veronica ran down the a la carte dishes. "Sirloin, baked potato, vegetables, salad, rolls, dessert, coffee. Perhaps I should have ordered wine instead of beer."

Fran looked considerably cheered up. She loved restaurants and the sense of anonymity which, she said, they gave her. And she had, it seemed, determined to forget the little interlude back there at the house, and Veronica's oblique remarks about her mother. "You're feeling good, aren't you?" she said, smiling. "However, I'd stick to beer if I were you, or it might be *my* turn to take *you* home."

Veronica shook her head. "No one is ever going to have to do that for me."

"Not even Chris?"

Veronica looked reflective. "Can't say I've thought of Chris in that role."

"You haven't!" Fran was elaborately surprised. "I'd say it would become him as well as any other."

"As a husband, I suppose."

"Naturally."

"It would please you if I were to get married, wouldn't it, Fran?"

"Of course it would." George was approaching with their drinks. He made a point of serving his favored customers their first drink, leaving the later ones for the waiters. "I've already told you how much I liked Chris Wallingford. Handsome, sensitive, and bright. What more could one ask?"

"I'm surprised," Veronica said, off-handedly, "that with your experience of marriage you'd still recommend it as a way of life."

"As a way of life, I'm not sure. As insurance against a lonely old age, I am sure."

George set their glasses before them, flicked an invisible crumb from the table-cloth, and retired. "I don't know," Veronica mused. "I see these old married couples around. They look bored to death. Lonely, too. With that kind of loneliness you feel only when you're with someone you don't want to be with."

Fran, glass in hand, gave her a sharp glance. "When did you find that out, at your age?"

"I'm a thousand years old really. You and Delia don't seem to realize it, but I am."

"You give me the willies," Fran murmured. "All you bright young people give me the willies. Why not wait until you have some back log of experience before deciding on a career of pessimism?"

"I'm not pessimistic. Observant, merely. It's my business to be."

Fran took a sip from her glass. "Tell me something about your novel. I think it's outrageous that we should be expected to wait till God knows when before being allowed to read it."

Veronica hesitated. "It's a novel about people, like most novels. Complications, misunderstandings, tears, laughter. So on."

"Well, I admire your courage in tackling such a project. As a failure myself, I drink to your success."

She drank, and Veronica, tasting her beer, thought: I have a feeling this is going to be one of those nights. I suppose I should do something about it, but do what? She shouldn't of course have had that martini at the house before we started out. Now it's too late. Should I threaten to walk out on her if she orders another round? It wouldn't make any difference. It never does. Besides, she's not my funeral. She's strictly Delia's. She's more Delia's funeral than Father ever was, or than I am, and of course Nick has never counted as funeral. And what about my funeral? I've had one. Is the next to be Chris? This deadly, devouring jealousy I have for Chris? Or is it to be the book—the ghastly ignominy of failure? And if not either of those then the other thing, the facing up to *that*. They'll say I've crucified Delia, but that's something between Delia and me. And why should I care when there's the whole future, years and years of future! And if you were to know the truth about every single book that's ever written you'd find crucifixions enough, no doubt about it. Anyway it's between Delia and me and even that's incidental compared to the thing as a whole, the germ grown into the flower, the means justified by the end. But what about Chris? Did he really go to Miriam's apartment that day, and if he didn't, how did the lighter find its way into her sofa? Oh, damn Chris and his charm, damn the way he has with women—even with women like Fran—making one despise oneself for being one of them and falling for the same old tricks. Chris and Miriam, Miriam and me, and heaven knows how many others. All of us sharing the memory of his mouth, the special expression in his eyes which each of us fancies is there just for *her* . . . his voice husky in the darkness, the practised way his tongue finds your ear, the smell of his skin!

Well, all right. Think of all those old couples I just mentioned. The Goodhues, the Robertsons, the Fays—to mention only a few. Married fifty years. Did they start out like Chris and me, filled with desire and distrust, rivals from the beginning, expecting to fuse all their uncertainties at the altar, knitting themselves into the formal situation stitch by stitch, adding convention to convention, adding children, possessions, friends, responsibilities, dogs, cats, potted plants and life insurance to the barricade which was to preserve them for ever against the plain truth that it just isn't in the cards you'll be able to face each other across the dining room table in ten years' time without wanting to scream? And you don't have to go back as far as the poor old Robertsons or the Fays. There's Fran and Herbert Hight—how long did *their* marriage last? Six years. There's Mother and Charles. How long was she faithful to him? A happy marriage, everybody believed, until his horse fell on him. Conventional Mother, with her continental ideas about the marital tie! Who'd have believed it?

Across the table Fran sipped her martini with a sense of pure luxury. Veronica had ceased to bother her. She was a heartless little piece but she'd find out one of these days what it means to be alone, to feel yourself a stranger not only to other people but to yourself, and that no matter where you go or what you do there is no escape from strangeness. Maybe she'll even find out that strangers will put up with you when your friends give up. Maybe Veronica will learn to tip the headwaiter to smile at her, and to remember, after a year's absence, that she preferred an onion to an olive in her martini. She was sitting pretty now with her youth and freshness, with her young man, her talent, her future. So was I, once. And will *she* ever learn what it means to have to develop your particular vice for no better reason than that it helps bring you into contact with other people and compels them to acknowledge your existence even while they might be wishing you dead? Maybe she never would learn. I hope, Fran thought, beginning to feel her liquor, I hope she won't learn the horror of a certain kind of self-knowledge, and the gasping relief of abandoning oneself to a recognizable indifference or a tried and unfailing love. The vocabulary of suffering is a separate one for each of us; arrogant as she is I wouldn't have it that she should master mine.

Veronica broke the silence which had fallen between them: "You know, Fran, I sort of wish you lived nearer us, so we could see more of you."

It was spoken on an impulse and Fran looked at her in surprise.

"That's nice of you, Nonny. I often wish it myself."

"Have you ever thought of selling the place in San Francisco and moving to New York? There's nothing to prevent you, is there?"

"Just the house."

"You can't build your life around a house!"

"I've had to. It's all I've got, and I'm fond of it."

"I can understand that," Veronica said, nodding. "It's the way I felt about our house for a long time. But one gets over it."

Fran sipped and said nothing and Veronica went on: "You could rent it on a long lease, I suppose. People do."

"I have, for a year. But I hated to do even that. Whatever happy memories I have of Herbert—of my married life—are centered in that house."

"It is nice," Veronica agreed. "I remember it from the time we came to visit you after Father died. I remember the palm trees and the poinsettias in the garden, and the sun everywhere."

And everywhere the sense of emptiness which seemed to be an extension of the emptiness she had known in her own home when Charles had died. Some one, some thing had died in Fran's house too, and Veronica had felt the air tremulous from that double loss as, a little girl of ten, she went from room to room, seeking she could not have said what or whom in all that alien green gold sun and in the gaudy beds of flowers which bloomed fiercely in a crooked season. Missing something, she was. Some large boisterous comforting presence that would restore the balance in her bereft and too feminine world. Nick had been too young to understand, but not so young as to have been insensible to his sister's yearning, for he asked her once where Fran's "father" had gone, and whether like his own he had fallen from his horse and been killed in the Park. No, even Nick had not been so young as not to sense the orphanage air in Fran's lovely house and perhaps in Fran herself, and this had made him, even as a very small boy, tender towards her as he might have been towards some large old blind dog.

"I remember that year very well," Fran said with sudden animation. "It was the only time you ever came west, you and Nick. Right after Charles' death. I tried to persuade Delia to stay, but you were having none of it. Such an act as you put on when you heard that you might not be going back to the house on Sixty-eighth Street!"

Veronica looked at her serenely. "I probably felt about it the way you feel about yours. Possibly even for the same reasons."

"Nonsense. You weren't married to Charles." She gave an abrupt laugh. "Though I must say you've sometimes behaved as though you thought you were. Freud would have loved you, deary. He sure would have loved you."

The gin was working and Veronica thought: I asked for this. Now what? Temporisingly, she said: "Well anyway, it's a good thing you have the house and that you love it. Must make it easier to be alone."

"Nothing ever makes being alone easier for anyone."

"Not after twenty years?"

"You'll find after you've had a man around for a while that you never again get used to life without one."

Veronica resigned herself to the inevitable. The last time they had dined here, a year ago, Fran had got started in exactly the same vein. It sometimes took two drinks, sometimes not more than one, to prick the stopped arteries of bitterness and regret.

Tonight the double martini on top the one she'd had at home was having its usual effect, all the quicker because of the abstinence she'd practised for the past week. Now, emotions which seemed to replenish themselves at every spending brought a dark flush to her face and a spurious brilliance to her eyes. She bore a grotesque resemblance to her sister, though Veronica realized that by the time she'd finished her glass her whole appearance would have succumbed to that familiar, young-old mask of the dipsomaniac with its seared fixity giving way to the swivel-glance, the maudlin grin contrived, with pitable artifice, to include friend and stranger alike in its none too ambiguous allure.

She began at once to talk about Herbert in the days of their engagement, Herbert, shy and passionate, swept off his feet by her early beauty and high spirit. "You never knew me in those days, Veronica! I looked more like Delia than I do now, but I was always much more of a devil that she ever thought of being. We were always considered good foils for one another. Father used to call us 'War and Peace,' because I was the agressive one and Delia quite the reverse."

Herbert had been quick to appreciate Fran's talent for the stage, and had encouraged her ambitions, till, like everything else vital and positive in her character, it played itself out in a dead end. She did not hesitate to speak of her failure and spared herself nothing, giving Herbert credit for the brief hope and happiness that had been theirs during those first years. "You know I'd been drinking since I was sixteen, but he didn't know it. My parents knew it. They'd known for some time but they kept it from Herbert. They were worried about my future and I suppose wanted to get me off their hands while the going was good." She laughed, peering down at her nearly empty glass. "And yet they were thoroughly respectable, God-fearing, church-going people. Small town, of course, and of course unlike us—my generation I mean, and heaven knows even more unlike yours. I'm sure it never occurred to them for a minute that they were doing an immoral thing in palming their incipient dipsomaniac of a daughter off on to a perfectly decent, unsuspecting man. The great thing was to get us married, Delia and me, and in Delia's case anyway the husband wasn't being fooled."

She signalled a passing waiter. "Another martini, please. And you, Nonny?"

Veronica shook her head and when the waiter had gone Fran continued: "If I hadn't had the constitution of an ox I'd have died long ago and saved everyone a lot of grief. Grandfather Cranshaw—your great-grandfather—drank himself to death, but he survived till he was ninety-three, so it didn't help much. If I don't get hit by a cab one of these days I'll probably live to be ninety-three myself. Poor Delia!"

The waiter came back with Fran's martini and Veronica suggested they order dinner. Fran seemed slightly annoyed by the interruption. "You order for both of us, Nonny. I don't care what I eat."

Veronica ordered steaks, baked potatoes and salad, and when

the waiter had left them Fran picked up her life history where she'd left off. Veronica knew the story by heart, knew it in every one of its many versions—Fran's, Delia's, their friends'. But for Fran the theme was perennially irresistible—after all she had no other—and it remained unaltered through every recital down to the day when, after her divorce and her shocked realization of what she had blindly and single-handedly wrought, she came flying east to cast herself and her overwhelmed heart on her always-to-be-depended upon twin Delia, married now to Charles Dalton and living in New York. Fran's version always ended with her arrival at the house on Sixty-eighth Street and a paean of praise for Delia and Charles for having taken her in and sheltered her in her hour of direst need.

When she first heard the story directly from Fran, Veronica was thirteen years old. It happened during one of her aunt's periodic visits to New York—again the occasion of her own and Delia's birthday. The day following her arrival, on Nick's urgent request, Fran had taken both children to walk in the Zoo. It was a cold bright November day, the air lively with balloons and the turning flight of pigeons, and Nick, tugging at his aunt's hand, led them unerringly to the lions' cage—his current passion, before which he would stand entranced for as long as he was allowed.

Veronica too had shown signs at that time of having an absorbing passion. She had started to write short stories, and her moods of silent abstraction, livened by sudden bursts of animation as she surfaced from the depths, were now more or less taken for granted by the household, as were her questions, usually unexpected and for the most part irrelevant to whatever conversation might be going on at the time. At other times they were apt to be rather more relevant than her hearers realised. She had early developed the artifice of a self-conscious personality—that of appearing not to be so at all, and she was always all ears.

One detail which eluded Veronica for a long time was what

exactly prompted Fran suddenly to start talking about "your Uncle Herbert" at the moment when the three of them—Fran, Nick, and herself—happened to be standing side by side at the outer rail watching the great drowsy beasts behind their bars. Later she recalled that there had been some preliminary discussion on the question whether lions were more afraid of people than people of lions, and it was at this point that Fran volunteered the information that "your Uncle Herbert" always held the former view, and that he ought to know because as a young man just out of college he'd hunted lions in Africa, and had brought home a lion skin to adorn—not the baby bunting—but the living room hearth of his house out West.

Nick, interrupting his vigil—it took the mention of lions in any form to do it—wanted to know what had happened to the lion skin since the day when Uncle Herbert ceased to be Uncle Herbert and became complicatedly someone quite different and unattached. Fran explained that Uncle Herbert had taken the skin with him when he went away, adding on a note of melanhcoly that it had been just about the only thing he'd apparently thought worth taking, and that, stuffed though the house was with beautiful and valuable "things," the selection of the lion skin was "just like him."

"Didn't he think that *you* were worth taking?" Veronica had put the question with a relevance that would not have passed muster had her aunt confined herself to black coffee with her lunch.

"Me?" Fran had given an astonished laugh, whereat one of the slumbering lions opened its agate eye, gazed at her briefly, and closed it again. "Herbert take me with him? He left me, didn't you know, silly?"

"Did you want him to?" Nick said absent-mindedly.

"Did I want him to what, dear?"

"Take the lion skin."

Fran had laid her hand on the pussy-willow shine and shape of Nick's head. "I didn't care. What'd I want with a beat-up old lion skin?"

"You could have given it to me."

"But you'd have liked Uncle Herbert to take you with him, wouldn't you?" Veronica had pressed, as resting her hands on the crossbar before her she levered herself on her toes towards the cage, at the same time peering up at her aunt, who in her turn gazed thoughtfully at the sleeping lion, perhaps seeing him dead and flattened before her hearth at home. "I'd just as soon he would have," she said after a pause. "If you must know, I'd just as soon your Uncle Herbert had stayed with me."

"But he's not our Uncle Herbert any more, is he?" Nick asked, his interest deriving less from any sense of the complexity of the relationship—he'd never set eyes on Uncle Herbert—than from a private vision, not unlike Fran's, of a dead lion magnificently adorning his own bedroom floor.

Veronica had taken it upon herself to answer her brother: "No, how could he be our uncle when they're divorced?"

Nick had promptly lost whatever curiosity he might have had in the subject, but Fran, with a glance at Veronica, inquired just how much she knew about the business, to which Veronica replied with great self-possession that she knew only what Delia had told her—simply that Aunt Fran and Uncle Herbert had not been able to get along and had therefore decided to be divorced, and that was all.

At this point one of the lions rose and stalked over to a farther corner of his cage, where he flung himself down, his great rosette of a head on his paws, and engaged in an hypnotic contest with Nick, who moved down the length of the cage to face him.

Still balancing on her toes with the crossbar under her stomach and leaning dangerously forward, Veronica then queried with an air of polite compulsion whether Fran missed Uncle Herbert, to which Fran replied that of course she did.

"Why don't you go back to him, then?"

"Darling! He's married again and has four children."

"Does he like children?"

"Apparently he does."

"What a pity," Veronica murmured, wide-eyed under her childish brows, and seemed about to submerge into one of her moods, when Fran asked why it should be such a pity. Veronica shrugged her little shoulders. "Just that you didn't have any, that's all."

There the conversation had paused, hung on some agreed-upon nail between them, to be taken down and resumed a little later when they continued their round of the Zoo, past the sea lions where Nick engaged in a piercing duet with one charming slug-like creature sunning herself on her piazza, past the polar bears to the restaurant for hot dogs and Coca-Cola, thence to the drome-dary cage, the elephants, and finally to the ponies where Nick insisted he be allowed to ride. They watched him trot away, a miniature Charles complete with hound's tooth jacket and imita-tion spurs.

Waiting for him to come back, Veronica fed peanuts to the squirrels and listened as Fran, worked up to a revery, described how she had come all the way from California to weep on Delia's neck. "I couldn't stand the house without Herbert. And when I'd been with your mother and father, I couldn't stand them either. They were together. They had each other. And I had nothing." And at that—it always happened—the drama came to an incon-clusive end, leaving the audience of one disappointed and in-credulous, since even at thirteen this didn't make the kind of sense which her creative instinct assured her it should.

"But what happened after *that*? What did you do—go back to California?"

"Eventually, yes."

"Why didn't you stay with Mother and Father?"

"I couldn't very well, darling. They had their own lives."

"Why didn't you marry someone else, then?"

Fran, smoking a cigarette and watching the child as she knelt on the grass, a squirrel gingerly appraising her outstretched hand, replied in a heavy voice: "I never found anyone I liked as much as I liked your Uncle Herbert."

Veronica, seeming only half attentive—the other half concentrated on the squirrel—inquired with the barest relevance: "Did Mother, ever, like anyone else?"

Fran too, was only half attentive, the other half concentrating on the blank that she found herself facing—that she always found herself facing, at this juncture of her story.

"No," she answered the kneeling child. "So you see, we're in the same boat, your mother and I."

The squirrel hitched itself closer and Veronica's long, graceful hand remained motionless, a peanut balanced on its index finger.

"But Mother had lots of friends. Don't you like Mother's friends, Fran?"

"Friends?" Fran seemed to speak from a distance. "Friends aren't the answer."

"You mean, to marry them?"

"Darling, you'll understand these things better when you grow up."

Veronica stayed silent for a moment, then in a softly matter-of-fact voice she addressed her next question to the squirrel:

"Had Mother started me when you came to stay with her?"

Fran looked suddenly at the glossy dark head, half concealed under its red beret, at a dark eye just visible under its delicate brow. "Had your mother *what*?"

"Started me. You know—was I going to be born when you came to stay with us that time after Uncle Herbert left you?"

"No," Fran said. "No, you weren't. You didn't arrive until the following year."

The squirrel, snatching the peanut from Veronica's hand, scuttled off with it, and that had been the end of Fran's story for the time being.

Their dinner arrived and Fran, finishing her drink, ordered another. Veronica murmured a protest: "Hadn't you better eat something? That makes *four*."

"Observant, aren't you?" And she added with sharp petulance:

"I don't believe you've listened to a word I've said for the past ten minutes!"

Veronica gave a half laugh. "I have! Honestly I have, Fran. You were saying you don't know what you'd have done without Delia. But then," she gazed consideringly at the hunk of prize steer on her plate, "but then you're always saying that."

"Am I?" Fran sounded anxious. "What a bore I must be. That's the trouble with this stuff. Makes you repetitious. What Herbert used to tell me. 'For God's sake, Fran! You've told me that already, don't you remember?' When I was off on some story about something or other. A friend. My acting. Got so we quarrelled over it. About everything. Trivialities."

She glanced without interest at her plate, and Veronica thought: All of five bucks' worth and it'll go back to the kitchen untouched. Like last time. I wonder how much money she's thrown away on meals she orders and never eats?

"All the same, Herbert was a damned good husband. Always gentle, treating me as if I were sick, or a child." She smiled mawkishly and Veronica thought: If she'd killed him with an ax instead of just driving him away, she'd still go on about him in this fashion. Mea culpa . . . mea culpa . . .

". . . Carry me up to bed in his arms and tuck me in and bring me aspirin and sit with me until I went to sleep."

The fourth martini arrived and Fran's smile settled into a kind of mask, as though she'd had a stroke.

"I was so goddam stuck on myself as an actress, but I had reason to be. Set my heart on taking the part of Medea in a stock company I'd managed to get interested in me . . . year before Herbert and I busted up. Guess I didn't know how close we were to it . . . guess he didn't either. Caught us off balance, and the horrible part of it was I'd just gotten back into the swing of work. I was crazy about the play . . . and one night—sober, mind you! Sober for the first time in weeks . . . I asked Herbert to listen while I read the bit, towards the end, where Medea kills her children. Remember when Jason comes in and asks her what the stain is on her hands, and she answers: 'The wine I was pouring for you spilled on my hand!' "

She slid back into the part, raising her voice, and several of the diners glanced at their table. Fran's eyes were glassy. "Know what happened? Herbert laughed. Couldn't help himself, couldn't stop."

Trembling, Fran tried to light a cigarette. "Laughed and laughed. And it wasn't put on either." She got the cigarette lighted and pushed aside her plate of food, untouched. "He never had laughed at me before, and we knew, now, that that was that."

CHAPTER

I X

IT was after midnight when Delia let herself into the house to find Veronica in pyjamas, curled up on the parlor sofa with a book. "Nonny, you weren't waiting up for me, were you? Where's Fran?"

Veronica put down her book. "Fran's still out."

Delia began to pull off her gloves. "Where did she go? I thought you were spending the evening together."

"I thought so too, but she overdid at dinner, and then we found that neither of us had enough money to pay the bill, so she suggested that she wait at the restaurant while I came home in a cab and get the travellers checks she said she'd left in her bureau."

Delia took off her coat and laid it with her gloves at the foot of the sofa. The glow resulting from her own pleasant evening drained out of her, as she said slowly: "I don't understand. Where is she now?"

"No idea. She phoned to say she'd decided to fix it up with George—he runs the restaurant where we ate, you know it, on Fifty-second and Madison—and George said it was O.K. She could stop in and pay him later. And since we'd missed the second show and it was such a lousy night, I didn't feel like going all the way back. Fran said she'd take a cab home."

"But why in the world couldn't she have arranged all that with George without sending you back for the travellers checks?"

Veronica shrugged. "Guess she wanted an excuse to get rid of me."

Delia winced. "When did that occur to you?"

"Frankly," said Veronica, "I'd had all I could take long before we were halfway through dinner. I was quite glad to leave."

"Oh Nonny, when you saw she was tight!"

Veronica looked sullen. "What was I supposed to do? You know how she gets. And she made it quite clear that she didn't want me around."

Delia took an agitated step or two, then faced her again. "How long ago was this?"

"About two hours since she phoned."

"From George's restaurant?" Delia started towards the telephone, but stopped when Veronica said: "She's not there now, because I've called, and they told me Mrs. Hight had paid her bill and left."

Delia sank into a chair and for a moment neither spoke. Veronica said at last: "She had the dough all the time, and she could have stayed at George's and gone on drinking, but I suppose she knew we'd come after her, so she took herself off somewhere else." And after a moment she added slowly: "She never gets so drunk but what she has things worked out, have you noticed?"

Delia stared frowning at the floor. "I wonder where she would have gone. My God . . . there are so many possibilities!"

"Why worry? You don't when she's not around."

"Don't I? That's what you think." She stared at Veronica. "Was Fran *very*?"

"Very. She'd finished with Medea and had got going on 'The Constant Wife,' about the time I decided to leave."

Delia's smile vanished almost as soon as it appeared. "You poor child! But she'd been behaving so well, and as usual I'd let myself begin to hope . . . One never learns."

Veronica thought of her aunt as she had last seen her at the restaurant, ogling George. Where would she end up, and how far could she be expected to navigate in the state she was in? I shouldn't have left her, Veronica told herself, guiltily. I could have stayed, or called Delia or something.

Delia said abruptly: "It's terribly slippery out, and that worries me too." She rose. "I think I'd better try to locate her."

"How in the heck can you locate her? There must be half a million bars in town. You can't call all of them!"

Delia laughed shortly. "I have a little list," she said over her shoulder as she went towards her desk. "Like the Lord High Executioner—I have a little list."

This was news to Veronica, who watched curiously as her mother sat down at the desk and took a notebook from one of the pigeon holes. Delia leafed through it until she found the page she wanted, then dialled a number. While waiting for an answer she smiled bleakly at her daughter. "Fran has a certain round," she explained with forced lightness. "Whenever I find out some place she's been to, I make a note of the address. It's worked a few times, though I suspect she usually refuses to take the call, or else doesn't hear it. Hullo?" She turned to the receiver. "Is this Pat's on Third Avenue? Would you please page Mrs. Frances Hight? Hight." She spelled it. "Thank you. I'll hold on."

She looked at Veronica. "You must promise not to mention this to Fran. She'd be furious if she knew I kept a list of her favorite dives. On the rare occasions when I happen to find her I pretend I was just going on a hunch."

"I don't see why you bother," Veronica muttered. A peculiar and unexpected sense of shame made her add quickly: "Sorry I let you in for this. I should have stuck with her."

"I'm glad now that you didn't. I'd have two of you to worry about."

"You seem to like worrying," Veronica burst out, flushing. "As I said before, Fran seems to make out perfectly well when you are not around to act the wet nurse. She's lived to be fifty!"

"Let us suppose for the sake of argument that Nick was always getting into trouble, and that he had learned to depend on you for help. What would you do?"

"If he was the pain in the neck that Fran sometimes is, I think I'd let him stew in his own juice."

"Not if you loved him, you wouldn't."

Veronica closed her book with a gesture of impatience. "You can love someone without allowing yourself to be made a monkey of. Fran's got your number, that's the trouble. She *knows* you'll always come across. If she didn't know it. . . ."

Delia turned to the phone. "Yes? No answer? Well, thank you very much. I'm sorry to have bothered you."

She glanced at the notebook, and dialled again. "I'll try Smithy's on Greenwich Street. They're usually good about paging people."

Waiting for a response, she said slowly: "Yes, Fran knows I'll always come across, and I know it. I haven't got your stamina, Nonny. I often wish I had."

She interrupted herself to speak into the receiver. "Yes, Smithy's Bar? Mrs. Hight doesn't seem to be there? Thank you."

She sat for a moment, gazing at the notebook, then: "I don't believe they even tried to find her, that time. Well, there's always Lou and Barney's. I'll try them."

Veronica returned to her book, behind whose shielding covers she reviewed the evening that was to have been a celebration of her decision to send the manuscript to Chris's father. Some celebration! Once more she caught herself remembering Fran's face in the restaurant. It possessed a kind of macabre fascination for her, with its suggestion of a family likeness to her own, to Nick's, and of course to Delia's. How deep did such a likeness go, and from what other source could she expect to hand on her own? How did one excise what one did not want, except perhaps by some prodigious effort of the spirit *not* to be like these others, like any of them? Not to participate in any degree whatsoever in the strength of one or the weakness of the other—to render one's fate uniquely, stubbornly one's own, one's purpose a clear triumph over the commonplace of flesh and blood. *I was not wanted, therefore I shall not want.*

Leaving Fran tonight she had rushed back home in a taxi and had gone straight to the telephone and called Chris's number in Cambridge. Then she'd had to wait, listening to the sound of the bell ringing in his room, ringing, ringing, its imperious summons drilling into her nerves. There'd been no answer and she'd finally hung up, feeling sick and cold, and almost at once the phone had rung, and it was Fran, telling her not to come back to George's, that she'd take a cab home. Veronica had thought dully: It's always someone else, someone you don't give a damn about. At the moment of greatest intensity there would be some drunk mumbling into your ear, or some asinine inquiry whether your feet were dry, or had you finished your book, or what would you like for lunch?

"Piero's? Is this Piero's bar on University Place? Would you please page Mrs. Frances. . . ."

Delia gave an angry exclamation. "The beast's hung up on me!"

The Dolphin on MacDougal Street, Pete and Nelly's on East Fourth, Granados', Fitzy's Pop-Inn, Lucky Jim's, The Cup and Stirrup. . . .

"No soap," Delia said at last, sighing. The clock on her desk chimed the hour and she rose. "Better go to bed, Veronica. I'll wait up."

Yawning, Veronica swung her legs off the sofa.

"You're not going to stay up all night, are you?"

"I hope I won't have to. Good night, dear."

Veronica hesitated. "I wouldn't worry too much if I were you, Mother."

"I'll try not to."

She watched the girl walk to the door, then called after her:

"Veronica!" And as Veronica turned: "Your book. Have you sent it to Watts and Wallingford?"

"Tomorrow," Veronica said, and stretched her thin arms above her head. "Tomorrow, probably. Good night, Mother."

When she'd gone Delia rose and went to the kitchen to heat water for coffee. It looked like a long vigil, one of many she could remember. Equal though she knew herself to be, most of the time, to these recurring crises in her existence, there were moments when she craved the solace of masculine companionship, the intimacy and the support of a personality other than her own. Why, she asked herself angrily, when I had the chance didn't I take it? There'd been more than one, but of the three men who had attracted her two were married; the third, younger than she by ten years, had been adoring for almost as many, but had in the end yielded to her sudden and—to him—incomprehensible refusal to make fools of them both, and had gone away. She missed him, and there were moments when she could find it in herself to think wistfully of Charles, who could at all events be counted on to sound a cheerful note, if nothing else.

Her thoughts turned gratefully to her friends the Bowers. Already the genial memory of her evening with them was fading under the strain of anxiety, but she recalled it now, trying to warm herself in the glow of their affection for her and for each other. Twenty years married, their life together was a kind of lodestar to which she had hitched her somewhat rickety faith. Should she call them on the phone, just for the sake of hearing a normal reassuring voice and an immediate offer to come over and bear her company? She was tempted, then resisted the impulse at the recollection of just such another evening when Fred Bowers had helped her put a rampant Fran into bed and hold her there until the sleeping powder, dropped into a glass of whisky, had done the trick. No, Delia admonished herself, resolutely. I can't call Fred and Nadine tonight. I'll have to sit this one out alone. Coffee would help, and a book, and the telephone might ring at any moment. She had to be braced for that emergency, for the sound of her sister's voice, thickly incoherent, or for the accents of a total stranger or those of a precinct policeman spelling out a litany of sordid facts which could come as no great surprise.

It was after three o'clock in the morning and she'd fallen asleep on the sofa when she heard Fran's voice clear and strong in the parlor door: "Delia! Can you let me have something to pay the cab?"

Delia sprang up, almost weeping with relief. Fran was hatless, her coat flapping open, her cheeks a dark red. "God, what a night! I thought we'd never make it. What are you doing up at this hour?"

"I was worried sick about you. Here, come in and get warm. I'll take care of the cab."

She went quickly out of the house, down the steps to the waiting cab. When she came back Fran was standing beside the sofa lighting a cigarette. Her hair had come down and her hands were shaking as though with ague. "Fran, are you all right?"

"Of course. What's the idea of sitting up for me all night?"

She dropped the match, then the cigarette. Stooping to retrieve them she fell on her knees, but rose at once, clutching the sofa for support.

"Better sit down," Delia said gently. "I'll get some coffee. I have some all made."

"Trust you," Fran said, distinctly. "Trust you to have it all made and the bandages all laid out. Always the Girl Scout. What they call'm? Den Mothers. That's you all over—Den Mother."

She lowered herself on the sofa and stared at her sister with a malevolent grin. "What's the idea, waiting up for me?"

"I wasn't sure you had a key. It wouldn't have been the first time that you'd locked yourself out."

"All by yourself?"

"Nonny went to bed."

"And Fred?"

Delia looked at her. "Fred who?"

"Fred Bowers. Your old buddy boy Fred."

"I left the Bowers at twelve o'clock, to be exact."

"You're always so exact."

"I'll go get the coffee," Delia said, turning away, but Fran called after her: "I'd prefer a drink, if you don't mind. Though I'm sure you do mind."

Delia came back to the sofa and stood looking down at the other, who sat quite erect. Except for her bloodshot eyes and trembling hands one would not have guessed how drunk she was. Delia said evenly: "I will get you a drink on condition that you go right to bed. It's after three and I'm tired. You must be, too."

"Don't be so Christly Florence Nightingale. It couldn't have been such an ordeal for you with old Freddy to keep you company. Why didn't he wait for me? Did last time, remember? Tried to get into my bed, and you spoiled the fun. Den Mother, you are. After all Nonny doesn't give a whoop what I do—why should you?"

Delia left her and went to the pantry, where she poured a stiff shot of whisky in a glass, added an ice cube and a dash of water, and brought it back to Fran. "Here's your drink. Would you like something to eat?"

"Veronica ran out on me."

"You made an excuse to get rid of her, and you know it. Finish your drink, Fran, and let's go."

"I was boring her. Well, she was boring me. Know something?"

Delia waited. She realized that there could be no rushing Fran at this stage. She was far gone, but not far enough. Nothing to do but wait for it to hit her and she'd keel over as though from a hypodermic.

"I'm getting good and sick of Nonny's airs and graces. So she's written a book, so what? What's she got to write a book about? I could give her a few pointers that'd make her sit up. So could you."

Delia's face hardened. "I know you're drunk, Fran, but just get this, will you? Lay off Veronica. Do you understand me? Lay off her. And don't pretend you don't know what I mean. You do."

Fran put the untouched glass on the table. "Airs and graces. Like to hear what she thinks about you? She told me." Fran laughed. "She's got us mixed up, Delia. Gives you credit for all my vices except the booze. She *knows* you don't do that. But she thinks you're sleeping with Freddy Bowers."

Delia continued to stand, looking down at her, saying nothing. She had to hear it, and decided that perhaps it would be just as well if she heard it all. Fran laughed again, the guttural private laugh of the alcoholic seeing visions. "Thinks you must be, because what could an attractive woman do about her sex life unless she slept around with her friends' husbands? Nonny's got you taped, darling. Tisn't fair. Someone ought to put her wise to us, Dele. To you and me. Somebody should. Duty."

Delia said with deliberation: "If you say one single word to Veronica about anything, its finis between you and me, Fran. Do you get me? Finis."

Fran's eyes flickered. She took a sip from the glass and made a face. "Don't talk nonsense."

"I asked you did you get me?"

"I do, but she doesn't. She thinks you're deep. Why'd you let her? I've a good mind . . ."

Delia leaned down and gave her shoulder a savage shake. "You hurt just one of those children, Fran, and it will be the last time you'll see them, or me. Tomorrow, when you're sober, I shall repeat this. But sleep on it tonight, if you know what's good for you."

Fran's smile trickled into her face like water into sand. It seemed as though she had not heard a word Delia said, as, her whole face darkening, she muttered suddenly: "Some bastard stole my pocketbook. All my travellers checks, driver's license, everything. Didn't have a cent to pay the taxi."

"It was over five dollars," Delia told her dispassionately. "I read the meter."

"Why wouldn't it be? Brought me all the way from 125th Street, somewhere. Only cab that'd stop in this stinking weather. And I didn't have the price of a tip."

"Where did you get the money to pay for your drinks?" Delia asked her. She felt dry and empty, the passion dead in her.

"Guy lent me the dough. Got his address some place so I can return it. Had a hell of a time getting away from him, too. Real bastard. Just because he thought I was in a spot."

"But who do you think it was took your pocketbook? And where did it happen—at George's?"

"Never lost anything at George's. He's a good guy. Good friend. Always remembers me. Like old Dipper at the Leonard. Dipper always remembers me too. No, I lost the damned thing after I left George's. Probably left it in that first taxi going to Alonso's, uptown. How the devil'd I know?"

"You just said you thought somebody stole it, and if that's the case we ought to tell the police."

Fran grunted. "You think of everything. When'd the police ever do anyone any good? Guy stole it was the guy lent me five bucks, probably. Swiped my pocketbook so he'd have an excuse to pick me up. But I've got his address, if it's the right one."

"It was obliging of him to leave you his address," Delia said with sudden weariness. "Are you going to finish that drink, or shall we go up?"

"Don't you get bored with yourself sometimes, being so superior?"

"Yes," Delia said. "I do, often."

"Knew it was a mistake for me to come here," Fran declared, shaking her head. "Always a mistake. We've tried it and tried it and it doesn't work. And Veronica thinks it would be a good idea if I was to live *here*! If that isn't innocence for you." She stared at Delia. "Know what I'm going to do? I'm going to move into the Leonard. Dipper'll take me in. Always has a room for me. Always."

She rose with great stateliness and started to button her coat in preparation for what, as Delia knew, was intended to be a grand exit. She had apparently lost her gloves with her pocketbook, and now Delia noticed that there were bruises on the backs of her hands and another on her temple. "Fran!" she exclaimed. "How did you get those things? You're hurt!"

Fran turned on her in a kind of fury, then reeled, striking the coffee table with her knee and knocking the crystal bowl which she'd given Delia, to the floor. "You can go to hell," she announced thickly. "You can go straight to your superior hell and leave me out of it!"

Delia caught her in her arms. "Fran, dear, let me help you."

Fran was weeping. "I had to fight him. And he seemed all right in the beginning. Said he knew people I said I knew out west. Quite decent. Then in the cab going to Alonso's, his idea, I had to ask the driver to stop and let me out. Told the driver I was his wife and having a tantrum, that I'd drunk too much, and the driver said we could both get the hell out for all of him. Then he followed me into the bar."

"Who followed you?" Delia was helping her towards the stairs, trying to talk in whispers so as not to arouse Veronica.

"Guy who picked me up at George's after Nonny left. But he was a bastard, a real bastard."

"But those bruises!" Delia murmured in anguish. "How did you get such awful bruises?"

"That was afterwards, when we'd got out of the cab. He tried to push me into a doorway and it was dark and no one around. We struggled and he hit me, I guess. I got away at last and ran down the street and another cab came along and stopped and I got in, and it brought me here."

They went into Fran's bedroom and Delia undressed her and put her into bed. She begged for another drink and Delia went down to get it, knowing that there was nothing to be gained by an argument, and that the sooner she knocked herself out the better.

Back in the parlor she picked up the bowl. It was not broken, but a deep interior flaw marked its shining circle, a wavering undulation which, as she studied it, seemed to move like some evil water snake in a phosphorescent void.

In her own room at last, Delia lay wide awake with her door ajar and a night light burning in the hall outside. She listened to the faint nocturnal sounds of the house, for to the wakeful there is no such thing as silence. Nor was there room in her tired mind for resentment or even despair. She found herself in the clasp of that dull resignation to which people accustom themselves, as they do to the tension of scar tissue in their flesh. This, she reminded herself, was what she had known was going to happen as soon as Fran arrived, and she thought of herself as the hero of Somerset Maugham's *Of Human Bondage*, tied to another person's fate for as long as they two should live, only this was a more insoluble bond than that which binds lovers, or than the bond of marriage itself. If Fran and I were Siamese twins, thought Delia, the surgeon's knife might sunder our flesh. Separate, we remain irrevocably joined.

She dropped off into a light sleep, but wakened almost at once and springing out of bed ran to Fran's bedroom two doors down the hall from her own. Fran's door was open, the light from her bed table shone on the bed and on the overturned glass beside her. A lighted cigarette had fallen among the blankets, setting fire to them, but Fran lay oblivious, groaning in her sleep, the bruise on her temple standing out like some terrible flower in the tangle of her hair.

CHAPTER

X

A GLAZE of sunlight lay on Veronica's window sill and she could see a pigeon sunning on a cornice of the building next door, above the first, fast melting snow of the year. A liner coming in to dock lifted its voice in a great cry of arrival, and as the sound died away she heard the pigeon crooning in its little private zone of light from which the snow had already gone.

Veronica took Donald Wallingford's letter from her pocket and spread it on her desk to read over again. It was typewritten on heavy white paper of formal note size with the firm's name and address, its telephone number, expensively embossed, and Wallingford's signature scampering like a large black insect almost the width of the inside page.

Veronica read it as she might have read a love letter, a luminous incredulity tingling in her veins.

Dear Miss Dalton,

Mr. Watts and I have now both read your manuscript, 'Who is Silvia,' and I am anxious that you should know our reactions without delay. We like your book. In fact we think it quite the most unusual piece of writing that has come our way for a long time—I was about to say 'from a young lady of your age,' but any qualification would be impertinent in every sense of the word. We do of course want to publish the book, subject to some minor conditions which we should like to discuss with you at your early convenience. If you will telephone me here we can arrange for you to meet Mr. Watts and myself, and it would give me pleasure if you will let me take you to lunch afterwards.

Yours sincerely,

Donald Wallingford.

P.S. If this were not to be a strictly business session, I'd say I wish Chris could have been with us!

Veronica replaced the letter in its envelope, where it had at once a marvelous, mysterious, and intimate air. She told herself that she was being extremely silly and naive to get so worked up over something that was after all hardly more personal than an ordinary business deal, but the fact remained—she *was* worked up. Even in the recaptured moments of her keenest childhood joys, even in love—and this too she could admit to herself—she had not experienced this particular thing, this aeration which seemed about to lift her off her feet into some ineffable element from which she slowly, diaphanously settled down to earth as she heard Katie dragging the vacuum cleaner along the passage towards her door.

"About time you let me pick up in here," Katie said as she entered. Then catching sight of Veronica's face she came to a full stop, and smiled. "Good news, honey?"

"Wonderful," Veronica replied, and put Wallingford's letter in her skirt pocket with one from his son.

"Well," Katie said, "you wouldn't go down to your mother's desk and send him an answer, would you, while I'm raking out this parrot's nest? And be sure to give him my regards. I like that Chris."

Veronica smiled and decided to let Katie think what she would. Delia and Fran were both out, Delia doing her stint at the rummage shop, and Fran settling down at the Leonard Hotel downtown, where she'd moved the day before, and from whose dingy fastness she intended to scout around and find herself a job—or so she'd announced in a typical excess of zeal following her recent bout and after setting fire to Delia's guest room bed. Sober, Fran made sense as usual, over-riding Delia's weak-kneed plea that she stay with them at least until she found a job.

"What's the use?" Fran had asked, shrugging. "I can't promise it won't happen again, and I'm not going to put you and Nonny through another session like the last, if I can help it."

"But if it should happen when you're alone at the Leonard!"

The sisters argued it out, pro and con, in Veronica's hearing, but Fran carried the day, promising to keep in touch, treating her infirmity as though it were epilepsy she was prone to, or some affliction of the heart! In the end she departed with her suitcase, a penitential yet somehow heroic figure, and the great game of wishful thinking started all over again.

"Maybe it will stick a little longer this time," Katie had volunteered hopefully to Delia as, between them and with Veronica's assistance—she'd come into the room and found them contemplating the pyre, speculating what could be salvaged, what not—they carried blankets, sheets, and mattress out to the sidewalk for the sanitation truck to take away. "May be a burned child can be made to fear the whisky—h'm?" And they'd laughed, somewhat on the grim side.

A faintly acrid smell of burnt wool still hung about the hall as Veronica left Katie to her vacuuming, and pausing at Delia's door she hesitated, thinking: "Should I call her and tell her . . . and tell Fran about Mr. Wallingford's letter?"

She had a sudden spontaneous impulse to share her happiness when she caught across the room her own reflection in her mother's mirror, the face, as she saw at once, of a young woman passionately in love. A swift frown shattered its radiance, and she turned and went quickly downstairs to the parlor and sat down at Delia's desk.

From Cambridge Chris had written briefly and with the strain of their last parting evident in every line. The letter was edgy, boastful, and full of innuendoes. He'd been working on that essay about Joseph Conrad and it was going well. He had a hangover from a terrific party at Marblehead the night before. Interesting

women, and the most promising little Polish girl from somewhere out west, whom he was taking out to dinner and dance as
soon as he'd got over the party at Marblehead. About Thanksgiving, he couldn't really make up his mind whether he wanted
to spend it in New York or with friends in Providence who had
invited him a long time ahead. Had Veronica sent off her manuscript to his father? Or was she still exercising the privilege of her
sex and playing hard to get? "Don't overdo it, honey. Budding
authors come a dime a dozen these days and you wouldn't want
the old man to cool off . . ."

Re-reading this missive, Veronica's eyes glowed with temper.
The condescension of .it, the nerve! He had expended all his
meager store of generosity in that gesture of an introduction to his
father, and now no doubt he hoped—and with what Olympian
pomp he'd deny that he hoped—that her novel might be turned
down, and he himself be restored to the eminence of the superior
being who'd done his best for her against his private judgment of
her talents, and to whom she would now return in all humility for
solace in love.

"If he knew how much I really did owe him!" If he knew that
all it had taken to goad her into sending the manuscript to his
father was finding his cigarette lighter tucked away among
Miriam's sofa cushions! A little thing like that . . . a little insignificant thing . . . only it wasn't little, it wasn't insignificant. It was
enormous, hideous . . . a great hydrant unlocked! But how right
I was not to let Chris read the manuscript first, not to have risked
the chance of allowing his opinion to affect my decision, his praise
or condemnation to spark the daring which it had taken to let it
out of my hands at last.

Well, she'd had her revenge and it should have tasted rather
sweeter than it somehow did. And now what? Should she write
Chris a gay friendly note, inclosing his father's letter, with a casual
postscript to let him know she'd found his lighter, and asking
whether she should return it to him or keep it until his next visit

to town? No need to mention *where* she'd found it. Let him work that one out for himself. Better still, why not mine the situation for every ounce of the irony in it, simply by keeping quiet and letting Donald Wallingford do the talking?

Undecided, Veronica sat and studied the objects arranged neatly on her mother's desk, a beautiful mahogany piece someone had given her at the time of her marriage to Charles. Like everything that belonged to Delia this had its particular orderly appearance from the space reserved for the telephone, pigeon holes stacked with stationery, letters, bills, bank statements, an ebony tray containing pens and pencils, to the small antique snuffbox in which she kept postage stamps. In a central recess under the carved scallop shell design stood a sectional frame from which three faces peered back at her in varying degrees of solemnity: herself, Charles, and Nick, taken when each of them could not have been more than four years old, contemporaries except for the frou-frou and ringlets of Charles, caught in a doting era when frou-frou and ringlets were the thing even for small boys.

As a child Veronica liked to sit at this desk and pretend to write letters and pay bills. Delia had let her take over one of the pigeon holes and it was still marked with the initials V.C.D. for Veronica Cranshaw Dalton, scratched into the wood when she was six years old.

As she sat, now, absently cataloging the objects before her and wondering whether she should write to Chris, whether she should call Donald Wallingford immediately to set a date for their meeting, or whether it would be better to wait, so as not to appear over-eager; reddening at her own folly, calling herself a dope, self-conscious as any spotty-faced bobby-sockser faced with her first serious date—as she sat, a prey to these interior conflicts, inevitably as a picture out of focus adjusts itself on the screen and *fits*, so the small panorama on Delia's desk wavered before her eyes and lost, for a second, its familiar physical components, then came together sharply as a paragraph of symbols in another context: "Silvia was tidy. You could see this tidiness in the way she kept her belongings, her desk for instance . . ." followed a catalog of every article on Delia's desk. ". . . tidyness, cleanliness, a soignée appearance were, in her set, a public mirror reflecting a private grace. They knew no better. Nor did she."

With a queer, half appealing, half defensive gesture Veronica rose from her chair and at that moment the telephone rang, shattering the image and restoring the original view.

"Veronica darling!"

"Chris."

"Can you hear me, Veronica? You sound awful far away."

"Well, I am!"

"Listen, I just this minute got a letter from Dad. Have you heard from him?"

"This morning." She picked up a pencil and began to doodle on Delia's engagement pad.

"Holy smoke, Nonny! They like your book. Dad writes that they're all enthusiastic—the other editors, I mean, including old Bunny Watts. But you know all about it, don't you? He's written you—told me he had."

Veronica drew a figure-eight round Delia's reminder to herself that she call the cleaners about Nick's tuxedo and telephone Fran about tickets for *The Threepenny Opera* Thursday night.

"Nonny, I'm so happy for you. Right off the bat like that! And Dad means what he says. You're going to see him, aren't you? At once? Has he called you yet?"

"I'm supposed to call him." She was breathless. "Chris, are you really pleased?"

"Are you really crazy? Did you expect me to be anything but?"

His voice had the high, silly ring it got whenever he let himself be carried away. "Listen, Nonny. You'll like Dad. He's the easiest, nicest guy in the world. And he understands people. I mean shy, difficult people like you."

"Am I shy and difficult?"

"Are you! No, but listen. He's the real McCoy. Oh damn, I wish I was with you now, this very minute."

"What about Thanksgiving? You're coming, aren't you?"

"If I can hold out that long."

"And what about the friends in Providence? And the Polish girl in Marblehead?"

She heard his muffled laugh. "The hell with her. She's got shoulder blades like a shark's fins. Nonny!" His voice wavered.

"Nonny, make the most of this, won't you? It's . . . I don't know whether it's the greatest moment in a person's life—an ordinary person, I mean. But in a writer's life there's never anything to touch it. I know what I'm talking about."

"They haven't actually taken it, yet." Childish, she told herself, playing naughts and crosses on the engagement pad. Childish, just because somebody has said something you've done is good . . .

"Nonny, are you listening? I said I knew what I was talking about . . ."

She, too, knew what he was talking about—she knew that for the moment at any rate some source of generosity had fountained in Chris, and that she should be grateful—for the moment.

It was not until after they had said goodbye and hung up that she remembered she had not mentioned the cigarette lighter, but the oversight didn't seem to matter much for the remainder of that day.

CHAPTER

XI

DONALD WALLINGFORD's office was an unpretentious affair of panelled walls hung with photographs of sailing boats and views of the Maine coast. There was a minimum of furniture—three chairs, a desk, a bookcase filled with copies of the firm's recent publications, and an old-fashioned hatrack of the type one finds in small backwoods hotels, from which there hung a felt hat and a raincoat from which the lining had parted company, giving it a frowsy effect.

The air smelled powerfully of tobacco smoke, and as Wallingford's door opened, a small, pale, pointed face like a rabbit's appeared and a voice exclaimed querulously: "God in heaven! You could cut this with a knife."

Wallingford put down his corncob and rose. "Hullo, Bunny. I'll open the window a crack."

He did so, and his partner stepped shrinkingly into the room, nibbling the air with his nose. Mr. Wilfrid Watts was one of those people whose striking resemblance to some other member of the animal kingdom endues them with a blessed immunity to the charge of age. At sixty, ten years Wallingford's senior, he might have been taken for an over-sized elderly rabbit or an under-nourished young one, and only his eyes, crepuscular and dark, gave any hint of his awareness of this possibility. In their melancholy way they seemed to be saying: "I know what you think, but you're wrong. I am not a rabbit!"

Watts, as his colleagues suspected, must early have decided to become a *character* complete with phobias, manias, tics, for only by such means could he hope to compete with the introverts he had to deal with, equipped as they were with a similar armament. From Monday morning when he arrived at the office on Madison Avenue to Thursday evening (he took Fridays off from work) Mr. Watts went through life with the distempered air of a rabbit that has been out in the rain. This was never more pronounced than when he knew he was faced with the ordeal of an interview with an author, and a woman at that, for if there was one thing Mr. Watts detested more than he did authors it was women authors, and should there be any residue of venom left over it was quickly expended on the kind of books they chose to write. His aversion to male writers had a more complex base. He had always held that the sword was mightier than the pen, and felt bitterly that in exchanging one for the other his sex was supinely surrendering the sole prerogative remaining to it in a lop-sided world.

Wilfrid Watts was, in short, a misogynist, though a not unsuccessful one. If through the accident of poor physique (he'd once confided to Donald Wallingford that the thing he'd yearned for in his youth was a military career, but they'd turned him down because of his eyesight and his feet—brains, as he pointed out bitterly, being at a discount in the army) he'd found himself pursuing a livelihood for which he believed he was temperamentally quite unfitted, he at least had the filial consolation of knowing that he was carrying out the last deathbed wish of his father, who had laid it on the line that the one-hundred-year-old firm of Watts and Son should not perish from the earth.

But if the fine art of publishing books was, for Wilfrid Watts, scarcely his metier, celibacy certainly was, and he had managed to make a considerable success out of both, at the same time taking out his aggressions on writers in general and women in particular by the simple device of making their literary existence, in so far as he had anything to do with it, as tortuous and exasperating as he knew how. But he was subtle, and used his known reputation as a fussy egocentric to get by with an arrogance which might otherwise have misfired. One of his better known tics was an abhorrence for the use of the semi-colon. He held this to be a pure literary affectation and made a great fuss whenever he came upon one, as though it were a fly which he'd found floating in his soup. Euphemism no matter how legitimate was another bugbear, so were most analogies. A novelist who once spoke of the running sea found this objection sarcastically embellishing the margin of his galley proof: "Since when has the sea had legs?" To which the angry author made reply: "Will you concede that the damned thing has a bottom?"

Watts had let it pass. He had a sense of humor, and what's more, like most eccentrics, he knew when his bluff was being called.

This morning, hopping into his partner's office, he flung a heavy, elaborately bound manuscript on Wallingford's desk, then perched on the edge and swung his little foot.

"What's this?" Wallingford asked. "A Missa Solemnis or something?"

"Snuffles, the Life History of a Corgie."

"You read it?"

"Bits. Murray has, though, and thinks it might have a certain appeal."

Donald turned the cover with a gingerly finger and read the title page, with the author's name: Frankwood Honeywell. He looked at Watts. "Boy or girl, want to bet?"

"I do not."

"Girl," Donald murmured. He turned another page. "Girl, aetat around sixty, I'd say. Relict of copper magnate or oil baron. Childless, of course. Two maids of the same vintage as herself, elderly chauffeur, black Rolls Royce circa 1926. Lives at the Westbury and wears black silk bloomers. Did you read the dedication?"

"I did not."

"I will then. 'For Snuffles, who made *my* life worth living, and who died in my arms!' "

Wallingford sighed wistfully. "Sure you don't want to bet?"

"You might be right about Frankwood Honeywell being a female," Mr. Watts conceded after some hesitation, "but what the hell is a corgie?"

"It's a breed of dog."

"Could be a breed of Seaforth Highlander for all I know. Well, I don't see it myself, but Murray seems to think you ought to give it the once over. You have a nose for these things."

Wallingford picked up his pipe. "I'll look at it. If it passes muster with the S.P.C.A. and I have a hunch it will, there's always a public panting to read about dogs. Not to mention cats." He looked at his watch. "Veronica Dalton ought to be showing up. Would you rather I saw her first?"

"You have that knack with women which I haven't."

"They're always keen to meet the head of the firm, though, Bunny. Why not just drop in casually, say something fatherly, and I'll take over from there?"

"Remember what happened last time I took your advice? It was with that Tibetan holy woman who'd written her memoirs. You bet it was a man, and I was stuck with her for months."

Donald laughed. "She made the Literary Guild though. Worth it, wasn't it?"

"It was weeks before I got the smell of yak butter out of my clothes." He flushed with indignation. "She carried it around with her, in a cold cream jar, and it leaked."

Wallingford laughed again. "She invited you to visit her in her monastery. 'Tisn't every one gets an invitation like that." He pondered a moment. "Well, you don't have to take Miss Dalton to lunch. I've asked her to lunch with me. Seriously, Bunny, the girl's good." He tapped Veronica's manuscript which lay on one side of his desk. "I've been re-reading it, and find myself impressed all over again."

Mr. Watts nodded grudgingly. "She's bright, but morbid.

That Oedipus stuff. Mother hatred, father love and the rest of it. Glad you're handling it and not I." His lips quivered in a rabbit version of a smile, as, pointing his toes, he hopped down from the desk and started for the door. "Let me know when your young genius shows up. Towards the end of the interview, if you don't mind."

He turned at the door. "One of Christopher's girls, did you tell me?"

"He likes her, I know. She's his find."

"Always thought he'd make a good editor," Watts remarked. "Got a nose for it, as you have. Tell by just listening to him."

"He hasn't had a chance to read this," Wallingford said, thoughtfully. "She wouldn't let him. Nobody's read it except ourselves. You and I, Murray, Joan Spears. Author the self-conscious type, I guess. Unsure of herself, according to Chris."

"Then you'd better tell him to watch out," Watts warned, his hand on the door knob. "Self conscious *and* morbid! They're the worst."

He vanished as though into a burrow as he caught the flourish of a lighted match in Wallingford's hand.

Alone, the latter lighted his pipe and sat for some minutes musing. Watt's parting words stuck in his mind. He thought about his son, and this attachment for Veronica Dalton about which Chris had made no secret. She was not the first, of course, nor, probably, was she alone in importance where his interests were concerned. There was Miriam Werth, or rather there *had* been Miriam, of whom Donald Wallingford had become extremely fond, thinking she'd make just the kind of daughter-in-law he would like. Lately however there'd been little or no mention of Miriam, and Donald was not the type of father who believes in asking questions of a son old enough to know his own business. Still, this was the first time he'd experienced anxiety on the boy's account. They were good friends but they left each other alone. Chris's confidence about his affair, if it could be called that, with Veronica Dalton, had come as a surprise with Miriam still apparently in the picture. The business had started with Chris's sudden, unrestrained enthusiasm for the newcomer as "a girl with a real mind," and Donald had protested that as far as he could judge there was nothing wrong with Miriam's mind, either. But Chris had gone on to speak of Veronica in a way which left the father with little doubt as to what was happening to him. Chris reported that he'd read Veronica's poems and a story or two; he'd spent hours talking to her, mostly about literature—Donald could hear them!—and that she had *something*. She had the stuff. And now she was finishing a novel, and he'd suggested that when it was done she bring it to his father at Watts and Wallingford before showing it around. "I haven't seen it, Dad. She's shy about letting her friends see it . . . first really big thing she's attempted. But you might take a look at it. No telling, you know. It might be damned good, then again it might not."

Donald agreed to read Veronica's manuscript whenever she brought it in, and had let it go at that. But as the months passed he'd become increasingly aware of a change in Chris, whose habitual sang-froid seemed to have deserted him; he seemed abstracted and moody, pessimistic about his future, touchy on the subject of his writing, about which, until now, he'd always been expansively self-assured, and in fact gave every indication of being up to his ears in a not too happy love affair. To Donald's few and tactfully worded inquiries the boy replied that Veronica was turning out to be rather more of a complicated piece of goods than he'd realized, but that he was mad for her and God knows where it was going to end. Tentatively, Donald suggested a logical place, but Chris had shaken his head. "She won't. She's got a thing about that, too. Maybe she's just the respectable type, though I doubt it."

Musing on the actuarial logistics of the situation, Wallingford was not disposed to lose sleep over it at the time. He knew his Chris. However, when Veronica's manuscript finally arrived and he had read it, he began to ask himself certain questions. That the girl was bright—brilliant even, there could be no doubt. Although according to Chris and to her own accompanying letter this was her first novel, she handled it like a professional. And that her theme should incline to the tragic he could understand— the young have to acquire a sense of proportion, and the light touch is not for them. What bothered Wallingford was a certain *tone* in her style, an obliqueness, a barbed insight that would have been notable in a seasoned writer, which he knew she was not. It bothered him because of her relation with his son, for if he was old-fashioned in any respect at all it was in his wish that Chris should make a happy marriage. His own had not been happy, and if he was not too blind to see the wood for the trees, not too bemused by the rush and impact of the story to be indifferent to its implications where the author was concerned—and he believed he was not so blind—it did seem to Wallingford that this young woman in her twenties, gifted, sensitive, discerning, had little use for happiness, nor indeed any belief in it as an essential ingredient for life.

And now he began to think of his wife Clare and of their divorce and his resolve never again to take anything, least of all women, seriously. "I'll be damned," he adjured himself years before when Clare ran off with her food faddist, "I'll be damned if I'll sit around and be an object of derision to my friends, but I'll be doubly damned if I'll take refuge in the last refuge of a cuckold and marry again. Liberté, egalité, fraternité . . . that's for me."

Coming into his office one spring morning six months after the divorce, Wallingford had sprung upon his partner and embraced him. "Bunny! How can I thank you?"

Watts flung him off. "What's the matter with you? Drunk at this hour?"

"Free at this hour!" Donald scaled his hat across the room. "Listen, Bunny. I woke up this morning knowing beyond cavil that I was a lucky man, and I could hardly wait to thank you."

"Thank me?" Watts stared at him in concern. In an undemonstrative way he was devoted to Wallingford, and the break-up between husband and wife had seemed to him to be tragic, not less so because it seemed to justify his own Horatio-at-the-Bridge attitude towards the married state.

"Who was it introduced Ridingdale McKennicot to the great diet-conscious American public, you or I?"

Watts smiled weakly. "I know, and except for the incredible sales, I've regretted that day I ever set eyes on him. But at least you had the satisfaction of winning the bet. I'd have sworn it was a female."

"You lost ten bucks, and I lost Clare. Lost her to the Ridingdale McKennicot Way to a Better Life. How to eat only half what you don't need anyway, and like it. Yogurt and wheat germ for breakfast. One carrot, two peas, and a cup of skimmed scum for lunch. Cottage cheese for dinner. Nothing between meals, not even women. And aside from a perpetual obsession with peristalsis, never let your thoughts sink below the navel, for that way madness lies."

Mr. Watts looked at him with genuine concern. "How was I to guess that Clare would fall for a bird like that, after being married to you?"

"Bless you, Bunny! It wasn't your fault. It was fate in the form of an advance copy of the goddam book which I took home to read as a matter of plain duty." He laughed. "The turning point in my life! Would you have believed it would come like that?" And he'd added meditatively: "Something had been slumbering in Clare all those years, and it took McKennicot to awaken it."

"I don't like to hear you talk like this, Donald. I liked Clare. I always thought she was a nice woman, as women go."

"She is a nice woman. Ridingdale McKennicot is nice too. I wish them both happiness, and improved digestion."

Watts shrugged. "And Chris? What about him?"

"No problem. I don't intend that there should be. I'm not wishing off any of my emotions on him, and he knows he can see his mother whenever he wants, which I suspect won't be often. Clare has never been the maternal type, and Ridingdale doesn't like children. He and Clare are dedicated reformers and they already have half a million souls on their agenda to win over from fleshpots to cole slaw, without bothering about Chris and me. Queer, have you noticed? Scratch a faddist and you find a fanatic every time."

In this fashion Donald Wallingford had managed to persuade his friends, and eventually himself, that the break between him and his wife was all to the good in the long run. He trained himself to think of her—when he did think of her—with strict objectivity, even when he remembered the early days of their courtship and marriage. At twenty-eight Clare Frothingham had looked like a figure by Veronese, her voluptuous proportions encased in the standard livery of every well-bred Boston virgin—a sweater, a skirt, and a string of pearls. In addition she boasted a Phi Beta Kappa from Radcliffe, and an encyclopedic mind which seemed determined to exclude from its universal categories most of the facts of love and quite a few of the facts of life. Donald's favorite recollection of her in later years was when, in the course of an earnest discussion on homosexuality, he heard her confess without a trace of humor that she'd always believed pederasty must be a form of athlete's foot. But she had been handsome then, and gave an impression of great vitality, and of secret talents in bed. When he met her Donald was five years younger than she, a small town boy, impressionable, green as an August apple, and bursting with sex. Clare, who so far had had no luck with nimbler men, quite over-awed this sensitive plant. They were married, and at the end of the second year there was Chris.

They got along after a fashion. Clare knew the right people, she belonged to the right clubs, groups, associations, and she had a passion for good works. It was, as Donald soon realized, just about the only passion she did have until she met Ridingdale McKennicot, an evangelical type with a soapy manner and total lack of wit—a faddist after her own heart. When the blow fell the sense of humor which eight years of marriage to a humorless woman had intensified in him as a sort of shock absorber, came to Wallingford's rescue and helped prevent him from making the kind of fool of himself which he might otherwise have done, for he had his fair share of vanity and McKennicot as a sexual rival had been a good deal harder to swallow than his own much advertised brand of breakfast food, black strap and all.

The divorce had been expeditiously and discreetly consummated in Mexico City, and Chris's vacations were spent partly with his mother in Monterey and partly with Donald in New York and Maine. By the time he'd reached college the boy seemed to have taken on more than a little of his father's sardonic philosophy, and what bruises he might have suffered from the break-up left him to all intents and purposes physically and emotionally unimpaired.

Wallingford took his pipe from his mouth and shook the moisture from the stem. Was it to be Chris's turn now? One could laugh at a woman like Clare. One could even forget, after a while, what she looked like. But he had a suspicion that Veronica Dalton was going to be quite another story.

CHAPTER

XII

THE weather had turned bitterly cold and a sharp wind was careening down Madison Avenue, when, several hours later, Veronica bade goodbye to Donald Wallingford outside the restaurant where he'd taken her to lunch. After shaking hands he'd continued to hold hers for a moment, and his gaze had a steadying kindness which outlasted hers. "I think we've covered most of the ground," he said. "But you'll call me if I can be of any help in the revision?"

"Of course. And thank you."

She was no longer half paralysed with nerves as she had been earlier when she walked into his office. "You've been very kind, Mr. Wallingford. I was nervous, meeting you for the first time."

"Did I seem such an ogre? Chris should have prepared you."

"He did. It was my fault. I have this stupid thing about people."

"I take it you mean to hold me to my promise about the manuscript—that no one is to see it except my colleagues?"

"Do you mind? I know it must seem silly to you at this stage. I just have to get used to the idea . . . you know!"

"Authors will be authors. And since you tell me you haven't kept a copy, see that you don't lose the one you have. Yes?"

He gave her a slight, reproving smile, murmured something

about the incorrigible carelessness of certain people—what would she do if the precious thing were to get itself lost, stolen, or burned?—then lifted his hat in farewell and she had a full view of him in that strong, clear light: a man of medium build with alert brown eyes, graying hair, and something of the look of a sailor, which made him seem queerly out of place on this crowded city street. Then he was gone, striding down the Avenue in his shabby raincoat and shapeless hat, hands dug into his pockets and pipe at right angles, into a ruck of plodding figures with downbent heads, bucking the wind.

An uptown bus carried Veronica past her home stop, but she made no attempt to pull the cord, and continued in a kind of dream up Fifth Avenue, past the Zoo, past the Museum, on towards 90th Street. She felt that she could not have borne any ebb in the tidal excitement which filled her, so it seemed, to the very brim, nor any intrusion on the new direction of her thoughts, the new vistas which crowded upon her mind.

"Make the most of it!" Chris had admonished her over the phone only three days before, but now Chris's voice was lost in a deeper cadence, his image blurred.

Walking into Donald Wallingford's office this noon she had in a confused way expected to find another Chris, a *simulacrum* perhaps; no more, but certainly no less, and there was no accounting for the shock of relief she'd experienced on discovering the father to be so totally unlike the son. Yet . . . what had she expected, really? A man who, like Chris, would put her on the defensive and so force her into a role she dreaded and detested in herself and which others had learned to dread? She didn't want that to happen. She never had wanted it, and yet it was always happening, catching her off balance, poisoning her relations with people wherever she went.

With Donald Wallingford there had been nothing of the sort, and now, as she gazed out of the window of the bus she reviewed the events of the past few hours with a feeling of sensuous luxury, like an addict of some solitary vice. It was all hers as it had not been in actuality for now there was no sharing. She had the memory to herself.

That office! Crossing the threshold on icy feet, she'd looked for something resplendent with books bound in expensive covers, an imposing desk, an executive elegance which for some reason she associated with Chris and his sybaritic tastes. Instead there had been that half familiar atmosphere of a country post office, reminding her of the one in Marbury where they spent their summers. And there was that bewhiskered raincoat on its hook, a hat which looked as if its owner used it to catch butterflies, and the modest figure of Wallingford himself as he rose from a back-tilted chair to greet her. "Miss Dalton? I am very glad to meet you."

Meaning it, too, meaning it with eyes and lips, whereas Chris's eyes always had something different to say. Not as tall as Chris, not as slender, with nothing of Chris's indolent delicacy, nor the charm one mulled over afterwards—that confiding, intimate, erotic charm! Not a trace of Chris's classic good looks—it was Miriam who'd first used the word classic to describe them, adding, as Veronica now recalled, that although the son in no way resembled papa, both had what it takes, whatever that might be, and one could only guess. Well, looking at Donald Wallingford, one did not have to guess. And oh the relief of not being compelled to guess . . . will he like me? Will he scare me? Will that something in me that always puts people's backs up come between us— that ghostly something, not so ghostly but that I once saw its face—the face of hatred and despair. Delia's face without Delia's beauty, Delia's soul sitting in her eyes!

Wallingford's glance had seemed to take in, at once, the puerile anguish that gripped Veronica, and to discern the reluctance even to mention her book or to broach the subject which had after all brought her to his door, the heavy consciousness of which kept her glued to his carpet until he drew up a chair for her, and began, himself, easily and naturally to talk about Chris. Well, what else? What better way to break the ice than by a topic so warm to him, one he must have reason to suspect might be warm to her also?

From Chris it had been no more than a step or two to the framed photographs on the walls, to which Veronica followed him and stood like a child in school while he expatiated on them, using the stem of his pipe for a pointer. There were snapshots of Chris sailing a boat, of Chris fishing, of Chris and himself standing at the door of a small white house with pines in the background and the shadow of some third person staining the sunlit grass between. "Miriam Werth took that one a couple of years ago. You know Miriam, I believe? We're very fond of her, Chris and I."

There was another picture of a small harbor and slender white boats, a fragile pier reaching out into it, and fish nets drying in the sun. There were photographs of lobster buoys, gulls, rocks. This was Todd's Harbor, sixty miles east of Mt. Desert Island, and Donald's grandmother had been a Todd, and he himself had grown up in that little house with the pines in the background and the rocky cove in front. Did Veronica know Todd's Harbor? No, she didn't, but Chris had spoken of it so often that she felt she did.

"Take a look at this," Wallingford urged her, enthusiastic before a view of the cove in a half circle of savage rock upon which the spray was breaking like a feather bed. "Our cove. Good anchorage, and fine for swimming if you don't mind cold water. Goes off deep and sudden and Chris almost drowned when he was a kid learning how to swim."

The boat riding at anchor was an auxiliary sloop they'd bought the year before. Something of a come-down, Wallingford indicated with a smile and a shrug, and in bits and pieces he filled in the lacunae which Chris had left in their background—this background of sailors in the era of spice ships that plied between Portland, Maine, and the East Indies; ships carrying ice cut in the fresh water ponds back of Machias, all the way to Calcutta via the Celebes, and, in a later and less romantic age although still one of the windjammer, lumber from Nova Scotia as far south as New Orleans.

As she listened, Veronica felt relief mounting to her head in the crazy hope that perhaps after all the book would not be mentioned today and that this encounter might pass as nothing more than a friendly visit, and the business which had brought her here be conducted at a later date, preferably through the United States mail. Oof! What an escape. Like being told by the doctor that you don't need an operation after all. Like a hundred escapes she'd had before, narrow and wide, always followed by this heady sense of having been somehow singled out for the hair's breadth . . .

But that was not to be. Turning from the photographs to look at her, Wallingford said without noticeable sentiment: "There you have it—Chris's great-grandfather a sailor, his grandfather a doctor, and his father a publisher of books."

He waved her to a chair and went back to his own, saying gravely:

"You know, this is almost as tough on me as it probably is on you. In fact I rather fancy it's tougher on me."

Veronica gave him a look of pure alarm. "Is it? Why?"

"Well, to tell someone that she's written what might prove to be something of a masterpiece must sound like the crassest sort of flattery. Does it?" His eyes, she decided, were watchful, though his smile lingered as though smiling were his habit.

She felt herself flushing. "Masterpiece? Isn't that going a bit far?"

"I don't think it is."

Wallingford had continued: "Your novel has something that doesn't happen by accident. It has balance, maturity. Yet you tell me this is your first book?"

She nodded, looking past him at a calendar with the picture of a full-rigged ship, the kind of thing one finds in a small general store selling rope and paint in a country town.

"Of course I suspect there are some autobiographical touches," Wallingford said, picking up his pipe and peering into the bowl.

"Oddly enough I thought I recognized some biographical ones. My own!"

"I don't understand," said Veronica, thinking: It isn't really a smile. It's just the way his mouth is shaped.

"Well, as a small child I felt myself to be—not unloved, like the hero in your story, but unwanted. My parents, unlike those you describe, were wrapped up in each other and I felt left out. What I admire so much in your book is that you have taken something which in the hands of a lesser artist might have amounted to no more than a situational cliché, and have given it intensity, largely through your utilization of those little true facts which always fascinated Stendhal."

Listening to him, she'd felt her face burn and felt it burn again, remembering. "I don't see how you can know whether they are true facts, or not, Mr. Wallingford." She'd added with a laugh:

"A realistic picture rests on the truth anyway, doesn't it? I mean, it has to."

"Sure. And art occasionally rests on the ability of the artist to catch the truth that others miss. *His* truth, peculiar to him, of course, but at the same time a reflection of everybody else's."

"The universal," she murmured.

"It's what I'm trying to say. Mind if I smoke?"

She didn't mind and he went on: "Another thing: you've managed to avoid sentimentality, and that's not always easy when writing about a child. An unusual child, of course. A victim, yes. But something of a little fiend, too." He laughed. "I can remember when I was about the age of your Larry . . . nine, was it? Going on ten? I had that same sense of life being on an exact level with my eyes, and it gave me a great advantage over the grown-up world. The advantage—you've described it—which a submarine has over an aircraft carrier." He laughed again, delightedly. "And what torpedoes you *do* shoot!"

Chris had never talked to her like this.

She said after a pause: "You don't think the book's too contrived—I mean, too much so. Creakily? Larry's constant but always innocent spying on his mother, for instance?"

"Of course it's contrived, beautifully contrived. And he had to spy, didn't he, just in order to survive? That bitch of a mother!" He corrected himself thoughtfully: "No, not bitch. Not as obvious as that. Not obvious at all, in fact. And that's part of the beauty of the contrivance." He smoked comfortably, looking at her. "Have you any idea what it means to a publisher to be able to give praise, and mean it?"

"I don't know," Veronica murmured.

"But you must know! You surely can't have any doubts?"

"You mean about the book?"

"What else?" She was silent, and he continued:

"I have a feeling that it could have been happier. If I had any criticism at all to offer, it would be on that point."

"You mean that virtue should be made to triumph instead of the other way around?" She looked at him in surprise. "But that is the whole point of the book—I mean, that virtue doesn't triumph."

"I suppose," Wallingford said after a slight pause, "I suppose that what I'm trying to get at is the *felt* attitude of the writer. It comes through—given the caliber of the writing it was bound to come through—that she herself holds to the belief that virtue doesn't triumph. Rather, that it doesn't pay."

Veronica took him up quickly: "There's a difference! What's meant to come through is Silvia's preoccupation—not with triumph, necessarily, but with payment. She likes to be paid, if in every sense of the word, other people do the paying." And she added anxiously: "Does it ring a bell, or doesn't it?"

"For the reader? Oh, it'll ring a bell all right. A whole carillon —or do I mean a death knell?"

"I felt it," Veronica told him in a low voice. "Intensely, while I was writing."

"I understand. One has to submerge. But may I say something?"

She'd looked at him with a recurrence of anxiety. "Of course."

"Perhaps I'm being captious—the book is so good, I feel I can risk a word here and there, and that you can take it."

"Well?"

"Well, Silvia, for instance. She does strike me as being a bit on the perfected side."

"She certainly wasn't intended to be!"

"Not in the virtuous sense, of course not. But perfect in her own way and in no other way that I've ever encountered in fiction, and hope to God I never do in life."

"You mean she doesn't come off as a character?"

He hesitated, giving an impression that he did not want to quibble, but that he considered it his duty to clear the last of the underbrush between them. At last he said: "She comes through, all right. Reading, I believed every word. It is only on reflection that I find myself wondering, a little. She is so hard, and yet her husband loves her, and so, until he finds her out, does her child."

Wallingford took his pipe from his mouth and leaned forward, resting his elbows on his knees. "They'd been married ten years, yet the husband never did find her out, did he?"

"He would have had he lived. I make that point, you remember?"

"He might have, if his horse hadn't fallen on him. As it was, he died happy."

"Innocent," she amended, her voice stiff. And then before he could say more she came out with it: "I think I can guess what's on your mind, Mr. Wallingford. Chris will have told you that my own father was killed in a horseback accident, and perhaps you're wondering how I could bring myself to use anything so personal, to me, in this context. Well, let it go as one of those little true facts you just mentioned—though not so little, at that!" She met his gaze squarely. "You know—you must know—what happens in a writer's consciousness once he has started to write. There is very little that isn't grist to his mill."

"I do know, which is why I venture to question the nature of the grist that goes to make Silvia."

"I still don't think I quite get you."

"You've made her so perfect in her horribleness that I find— but only on reflection, mind you!—I find her just a little hard to take. To believe in, I mean." And he finished quickly: "You've left her without a chink in her armor, and by making her invulnerable you've made her—may I say it?—just a shade less plausible than she might otherwise have been."

Veronica thought fleetingly: In some ways he *is* like Chris. The flush still high in her cheeks, she said slowly: "Silvia doesn't convince you, then, does she? I mean in what you call her horribleness."

"Only because you have endued her with nothing but horribleness. Even her beauty becomes horrible, and horribly becoming!"

Ninety-fifth Street slipped past. She'd have to get out at the next stop if she was to get home before it got quite dark. Before the end of that session in his office, she had brought herself to ask Wallingford the question to which she knew he must give an unequivocal answer. "Mr. Wallingford . . . would you say that in the artistic sense purely . . . I mean, independent of everything else, and reading it *straight*, . . . that the book stands on its own feet?"

"I would say that it most certainly does."

He rose as a noiseless presence emanated behind her.

"Miss Dalton, may I present my partner Mr. Watts?"

The little man hopped into view, and Veronica had the impression of something furry, timid, and fierce, all in one piece. He took her hand, wrung it, and dropped it at once.

"Miss Dalton, very happy. Proud. Remarkable book. Rare in one so young. Life time of publishing, few rewards. Snuffles mostly. Private lives of goldfish by doting dowagers. Mr. Wallingford will explain our conditions of contract and you do understand no possibility of publication before next summer? Congratulations . . ."

He popped out of the room as unobtrusively as he had popped in, and the bushes closed behind him. Wallingford took the beaten-up hat from its hook and turned, smiling, to Veronica.

"Now," he said, "we can go out and eat."

CHAPTER

XIII

THE bus came to a stop and Veronica saw the Harlem River already paling in dusk. Startled, she realized that except for the driver she was the sole remaining occupant of the bus, for this was the end of its run. She'd been riding for almost an hour, and now it was four o'clock and she had the choice of another long bus ride home or of taking the subway or a cab. In no hurry, she decided on a bus.

The air stung her face and made her eyes water while she waited for one to come her way, but the weather, like her surroundings, had a kind of unreality, so she scarcely felt it. Memories of her interview with Donald Wallingford and of the luncheon that had followed filled her mind to the exclusion of everything else. They had continued the discussion of her book, and she'd been impressed by the skill with which he led up to the points of criticism—the small, weak joints in the story which in his opinion required, as he put it, tightening up here and there.

There was for instance the question whether a child of ten— the protagonist in the novel—would be as preoccupied as she'd made him out to be, with a problem in connection with his parentage.

"The psychological phenomenon of a child's wonder about his parents and about his physical bond to them is a common one, of course," said Wallingford. "I'd say that there was scarcely a boy or girl between the ages of say three to twelve who doesn't at some time or other torment himself with the mystery of who he is and whom he belongs to. He probably doesn't need any particular stimulus to trouble his dreams—they're part of his developing consciousness, his awareness of himself as a creature separate from others, vulnerable and alone. It's not enough to tell himself that he is Tom, Dick, or Harry. That doesn't answer his question —one which he probably doesn't even dare put into words: 'Who am I in relation to my mother and my father?' And if he happens to be high-strung and over-sensitive like the child in your story, with, as you have described it, some long-forgotten grievance imbedded deep in his infantine unconscious, he might very well go a step farther and ask himself: 'Are these people my parents, or is there a mystery here, some black unexplored corner into which I dare not look, some door left terrifyingly ajar and leading into a creaking nightmare of the Unknown? Am I the child of my parents or am I a changeling thrust upon them by some mistake of which they are aware but of which I am not . . . or worse still, a mistake of which they are not aware either, and might there not come a day when they will unearth the hideous truth and stop loving me and throw me out?' "

Wallingford had continued, musingly: "In the case of the child you write about it does occur to me, though, that you might have over-stressed, somewhat, the obsession in little Larry's mind. He's still an infant, after all."

"But doesn't it all depend on what kind of an infant?" Veronica demurred, sipping the Dubonnet she'd ordered instead of a cocktail. She went on:

"We agree that he's unusual—a victim, but something of a little fiend, as you pointed out back there in your office. Knowing himself to be deeply loved by one parent, his father, disliked by the other—his mother—his special brand of fiendishness is more or less forced upon him by his sense of his own helplessness. He wants his mother's love and cannot understand why she denies him. His sense of deprivation increases as he begins to understand her for the hypocrite that she is, for she's not above playing the mother in public as further enhancement of her charm, and as a means of keeping a hold on the husband whom she doesn't love, but whose protection and support are necessary to her. Silvia can fool her husband because of his involvement with her, but it isn't so easy to fool a child who has no experience of deception to deflect him . . . life, as you said, is on a level with his eyes, something that the grownup world forgets, moving as it does on another plane."

Amazing, Veronica thought, how easy it is to talk to this man. I've never talked like this to anyone in my life, not to Miriam, not even to Chris.

Wallingford gave her a considering glance. "Look, I'm no more carping about little Larry than I am about his mother, Silvia. Not really. If what you have done with him, and what you have done with Silvia, *is what you intended to do*, I'm satisfied." He smiled. "I just wanted to be sure that *you* were sure."

Veronica said slowly: "I'm sure . . . yes, really, I am sure!"

Later he said: "You've managed to put a child's whole attitude towards this problem of relatedness in a nutshell. In a way, as I read it, I found myself thinking about Chris."

She was surprised. "Chris?"

"At the time when my wife and I were divorced, I had some tough explaining to do to Chris. He was very young, and I found it difficult to define, for him, the stark process of alienation between two people—to explain the invisible dissolution of an invisible bond! After all how does one explain it to a child? To talk to him about the facts of life . . ." he shrugged. "All he wanted to know, as your Larry wanted to know—and know with all his five senses—is how, if you are his father or his mother, you can ever *not* be? And if one or the other doesn't exist in the sense—the legitimate sense that his father didn't, for Larry, how explain that? And if you do succeed in getting it across, what is he supposed to do with all that pathetic store of affection, gone for nothing?"

Veronica asked after a pause: "Did Chris suffer much? After all, he had you, hadn't he?"

"Yes, he had me, and he could have had his mother too, if either of them wanted it that way, and as it turned out, they didn't."

Veronica sat for some minutes silently contemplating the last drop of crimson liquid in the bottom of her glass. Under cover of the voices that rose round them in the crowded restaurant, the thought crossed her mind in a kind of parenthesis that Wallingford had revealed more of himself and his past in that one sentence than she had gathered from Chris in the six months of their intimacy.

Donald continued: "In the case of the boy in your novel, the search is not for an alternative, but what—for him—has suddenly become irrecoverable. If the death of his father, the physical death, were not also a symbolic death, it might put something of a strain on the reader's credulity in Larry's later experiencing a kind of relief at the thought that the man he has always adored as a father should have died without discovering that his wife was what you've so expertly made her out to be." Donald had finished almost as though talking to himself: "To me the most poignant scene in the book is towards the end, when Larry sees his father killed by the horse. Under the shock and terror of it, one senses the pure wonder of a child's first experience of death. And then the turning, the inevitable turning to the only person left for him to turn to, his mother, and the plummeting descent from wonder into unavoidable recognition of truth he has only—till then— dimly comprehended, when he rushes home to tell her what has happened, and finds her in another man's arms."

It was getting dark when Veronica finally left the bus and made her way towards home. She hadn't gone far when she recognized a figure hurrying in the opposite direction, and ran in pursuit:

"Miriam!"

Miriam Werth turned and came slowly back. "Veronica! Where the devil've you been?"

They met at the foot of the brownstone steps below Veronica's door. Lights burned in the downstairs parlor, the curtains were drawn, and as she noticed these things she had a sudden sense of luxury, a satisfied, sensuous fatigue in all her limbs. "Where have I been? Come in and I'll tell all."

Miriam peered at her short-sightedly. "I called you on the phone and Katie said you'd left the house before lunch and didn't know when you'd be back. Since I was uptown anyway I dropped in to see if you'd gotten home. I found Delia alone, and beginning to wonder where you'd got to."

Veronica took her arm. "Come in and have tea. I'm tired and half frozen."

"Can't. Delia gave me tea, and I've got to get home. People coming in later. Nonny, why in the world didn't you tell me that Watts and Wallingford were taking your book?"

Veronica hesitated, and Miriam went on with unusual vehemence:

"I just spilled the beans to your mother. Didn't mean to. I took it for granted you must have told her. Chris wrote me about it, and he was thrilled to pieces. So am I! But I could slay you for being so damned secretive."

Veronica laughed. "I was going to call you up tonight. I had lunch with Donald Wallingford today. I've just come from there."

"Just come from having lunch? It's after five."

"I took a bus ride because I wanted to think. You know."

"Do I? I'm beginning to wonder. But look, Delia's waiting for you. I'm sorry I mentioned the book, but how in heck was I to know you hadn't even told her? She was very nice about it, I must say." She put her arm round Veronica. "Nonny, I'm so glad for you. I've some idea of what this must mean, after the way you've worked, and with all the promise you've shown from the start. But even promising people don't always make it, do they? You have." Her eyes glowed.

"For most of us, things just happen. But you made something happen . . . it's no slight thing to have had a hand in one's own fate by creating something outside it. Oh hell! Call me tomorrow. Or better still, come around."

She was gone, fighting her way up the street against the wind, and Veronica went up the steps to the house.

Delia was finishing a cup of tea in the parlor, which was suffused in a pale aqueous glow from the single light beside the sofa where she sat. This was an hour and a scene which in her childhood used to excite confusing emotions in Veronica. The painted water-lilies above the mantel seemed to quiver and spread their fragile scent into the room, and a minute passed before she realized that the perfume came from Delia's clothing and that it accompanied her wherever she went. Chairs and tables were poignant reminders of something, a personality, perhaps, which had touched them once and left its impress on their prosaic shapes, and the figure on the sofa assumed in this light an air of mystery at once alluring and aloof. When as a child Veronica lay in bed in the darkness a scene such as this would rise in her memory and she'd feel that her heart must burst with its secret longing, and she'd clench her eyelids to squeeze out the vision, and the tears with it.

As the girl waited motionless at the open door, Delia saw her and said: "The tea is still hot, if you'd like some, Nonny." And as Veronica entered she added: "You just missed Miriam Werth. I urged her to stay for supper, but she had an engagement."

"I met her outside," Veronica said. She sat on the sofa beside Delia and poured herself tea, and without looking at her mother, added: "I had lunch today with Chris's father, Mr. Wallingford."

"You didn't tell me you were going to."

"Should I have?"

"Not if you didn't want to, no."

Veronica stirred her tea. "They're taking the book, Mother. Actually I knew it several days ago. I didn't tell you because I wanted to be absolutely sure. That was what the lunch was about."

Delia said calmly: "Miriam told me she'd heard about it from Chris. She was upset, I think, for fear she may have betrayed some sort of confidence." With a quick, shy movement she laid her hand on Veronica's knee. "Darling!" she said in a moved voice, and the color rushed to Veronica's face.

"Mother, they like it!"

Delia gazed at her intently. "This has made you happy, I can see. But did you doubt that they would like it?"

"No matter how good one may think oneself, or believe in one-self . . . it doesn't amount to anything unless . . . you know . . . other people recognize whatever it is one has tried to do."

She put down her cup and began to talk excitedly, breathlessly as her friends sometimes heard her talk, but as Delia seldom did, and the latter reflected, with a pang: It's almost as though she'd forgotten she was talking to me!

"To be justified!" Veronica exclaimed, and stared raptly into her mother's face. "That's it, that's what counts."

"Of course. And he made you feel that, did he? Mr. Walling-ford, I mean."

Veronica looked like a girl who'd been invited to her first prom. There was an almost terrible innocence about her. "Mother, should we ask him to dinner one night soon? When Chris is here, and Nick?"

"Why not?" said Delia. She began to set the tea tray in order, collecting the spoons, smoothing the little linen napkins marked with her initials that Fran had brought from California years be-fore. "We should have done it months ago, considering our friend-ship with Chris. I suggested it, if you remember, but you were not too keen."

"Now the ice is broken I think we should."

Delia stared at her in wonder.

"Thanksgiving, then," Veronica offered, like a child contem-plating a party. "Chris will be here. Or perhaps Thanksgiving eve in case they've made other plans for Thanksgiving. Should we ask anyone else?"

"It's your party," Delia said with a smile. "Ask who you want. Miriam Werth, I should think."

"With Nick, that's two. You and Chris and his father and me."

There was a pause. "And Fran?" Delia asked.

Veronica frowned. "Should we? I'd be afraid of what might happen."

"I am too, but we can't hurt her feelings."

Veronica considered the problem, her lower lip caught in her teeth. "If we have her Thanksgiving perhaps we can get away without even mentioning a party the night before?"

"We'll work it somehow," Delia said, and added in a troubled voice: "I haven't heard from her for a couple of days."

They talked a little of Fran, a kind of normality descending upon them as though both had come back from a journey and were reviving an old relationship. "I called the hotel, but I hate to keep doing it. They're so uncouth there, and last time I tried to get her the man at the desk hung up on me. Yesterday when I went to see her she wasn't in. Nor was she in today."

"Off on another binge, probably," said Veronica, lightly. All of a sudden, nothing could touch her. She stood above the world and its sordid repetitions, above the perverse stupidities of people who could not help themselves and would permit no one else to do so.

Delia rose and picked up the tray. "Will you call Nick tonight and tell him about your book, Nonny? He'll want to hear."

"I'll call him," said Veronica. She sat motionless, hardly aware, now, of Delia, her face curiously vulnerable and soft as even Chris had never seen it.

CHAPTER

XIV

"OLD IRONPANTS," Nick said, and dodged behind the kitchen table as Katie came at him with a mixing spoon. "Honest to goodness, honey, you're tough. Almost as tough as your own cookies."

"That all you learn in that high-priced boarding school?" Katie demanded, simmering. "To pinch women till they're black and blue—and you not sixteen yet!"

"It's considered part of our homework. Teaches us the art of togetherness. Tell me, Katie, have you missed me? Has it been hell on wheels here without me?"

"It's been heaven, that part of heaven that's farthest off from the nursery." She went to the stove, started to bend over to peer into the oven, thought better of it, and gave him a menacing glance over her shoulder. "Why don't you make yourself useful instead of hanging around pestering people?"

"You'll give me a trauma, rejecting me so." He perched on the table and swung one long, stork-thin leg. He and Katie were old friends, for she had helped Delia bring him up, and she knew that she could usually reduce him to cringing compliance by the threat of producing, for public consumption, a snapshot of him taken at ten months, nakedly sprawling in her lap.

"I've missed you, Kate. Kiss me, Kate."

Ignoring him, she pulled a stool to the table and sat down, her capable hands shaping bread into little rounds, squares, triangles, arranging cheese on them, caviar, chopped egg. Making a long arm Nick helped himself and spoke with his mouth full: "Tell me what's been going on behind my back. Gossip with me. I know you're bursting with tidbits. I can see two of 'em from here."

Her face quivered. "You know what's been going on as well as anybody. You've been home since noon and you haven't stopped asking questions yet. 'Where's my waterproof match case? Where's my tapered trout line? Where's my sheath knife? Where's my this, where's my that.'"

"I'd tell you," he said softly, "but I think you know. You're getting to be a big girl now."

She gave an angry burst of laughter. "Grow up, won't you?"

"And have them put me to work earning my living?" He selected a piece of bread, heaped it with caviar, and ate it. "You make the best canapés. What's for dessert tonight?"

"Rum baba with ice cream. Cordials with coffee, afterwards."

"Mother's really laying it on, isn't she? When I think of what they feed us at that sweat shop while my relatives gorge at home!"

"This party's in honor of Veronica's book. Why don't you write a book? Keep you quiet for a while."

"Not me. I have enough of them in school." He bellowed the Knife Song from *The Threepenny Opera*: "O the shark has pretty teeth, dear, and he keeps them pearly white!"

"Keep yours out of the caviar, will you, dear? It's all we've got."

Nick frowned absent-mindedly, drawing his heavy brows together over a prominent, hawk-like nose. Painfully thin, too tall for his age, he seemed disposed to spread-eagle into manhood at any minute, and as Katie looked at him she felt a pang of tenderness somewhere in the center of her being. "Here," she said, "eat some more if you want, though it does seem an expensive way to get sick. You don't look more than half nourished to me."

"I'm not, but that's because of my high rate of metabolism. Like the hummingbird's. Did you know that hummingbirds have the highest rate of metabolism in the world?" He dipped a knife in the caviar. "If Veronica's going to turn out to be a famous author, maybe we'll be able to afford to buy this stuff by the keg. By the way how's Chris Wallingford making out, Kate?"

"Making out?"

"With Nonny, stupid. Is he still—you know, up to his ears?"

"She got a letter from him the other day made her look like *she* was."

"Can't be sure with Nonny. These girls that're all brains and no breasts . . ."

"That'll be enough from you, Nick."

"Intellectual type. There's been one on my trail up there at school. Sister of one of my classmates. Must weigh about a hundred pounds more than you do, which makes her around three hundred even, I'd say. I don't have to run from her. Just walk, kicking stones as I go."

"What you got against the intellectual type?"

"In the first place they can't cook. Second place they're apt to be competitive, even in bed. So I've been told."

She gasped. "When I was your age . . ."

"You don't look a day over sixty right now. But to get back to Chris. I like him. Got to think up some way of reviving the subject of that invitation he handed me last time I was home. Visit at his old man's place in Maine. Sailing and fishing. M'm."

"Chris's father's coming to dinner tonight so you'll get your chance." She sighed. "I can't get over Veronica, though. Working away so quiet like she's done all year, never opening her mouth, nobody getting so much as a hint what she was up to except of course we knew it was to be a book. Then off she goes on her own and gets the publishers to take it. That's what comes of having brains!"

"The implication being?" He reached across the table with lightning speed and Katie gave a squeal of outrage. "Now Nick!"

"I can't resist you . . . *you butterfly!*"

His face darkened suddenly. "I wish they were asking Fran tonight. Dirty trick to leave her out."

Katie shook her head. "It wouldn't work. You know well's I do, what'd happen."

"You mean she'd get drunk. So what? That wouldn't be news to anybody, would it? And she's going to be awful hurt, you know she is."

"She's coming for dinner tomorrow noon. We'll make it up to her then."

"How you going to keep it quiet that we had a party here tonight and didn't ask *her*?" His frown became forbidding. "Treating her as though she were a skeleton in the cupboard. And it's been a whole year since I saw her."

Katie repeated patiently: "You'll see her tomorrow. Quit griping."

"But you like Fran! Do you want to hurt her feelings?"

"There's other people's feelings besides Fran's that might get hurt if she was to come tonight."

"You mean Veronica. Well, she can take it. Fran can't."

She said soberly: "I like your Aunt Fran. She's as nice a person as there is, when she isn't drinking. But the plain truth is there's hardly a time when she isn't drinking. Think of all the times she's come to visit, and not a time but what she's done something awful. Seems as if she must save up for when she knows somebody's around to take care of her."

"In that case, why not have her here tonight?"

It was, she guessed, part of his innocence to be difficult about the most unexpected things. And his loyalties went deep.

"You've seen something of Fran when she's putting on one of her acts. Look, honey. There's not going to be any hurt feelings because she's just not going to know we had a party tonight."

"And if she walks right in the middle of it, what do we do? Tell her she's a dream, walking?"

"She won't. She's been led to believe that the whole family's going out to dinner some place else."

"I hate that. It stinks."

"Well, you fight it out with your mother and Veronica. It's none of my business."

"But damn it!" He made a feint at the air with his fist. "Nonny's book, and her publisher coming, and Chris, and me back from school for just forty-eight hours, and a whole year since I last saw her!"

Katie was silent for a moment, then she said slowly: "They didn't tell you what happened right after she got here this time. Maybe I shouldn't tell you, but since you're so worked up, I will. Mrs. Hight stayed off the bottle for several days, and we all breathed easier. Then she and Nonny went out to dinner one night, and Mrs. Hight overdid. Your mother had to put her to bed, and towards morning what happened but she smelled smoke coming from your aunt's room, and there she was—your aunt—asleep, kind of drugged with all the liquor she'd put away, and her bed on fire from a cigarette she'd dropped in it, and the nightgown burned right off her. Next day we had to take everything downstairs for the sanitation truck to lug off. Nice looking mess it was too—like a cremation. If your mother hadn't been home the whole house might've burned down."

He looked unimpressed. "Well, it didn't burn down, did it? People are having accidents all the time. Automobiles. High voltage wires. Drowning. Fran's not much worse, or she wouldn't have lasted."

"You ever heard of anybody dying of drink? They don't. They get kind of embalmed, that's all. They live for ever, just about. Think of your own great-grandfather. Mrs. Dalton's told me all about him. It's where Fran gets it, I guess."

He sat morosely swinging his legs. "Why didn't somebody make her join AA or something?"

"She did join AA. She's been in and out of that and in and out of sanatoriums. I'm not telling you anything you don't know." And in a gentler tone: "Seems like your aunt brings a blight wherever she is. Like those people who carry typhoid, poisoning other people's lives."

When he was silent she finished: "Veronica's no great help, either. Your mother's had to take this alone."

Nick's frown gave his young features an odd look of maturity and he gazed at Katie with an unseeing, concentrated gaze. "But what's everybody so afraid of? That Fran'll disgrace them in front of Mr. Wallingford and Chris? If Chris and Nonny are going to be married, the sooner he knows about Fran the better. And he's no stick. I think he'd like Fran if he knew her."

The pantry door swung open and Delia came into the kitchen carrying the crystal bowl which Fran had given her. "This leaks, Katie."

Katie rose and taking the bowl from Delia held it to the light.

A fissure in its center writhed like a green snake as she turned it this way and that. "What a pity! It sure is a lovely thing, and must have cost a mint."

Delia glanced at her son. "Anything wrong, my sweet? You look like a thundercloud."

He said impetuously: "Mother, what about Fran? No, listen. Why can't she come to the party tonight? I think it's a stinking trick not to ask her."

She put her arm round his neck. "We've discussed it once, haven't we? You can't love Fran more than I do . . . and she's coming for dinner tomorrow anyway."

"Yes, and you know what'll happen then! Everybody having to keep quiet about tonight . . . watching our step for fear she'll find out we had a party and didn't ask her because we're ashamed of her!"

Delia rocked him gently against her. "If she finds out, I'll be frank with her and explain why we didn't ask her tonight. If her feelings are going to be hurt, then they will be hurt, but there's no point in asking for trouble, is there? This is Veronica's party. It's Mr. Wallingford's introduction to the family, and I want to make it as happy an evening for Veronica as I know how."

"Veronica Veronica! Everything for Veronica. Just because she's written a goddam book, everybody's got to give in to Veronica!"

Veronica came into the kitchen and looked coolly at her brother.

"All right, Sir Walter Raleigh. Where's your fine scarlet cloak?"

Katie laughed. "You know something, Veronica? Nick doesn't care for the intellectual type. He told me so."

Nick's brows were a solid ridge above his eyes. "*Women!*"

"Nick darling," said Delia. She'd run into this before, with him. It was, she supposed, a generosity that would pass from too much giving, but it could still melt her, and there were moments when she blamed herself for sheltering him as she had done, for having kept him too much in the dark. But she felt that she'd had, in the beginning, not much choice.

"Listen, Nick. We'll make it up to Fran tomorrow. I've got tickets for the Teahouse of the August Moon . . ."

"Bribery," he interrupted, coldly. "Doing something mean, then trying to make up for it by bribery!"

She flushed a little, paying a further price for this innocence which she'd made so great a point of cherishing, but before she could protest, Veronica wanted to know what it was all about. She passed them as she spoke, on her way to the sink with a florist's box in her hands.

Nick followed her with his eyes. "I didn't think anyone could sink so low as to be ashamed of a member of their own family!"

"You don't have to be ashamed," Veronica retorted without heat. "You can be just plain bored."

She untied the box and lifted out its contents, a camellia, dusky red and glowing among its shining leaves. The color which rose to her cheeks matched the flower as she stood staring at it—matched her lips, the curve of her smile.

"From your publisher?" Nick asked sarcastically, and the sudden flash of temper in her eyes betrayed to his quick understanding—and to her mother's—that this was exactly what she must have hoped for. But the card attached bore—not Donald Wallingford's name, but Chris's, and as she turned away it was Katie who caught the fading radiance in her face.

"My Lord!" Katie exclaimed, and stared at the bowl which she'd been drying, now in two pieces in her hands. "And it wasn't even broken!"

"It's all right," said Delia. "Not your fault, Katie." And she added with a slight laugh: "And that's another secret we must keep from Fran, or she'll go out and buy another. And as you say, they cost a mint."

CHAPTER

XV

SHOWERED and powdered, Delia sat before the triplex mirror on her dressing table, and taking the pins out of her hair let it cascade to her bare shoulders. It had long since lost the effects of Mr. Ramond's ministrations and she'd been too busy lately to make another appointment. Besides, she reflected with a shrug, Nick is the only person who gives a damn what I look like. Thinking about her son, her face softened. She loved him altogether too much for her own peace of mind, and she sometimes feared that he might love her too well for his own. Such love makes one vulnerable and she did not want him to be vulnerable—not yet at any event. As for herself she was vulnerable enough, thanks to Fran and Veronica, thanks to Charles, too. Yes, even now, thanks to Charles. Substantial and insensitive as he had been in life, in death Charles had found a way to make himself felt. This afternoon for instance that look on Veronica's face when she opened the florist's box and lifted out the camellia which Chris had sent her. That flash of temper in her eyes at Nick's teasing question: "From your publisher?"

Delia remembered such an expression in Charles' eyes when something happened to anger or frustrate him. The expression of a child bent on having his own way no matter what the cost—a look which dared the impossible, dared death even. So he must have looked when his horse balked with him on that April afternoon as he drove his spur into its flank, causing it to rear up on the grass and crush him in its fall. Could it be that Charles' daughter had taken on an equivalent pride—or ambition, rather, one that reached beyond the pure mastery of her art and sought to seize and rowel the tenderness in life till nothing was left? Charles had had no use for tenderness. He would, had it been feasible, have worn his spurs to bed. But Nick! She caught her breath, remembering his swift response to her pleading glance as he moved to deal with that small emergency this afternoon, moved towards his sister where she stood with her back to them all, Chris's unwanted flower like a wound against her breast.

Sensing that something was wrong, and forgetting his sulks over Fran, Nick had plucked the camellia from Veronica's hand and set it behind his ear. Then taking her in his arms he danced with her to a whistled accompaniment and Katie's drumbeat with mixing spoon and bowl. He danced like a Negro, with a loose-jointed grace, losing himself in the rhythm and taking Veronica with him, his cheek on her hair, holding her until she smiled, a little uncertainly at first, then, her eyes closed, in grave surrender to his mood. In their unthinking and sensuous relaxation both had looked very much like Charles, and catching Katie's eye Delia read the thought in hers.

Now, coiling her hair into a shining cable, she thought with revived hope that between Nick's versatility and Veronica's new dress, things might not go so badly tonight, after all. Two days ago Delia had made a reckless foray into the department stores, and the dress which she'd chosen for Veronica, subject to Veronica's approval, had seemed to Delia so absolutely right that she'd allowed herself to be tempted beyond all sobering considerations of price, and had bought it. Veronica had approved. She had even, rather shyly, kissed Delia as she tendered her thanks, and Delia had thought: I could count those kisses, over the past ten years, on the fingers of my two hands.

There was a knock on her door and Nick's voice: "Can I come in?"

"Come," Delia called. Dressed, she was fastening an earring as he entered and stood behind her so that their two faces were mirrored in the looking glass. Nick had an incongruous elegance in his dinner-jacket, already a little too tight for him, the shortened cuffs giving his large knuckly wrists an amputated look. He put his arms round her and dug his chin into her shoulder. "New dress?"

"As of last year, yes."

"Cool."

"Is Veronica dressed?"

"I'll say. Stunning in that new thing you got her. And I mean stunning."

Delia fixed the other earring while he watched her. "You'd give Nonny a run for her money though, any day."

"Oh, Nick, no. Don't say things like that."

"What the heck, you can't help it, can you? I mean, being what you are." Then impatiently, "Oh I know, you're thinking of her inferiority complex. I don't believe she's got one."

"You were nice down there in the kitchen this evening, Nick. She seemed upset about something, and you saved the situation."

"If Veronica'd only get over wanting everything!"

Delia gave him a quick glance. Was he really so innocent? He could give her moments of doubt, making her wonder whether she perhaps took that innocence too much for granted, made too much of a thing out of it now that he seemed to be growing, not only out of his clothes, but, in little spurts, almost out of her reach.

She said slowly: "Maybe now, she will. With Chris, and success . . . maybe she will get over wanting everything."

"Miriam Werth's downstairs and she and Nonny are tearing modern poets apart on the sofa. Whole place drips with gore."

He took a black lace stole from a chair and wrapped it round his head like a turban. "Why, when brainy people get together, can't they ever find anybody or anything to talk about that they *like*?"

"They're being what they call objective," Delia said with a

little laugh. "The way you get when I venture to suggest that you do a bit more reading and not keep flunking your literature courses."

"Crap. And I don't see why if Dylan Thomas wants to talk to himself under a milkweed, anybody should object. Miriam says he's just another Edgar Lee Masters, and Veronica takes that as though *she* thought it was the kiss of death. Miriam says all our modern poets are over-rated. And Veronica says that that's because they're afraid of pure poetry. What *is* pure poetry?"

"It's one of the things you're supposed to be finding out at school. I got another letter from Mr. McAllister, Nick. A very discouraging one."

"Old Mac? He was born discouraged. Trouble is he can't grasp the elemental truth that to an intelligent mind like mine, the printed word a printed word is, no more."

"But Nick, you've got to learn something!"

"When I was a kid I wanted to learn how to be a wild animal, a really wild animal like one of those in the zoo. I used to go from cage to cage trying to make up my mind which animal I'd rather be. Sometimes I'd settle on a lion, sometimes on a polar bear. Then one day I watched the polar bears making love and I decided I'd rather be a seal. They seemed more refined."

"You didn't think of one of those monkeys—the ones with the purple behinds?"

"Mother!" he cried, horrified.

She laughed. "Well, when did you finally give up the idea and decide to be just a plain ordinary human being?"

"I'm not sure that I have made up my mind."

"But you've got to be educated," Delia protested. "You've got to have a profession, earn a living."

"Maybe I'll settle for playing the accordion in a night club."

"Nick."

"Or I might become a magician." He touched the folds of his turban. "A magician, so that by the merest wish I can disappear any time I'm expected to do something I don't want to do."

Delia took the stole from his head and draped it over her shoulders. They crossed the room towards the door, the boy's arm round her waist. "Has Nonny given you any idea what her book's about?" Nick asked suddenly. Delia shook her head. She had a glimpse of herself in a tall mirror as she passed. Slender, the gray-blue of her dress drawing a moonstone pallor from the light, Nick's Spanish comb like a dark hand in the coil of her hair.

"You mean she can let a complete stranger like Wallingford read it, and not you and me?"

"You know Nonny. Besides, Mr. Wallingford's firm is going to publish it. Naturally, he has to read it first."

"But even Chris hasn't seen it, even Miriam! How crazy can you get?"

She chaffed him: "Don't tell me you want to read Nonny's book? It's a book, mind you. A b-o-o-k!"

He said indifferently: "I don't want to read it, I just want to know what's it about. Maybe it'll get on TV, then I won't have to bother."

The Wallingfords arrived as Delia and Nick entered the parlor, and as, with Veronica, Delia crossed the room to greet them she had a moment for a first swift appraisal of the father as she'd already had ample scope for appraising the son. Looks like a decent sort, she told herself, relieved, and with a touch of remorse that there should have been any doubt in her mind. A quite obviously decent sort, even allowing for the brevity of the impression as it stretched minute by minute into a larger, confirming view. And Delia's smile, as she shook hands with Donald, was warmer for that first doubt, born of her knowledge of his divorce and her ignorance of its long-lost details, and of certain uneasy reflections on the nature and possible consolations of sophisticated and unattached males.

As a matter of fact Delia felt that there was some excuse for such reservations on her part. After all, Charles had left her with few illusions, and her sister Fran had taken pretty effective care of those. It was in the somewhat meager light of what was left that she'd found herself speculating on Veronica's recent extraordinary change of mood from reserve to impulsive warmth, a change which in Delia's eyes could just possibly have more to it than a mother might have reason to be grateful for. It bore looking into, and she'd quickly decided that this evening's encounter with Donald Wallingford would present her with the perfect opportunity for doing just that.

These reflections flashed through her mind under cover of the greetings and introductions, and her eyes, her ears, practised in such matters, singled out Chris's father for a special and as she imagined, cleverly concealed scrutiny which was not for an instant lost on him, since his first glimpse of her as he entered the room had been enough to obscure almost totally every other person in it.

"Mr. Wallingford," Veronica presented Donald as Chris's hand, cool and possessive, slid down her bare arm to her wrist. "Mr. Wallingford, my mother. You know Miriam. And this is my brother Nick."

She did it nicely, with scarcely a hint of inner commotion, and as Wallingford shook hands she stood between father and son like a slender pencil of flame in her golden dress, Chris's fingers on her pulse, taking its heightened beat for himself.

"I apologize for being late," Donald said, turning once more to Delia. "I had an appointment which kept me longer than I thought it would, then Chris couldn't find his shoes."

"Let's stick to that appointment," Chris said. "It's entirely due to Mrs. Frankwood Snuffles that we're late." He smiled at Veronica. "You've got a rival at Watts and Wallingford's, kid. Dad says she's a wow."

"A bow wow," Wallingford corrected him. He turned to kiss Miriam Werth. "And I would like to inquire, in passing, what Chris's friends do when he's not around. They never seem to bother their heads about me."

Miriam linked her arm in his. It was evident that they liked each other. "The question of what you do when Chris isn't around would seem more to the point."

"I mope."

"Don't believe him, anyone." Chris swung Veronica's hand to and fro in his own. "He takes lady authors out to lunch and cocktails and tries to smooth down their feathers after Uncle Bunny Watts has got them all ruffled up."

"I have a somewhat temperamental partner," Wallingford explained, impartially, to the group. "And the smoothing process can be more arduous than Chris would have you believe. Today for instance I spent the entire afternoon over tomato juice and pretzels—my new author doesn't take inebriating liquors so of course out of politeness I couldn't either—and we discussed corgies. A corgie, in case you are not aware of it, is a breed of dog. Small. Brown. It has, apparently, a long history. This example embraced all of five hundred pages, and Mr. Watts had suggested to the author that the biography might be improved by cutting it to half that length."

"She threatened to leave Watts and Wallingford and go to Scribner's," Chris said, happily. "She said she spoke for dog-lovers all over the world, and that five hundred pages didn't begin to do justice to the subject. She wasn't going to have it cut by a single comma. What happened then, Dad?"

"Bunny suggested that as a compromise she leave out the dedication, which, he declared, was pure slop. I came into his office just as she was on the port tack, headed for the elevator and Scribner's."

"And then?" Chris prompted, grinning.

"I introduced myself and said that as a lover of dogs I felt strongly that she and I could perhaps arrive at an understanding of the problem, and invited her out to lunch. We talked dogs all afternoon. I walked out of that restaurant practically on all fours."

He turned gravely to Delia. "The sad part of the story is that if I could have persuaded my partner to take me up on a bet, I'd have won hands down."

Chris elucidated. "Dad's clairvoyant about people, you know. When a manuscript comes into the office under a peculiar name like Frankwell Honeywood, for example. . . ."

"Frankwood Honeywell," his father murmured deprecatingly, with a glance at Delia. Under the nonsense, she sensed a carefully directed interest. So he, too, was curious. Well, why not? As Chris's father he had as much reason to be as she had . . . as Veronica's mother.

"Whenever a manuscript arrives with a funny name Dad and Mr. Watts make bets on the sex and psychological composition of the author, but Dad's won so often that the old man's afraid to play any more."

"I had this one's number from the start," Wallingford said with pride. "Widow of a Texas oil magnate who left her with half a million and this corgie dog. The dog died last year, and this biography, the author assured me, has been the raison d'etre of her existence ever since. Snuffles, it seems, had the intelligence of something more than human. He could do everything except play the stock market, and was of such delicate sensibilities that he always turned his back when she took her bath."

Nick shouted, then suddenly shot a question at him: "And Veronica's book—is that biographical?"

Wallingford smiled. "Here's your sister. Hadn't you better ask her?"

"It's about sex, of course," Nick said, shrugging. "That's the only thing women want to write about. In novels, I mean."

"Wrong again," Veronica twitted him composedly. "And there's no use your going on about it because it won't get you anywhere."

"Boy meets girl," Nick persisted. "Girl meets boy. Boy meets boy. Girl meets girl. Listen, it *has* to be one or the other or it won't be a book."

Delia put her hand on his shoulder. "Bring the drinks, will you, Nick? We can mix them in here."

"Let me help," said Miriam. They left the room together. Chris led Veronica towards the fireplace and Wallingford sat down beside Delia on the sofa and began to talk lightly about unimportant things—the atmosphere of the room, the special fitness of the water color over the mantel—a Peirce, wasn't it? He'd guessed as much, for he had one of the painter's canvases at home. Did she know the work of two other favorites of his—both painters of the Maine scene, Hartley and Marin? She did, and admired them greatly. It was easy to talk to him and she asked herself impatiently why she should have expected anything else from a man as adept as he must be in coping with the complex, the difficult, the dull. A wary outlook on life had taught her to look for the same trait in others, and on not finding it to tell herself as she now did that if anything should occur to faze this man, he would be careful not to show it. She had a sudden incomprehensible desire to like him, which sprang, as she was to confess to him much later, from that vacuum in which she'd lived for so long. Clinging to the few friends whom she knew well, she had learned to dispense with strangers who were forever putting her on her guard. She'd forced herself—for the children's sake—to play the hypocrite, to meet their friends and make them feel at home, and it usually paid off, leaving her ashamed of her initial cowardice.

Now in the small island of privacy in which she found herself alone with Chris's father she heard him say in a matter of fact voice:

"I'm so glad to be here, Mrs. Dalton. Chris has spoken of you so often and so glowingly that it seems incredible we shouldn't have met before this."

Delia explained that as a family they led a rather uneventful life, and that it had really been up to her to do something about it.

"One gets into lazy habits . . . and meeting people, new people, seems to become more and more a matter of luck."

"Liking them when you do meet them becomes even more so." He took his pipe from his pocket and looked at it, then put it back. "Guess I better save this thing for after dinner." He looked across the room at Chris and Veronica. "You know, I'd like very much to talk to you about your daughter's novel, but she's exacted this silly pledge of me, so my lips are sealed. Am I right in supposing that you haven't read it?"

"Veronica is absurd about her writing, but I've learned to control my curiosity!"

"Well, there's no reason why you shouldn't be told that in my opinion, and my colleagues', you have every cause to feel proud."

"I am proud. We're not an intellectual family—in the formal sense of the word. That may, in a way, account for the isolation in which she works." She looked at him gravely. "But perhaps success will help bring her out of it, a bit."

He started to say something but the words seemed somehow to run away from him, and his eyes had a flash of brilliance as though a light had shone in them, and she felt the warmth, like the touch of a hand.

CHAPTER

XVI

"Like it?" Chris asked. He brushed the camellia on Veronica's shoulder, letting his hand linger on the warm skin of her neck.

"I got the biggest and most expensive one I could find."

"It was sweet of you."

"I see you're wearing make-up. How come this sudden departure from the norm?"

"I decided I'd better do something about changing my personality. Think that's possible—at my age?"

"The witch doctors says forty is the dead line." He looked at her curiously. "Happy? You ought to be."

She nodded, her entire consciousness directed towards the sofa, where his father was talking to Delia. "So you changed your mind about coming home for Thanksgiving," she said to Chris in the same light tone. "What about those mysterious friends in Rhode Island?"

"I came home because of you, as you know goddam well."

"I wasn't so sure, judging by your last letter. It was on the coquettish side—and you know how I feel about male coquettes."

"I'm not so crazy about the female variety, myself," Chris replied, then, quickly: "Quit it, Nonny! Tonight of all nights. And you're looking nicer than I ever remember seeing you. It's the book, of course. I'm not so conceited as to imagine it could be because of me!"

154

"What is it you want me to quit?"

"I don't know . . . yes, I do. This distantness, with me." He moved closer so their shoulders touched. "Let's throw everyone for a loop by announcing our engagement—now, this minute!"

She was silent and he pressed: "Why not? You know it's what we both want. And everybody'd be pleased."

"Would we, still, after a year or two?"

He laughed impatiently. "One can always call it a day!"

"Yes, of course. One always can." Reaching up to the mantel she took down his cigarette lighter. "Before I forget, you left this lying around last time you were here."

He glanced at it and slipped it into his pocket. "Thanks. Look, Nonny. Soon as I graduate, the army's going to grab me. If we got married we could still have a little time together, in Maine if you liked, or we could take a quick trip to Europe. I've been thinking about it. And if they send me to Germany or to Japan, maybe you could come along. You could continue your writing—but we'd be together."

"I don't get this eagerness for marriage. We can be together without it, can't we?"

He looked at her steadily. "If you'd rather have it that way, yes, we can. But what have you got against marriage?"

She seemed to think it over before she answered: "The sense of obligation, I suppose. And the knowledge that while it is taken so solemnly by everyone, it can still end with a bang or a whimper the very next day."

Chris's eyes narrowed in a way she'd seen them before—a way that could always half frighten her and half attract. His whole manner changed, became superficial. "I take it I'm being given the polite brush-off?"

Panic rushed her suddenly. "Chris, don't. I'm sorry. Let's not talk about these things now. Not here."

He shrugged. "I'd like to talk to you about a lot of things. About your book, for instance. I can't, though, until I've read it."

He made an effort at friendliness. "Anyway I guess Dad's said all the things you'd want to hear about it, hasn't he?"

"He's been swell."

"I told you he would be. And he likes you." He glanced across the room. "Rather looks as if he liked Delia, too, though I always took that for granted."

"Naturally."

"He's coony about women as a rule. Guess he's had to be."

"It seems funny that he should never have married again."

"Well, he's a self-sufficient old son of a gun, and I rather fancy he has his consolations. Women seem to like him."

She asked, guardedly: "Was it a very unhappy marriage, his and your mother's?"

"I suppose if I say yes, you'll use that as another excuse for your scunner against marriage! Actually, no, I don't think they were so unhappy. Just bored each other to death, so decided to call it off."

This was not the first time the subject had cropped up between them, and that it should do so at this juncture was a measure of the loss at which they found themselves. Chris glanced up to find Veronica gazing at him with a strange and quite lovely smile which sent a shock of desire through him, banishing his anger and frustration. "Nonny," he muttered. "God damn you!"

Nick and Miriam appeared with the drinks. and Veronica turned away, composure like some plastic sub⸱ ⸱⸱ured over her by an invisible hand.

"We've been talking about dreams," Miriam told them gaily. "Katie had a lulu last night. She dreamed she'd become radioactive and was afraid that if anyone found out she'd be executed for the common good."

"Tell them about yours," Nick suggested. He had provided himself with a can of beer and pretended not to notice Delia's lifted brow. "Go on, tell them, Miriam."

"Mine wasn't anything. Just one of those occasions that sound so scintillating when one dreams about them."

She took a cocktail from the tray and sat down beside Donald, who put his arm round her. "I was in some sort of lecture hall, postulating a theory that the soul of man was about to lose individuality and coalesce in a kind of generalized social conscience which, in my dream, seemed to have terrifying implications. I wanted the audience to do something about this—to arouse them to a sense of urgency, but there they all sat, apparently quite undisturbed by the possibility that they might each one be about to lose his soul, an event which *I knew* would be every bit as serious for them as losing their legs. I finally became so worked up that I started to shout: 'Don't you realize the awful thing that's happening to you?' And at that the entire room full of people began to laugh and jeer, and I realized I was licked."

She took a sip from her glass and laughed. "Suddenly I spied Chris, who got up to challenge my thesis. And quite intelligently too, I will say."

"Sounds like me," Chris said, loftily. "Quote me, Mim."

"Can't remember, but it *sounded* good. Anyhow we all got into a fight, and people pointed at me and yelled: 'She's the enemy!' And just as I feared they were going to attack me—Chris among them—they all made a dash for the exit and I was left alone in the huge, empty hall, and that was worse than being mobbed."

She smiled at Wallingford. "Then I woke up. But it was regular Kafka stuff while it lasted."

There was the briefest pause, then Wallingford turned to Delia.

"That's what comes of being an anthropologist. Writers and anthropologists generally, I find, are quite unable to keep their subconscious down under, where it belongs."

"Tell us about that other wacky dream you had once," Nick urged Miriam. "Chris was in that one too, remember?"

Chris looked at him. "That a whole can of beer you're drinking, Nick?"

"I missed Mother and Fran's birthday party. While they were

guzzling champagne I was being made to swill milk and prune juice in that house of detention Mother pays three grand a year to keep me in." He raised his glass to Veronica. "Here's luck to the novel, sister. If it should happen to make a lot of dough, I could use another trout rod."

Wallingford smiled at the boy. "We have a trout brook near my place at Todd's Harbor. Better come down next summer and take a crack at it."

Nick beamed. "I'll take you up on that!"

"It's wonderful," Miriam said. "I caught a trout there myself last summer, but it was under age or something and Donald made me throw it back."

"Come back next summer," Donald told her, affectionately. "Maybe the trout will have reached the age of consent."

She shook her head. "Next summer I'm going to my cousins at Martha's Vineyard. Thanks just the same."

They went in to dinner and Chris began to talk with animation about Cambridge and his anxiety to get out of that educational factory and down to the business of making a living. "Or just living." He did not look at Veronica. "The business of living some sort of a private life before the army makes me into another kind of private. Two years snatched out of a guy's life, just like that! I sometimes think that the C.O.'s have something."

Donald looked at him in surprise. "You do? I'd say you were hardly the type."

"I'm not so sure." He sounded a shade defiant. "I haven't run into a single guy in my class who's sold on soldiering. But they're not sold on the idea of the individual protest, either."

"Makes me think of my dream," Miriam murmured, looking at him through her glasses, her eyes strangely distant.

Donald said thoughtfully: "Wish I could see some hope for the individual protest. I respect the principle involved in conscientious objection to anything, but it does seem to become less meaningful as time goes on."

"Meaningful to whom—the crowd?" Miriam shook her head.

"You have to go on protesting, even if there is no one to listen. The other way madness lies."

"For the individual yes, for the crowd, no." Donald went on quickly: "We're rapidly becoming a syndicate of timid souls which believes—and which has the means to enforce its belief— that safety lies in numbers, and that without conformity you perish."

Delia agreed. "Numbers and more numbers! I get a feeling at times that every individual gesture has been taken over by the crowd and made valueless by sheer repetition. Nothing really moves us anymore, or if it does, it moves us *conventionally*. There is something stupefying about the scale on which things happen— perhaps the word saturation sums it up. We hear of saturation this and saturation that—advertising, buying, spending, *bombing*! How can the individual register an equivalent reaction, or make what he has effective against this . . . enormity!"

"He can't," Wallingford said, his gaze intent on her face. "Which brings us back to the conscientious objector. He's already a gone goon, since society won't even allow him the brief and lonely splendor of martyrdom. All it does is stick him in an internment camp and forget all about him."

"He'll at least have had the consolation of acting according to the dictates of his conscience," declared Chris after a pause.

"And the individual conscience is always in a minority, so there we are."

Nick asked to be told the difference between a pacifist and a conscientious objector, and Wallingford explained that there wasn't any difference, really. "It's just that as people become more civilised they become more agressive. It's against this organized aggressiveness that the C.O. makes his objection."

While they were talking, Delia had become increasingly aware of Veronica's silence. Am I doing something wrong? she asked herself, uneasily. Talking too much, perhaps . . . having too good a time? Her silence is aimed at me . . . I can feel it.

Donald was speaking: "It seems to me that modern war isn't

really the barbarism it's supposed to be. No barbarian ever dreamed up anything like the horrors we've invented. They acted, by and large, in the spirit of passion, man against man, and there was always room for the individual gesture of forgiveness and pity. But not anymore! Not in this push-button age."

It seemed that almost in spite of himself, he addressed his remarks to Delia, his eyes drawn again and again to her face.

"Our idea of war is the ultimate example of everything in our society. As sophisticated, as conventional, as amoral. Your conscientious objector hasn't a prayer."

"And where would you say that the artist comes into this picture?" Miriam asked after a pause. "The artist, with his aesthetic sensibility, the individual par excellence!"

"He'll be starved out," Wallingford replied with a shrug. "Starved out, or taken over, like everyone else."

"Pessimist!" cried Miriam. "Stop him, somebody! He's spoiling my Lobster Newburg." She turned to Veronica. "What about it, Nonny? As a writer you must have some ideas on the subject."

Veronica looked as though she were just waking up. "What subject? *Morality?* Old hat, isn't it?"

She managed to make it sound outrageously rude, but Donald laughed. "Come!" he gibed. "No one could have written the novel you've written without having very positive ideas on the subject."

He caught himself up quickly. "I'm sorry—but I didn't give anything away, did I?"

She forced a smile. "No, it's all right."

Nick decided that the moment had come to change the subject to one nearer his interests. "Mr. Wallingford, did you mean it about the trout fishing next summer?"

"Of course. August is a bit late for trout, but we might find some. And there's deep sea fishing, and a boat, if you happen to like sailing." He glanced at Delia. "This is a bona fide invitation to the family. We have ample room."

"For you, too, Miriam," Chris turned to her urgently. "It'll be the best house party yet."

"I've promised my cousins. Try me summer after next."

"Damn it, how'd I know where I'll be summer after next? On Okinawa maybe, or a space ship over the Caspian Sea!"

Delia returned Wallingford's steady gaze. "Yes," she said with sudden decision. "Of course we'll come. We'd love to."

CHAPTER

XVII

NICK was alone in the kitchen where he'd gone to help Katie carry out the dishes when the telephone rang, and, unthinkingly, he lifted the receiver. It was Fran. "Nick!"

"Fran, how are you?" He muffled the receiver with his hand to keep out the sound of voices from the dining room. "Where are you, Fran?"

"At the Leonard, where else? I felt at a loose end and thought I'd come over and see you." She sounded sober, her voice clear, affectionate. "Honey, when did you get home? I'd have come over earlier if I'd known."

He did some fast thinking. "Why don't you stay where you are, Fran, and I'll come see you? The family are all off at a party, so it'll be just me." He could hear Katie push her way past the swinging door into the pantry, ushering in a burst of voices.

"I'll be right over, Fran. Stay put, h'm?" He hung up and went to the sink to pour himself a glass of water as Katie entered the kitchen. "That the telephone?" she asked, setting a tray of dishes on the table. "Who was it?"

"Wrong number," he told her smoothly, with a pleasant sense of being, for the moment, master of a tricky situation. "Girl mistook me for her sugar and we were getting along nicely until her mother or someone came along and she hung up on me."

Five minutes later Veronica, passing the hall door, saw him putting on his overcoat with an air of stealth quite unlike him.

"Where are you off to at this hour?"

"None of your business," he growled. Then, quickly: "Listen, Fran telephoned and she was all for coming over here, but I headed her off by saying I'd drop in and see her for a few minutes. Tell Mother, will you? I won't be gone long."

She looked at him dubiously. "I don't know. It's after ten. Should you?"

"Got to, now. Said I would." He wound a muffler round his neck. "She's quite apt to show up if I don't, and that wouldn't be so hot. What'd you and Mother tell her anyway—about tonight, I mean? Better brief me so I won't pull any boners."

"I didn't even speak to Fran. I've no idea what Mother or Katie may have told her. You'll just have to use your head, I guess."

"That's for me," he said, nodding. "Tell the others good night, will you? Use *your* head. Friend in distress, or something."

She went to the door with him. "Was Fran all right?"

"Sounded all right to me. Sounded fine, in fact. Probably wouldn't have done a bit of harm to have asked her to the party."

He gave her a look of heavy disapproval. "All your fault, and Mother's, that I have to run out on you like this. G'night!"

He let himself out of the house and the brown, cold air felt fresh on his face as he headed towards Madison, hoping to get a bus. None appeared, and he started down the avenue towards 59th St. and the subway, feeling light-hearted, adventurous, and responsible. Poor old Fran had sounded terribly lonesome and it made him angry all over again to think of her frowsting in her dingy hotel when everyone else was having a good time. He understood his mother's feelings, sure. Fran might easily have fouled up the whole shooting match, but then again, she mightn't have. Anyway he was glad to be going to see her—he felt grown-up, only faintly guilty at having run off without telling his mother, and pleasantly defiant. Striding along in the cold, he began to sing:

"*When the shark bites*
With his teeth, dear,
Scarlet billows start to spread,
Fancy gloves though
Wears Macheath, dear,
So there's not a trace of red . . ."

Store windows on his right were filled with a condensed glow of light and only a delicatessen or two remained open at this hour. The autumn darkness was pierced by metallic gleams of tinsel and a pointillism of color—holly, though it was four weeks to Christmas, gay boxes of candy, fat plastic turkeys, a suckling pig revolving horribly on its spit, eyes like marbles, tail a piteous question mark which made him feel a little sick. He thought: things one eats should never bear any resemblance to life.

In the subway the foetid air cut into his sinuses. Why did these places always smell of urine? People were stinkers by nature. You imagine they're nice, that they're decent, human actually, but just coop them somewhere all together and you soon found out that they were stinkers. He thought of the conversation at the dinner table tonight, paraphrasing it to fit his own understanding. A great goddam sort of school, is what Mr. Wallingford meant when he spoke of the new society we were coming into. Something like the joint I go to. Not too bad, or you wouldn't stay. You were fed, clothed, exercised, taught things, given to understand that you carried the torch for the future. A bore of course. Crap, mostly. But you took it because there didn't seem anything else to do, unless you were one of those undisciplined nuts like Ponty Schumacher who spent all his time running away and being brought back, and the school only kept him because his family had a lot of influence or something and probably paid more to have them put up with Ponty's queerness.

"Tokens, please."

The man in the upright coffin of a cage took Nick's money and flicked the tokens under the grille. He had an eye like a lead bullet and looked as though he'd never known a moment's fun in his life.

Nick sauntered up and down the platform, waiting for his train, whistling the Knife Song through his teeth. I'm lucky, he told himself. Don't have to empty garbage or sell newspapers or deliver late baskets of groceries at people's back doors for a little extra dough. Two hundred guys at school don't have to, either. Multiply Holyrood by several hundred and you'd find there were a hell of a lot of lucky bastards around, taking it all in all. Good thing Father left Mother fixed up so *she* doesn't have to scrub floors or get bleary-eyed typing some fat bastard's letters for him. Nick thought of Delia with a sudden spasm of tenderness. She'd looked beautiful tonight. Young, a figure as good as Veronica's, even better. And loving and delicately scented and soft and seeing into your mind and through your eyes, but never making a thing out of it, never making you feel that you were a sap . . . Never pushing, prying, accusing. Even when he got those lousy marks at school and couldn't bring himself to tell her about McAllister, the goddam flit, and why he'd given him those marks for conduct . . . *demeanour*, they called it! "Very well, Dalton. We won't say any more about it. Remember, he who accuses others accuses himself."

The bastard, with his fine gray hair and his suntan and too-tight pants. Boy, the stink I could arouse by letting them know the kind of guy they hire to teach us English Lit! But Mac had never tried it again, not after that first night when I pretended to be asleep and swatted him in the eye with my fist just as though I didn't know it was him and what he was trying. . . . Had to go on pretending ever since that I didn't know, or remember. 'He who accuses others accuses himself.' True, all right. Mac had it worked out, which is how he'd lasted as long as he had at Holyrood, which had a reputation for being one of the best run private schools around. But Delia . . . she mustn't know. She'd understand, of course. No doubt about that. But she'd whip him

out of there fast, and there'd be bound to be questions, accusa-
tions, denials, and a lot more people than he would be involved.

The express came tearing into the station. Nick found a seat
and braced himself with his hands deep in his pockets and thought
about his Aunt Fran. She'd sounded O.K. over the phone, and if
by some chance she happened to be sober, or sober enough, there'd
be all the more reason for him to watch his step about the party
tonight. She's always been darned nice to me, he reflected, thinking of the presents at birthdays and Christmas—she made a point
of finding out just what you'd be likely to want most, and then
going out of her way to find it for you. Latterly she'd sent checks
. . . for sums he was sure she couldn't afford. And she'd always
treated him as though he were grown-up and an equal, and had
done it without that slimy hypocritical air most people use when
they think they're putting a younger person at his ease. And she
could be fun. She liked to tell a dirty story occasionally, and liked
to hear one. Nothing of the prissy old bag about Fran, not like
some of those dames who showed up at school over weekends to
see their nephews and sons, or the sons and nephews of their
friends.

Damn it, yes, they should have had Fran over tonight. She was
one of the family and what was the point of trying to keep her
under wraps? People found out about you sooner or later, about
your parents, your relatives, your friends. There was the case of
that guy at school for instance—Patrick Wilson, had a sister that
was born without arms or legs—without a single arm or a leg,
and no one ever knew a thing about it, it being taken for granted
Patrick was an only child. And then one day this sister of his was
in an automobile accident—she'd been taken for a drive by her
mother or someone—and she was killed and it was all in the
papers, with photographs and the name of the family and everything, and it mentioned that she'd had a brother, Patrick, a stu-
dent at Holyrood, and when it came out like that and everyone
interested, naturally, Patrick Wilson had some sort of a nervous
breakdown and had to leave, and everybody said what the hell!

Wouldn't have made any difference to them, except for the excitement of not *knowing* he had a kid sister that hadn't arms and legs like everyone else.

As far as Chris was concerned, he'd already met Fran and knew she was something of an old soak. Why shouldn't his father know it too? He looked as if he could take it. A swell guy. No crap about him. And the way he kept looking at Delia tonight, as though his eyes had gotten stuck. And I don't mind about that either, Nick assured himself, feeling a sudden weakness of his stomach muscles. I don't really mind if some good guy comes along and falls for her and wants to marry her. Only reason it hasn't happened already probably is because of Veronica and me, because Mother's always had us hanging around her neck like a couple of albatrosses or something, and she's got into the habit of passing up things on our account. Katie's said as much, and she ought to know. Things she might have had and didn't because she was afraid there mightn't be enough dough left for us to have what she wanted to give us. So she's gone without trips, new dresses, the opera—things women seem to like. Gone without guys too, because if she hadn't where the heck were they? With Father dead ten years there must have been guys around she could have married. But Nonny probably took care of *that*. No one was going to take Father's place if Nonny could prevent it. Katie had had something to say about that, too. She'd come out with it almost as though she couldn't help herself one day last year when she and Veronica were having a row about something, and Veronica had sulked for hours afterwards. And tonight! Putting on the sour puss just because Wallingford was giving Mother the eye instead of giving it to *her*. Jeepers! Wasn't Chris enough for her? But Veronica never had had enough of anything, and that was her trouble. He'd told Delia so. She wanted everything, everything, everything, and all the time there was Miriam Werth who'd give her eye teeth for Chris and by Jesus it would serve Veronica right, damned if it wouldn't, if Miriam were to snatch him right from under her nose.

He told himself uneasily that this didn't mean he wasn't fond of Veronica. He was. There were things he knew about her that he was willing to bet no one else knew. That she sometimes cried in bed, for instance. That, unable to sleep, she came into his room and curled at the foot of his bed and smoked one cigarette after another, and ordered him to talk to her. "Talk about what?"

"Anything. I don't care—anything."

So they talked about ordinary simple things that happened at his school, and the best kind of lure to use for trout in April when the water was high, and about Patrick Wilson and the sister without arms and legs, and even about McAllister, and Veronica laughed and asked him to tell her some more, and she never lectured him or told him to watch his step, but just to keep talking so she wouldn't, she said, have to think. Alone with him Veronica could be quite another sort of person than the bitch she could be with other people. With Delia especially. She was jealous of Delia, that was why. But with him there was something else, something he couldn't discuss with anyone, something he was shy of even thinking about. Veronica liked him. She liked him with a kind of desperate eager, little-girl liking she never showed before other people, and which he sometimes suspected she didn't realize she was showing *him*. That was something he couldn't forget. Even when he wanted to beat her up for her meanness to Delia, it was something he couldn't forget.

CHAPTER

XVIII

Emerging from the subway on Eighth Street, Nick made his way to Fran's hotel a few blocks away. Unpainted for years, ill-lighted, with a scabrous look to it, the Leonard was an uninviting dive even by day. At this hour it struck Nick as being a cross between an undertaker's establishment and a warehouse. A torn canopy hung across the sidewalk, a light shone drearily over the front entrance, and as he walked up the wooden steps he tripped over a pail of water and almost fell on his face in the lobby.

Inside, the place looked as though it were in process of being dismantled. Paper hung in strips on one wall, revealing an original screaming pink. A few decrepit chairs were scattered around, and people were sitting on these in deathly silence, their attention focussed on Nick as he paused by the door, wiping his wet shoes on a scrofulous mat. There was no sign of an information desk, and he tried to remember the number of Fran's room, which she'd given him over the phone.

Near by sat an old woman in a pink knitted beret and a green dress, a blazing spot of rouge in each cheek. The first to spy Nick as he stumbled into the lobby, she trained a cold eye on him as he searched his pockets for an imaginary address book while summoning up nerve to ask her the whereabouts of the room clerk. Then he heard a sound on his left and saw a thin, elderly man being sick in a paper bag.

"Want something?" the woman in the pink beret demanded gratingly of Nick, and he fancied he had a glimpse of her tongue, pink and forked like a dragon's.

"Could you tell me where'd I find the information desk, please?" he asked, and for a moment she continued to bore at him with her gimlet eyes, then jerked her head sidewise. "Round the corner to your left."

He crossed the lobby in the direction she indicated and found the information desk, and behind it a fat, bald man with nostrils like stuffed snails. "Want sum'n?" this character asked Nick in surprisingly human accents. "Or just lorst?"

"My aunt, Mrs. Hight. She's staying here."

"Room number?"

"I don't seem to have it, but she's registered, I know. Mrs. Frances Hight."

The name sounded reassuringly familiar, even aristocratic, in this sleazy atmosphere, and Nick waited while the clerk reached out a dirty hand and ran a finger down a list of names. "Hight. Mrs. Frances. Thatter?"

"Yes, my aunt. She expects me."

"Number four thirty-two. You c'n use the house phone ovtha."

Nick called Fran's room and she answered at once. "Come on up, baby. Fourth floor. Turn to your right as you get out of the elevator and mind you don't fall over the stiff in the corridor."

The stiff! Nick had a moment of panic, thinking that anything was possible in this hole, then realized that this was Fran's idea of a joke. "Be right up!"

Leaving the phone, he couldn't find the elevator, the clerk seemed to have vanished, so he wandered back to the lobby and its two weird occupants, to whose number a third had been added —a big red-faced woman in a tight black skirt and tighter sweater, in animated conversation with the pink beret, apparently about the elderly man who was still being sick in his paper bag.

"He could help himself if he wanted," the big woman declared emphatically, blowing smoke from her cigarette. "He just don't want to. You take these characters they don't drink to drownd their troubles, they want for their troubles to drownd them."

Nick looked vaguely around in search of the elevator, and failing that, a staircase. There seemed to be neither.

"He killed my kitty," the woman in the pink beret was saying vindictively, glaring at the sick man who seemed oblivious to everything except the state of his health.

"I know he killed my kitty and I'd kill him only it'd be murder and I'd be made to burn for it, the bastard."

"You don't have to lift a finger," the big woman told her soothingly. She crossed her legs and Nick had an impressive view all the way up her thighs, as she perhaps intended he should have.

"You don't have to kill nobody, kid. Just sit right where you are and let him drown in his own juice. Looks like he's more'n halfway to doing it already, the smuck."

"He killed my kitty on purpose because he said she kept him awake nights, then he denies it and says she must of gotten run over or stole. Spends every cent I give him on booze, then goes kills a little defenceless kitty only three months old."

"The smuck! I wouldn't give him a bent nickel to put in the pay toilet."

"He'd bum it on the street if I didn't, and I got my self-respect to think about, haven't I?"

Pink beret turned without warning on Nick. "What you hanging around for?"

"I can't find the elevator," Nick said frigidly.

"Well, do I look like an elevator?"

The big woman laughed. "Look, kid," she said briskly to Nick. "This aint Grand Central. Elevator's behind that screen, first door next the one says Gentlemen, only you won't find no gentlemen in this joint. Who is it you want anyway?"

"My aunt. Thanks, I think I can find her now."

"Must be that dame Dipper had to carry upstairs to her room couple nights back," the woman in the pink beret volunteered with a grin. "She's been here before. Dipper tends out on her personally because he says she's the only lady ever comes into the place."

"Dipper must use the touch system, how else'd he know?"

Both shrieked. Nick found the elevator, a self-service one which stank and which mounted at such a leisurely speed that he was almost suffocated by the time he reached the fourth floor and sprang out.

Fran greeted him at her door, kissing him on both cheeks.

"Nick, lamb! Coming out at this hour just to see your poor old aunt. I thought you weren't expected until tomorrow."

She drew him into the room and he smelled the whisky, though she seemed perfectly under control, and smart in a dark suit with pearls at her throat and ears.

"Take off your coat," she said gaily. "I'll fix us a drink."

"God, Fran! Why do you have to live in this joint?"

She went to a table where glasses were set out, and a bucket of ice, soda, Coca-Cola, and a bottle of Scotch.

"You're spoiled, that's the trouble with you, Nicky boy. Prep school and life on Sixty-eighth Street has ruined you for the coarser things of life."

"I'll say."

"What's the matter with this joint? Not flossy, I admit, but it suits me. It's quiet, and people leave you alone. And above all it's cheap."

"How does Mother feel about it?"

"The way you do, I guess. What'll you have, sweet? There's Scotch, Coke, or plain fizzy water. Name it."

"Coke. But listen, Fran, those goons downstairs!"

"You mean the still-lifes down in the lobby? They're harmless. Besides, my deal is with Dipper, who runs the place and takes care of me."

"Yeah, and thinks you're a lady."

"He does? How'd you find that out?"

"The zombies downstairs." He repeated what he'd heard them

say, and Fran laughed. "Bitches! They're funny, though, don't you think so?"

Nick straddled a chair and rested his arms along its top.

"They act as if they'd escaped from a loony bin."

"You'll learn some day that the world is full of people like that."

"Oh, quit the preaching! Aren't you afraid you'll wake up some morning and find one of them's grabbed your pocketbook or something?"

"Only thing I'm afraid of is that I'll wake up some morning. Like a shot of whisky in your coke?"

"Are you crazy? I'm not supposed to drink."

He took the glass of coke she brought him and lifted it to touch hers. "Anyway, it's good to see you, Fran. One whole year!"

"And you've grown almost out of reach! I'd kiss you again only I'm afraid it might embarrass you."

He began to see that she was drunk, deeply drunk as he rarely saw her. Even at that it was an intermediate stage when she still retained a superficial control over herself, her astonishing vitality sustaining her against the creeping tide of alcohol which she'd been consuming without pause since she left Delia's house three weeks before. Nick knew that she could go on packing it away yet pull herself together and put up a good front, so if you didn't know her well it would take a little while to catch on to just how far gone she was. He felt a twinge of uneasiness, watching her spill the soda as she added it to the whisky in her glass.

Meeting his eyes, she smiled. "Cheer up, kid. I won't let the zombies get you."

"I don't see why Mother lets you come here."

"She understands my low tastes."

"That old man putting his lunch in a paper bag! Suppose he thought he was in an airplane?"

"Transatlantic flight, first class, going to Paris for his vacation." She sat down facing Nick. "How come you're all dressed up?"

He hadn't thought of that. "There was a party with the

Wallingfords, in honor of Veronica's novel. You know it's going to be published, don't you? Some time next year."

Fran took a swallow from her glass. "Yes, our brilliant Nonny has really done something. I always rather thought she would. Not like Delia and me. Aren't you proud of your sister?"

"I don't know. Haven't had a chance to read her book, yet."

"She makes me tired, all that hush hush stuff."

There was a slight pause, then he said, frowning: "Listen, Fran. Why didn't you stay with us? Or anyway, you could have found some decent place farther uptown."

"My dear, I'm broke. The Leonard is all I can afford, and if I'm a little behind with the rent, Dipper doesn't pester me. He knows he'll get his dough some time—which is more than I know!" She laughed again, on a tough note. "And then, I value my independence, what there is of it. To be bust is one thing, to be bust and living off relatives is another."

"Calling your twin sister a relative!" Nick growled. Talk about money always distressed him, made him conscious of his youth and inadequacy in a way he hated. That Fran should be strapped for funds and obliged to live in this shabby place filled him with confused feelings of guilt and shame, and perhaps guessing something of what was passing in his mind, she said with a smile:

"You know that whenever I show up there's apt to be trouble. Last year I had a row with your mother's dear friends the Bowers. They bore me and I got boiled and said things I shouldn't have said. Time before that something else happened, and there was a business with the police." She gave him a sidelong glance. "I don't know how much of all this you're supposed to know, but I never have had much sympathy with Delia's trying to keep you in ignorance where I'm concerned." Then, catching the offended look on his face, for he hated to hear his mother criticized, she went on quickly: "I don't intend to make a nuisance of myself, but it happens. The last night I spent under Delia's roof I damned near set it on fire, and I don't think she was entirely unrelieved when I decided to move out."

"But you could do the same thing here, couldn't you? Set a fire, I mean. And then what?"

He had a sudden horrible vision of Dipper dragging her in her nightgown down the elevator and into the lobby in full view of the woman in the pink beret, her big red-faced friend, and the man puking in his paper bag. He could just hear what they'd have to say about Dipper's lady friend! Fran was his mother's twin, they resembled each other, and he couldn't stand the thought of anyone who so resembled Delia making an exhibition of herself in, of all places, the Leonard Hotel. So all right, he was a snob, but he didn't care if he was. Dipper carrying Fran in her nightgown. . . .

"Don't worry," Fran said, shrugging. "You'd be surprised how careful I can be when I know there's no one around to watch out for me!"

Her outspokenness was always disarming, and he gave her an unwilling smile. "I like living like this. I have a weakness for crummy places and crummy people. You can take 'em or leave 'em. Degenerate, perhaps, but that's the way I like it."

Nick sipped his coke and thought of the party going on at home without him. The good food, the flowers, the friendly, familiar set-up, the reassuring touch of his mother's personality— and Fran here in this ratty joint with no one to talk to, dependent on *Dipper* to take care of her if she got in trouble!

Fran said suddenly: "What do you say we go out and get something to eat?"

He looked at his watch. "It's eleven o'clock. Restaurants'll all be shut, won't they?"

"I know a place that stays open all night. Down on MacDougal Street."

Nick felt with sudden premonition that it might be better if they were to stay where they were. "I'm not especially hungry, Fran. Suppose I dash out and buy us a sandwich and dash back?"

"A sandwich—when I haven't set eyes on you for a whole year? Not on your life." She rose to her feet and he saw with dismay that it cost her something to keep her balance. She stood for a moment gazing at him with an expression he found hard to define.

"Gosh," she said at last, with a sigh. "Why weren't you my son? Mushy thing to say, but I mean it."

"You and Mother have done pretty well between you, sharing Nonny and me all these years."

"Nonny!" She shook her head. "No one's going to share Nonny. She'll see to that."

On her way to the coat closet, Fran paused by the liquor supply and poured herself another slug. Nick rose, picking up his coat. "O.K. Fran, let's go and get something to eat." He added firmly: "I've got enough dough so you don't have to worry."

She gulped down her drink and said thickly: "You're such a nice kid. Nicest kid I know. Hope some bitch of a woman doesn't come along and mess up your life."

"She won't," Nick said soothingly. "I won't let her."

He helped her with her coat, and for a moment Fran stood with her hands on his shoulders, peering at him as if through a haze.

"Hope you're not going to look like Charles!"

"Why not? He was a good looking guy, according to his photographs."

She smiled with an unpleasant knowingness—he'd seen that smile before, but not at such close quarters, and it made him feel slightly sick. What was there about drunks, he wondered, that made them act as though they had the secrets of the world up their sleeves? He found her gloves and pocketbook and handed them to her. "Got your room key?" he asked, paternally. "I'd hate to have to ask Dipper to let us in afterwards."

"Dipper's all right. Trouble with you, Nicky, as I've told you —you're in danger of growing up to be a snob."

"You just said you thought I was the nicest guy you knew!"

"It's Delia's fault. She's set on keeping you respectable."

"Lay off Delia," he said, lightly.

"Don't look like Charles, and don't act like a snob." She turned to him suddenly, fear in her eyes. "I don't mean that . . . not really. I'd hate to think that a time might come when you won't have any use for your poor old aunt. Like Veronica. Pity, that's all. No love, no nothing. Don't think I could bear that, from you."

In his anxiety to cheer her up, he became indiscreet. "Who the heck was it ran out on a party to come see you, when the others . . ." He broke off, but it was too late. Perhaps Fran had had her suspicions from the beginning; perhaps, drunk though she was, she now divined the reason for his sudden flushing and the defiant silence with which he regarded her.

"The others, h'n?" She patted his arm. "I get it. And it doesn't matter. Let's go."

CHAPTER

XIX

To Nick's relief, the lobby was deserted when they emerged from the elevator, and even Dipper seemed to have vanished through some trap door into the unknown. Out on the street, Fran revived somewhat and took his arm. "So Delia and Nonny threw a party and didn't invite me?"

"That's not what I said."

"You don't have to say anything, baby." She pressed his arm and they turned in the direction of Washington Square. "They'd invited Nonny's publisher and were afraid I'd throw a wrench in the works. They were probably right."

He felt a sudden need for frankness. "It was silly. The whole thing was silly. But I guess Mother was thinking about Veronica."

"She'd do better to relax."

"And it wasn't Veronica's fault either, not really." Artless, he added: "Nobody knew what kind of guy Mr. Wallingford might turn out to be, I guess. What makes the whole thing so silly is that it wouldn't have made any difference if you had come and gotten tight. Wallingford is a nice guy. So's Chris."

Fran laughed. "So I wouldn't have been upsetting any apple carts?"

"You wouldn't have tried, would you?"

"Hell, let's forget it. What matters is that you loved me enough to leave the party and come see me."

He persisted anxiously: "You won't take it out on Mother, will you? I think she feels badly about it anyway."

She said nothing. They crossed the street, and suddenly she drew him to a halt and pointed. "See that place, that excavation?"

It was on the corner of Eighth Street, a great square hole protected by a board fence over the top of which they peered into the desolation below. The wan light of a street lamp illumined one wall, standing flat and one-dimensional with its frescoed outlines of what had once been rooms; bits of wallpaper and colored plaster still stuck to it, and the geometric progression of a vanished staircase mounted towards the sky. Below stretched an area of disaster with a few recognizable details—a blue-painted door propped against a rusted bundle of old wires, a section of mahogany balustrade, metal façades of a fireplace, and a marble wash basin tipped on its side next to a heap of broken bricks. Dominating the scene, morose and forbidding, stood the bulldozer that had wrought this havoc, mounting guard under the stars.

"That," Fran said, "used to be the Lafayette Hotel where your Uncle Herbert and I spent our honeymoon."

Nick remembered the place vaguely. "They're doing this everywhere nowadays," he said. "Hotels, churches, anything. Here one minute, next minute . . . poof!"

"A whole chunk of the past," Fran went on as though she hadn't heard what he said. "Herbert and I came here to stay whenever we were in New York. We always had the big room on the corner, so we could look out on University Place and Eighth Street. There was gold leaf in the old-fashioned wallpaper and the furniture had come from France, and every morning we had breakfast brought to our room. Croissants and strawberry jam and café au lait. The food was the best in town. Downstairs in the cafe there were red velvet curtains in the windows, and marble topped tables, and the waiters were French and temperamental, and you always ran into the same people sitting drinking and playing dominoes or chess. Sometimes we saw Bertrand Russell there, and Wendell Wilkie and Hendrik Van Loon, and Thomas Wolfe. The place had what people call atmosphere, but it didn't depend on artificial cobwebs and indirect lighting to achieve it."

She had spoken soberly and with strange feeling, and Nick stared into the abyss, which meant nothing to him. He was at that precarious and enviable age that is without nostalgia, lacking experience of extreme sadness and extreme joy—an early morning age when even shadows are without an added meaning, and so there was no way for him to understand the things that were happening to Fran as she stood with her arm trembling in his, contemplating a ruin she had once seen whole and vibrant with life.

"Like the war," the boy said at last, for something to say. "Like pictures of the blitz in London."

"Like the war that's always going on against the things that matter to a few people. John Sloan did a painting of this, and he's dead, too."

"It was only a hotel," Nick said, to comfort her.

"It wasn't only a hotel. It was a place where Herbert and I made love."

Embarrassed, Nick said no more, and when a taxi slowed expectantly alongside, Fran waved it to a stop and gave the driver an address on the farther side of Washington Square. "I haven't been there since the Lord knows when," she told Nick as they got into the cab. "It's probably gone the way of the Lafayette."

However, they found the restaurant she had in mind, small and dingy, with a few night hawks perched along the bar. Fran lost no time ordering a highball for herself and a beer for Nick, who decided that one beer wouldn't kill him, and that he'd call it a day after that. Heat, the stuffy atmosphere of the room, and a curious inner excitement had set the alcohol coursing through Fran's system and there was a touch of venom in her smile as she raised her glass to Nick. "Wonder what Delia and Nonny would say if they were to see you boozing in this dive with me?"

Nick frowned. "Mother wouldn't like it."

"Are you going to make a clean breast of it when you get home?"

"It's not so serious, is it? Though I guess I'd be in trouble if the people at school heard about it."

She stared at him speculatively. "So Delia and Nonny were afraid I might get plastered and disgrace them in front of their friends?"

"Do we have to go into that again?" Nick asked, sighing. "And you're coming to dinner with us tomorrow anyway."

"As a consolation prize, I suppose. Well, do you know something, Nicky? Maybe I'll decide that I don't want to come to dinner tomorrow after all."

He shrugged, saying nothing, and after a moment Fran asked:

"Did they know you were coming to see me tonight?"

"I told Nonny I was. Mother was busy with the guests."

Fran gave an unpleasant laugh. "So you sneaked out on her! Well, it shows a certain independence on your part, I must say. Congratulations! I was beginning to fear Delia would keep you in swaddling clothes until you grew a beard."

He reddened, taken aback by a mood he had not seen her in before.

"Nonny said she'd explain to Mother that I'd gone to see you. For God's sake, Fran! What's the matter with that?"

"Delia'll probably think there's something the matter, all right. She's always felt I was a corrupting influence on her young."

Nick sipped his beer, thinking: This was a big mistake. She's really pissed off, and it's my own fault for making that slip in the first place.

Fran said slowly: "Yes, you're evidently tasting the sweets of independence, Nicky boy. And as I say, it's about time. I've never worried much about Veronica—I knew she'd kick over the traces sooner or later, and she did it soon. But you're a different dish of tea." She smiled. "And you've changed in this past year, too. Growing up, with a vengeance."

"I'm fifteen," he told her in a low voice. "Better pipe down. They're not supposed to serve alcohol to minors."

"You look older than fifteen. Nineteen, easily. Don't worry— if any nosey parker comes asking questions I'll tell him you're nineteen and let him try and prove otherwise."

Nick thought: *She* hasn't changed, except maybe for the worse, and that makes Katie right after all. Back there in the hotel, Fran had spruced herself up in expectation of his visit, and he'd thought she looked pretty much as he remembered her from this time last year. But things had happened to Fran, and it began to look as if they could not have been the good things, the happy things. Watching a strand of hair slide free of its pins, and the silly, sly, lecherous smile of the drunkard crawl across her face, Nick thought: When you're fifty years old and like Fran, what can happen to you except the sad, bad, unhappy things?

"One whole year," Fran was saying over the rim of her glass. "Hell of a long time. It's in the kids you see time passing. They grow up, but Delia and I, we just grow old."

"Nuts," he muttered, at a loss. "Mother doesn't look old one damn bit."

"Darling," she murmured, shaking her head. "You're crazy about her, aren't you?"

"Why shouldn't I be? You ought to be too. Her sister."

The waiter came to their table and Nick ordered sandwiches for both of them, and Fran, her first drink still unfinished, ordered another. She leaned her elbows on the table and lighted a cigarette. "Why, when Delia goes to all that trouble about her looks, she doesn't do something about finding herself a man, I don't know. Do you?"

He retorted with sudden temper: "It's her business and I don't want to talk about it."

"You think I'm being critical of her, and I'm not. I'm concerned. I'd like to see her get a good guy. She's been lonely long enough."

He remained silent and she said insinuatingly:

"I suppose you're thinking why the hell I don't get myself a guy while I'm about it?"

"I'm not thinking anything."

"I'll tell you why. Because it's a goddam bore. After fifty, sex is a bore."

He shrugged. "O.K. so it's a bore. Let's talk about something else."

Fran's expression shifted to a kind of cringing. She put out a hand and touched his. "Don't get mad, Nick! I'm not criticizing Delia. I adore her. She's the only person left for me to adore on this whole earth. There's you and Nonny, of course, and I love you dearly, but it isn't the same thing as the love one has for one's own twin sister." She gulped. "There are times when I tell myself I've loved Delia even more than I ever loved Herbert. Why wouldn't I? She stuck by me when he didn't. She's done things for me no one would believe, except the few that know about it."

She took a swallow from her glass and Nick saw her eyes had filled with tears. Here it comes, he thought, dismally. He hoped, however, that she'd go back to the subject of Herbert and leave his mother out of it.

"Not that Herbert wasn't a wonderful person too," Fran meandered off into the desired track, and Nick drew a little sigh of relief. "God! Was he. You know I wanted to go on the stage. Always wanted it, and he always encouraged me. Everybody's heard the story . . . all right, so everybody's heard it, so what. You haven't. You've heard some of it but not all, because you've always been the baby and things have had to be kept from you. I see the point. Trouble was, I never could have enough—you know? Adulation. Wasn't in Herbert to give that to anyone. He had no use for *excess*, and I had no use for anything else, so I divorced him. And now let me tell you something, baby. Don't ever get a divorce."

"Maybe I better just not ever get married."

"Never get a divorce. Never go near any goddam lawyers. They're at the bottom of the trouble. Once you put yourself in a

lawyer's hands you got to get a divorce no matter what, even if
you want to change your mind, anything, they won't let you. Look
at me. I didn't want a divorce. Just imagined I did. It was an act—
like everything I did, it was an act. And I was good, I tell you.
George Baker once wrote me a letter. I've got it some place. Show
it to you. Baker'd ought to have known whether I had it in me
or not. And if I'd stayed off the bottle and worked, I'd have
got somewhere. Like Veronica. Look at Veronica. Twenty-one
and she's accomplished something already, without encourage-
ment, without the artistic background—all on her own! I tell you
I'm filled with envy. Admiration too. Makes me feel better about a
lot of things, but we can't go into that either." She stared at
him with dreadful intensity. "Nick, did you ever take a vow
about anything?"

He shook his head, taking his time over the beer, wishing the
waiter would bring the sandwiches before Fran went entirely to
pieces under his eyes.

"Well," she said slowly, with that mysterious, communicating
air of a drunk, "don't. Not ever. Never let yourself be put in a
corner and made to swear to anything even if they tell you it's
the only thing for you to do, for your sake and everybody else's
goddam sake. Don't do it, Nick. Don't. Take your chances in
the world. Keep your hands untied."

He felt puzzled, apprehensive, but realized that the only thing
for him was to humor her along. "O.K. Fran," he said, gently. "Go
ahead, tell me about the lawyers. What happened?"

"Sons of bitches, that's what happened." She brooded, a liver-
colored flush coming up from her throat to her brow. "Herbert
would have been proud of me, if I'd really worked. But I got so
I couldn't tell the difference between acting and exhibitionism.
All the time I thought I was fooling people I was fooling myself
one degree more. Fooled Herbert, yes. Even fooled the lawyers
into believing I wasn't fooling . . . if you get me."

The waiter came with their sandwiches, and Nick recklessly
ordered another beer.

"Six years," Fran said, looking at him glassily. "And the last two of them nothing but rows. Then one day I tied on a real one and told Herbert I was through and wanted a divorce, and he said quite coolly that that would suit him fine, and I saw at once that he meant it. I was thrown for a loop. I hadn't expected him to say it. I expected an act from *him* . . . pleadings, despair, self-abasement . . . Well, I didn't get it. Not a bit of it. If I'd left him anything at all after those years of marriage, it was his dignity, and he wasn't parting with that. And that left me with nothing to do except carry on to the next act. I guess I still had some crazy hope that I could ring down the curtain before it was too late, but that's the difference between life and the stage. In life you can't ring down the curtain just when you feel like it, changing your mind and your emotions with your make-up. So off I went to my lawyers and Herbert went to his and the coony bastards put their heads together and they must have known that there really wasn't the slightest excuse for that divorce nor any honest desire for it on either side—that it was just one of those things. A mood, a tantrum . . . an act! I still hoped madly that something would happen to stop the proceedings. That Herbert wouldn't let me go through with it, that somebody'd step in and save the apple cart. God, maybe. But nobody did step in, and the lawyers went ahead and sewed us up nice and neat in our shrouds. They knew Herbert had money and they'd get their percentage, and the tougher the going the higher the percentage. Adultery it had to be to make it stick, and Herbert agreed to take the blame, though we didn't have a thing on him, not a thing. And in all this mess the only person that tried to help us was Delia. She'd just married Charles, and she wrote begging me to drop the suit and come east and stay with them until Herbert and I had cooled off. But whenever anyone tried to get into the act it made more of an audience and I felt I couldn't run out on my part. That suited the lawyers fine. And once the papers had been served on poor Herbert, that was that."

She stared into her glass, and Nick thought of the boys he knew at school whose parents had been divorced. He'd never given the question any particular consideration until this moment, but now he experienced a sudden surge of relief and gratitude that his own parents should have stayed together, loyal and undivided, till death did them part.

"I don't see why you blame the lawyers," he said at last to Fran. "They only did what they were hired to do, didn't they?"

"Kites!" she said, savagely. "Vultures!" She finished thickly: "They got a nice fat settlement out of Herbert, for me, and in addition he had to pay my man as well as his own. Nice business, all around."

She made a dramatic gesture and knocked a glass of water on the floor. A waiter came and mopped it up and Nick felt embarrassed. "Better eat something," he suggested, pushing the sandwiches towards her. "Go on, Fran. Eat something."

Fran was leering at the waiter, who looked as if he were about to fall asleep on his feet. "I'd like to switch to a martini," she said with great deliberation. "Double, dry, and nothing in it."

The waiter nodded and went away, and Nick looked at her, aghast. "Jesus, Fran!"

"Quit that, Nicky. You're not in prep school now."

He thought quickly: Maybe I better find a telephone and call the house, ask Mother to come on over here. What a laugh, after acting so damned sure of myself!

The waiter brought Fran's martini and she downed half of it at one go. "When I realized everything was washed up between Herbert and me, I went to pieces. Knew I'd lost my audience for keeps. Only audience'd ever mattered."

"There was Mother," he reminded her, uncomfortably. "And Dad."

Fran gave a crazy sounding laugh. "Yes, there was your mother and Charles. I had them, and they had me. Delia's had me ever since, and I bet there's been times when she's wished she'd let me die in a ditch." She stared at Nick. "Know something, Nicky?

People like Delia are bad for people like me. They put up with us. They take everything we dish out. . . ."

He lashed at her suddenly: "You could be grateful!"

She was silent, looking at him with eyes in which drunkenness and a sort of cunning seemed to mix. "Grateful?" she repeated the word as though turning it over in her mind. "Grateful to Delia, you mean?"

"Why not grateful to Delia? And to my father, too. You said they were kind to you when you were out of luck, after your divorce, and you had nowhere else to go."

He couldn't take his eyes from her face, in which strange things seemed to be happening. A struggle made her lips, her eyes twitch as though she were in torture, and for a single terrific moment Nick had a distinct impression that he stood in some inexplicable, unprecedented danger, that Fran was going to say something, do something that must shatter him like a glass. Afterwards, thinking it over, he told himself that it had felt like a close shave in an automobile, or like the shock of contact with a live wire.

Nothing happened. Fran finished her cocktail and said heavily: "This place stinks. Let's go."

Relieved, he paid the bill and they went out into the cold, black street.

CHAPTER

XX

Nɪᴄᴋ wanted to take her back to the hotel, but there was no doing anything with her. "It's only a little after midnight!"

He protested. "They'll wonder what's happened to us. Maybe I better telephone the house."

"For God's sake . . . you're not in school."

"And I'm not supposed to go in bars and drink, either. If this ever got back, they'd kick me out."

"Best thing that could happen to you, to be kicked out of that snob factory."

"Listen, Fran."

She dropped his arm. "All right, run along home, kiddo. Give them my love and tell them I wouldn't have gone to their goddam snotty party if they'd asked me."

In the past, he used to be flattered when his aunt treated him as though he were her contemporary, but this reversal of the roles struck him as being neither flattering nor funny.

"Fran," he persisted miserably, "Fran, let's go back home together. To Mother's. Come on, Fran, please."

She was swaying on her feet. "All right," she said after a moment. "One more drink and then we'll go home. Just one, I promise."

He gave in because there seemed nothing else to do. Staggering through the gloom, passing up one frowsy joint after another, Fran finally dragged him with her into a bar filled with the dregs and drunks of the locality and the hour. Nick steered her to a table still littered with dirty glasses, spilled popcorn, and cigarette ends. She collapsed on a chair and a waiter came to take their order. "Rye on the rocks," she told him magisterially. "Two. And clean up this crap, will you?"

The waiter looked at Nick. "How old you, son?"

"Nineteen," Nick replied, with the faintest hesitation. "But you can make mine beer."

The man continued to look at him. "We're not allowed to serve liquor to minors."

Fran glared at him. "You heard him say he was nineteen. What's a person supposed to do—carry his birth certificate wherever he goes?"

The waiter departed and Nick laughed uneasily. "He doesn't believe us, that's plain."

"Goddam fool. You look nineteen anyway." She smiled at him suddenly. "Relax, honey. You're not in school."

"Do you have to keep saying that?"

"Have I said it before? Sorry. Mind must be slipping."

She opened her pocketbook and began tidying her hair and applying lipstick and for some reason the way she set about it embarrassed Nick, possibly because of the sudden interest of two elderly men at the adjoining table. Nick told himself that he ought to find a telephone and call Delia, then decided he'd wait till he'd had his beer and they were about to leave. He knew very well that he had no real desire to call his mother, that he dreaded to hear her voice and what she'd have to say. Unaccustomed to drinking anything more potent than an occasional glass of beer, the amount he'd drunk tonight was beginning to catch up on him, and he warned himself that this must be his last. And if Fran made a fuss and reneged on her promise to leave when they'd finished this round, he'd just walk out on her, and no funny business about it.

Fortified by his resolve, Nick glanced round him, wishing they had not chosen this particular joint for their nightcap. The air was laced with the smell of liquor and cigarettes and he felt his sinuses begin to puff up and his eyes smart, and decided he'd better go to the bathroom and douse his face with cold water. When he got back to Fran he found her in heated argument with their waiter, who had put her drink before her but had not brought one for Nick. "He told you he was nineteen and I tell you he's nineteen! What'd you want us to do—sing it for you in French?"

"Look," the man said patiently, "we serve liquor to kids, we lose our license and maybe go to jail. That's how it is."

"If that's how it is then you can take this drink and stuff it, see?"

The strangers at the next table laughed, and the waiter looked at her grimly. "Take it easy," he said, and walked away. Fran glared after him. "Son of a bitch. I'll finish this and then we'll go some place where they know their business."

"No, we won't," Nick told her angrily, feeling like more and more of a fool. "You promised this was to be the last, remember?"

"I'm going to see that you get your drink if it's the last thing I do," Fran retorted with a horrible air of meaning exactly what she said. "Nobody's got any right to refuse to serve a customer. Trying to teach me!" She took a swallow from her glass, and added ominously: "Think I'll go over there and give that guy a lesson in his duties."

Nick caught her arm. "No, Fran. Sit down. I don't want a drink, I tell you. Finish yours and let's go."

At this point one of the men at the next table hitched his chair closer to theirs and said politely: "I have a beer here I don't want. Glad to have the young man take it."

He must, Nick decided swiftly, have ordered it when he heard the altercation between Fran and the waiter. "Thanks," he told the rather woozy looking Samaritan, and shook his head. "Guess I won't, just the same."

"Go ahead," the man insisted, and put the full glass of beer on the table before Nick. He added with a grin: "It isn't a Mickey Finn! This is a respectable place and we're all good friends. Isn't that so, ma'am?" He appealed with great courtliness to Fran, who shrugged. "Don't know about that." Then impatiently to Nick: "Oh for Christ's sake! Take it, Nick, if he wants you to. Show that waiter where he gets off."

Afraid of starting a scene, Nick thanked the donor and took a drink from the glass. It was icy and tasted good, and he felt better. No point in acting stuffy, he thought. No point in wearing your goddam innocence as if it were a hair shirt just to amuse the public.

Fran smiled at the strangers, and Nick saw that her lipstick had skidded, giving her mouth a lop-sided look. "Thank you," she said. "And now you have one on us."

"Nothing doing," the man returned gallantly. "You down the one you've got there, and we'll have a round on me."

His friend smiled. He had teeth like a bear trap. "That's the ticket. And we might as well join forces while we're about it, may we?"

Fran said graciously that they might, and Nick found himself seated next to the man with the bear trap dentures, who patted him approvingly on the back. "Good drink, beer. Full of minerals, vitamins. A great thirst pacifier in the Orient, did you know that?"

Nick said he did.

"Been in the Orient?" the man asked him, interested.

"Borneo," Nick told him, deadpan. "Only vitamins we ever got in Borneo was from beer. They used to put in my formula to help my teeth grow."

"Good boy. It's different here, you see. The guys who run the place got to watch their step because it's a serious offence to sell alcohol to minors. You mustn't mind, though. I'll square it with Pete."

His friend was cosying up to Fran. "How about it now? Encorse, as we say in Fraunce?"

"Encora, as they say in Italy," the other man corrected him, and looked hard at Nick. "You ever been in Italy?"

"Milan," Nick said. "My father conducted the symphony orchestra in Milan in 1935."

"You look Italian," the man said, softly. "Olive skin, dark hair, dark eyes. Italian by birth, maybe?"

"Not by birth, no."

The other thought it over, let it pass. "Musical," he said at last, as though to himself. "Artistic type, I can see that. These things are usually inherited. Like a nice skin."

"And pianos," Nick said, taking a swallow from his glass.

"Pianos?"

"I inherited my father's piano. Not much good now, though. Termites got it."

The man said slowly: "I didn't know they had termites in Italy."

"Not in Italy, in Borneo. We took the piano all the way to Borneo to have the ivories fixed. Then the termites moved in."

"I see," the man said, and his eyes suddenly got a squeezed-up look too small for the rest of his face. "Well, I was wondering about you ever since I saw you come in here. Just that nice skin made me wonder."

He hitched his chair closer to Nick's while his friend planted a thick hand on the back of Fran's chair and began to talk to her in an undertone. Nick heard her laugh and thought: They reached the dirty story stage pretty quick. And what the hell does she think I'm going to do with this bird? Doesn't she see . . . can't she guess . . .

Another beer appeared on the table and his companion moved it unobtrusively over towards Nick. "My name's Smith," he said conversationally. "Piermont Smith. Got a nice place uptown, in the East Eighties. And you?"

"Brown," Nick said. He picked up the fresh glass of beer and looked at it critically. "John Brown of Harpers Ferry, Va."

The man smiled. "Bright kid. Ever see a movie called Rififi?

French. Hot stuff. Guy in it looks like you. Tall, dark, carries a razor and takes dope. Eyes just like yours."

"Funny thing about eyes," Nick said. "Either you have them or you haven't. Ever noticed?"

The other was silent for a minute, smiling straight into Nick's face. Nick thought: Why does one always want to hit them? There were other means of escape, of course. You could always get up and get out. But then there was Fran, damn her. She was laughing in a thick helpless sort of way, and the other man was bending over her, his back towards Nick and his friend. The latter said to Nick in a soft voice: "Don't be too smart, kid. It isn't becoming. Don't jump to conclusions either. It isn't smart."

A juke box was playing a familiar tune, and Nick, nervous now, began to hum it under his breath:

> Oh the shark has pretty teeth, dear,
> And he shows them pearly white,
> Just a jackknife has MacHeath, dear,
> And he keeps it out of sight . . .

Suddenly he heard Fran's voice crash like crockery in the dense atmosphere of the room. She was on her feet, her hair coming down, her eyes blazing. "You goddam homo! He's my nephew, and you try that and I'll call the cops!"

Nick shoved back his chair and rose as the man next to him made a grab at his arm. "Sit down, kid, and finish your beer. Never mind her. My friend'll take care of it."

Nick pulled himself free in time to see Fran take a swing at the other man with her pocketbook. "Flit!" she screamed. "Pederast!"

Nick reached her, seized her arm, and began trying to squeeze out of the crowded hole, dragging her with him. But the man whom she'd swatted came lunging after them and caught Nick by the collar, swinging him around. Nick stared into a face in which the veins stood out like mole-runs in turf. "Beating it without paying for your drinks? The hell you are!"

Nick spoke over his shoulder to Fran. "Go on out and wait for me. I'll settle the bill and be right with you."

He tried to sound twice his age and in command of the situation even while he felt the man's paw half strangling him. Fran's response was to aim another blow at Nick's captor while she shrieked "pederast" at the top of her lungs. The waiter and bartender now closed in and told the man to let the kid go so he could pay his bill and get out. "And stay out," the bartender added, looking at Fran. "Get out and stay out, the pair of you."

He turned to Nick. "O.K. that'll be eighty-five cents for her rye on the rocks, and thirty-five for your beer. Make it snappy."

The man gripping Nick's collar shook him furiously. "One beer! The little ——— had two!"

Nick found a dollar bill in his pocket and handed it to the waiter. "That's eighty-five cents for the lady's drink, and a fifteen cent tip for you. As for the beer, you're not supposed to sell liquor to minors, remember?"

A bar-fly draped over a stool laughed hoarsely. "You win, kid!" Then to the others: "Cut it out! This is Thanksgiving eve. Can't anybody enjoy his drink in peace and quiet Thanksgiving eve for God's sake?"

Nick, feeling his persecutor's grip relax, twisted round and planted his fist full on the man's nose. Then he and Fran were out the door, and the bartender addressed them distantly from the threshold: "Get out of here, and don't ever come back!"

"When we do, it will be with a cop," Fran told him, in a shout. "I shall have you thrown out of business for accosting minors and refusing to serve a customer, see if I don't."

Nick dragged her away, and when a stray taxi came by he hailed it and managed to bundle her into it, getting in beside her. All the way to her hotel Fran ranted on the subject of perverts, drug addicts, thugs, but Nick sat silent, savoring mixed emotions of elation and fright—elation that he should have slugged a man bigger than himself, fright for the possible consequences of this jaunt. Things have a way of getting around. It might even get into the papers. Some goon might have had a candid camera and taken a shot of him drinking beer with Fran and those other characters. Suppose it got back to the people at school, or to Delia. He laughed somewhat nervously and Fran said: "Scum! I wish I'd brained him."

"I still don't know what started it."

"He asked me what I thought I was doing with a kid young enough to be my son. Suggested that he and I go to a hotel together, and that his friend would know how to look after you. Said something else, too." She broke off and he felt her trembling.

"Never mind," Nick said. "The hell with it."

He felt a sudden overpowering longing for home, for the warmth, the quiet, the clear lights and the clean smell of home. Feelings he remembered having when he was a child, and when he first went to boarding school and longed for his own bed, his own room, his mother. He was too tired now to be ashamed of this feeling, too dizzy from the beer he'd drunk and the fumes of tobacco he'd been inhaling all evening. True, he'd played the man and there'd been a certain amount of fun mixed up in it—he'd enjoyed annoying that old homo back there in the bar—but now it was over and all that was left was a sick sensation in his middle and an aching head.

Beside him Fran began to weep—the easy, guttural weeping of a drunk, and he put his arm round her and told her cheer up, it wasn't so bad. She shook her head, sobbing. "I'm no good, that's the trouble. Everything's a mess. I'm a mess. Whass use pretending? Delia knows . . . I mucked up her life . . . mucked up Herbert's. Everybody's. You know what one person'c'n do? Muck up the whole world. Look'd Hitler. Mussolini. Stal'n. In a fam'ly it takes just one person like me."

"Why do you, then?" Nick asked wearily. She weighed on his arm like a sack of lead pipe.

"Why'd I? Because I'm evil. Evil all the way through. From the beginning. Delia knows, always knew. That's why she's worked at being everything I'm not. Beautiful. Kind. Brave. And damn her for it, damn her damn her damn her!"

Nick pulled his arm away from Fran's shoulder. "Quit it, Fran. You're potted, and you'll feel differently tomorrow."

"You and Veronica had to be brought up as unlike me as she knew how. She made me promise. Made me swear. Told me if I ever opened my trap she'd take you both and go away where I'd never find you."

She turned to him with sudden frightening urgency. "You know something, Nick? Delia's made of steel inside. She's had to be. Not at first, no. I know enough about how steel is made, how it gets to be what it is. Takes doing. It took doing, for her, when she was young and scared and hurt, and I was the strong magnetic brazen one . . . took doing . . ." She gave a sob. "But if she ever made up her mind to leave me . . . I mean really to leave me, she'd do it."

"You're getting her mixed up with Herbert," Nick said crossly. "How can Mother leave you? You're the one that does the leaving, sticking around a month or two, then beating it back to California." He tried to sound rallying, sensible, but he was bored and beginning to have an uneasy feeling that he might be going to get sick.

"It's part of the deal. I can come and visit her and you and Nonny. On condition. Because she doesn't trust me, see? She doesn't trust me . . . doesn't. . . ."

They were at the Leonard. Nick paid the driver and helped Fran up the greasy steps into the lobby, thankful to find it empty and Dipper still absent from his post. The place looked more like a morgue than ever, the elevator crawled, but at last they were at Fran's door and he said gently: "I'll leave you, now. You'll be O.K."

She clung to him. "Aren't you going to kiss me goodnight?"

He kissed her in a rather gingerly way on the cheek, and she held him closer. "Don't go away, Nick. Not at once. Stay while I have one drink, then you can go."

She pulled him into the room and shut the door. He turned on the light and the whole appearance of the place filled him with nausea, but he said nothing as Fran took off her coat and sank on the bed, looking an utter wreck. He thought, wonderingly: How in the heck did she ever get to be Mother's twin?

"Pour me a drink, Nicky. No water. Just whisky."

He went to the table where they'd left the Scotch and the glasses and poured her a drink and brought it back to her, sitting beside her on the bed while she drank it. Then he took off her shoes and pulled the coverlet over her, and she took his hand and held it, staring at him with terrible eyes. "Nick, I hope you won't ever know what it is to be alone."

"Go to sleep, Fran, won't you?"

"To be alone and to know nobody gives a damn, and to know it's all your own fault, that it needn't ever have happened . . . not ever."

He waited, longing to leave her, fed up with her, with this place, with everything that had happened tonight except that blow he'd given the man back there at the bar.

She said slowly, still staring at him: "If you tell Delia about this . . . my getting so drunk tonight . . . she'll leave me."

"Don't be a dope. How can she, with Nonny and me on her neck?"

"She can. You don't know Delia. If she gets desperate enough she'll leave me. She'll take you and Veronica and go far away some place I won't even know where."

He tried to inject a note of sanity. "She could take me, sure, but Veronica's not even a minor any more, so she couldn't take her. And I don't see Mother running out on her own daughter. Or on you either—her own sister!"

An expression which he'd surprised on her face earlier in the evening rose up on it, like a frost design on glass. "You know what Delia said to me last year . . . when I was here for our birthday and had that fight with the Bowers . . . that silly goddam fight . . . just because I was jealous of her fondness for them . . .

theirs for her . . . all that prissy nice responsible friends of the family crap! Know what Delia said to me? She said 'Fran, you drive someone into a corner and they have no way of getting out of it, they're going to push you out of the way, understand?' That's what Delia said to me, last year."

"Well?" He stood by the bed, his hand still clutched in hers, his face shadowed. "Why drive people into corners, then? You don't have to."

She brooded, her eyes flickering. "The truth," she muttered at last, incomprehensibly. "The truth . . . it would have been much better, much better, from the beginning."

He tried to release his hand. "Go on to sleep, Fran. You're coming to Thanksgiving dinner with us tomorrow, and you better catch up on yourself if you want to enjoy it."

"I'm not coming to any Thanksgiving dinner with anybody. Thanksgiving for what? My mucked-up lousy life? Ha ha!"

"Well, anyway, it's time I got home. We'll see you tomorrow. Mother'll probably call you round noon."

Fran's whole face seemed to have slipped to one side. He could hardly bear to look at her, but she suddenly dragged on his arm, so their faces were close together. "Kiss me goodnight, Nick."

He kissed her, and she flung her arms round him, kissing him wildly, feverishly, so he had to struggle to free himself. Then she wilted, and for a horrible moment he thought she must really have had a stroke and died. Shaking, he went to the window and opened it, letting the air play on his face. When he turned round he saw that Fran's eyes were closed and that she was breathing the heavy, stertorous breath of one under anesthesia. Quietly, Nick removed a package of cigarettes and the matches from the table next to the bed, then went through her pocketbook and took another package of cigarettes and more matches and put them in his pocket. After that he left her, closing the door noiselessly, and made his way thankfully out of the place into the dim, empty streets to the nearest subway.

CHAPTER

XXI

It was three in the morning, the air heavy with pre-dawn darkness as Nick left the subway exit and walked up Fifth Avenue towards home. Windows still lighted had the unreality of a stage set, and he wondered fleetingly what kind of people could be up at this hour . . . sick people, probably; people making love, or poor dopes working for a living into the small hours, or perhaps just waiting for other people to come home.

He shivered in his overcoat and thought uneasily of his mother. If only she was asleep it wouldn't be so bad. He'd feel better able to come through with explanations tomorrow morning. The beer he'd drunk had left him bilious and his head throbbed. It served him right, he supposed. He should have known better than to go and see Fran tonight. Tonight! It was already morning and somewhere on the eastern horizon the sky knew it, but hours must elapse before the city found it out and the stifling mortuary gloom gave way, inch by pallid inch, to the tremulous day.

There was a light in the hall when he let himself into the house, and another in the parlor. He'd more than half expected to find Delia waiting up for him, but the room was empty, picked-up and neat so you'd hardly have known there'd been a party. Nick stood in the middle of the room, listening; tired, yet all of a sudden very wide awake and restless. Delia's clock ticked on her desk, and from the kitchen came the sound of the refrigerator motor going on, and he told himself he might feel better if he were to eat something.

The kitchen had the same picked-up appearance as the parlor, the dishes washed and put away, the camellia which Chris had given Veronica wilting in a tumbler near the sink. Nick poured himself a glass of milk and made himself a sandwich, then he sat down on Katie's kitchen stool and lighted a cigarette, feeling better minute by minute. God, what an evening! He could smile at it now, at this remove and from the safe vantage of home. After all nothing very serious had happened—that is, nothing you could name as being really wrong. It was against the rules, of course, for him to be seen in a bar drinking and smoking, but he knew guys in school who did the same thing during vacation, and who got away with it. The important thing was not to be found out, and who was going to talk about it? Certainly not he. Of course there was Fran, damn it. Sober, she could be trusted, but drunk . . .

He felt a slight return of disquiet. There had been a moment in the restaurant before they went into that last joint when he'd had a very peculiar idea—more than an idea, a definite sense of there being something extremely unpleasant hanging over him, as though Fran were on the verge of saying something, or doing something momentous and catastrophic, though for the life of him he couldn't imagine what it would have been. The moment had passed and he'd dismissed it from his mind, yet it left an impression, and now as he sat in this clean, friendly room, secure between its four walls, he asked himself just what it could have been that he'd felt was about to happen. One of those things called a premonition. But what could poor old Fran have done to hurt him? Drunk she talked a lot of horse, saying things she shouldn't say, acting as if she were the repository of state secrets, and that you'd have to burn the soles of her feet with an acetylene torch to get them out of her. Drunk people often talked like that. He'd heard a few in his time. It wasn't as if he'd feared Fran might try to hit him, even scream at him. Nothing like that. Nothing even like that business at the end of the evening when he'd put her to bed and she'd kissed him in a way he didn't like. He reddened a little, remembering it.

Nick frowned at his cigarette. The hell with Fran for one night. He'd had enough of even thinking about her. He finished the cigarette, put out the lights and went quietly upstairs towards his bedroom, and saw that Delia's door was open, a column of light leaning across the hall from door to wall.

"Nick?" she called him in a low voice. "Come in here a minute, will you, dear?"

He went into the room and saw her lying in bed with a light beside her, and a book, and because the windows were still closed he knew that she couldn't have been asleep, but had been waiting for him to come home.

He sat down on the bed, and she looked at him quietly for a minute or two. "Hungry?" she asked at last. "There's some food in the refrigerator."

"I had some," Nick said. He picked up the book and read the title: *Persuasion*.

"Good story?" he asked, trying to delay the questions he knew were bound to come.

She continued to look at him. "What happened tonight, Nick? Tell me."

He stared at the crimson rug on the floor beside the bed. It was one the Bowers had given her for a wedding present and he had always liked it. Delia put her hand on his knee and said: "It was bad, wasn't it? I called the Leonard several times, and they said Fran's room didn't answer, so I knew you'd gone out. Then I tried one or two of her favorite haunts, and she wasn't there."

"I should have called you," Nick said, shrugging. "I meant to, but things got more and more complicated, and I didn't get round to it."

He met her eyes. "How was the party? Did they stay late?"

"Nick, I wish you'd tell me about this evening."

"She got plastered."

"Why didn't you leave her and come home?"

"Would you have?"

Delia drew a long, uncertain breath. "No, but that's different. Go on, tell me more."

"We went out to eat dinner, but you know how she gets when she's on a binge. Orders food and leaves it. Keeps ordering more to drink. After dinner we went to a bar and she got into a fight with a man." He laughed suddenly. "Fran handed him one on the ear with her handbag. A beaut. I bet he'll need a hearing-aid after that."

Delia didn't smile, and he said irritably: "You're not going to get stuffy about this, are you, Mother? After all here I am back, safe and sound. What's more I got Fran back to her hotel safe and sound, too. You owe me a medal—not these dirty looks!"

"What was the fight about at the bar?"

"There were a couple of old flits, and Fran was trying to protect me, I guess. It ended by me protecting her."

Delia gasped. "Nick, you're fifteen! If this gets back to Holyrood it wouldn't be so funny, would it?"

"Why should it get back to Holyrood?" He bent towards her suddenly, taking the end of her braid of hair and twisting it in his hands. "Look, quit fussing. There was no one round that even knew us. God, you should have seen them! And so all's well that ends well, for this round anyway."

She was silent for a moment, her eyes never leaving his face. Then she said: "What did Fran talk about?"

"Same old hat we've heard before. About her and Herbert and their divorce. That stuff." He made a face. "I better tell you, though, that she knows about our party here tonight. I guess it was my fault. I let the cat out without meaning to, and she can be pretty quick to catch on even when she's potted, so you'd better be prepared when you see her tomorrow." He added thoughtfully: "If you do see her tomorrow. I've an idea she'll spend it in bed with an ice pack on her head."

"What did you drink tonight?"

"Beer. And I smoked five cigarettes."

Delia took a piece of kleenex from a box on the bedside table and handed it to him. "Better wipe your face," she said coldly. "It's all over something."

Nick rubbed the tissue over his mouth and chin. It came off red from Fran's lipstick, where she'd kissed him. He felt himself flushing as he crumpled the tissue in his hand and tossed it into the waste basket. Then he said in a matter-of-fact voice: "You might as well know that she put on a gooey act when I tried to leave. Didn't want to be left alone, and all that. So I stayed until she'd had one more drink and had passed out, then I scrammed."

He played out the facts like a good fisherman, keeping a tight line. "I confiscated her cigarettes, though, and the matches, just in case."

For a moment neither spoke, then Delia said in a careful voice:

"Nick, I'm not trying to make you tell me anything you'd rather not. But when Fran puts on one of her melodramatic acts she never knows where—or when—to stop. You're old enough to understand some of this, now. And old enough, I hope, not to take any of it seriously."

He nodded. "I get it. Poor Fran! Nothing quite comes off with her, does it? I mean, the act. To have to sit back and see you and Veronica . . . you know, making a go of things, and to know she's a flop, herself." He was frowningly silent, then: "Isn't there something we can do, Mother? Can't she be made to snap out of it, somehow?"

Delia's lips trembled. "How far can anyone help another person? Oh darling, I hate to have you in on this! I've hoped for a miracle for Fran almost as long as I can remember. I go on hoping. Perhaps . . . some day . . ."

He shook his head. "Nuts. She doesn't want a miracle. She just needs to get rid of whatever's biting her. And something is, all right. Though God knows what."

"Is that what she said to you tonight?"

"Didn't say it . . . not like that anyway. Not like I've ever heard her before. Making less and less sense."

He yawned suddenly and rose, stretching his long arms over his head, his eyes spilling tears of sleep. "Four o'clock! Gads . . . I'm bushed."

"Nick," said Delia, gazing up at him.

He dropped his arms and looked down at her, seeming much older than his fifteen years. "Now what?"

"You're not worried, are you? About Fran . . . about anything?"

He grinned. "I was this evening, in spots. Not now though."

He stooped to kiss her, and Delia held him, her hands on his shoulders. "Honest, Nick?"

He kissed her quickly, abruptly, then stood up. "Quit fussing," he said with a laugh, and going to the window, he opened it, then left the room and Delia heard him yawning his way in small, puppy-like yelps along the hall to his own room.

Delia put out the light beside her bed and lay staring at the darkness. Tears which had been near the surface all evening drained slowly back to their reservoir, but she was taken with a violent shivering which made her body twitch uncontrollably as though she were in the grip of some malignant fever. And so I am, she told herself, trying to check it by an effort of will. So I am, a fever of rage, a fever of such intensity as I haven't felt for years, that I've suppressed, ignored, fought down, but never conquered. Quietly, relentlessly it has been conquering me, an invisible process of attrition, wearing down my nerves, my fibre, my soul.

"Fran," she uttered the name aloud in the fragrant gloom of the bedroom into which the pale shapes of the curtains from the open window streamed like ghosts. "Fran!"

Damn Fran. Damn her beastliness, her weakness, her special genius for ruination. And damn Veronica too. Damn them both, oh, damn them, damn them both!

Delia rolled over on her face among the pillows and lay shivering and struggling to control the violence which possessed her like an impulse towards murder. Images, visions, snatches of sound,

of dance music from the phonograph this evening, of Wallingford's voice when he'd taken her in his arms and they had turned
gently, intimately, to the rhythm of the dance which Chris had
selected from the collection of records under the bookcase.
Wallingford's arm supporting her, his hand clasping hers, his head
bent towards her: "That's a nice boy of yours."

"Nick, yes."

"I'm sorry he had to leave."

"It was an SOS . . . friend in trouble."

Friend in trouble! Lies. Why not have come out with it and
told him she had an alcoholic sister who was *always* in trouble?

This was to be Veronica's party and I wanted it perfect for
her sake, because you and Chris were to be here, and Fran would
have got drunk and shamed us all and ruined everything, as she
always does.

Delia's hands clenched on the pillow. And Veronica! Veronica's
rigid face next to the crimson petals of the camellia as she had
danced past in Chris's arms. Veronica's eyes like gun barrels boring
into my eyes, boring into my breast, my heart! Veronica and Fran,
Fran and Veronica, and the lies . . . How many lies have I told
for Fran's sake? For Veronica's sake? For Nick's, for my own? A
lifetime of lying to save something, to save some one. And how
should I have expected to win out? How much does one have to
surrender, to give up, make a present of in order to insure a victory
which, even if won, must run through my fingers like mercury, and
be lost? Give up . . . give up . . . give up! Go on giving up because
once you've started it you have no choice. Love. Faith. Honor.
Illusion. Confidence. Trust. Give them all up and grit your teeth
and carry on, not because you believe for a minute in the morality
of what you have elected to do but because you have no choice.
Every mistake we make is the direct consequence of the first mistake we made, every lie the child of the original lie. At fifty years,
a lifetime of lies stretching behind you. The only life that seemed
worth living—the life of youth, vigor, expectation, hope lies behind you. Mr. Ramond can't bring it back even if you were to go

to him every day and pay him a fortune. You will not keep your beauty, nor preserve for more than a few years the spurious look of youth and health that makes people turn to look at you in the street, and which brings that quick, meaningful look into a man's eyes as, tonight, it leaped for a little while in the eyes of Donald Wallingford.

Always on the brink of happiness, the chasm at your feet and the carefully timed blow at your back. Veronica . . . Fran . . . Fran . . . Veronica!

"You're lucky in your children," Wallingford had said, his lips against her ear.

"Yes, and so are you."

"In Chris? Very." He'd held her close, the rhythm going through them both like a single current. "Veronica's book is taboo between us for the present, but Veronica is not, nor is Chris. I'd like sometime soon to talk to you about those two, if I may?"

"I understand. Yes, of course."

"May I telephone you for lunch one day next week?"

"I'd like it very much."

She'd met his eyes, close to her own. "Not tired, are you?" he asked, making it sound as if it really mattered whether she were.

"Heavens, no! I haven't danced like this for ages."

Not since she danced with Kingsley Bates, and that was all of ten years ago. Ages!

"There's a good floor at the Drake, if you should feel in the mood any time."

The old thrill, the old flattery, making her feel alive.

Then it was time for him to leave, and as she and Veronica accompanied them to the hall, Wallingford held her hand and said coolly before the others: "I shall call you next week, then. Wednesday perhaps, or Thursday?"

Delia had felt Veronica's glance like a sword point. "Thank you very much, Mr. Wallingford. Next Thursday would be fine."

Later, the dishes washed and put away, the parlor tidied, Katie and Veronica gone to bed, there had been no sign of Nick. At the Leonard, Dipper growled into the receiver: "Mrs. Hight don't answer."

"Is this Pete's Bar? Would you mind paging Mrs. Frances Hight, please?

"Louis? Can you tell me whether Mrs. Frances Hight is there? Mrs. Hight. Thank you."

And so on down the list.

Afterwards she'd gone to Veronica's room and knocked on the door, and an expressionless voice answered: "Come in."

Delia stood in the door, gazing at her daughter. In bed, Veronica was lovely in her high-necked nightgown.

"Nonny, I'm worried about Nick."

The girl shrugged. "What am I supposed to do?"

"Nothing, of course. I just . . . he didn't say exactly where he expected to go with Fran, did he?"

"I told you all I know. He went to the Leonard."

"They say Fran's room doesn't answer."

Pause. "I wish I'd known he was going. I'd have stopped him."

"That was why he went without telling you." She looked at her mother. "Nick's growing up."

Delia caught her breath. "Yes, but he has a little way to go."

"What do you expect to do—keep him in diapers until he's fifty?"

The distance between them was oceanic, fathomless. And a few hours ago it had seemed to Delia that they had come close to bridging it.

"Well," she said at last. "It was a nice party even if we lost Nick. Did you have a good time, Nonny?"

"Yes, thanks."

"I'm so glad for you," Delia went on, wondering why she bothered, hypnotized by habit, like a parrot. Like Pavlov's dog. "I am, really, Veronica. And about the book. Everything." Her throat ached with tears. "Too happy for words!"

"Are you?" Veronica did not look at her. "One would hardly have gathered that tonight."

"What do you mean?"

"I mean you were at no apparent loss for words, that's all I mean."

Delia had left her then and gone back to her own room and undressed, and now she lay face down among her pillows, rage like a new lease on life beating her spirit to incandescence.

CHAPTER

XXII

"I'M SORRY," Fran said. "I have already told you so in my letter, and I repeat it now. I'm sorry."

The sisters sat facing each other across the murky expanse of Fran's bedroom, gloomy even at this hour though the sun shone brilliantly outdoors, flinging an oblong of light on the wall of an adjoining building, and Delia could hear sparrows twittering in the dirty area below.

More than a week had passed since she'd seen Fran. Thanksgiving had come and gone without a word exchanged between them, then Fran had written briefly to apologize for not showing up on Thanksgiving Day and for having kept Nick out to all hours the night before. Delia felt that she had to give herself time to get her own emotions under control, and finally, on a morning towards the end of the week, she decided to take a chance on finding Fran at home, and taxied down to the Leonard Hotel. That she didn't call up first to make sure of finding Fran was, as she knew, due to a fundamental aversion to hearing her sister's voice and perhaps also to an unconfessed hope that she might find her gone and the ordeal of a meeting indefinitely postponed. But this was not to be. Fran was at the Leonard, and after a perfunctory greeting Delia had come straight to the point: "I want you to tell me exactly what happened Thanksgiving eve when you took Nick out on the town."

"Isn't it enough for me to say I'm sorry? What more do you expect?"

Delia thought: How often have I heard her say she's sorry, and in exactly that tone of voice? How many notes of apology have I had to read? And what do I expect, at this stage of the game . . . just what exactly do I expect?

She looked away from the ravaged face before her and said quietly: "Nick is fifteen years old. Granted he seems mature for his age, but the fact remains, if the authorities at Holyrood were to hear of that performance the other night, he'd be expelled. It would be difficult, perhaps impossible, to get him into another decent school. Did you think of that?"

"Frankly, I didn't. But there's no reason why the school should know anything about it. Nick's certainly not going to tell them."

"No," Delia agreed, drily. "He's not. Nor am I." She stared at her sister. "But how many people have you told already?"

Fran shrugged. Her skin had a desiccated appearance and hung in folds under her eyes. "You always were one to make mountains out of molehills, Delia. It isn't even as if we moved in the same circles. Even if I were silly enough to mention it there's not much danger of its getting around so it could do any harm to Nick."

"No? Well, Monday night I had dinner with the Bowers. They told me they'd called you and invited you to join us, but that you excused yourself, explaining that you were recovering from what you described as a binge with your little nephew. You went on at some length about Nick's charm, his precocity, and how flattered you were that at your age you could still inspire chivalry in a masculine breast. That line!" Delia had flushed as she spoke, the internal mentor warning her to watch her step. *None of that. . . .*

Fran laughed. "And the Bowers were shocked, were they? I'm not surprised. Stuffed shirts, both of them."

"Stuffed shirts have their uses, as who should know better than you? They at least operate from a position of strength . . ." She broke off, struggling to control herself. Then, more calmly: "Fred told me that you were evidently feeling no pain when you talked to him over the phone. I don't know whether you remembered at the time that he is a trustee of Nick's school. He happens also to be a good and loyal friend of mine as he has in the past been yours. But even at that he was not disposed to take a casual view of a fifteen-year-old boy going in and out of bars in the small hours of the morning and getting into a drunken fracas which might have involved more than a brush with the police."

"All right," Fran said, violently. "So I behaved badly, outrageously. I admit it. What more do you want me to say?"

"I want you to tell me what you and Nick talked about that evening."

"How the devil would I know what we talked about? I don't keep a tape recording of every conversation I have with people."

Her mouth, shakily smeared with lipstick, looked like a red wound in her face. Delia stared at it in a kind of fascination. She said slowly: "He came home smelling of beer and cigarettes, his face all over lipstick. If he'd been out with anyone else—yes, anyone!—I might have thought it funny, or at any rate nothing to be too concerned about. I realize I can't protect him forever, and that with every year that passes my right and my ability to do so is so much less."

Fran stared at her. "I wish I knew what the hell you're driving at, but I don't and I'm beginning not to give a damn."

"When have you ever given a damn? As long as you can have your cake and eat it . . . go the limit, then wallow in self-pity and contrition!" *None of that!* But her heart was pounding and Nick's face swam before her eyes, his face with an expression on it she had not seen before. "Nick is growing up," Veronica had reminded her gratuitously . . . and Veronica had sounded like Fran too. It was not only the stuffed shirts who operated from positions of strength, and Fran knew it, and Veronica was learning.

Delia went on coldly: "You're sober now, so that even if you don't like what I'm saying, you'll at least understand it. I insist that you tell me what passed between you and Nick the night you took him out."

"We talked about Herbert and me. And about Veronica's book. What would we have talked about? And why didn't you ask Nick?"

"I did ask him."

Delia found a package of cigarettes and lighted one. "I did ask him. He told me just about what you've told me."

"Well? Didn't that reassure you?"

"No."

"For God's sake! Why not?"

"I know Nick. I know when he's being frank and when he isn't. It's very rarely that he isn't. And he wasn't, that night."

"Well, as you said yourself, he's mature for his age. Probably feels it's about time he was accorded some degree of privacy."

Delia looked at her steadily. "When you both came back here, to this room, you were drunk. Nick had been sopping up beer all evening—he told me he had. He told me that you made a fuss about his leaving, that you begged him to stay with you because you dreaded to be alone. So he stayed until you'd had one more drink and had passed out, then he left."

"Well?"

"What I want to know is what happened before you passed out."

Fran picked up an ashtray and emptied it in a waste basket.

"I passed out, period."

"And you made no . . . revelations before that?"

"If you mean, did I spill any beans, no, I didn't."

"And you didn't try to seduce him?"

Fran's face turned the color of raw liver. "Are you crazy?"

"Did you try to seduce Nick?"

"Why don't you ask Nick?"

"*Did you?*"

"Did I? I . . . no, I didn't. I didn't!"

"Will you deny that the thought was in your mind, that that was your intention when you brought him back here and kissed him?"

Fran was trembling. "Does it occur to you that you have no God damn right to ask me such questions?"

"I have every right," Delia replied in a hard voice. "Every right in the world, and no one knows it better than you do." She continued with an effort at steadiness: "Nick is the only person in this whole situation who has so far escaped being tainted by it. That I haven't had the same luck with Veronica is not entirely my fault. You know that too. But I have always been able to count on Nick. On his love, his loyalty. Whether you tried to seduce him or whether you didn't is something I shall probably never know. He'll never tell me, and I shall never ask him. I can only suspect and fear . . . and that has been the pattern of my life ever since I can remember, and I have you to thank for it."

Fran winced, and Delia went on remorselessly: "It seems as if you had a genius for timing your arrival—the moment of someone's imminent happiness, the moment of another's relaxation from strain—that is the moment you choose to come back into our lives."

She thought of Donald Wallingford and of the breath of happiness which had blown briefly upon the long drought of her existence, but of that she did not speak. "This time you had to come back to us just when Veronica is on the eve of a new, and perhaps the happiest and most hopeful phase of her life, when Nick is adolescent, at his most impressionable age, and sexually vulnerable, and I lulled into my usual asinine condition of wishful thinking on their account, on yours—on mine!"

Smoke from their cigarettes mounted the stagnant air, and the sound of sparrows outside seemed as incongruous as a Christmas carol.

Delia said: "Whenever you've been gone any length of time

and all I have to judge from is an occasional letter full of the usual lies and half-truths about a new job, new friends, new aspirations —and of course new debts, I can still enjoy the luxury of letting myself hope that perhaps it is not a lie this time. Distance makes all the difference between knowing the worst and hoping for the best. And when you write that you're coming back . . . you can't stand the loneliness, you need the contact with love . . . with me, with the children . . . I am overcome by feelings of guilt and pity, victimized by the habit of hope, the desperate belief in miracles. What I keep forgetting—there are things one must forget to remain sane—is that I can't change the past, and neither can you. We're stuck with it, both of us. And we're stuck with each other."

"Delia!" Fran breathed. Then, thickly: "I'll go away. If that will make things easier for you, and you say it will—I'll go back to San Francisco and stay there."

Delia went on as if she hadn't heard. "Lately I've had the feeling that my whole life has been passed in the dread of some kind of ambush, and of course that's exactly the way it has been passed. Psychologists tell us that one of the most severe shocks in life is a person's realization of *age* . . . well, I've experienced that shock and it seems to have opened my eyes, forced me to remember, to think back. Think about you and me when we were kids and I was afraid to do or say something which would make you angry so you'd turn your superior wit and sarcasm on me—as Veronica does now. I worked to make myself imperfect because that would be true perfection in your eyes . . . as it would be, today, in Veronica's. And because everyone admired you and considered you gifted, I did so too. Miss Jekyll and Miss Hyde, Papa used to call us—remember? War and Peace. Truth and Con-sequences. Sense and Sensibility. You were always accorded the positive and therefore the most flattering role, while it was taken for granted that I should be happy with what was left."

Fran was silent, her eyes filled with incredulity.

"One can't go too far back in the past," said Delia, slowly.

"One doesn't need to. Our parents were intelligent and sensitive and they loved us dearly and did their best to make us happy. They prided themselves on having modern ideas, one of which was the careful avoidance, especially in the case of twins, of sibling rivalry. I've read all about it since, in one of those books in Veronica's collection." She smiled. "I'm sure Papa and Mama prided themselves on their success with you and me. We were different to begin with, and all they had to do was play up the difference. So although I was the prettier of the two, you were the strongest, with a flair for life that was very swiftly squelched in me."

"Delia!"

"I'm not saying that our parents were mistaken in the things they did or in the decisions they made for our sakes. Their intentions were of the best. I'm not even prepared to say that I was mistaken when, for the first time in my life I tried to prove that I was as strong as you, and equal to a great emergency, and with as fine a flair for life, when I made what after all amounts to one of the most serious decisions a person can make, and you let me, because for the first time in *your* life you made it clear that you weren't equal to making any decision at all."

"Must you?" Fran muttered, shivering. "It's all done and buried long ago. We have a pact—a sacred pact you've always called it, never to speak about it even to each other, under any provocation whatsoever."

"Are you reminding me of that pact? Isn't it rather for me to remind you?"

"When it concerns me, if possible, even more than it does you? What kind of a damned fool do you think I am, Delia? What kind of an irresponsible, heartless fool!"

Delia stared at her with a peculiar speculation. "Fools are easily dealt with. It's clever people like you and Veronica who make the trouble. Veronica long ago decided that I didn't love her, or her father, and she's tried to make me pay for it ever since, just as you've tried to make me pay for my innocence."

"*I've* tried to make you pay? *I?*"

"Haven't you?"

Delia rose as she spoke, and picked up her coat. "But I didn't come here to talk about myself, or for that matter about Veronica. Where she is concerned, I realize I am helpless. Where Nick is concerned I am not." Her eyes ignited like sunlit ice. "Where Nick is concerned it's hands off. Do you understand me, Fran? It's hands off."

Fran seemed to pull herself together. She gave a sudden, unpleasant laugh. "I must say, you sound just like a jealous woman! And I'm through apologizing for that silly escapade the other night. Except to say that I think it did Nick more good to go on a binge with me than anything he gets out of that prissy prep school you send him to."

Delia, on her way to the door, turned and came back. "If Nick had gone on a binge with another woman—and I mean any other woman, young as he is, a child!—I'd have accepted it as part of the hazards of growing up. But not with you, Fran. Not with you."

They faced each other in that drab room, hostility naked between them. Fran laughed again. "God, what a prig you can be sometimes! No wonder the men don't come around any more. No wonder poor old Charles . . ."

Delia slapped her hard across the cheek. "Stay away from me from now on, Fran. Understand? I'm not taking any more. I'm not taking another damned thing from you."

Sparrows twittered in the silence, then Fran said in a low voice: "Don't worry, you won't have to."

Delia let herself out of the room and walked blindly down the noisome passage to the elevator, across the hideous lobby where the woman in the pink beret was smoking a cigarette and telling Dipper what a son of a bitch her husband was, out through the door into a nacreous light through which a few snowflakes were improbably, exquisitely descending. A taxi was standing at the curb and Delia got into it and gave the driver an address uptown.

CHAPTER

XXIII

ON HER way to meet Donald Wallingford, who had asked her to lunch with him, Delia's rage ebbed, and an old terror seeped in its place. Fran's face floated before her eyes like a death mask, her own words: "I'm not taking another damned thing from you!" and Fran's "Don't worry, you won't have to," seemed caught in her ears like the agonized buzzing of flies in a spider web.

Four years ago, after a similar scene, Fran had taken an overdose of sleeping pills and a mere accident of timing had saved her —the doctor made the distance from his office to her door in twenty minutes instead of forty-five. Would she try it again?

Let her, whispered the spider in Delia's ear. *Let her* . . . what else is there left for her in life, except this final gesture to end all gestures, reality the finis to an interminable saga of make-believe? And for me freedom at last . . . freedom to remember that twisted, smiling face, and the leaping imprint of my hand?

She won't do it. If there is one thing stronger in Fran than her instinct for destruction, it is the instinct for survival. She'll live to see us all buried. That was what the doctor had said when, his fingers on her pulse, he'd turned his head to look at Delia: "She'll live. Her body knows how even if her mind doesn't."

Delia closed her eyes, thinking: It has never been as bad as this. I've never slapped her. Her eyes have never looked at me as they did just now, with a kind of awakening in them, as though hell had opened for her and this time there was no out.

"Fran," Delia whispered between stiff lips. "Fran!"

She felt the current between herself and her sister running assertive, relentless in insidious communication: "Come back, Delia. If you ever expect to find me again, or expect me to find you . . . come back!"

Traffic blocked the taxi's passage up Madison Avenue and the driver's voice broke in upon her: "Which restaurant did you say, lady?"

Delia opened her eyes to a sight of his tweed cap and thick red neck. Light streamed on the crowded street and life was everywhere, urgent, indifferent, invincible. "Fran will live . . . her body knows how even if her mind doesn't. . . ."

"Le Roi's on West Fifty-seventh," Delia told the driver, and rubbed her gloved hands together as though she were trying to bring life back to the dead. "Drop me at the corner of Fifth and I'll walk from there."

She'd find a drug store and telephone the Leonard before meeting Wallingford. She'd call Fran and say something gay and light and silly: "How could we have been such nuts? Forgive me, darling. I must have been out of my mind. Come to dinner tonight and let's take in a movie. . . ."

Like lovers who'd had a quarrel knowing it meant nothing. Only they were not lovers, nor even as the years passed, loving. They were sisters. Sisters under the skin. The Colonel's lady and Judy O'Grady . . . *I am going nuts!*

At the corner of Madison and Fifty-seventh they were caught in another jam, and Delia, glancing at her watch, calculated that it had already taken them twenty-five minutes to get this far from the Leonard. Her panic reviving, she was about to tell the driver to let her out so she could find a telephone, when the jam broke and they proceeded west along Fifty-seventh to Fifth. Again they were held up, and Delia, beside herself, paid the driver and got out. She had to walk two blocks before she found a drug store, and then both telephone booths were occupied and other people waiting to use them. Frustration brought a measure of calm, and she decided to walk on to the restaurant where Wallingford was probably waiting for her—she was fifteen minutes late. She'd excuse herself and call Fran from there.

Wallingford was waiting for her on the sidewalk outside the little French restaurant, and she had a glimpse of him, his back towards her, sauntering up the street. Then he wheeled and saw her and his face lighted expressively. "This is sweet of you!"

He held her hand, his own gloveless, cold. "It was nice of you to ask me."

"We had a date, remember?"

They stood a moment in a kind of uncertainty, the snowy air on their faces, both of an age and in a condition of mind to realize that this was no fortuitous occasion. Though only their second encounter it made for a special charm, a heightened suspense. Once more Delia felt a subsidence of fear, and told herself wonderingly: The trouble is I live too much within myself and exaggerate everything.

Still holding her hand, Wallingford said: "Anything wrong?"

"Not really. But I have to put in a telephone call, do you mind?"

While he was checking his hat and coat Delia asked the hat check girl where she could find a telephone, and Donald said: "Let me order a drink for you in the meantime."

"A daiquiri, thank you."

He found a table and watched her slender, elegant back as she made her way to the telephone booth at the farther side of the room. A waiter came and took his order for the drinks, and he relaxed, trying to analyse the feelings which had come upon him when he'd turned to see Delia walking towards him up the street. It was true that she had been in his mind fairly constantly since their last meeting more than a week ago, but he had not been prepared for the sudden rush of pleasure which her reappearance brought him, and he smiled a trifle grimly, thinking: Better watch it, old boy. No point in falling on your face at this stage of the game.

She was lovely, all right. Lovelier than he remembered. But this second glimpse, fleeting though it was, had suggested something more than loveliness, something totally beyond the scope of his earlier impressions of her, and his subsequent speculation. He tried now to put a name to that something but it eluded him, leaving a kind of iridescence, the sharpened sense of stillness stirred, like phosphor, then lost.

Walking home with Chris the night of Delia's party, they had talked a little of the attractive household they'd just left, and Donald had observed musingly that despite Chris's often expressed admiration, he still hadn't been prepared, quite, for the special quality of Delia's charm. "I'd expected something . . . tougher!" He smiled to himself in the gloom. "Something of the nature of porcelain—you know?"

"I don't," Chris replied, surprised. "Delia—tough?" He laughed, then added soberly: "Funny that you should have got that idea of her, though. It's what Veronica thinks. They don't get on."

"Delia and Veronica don't get on?"

"Well, Veronica has one of those mother things. We don't talk about it much, because Nonny knows I'm fond of her mother, so talking doesn't get us very far."

They had walked on a little distance, then Chris said abruptly:

"Now you've had a chance to see something of Veronica, Dad, what do you think?"

"I'm not sure what to think."

"You admire her writing, though?" He had sounded anxious, almost bedevilled, and the older man, not much easier in his mind, had taken his arm. "Yes, I do admire her writing. It has an amazing quality—by that I mean, a quality of brilliance, depth, expertness. I ask myself whether this can be a mere tour de force and whether she is capable of the sustained effort . . . the long haul which goes to make your true writer. I don't know. Time will tell."

"But as a person . . . as a woman . . ." Chris left the sentence unfinished, and after a slight hesitation Donald said gently: "I think that you'd be happier with Miriam Werth."

Chris made a swift, angry gesture, freeing his arm from Donald's.

"What's Miriam got to do with it?"

"It was Miriam before it was Veronica, wasn't it?"

"But what have you got against Veronica?"

They were at Seventy-second Street and as they prepared to cross Madison towards Park Donald took his son's arm again. "Shall I say that I just don't think the girl knows her own mind, and that I would hate to see you made the victim of her indecision—or even of her decision?"

They reached the farther sidewalk and Chris asked in a strained voice: "Is that all you've got against her—that she doesn't seem to know her own mind?"

Donald was silent for several minutes, appearing to think it over. He felt irritatingly at a disadvantage. He was not free to explain to Chris that part of his uneasiness sprang from certain neurotic attitudes which he'd discerned in Veronica's novel, and which he had little doubt were to some extent her own, and that he had been further impressed by her peculiar behavior tonight. Accustomed to the unpredictable, he'd still not expected the revelation of jealous terror which he was sure he'd surprised more than once in the girl's eyes and in her manner as the evening wore on. He'd summed her up as being too proud, too reserved, or perhaps too repressed ever to let herself lapse into the ignominy of self-betrayal, yet that was exactly what had seemed to happen tonight, and he'd been on tenterhooks for fear Chris might notice it and guess its cause. That he had not done so was, in the father's eyes, added reason for concern. Chris was no fool, but he must be in a bad way of love to have missed the fact that Veronica was nakedly, unashamedly, making a play for his—Donald's—attention, and that she resented, and in a strange way seemed even to fear, the attention which ordinary courtesy demanded he pay her mother. Every job has its emotional pitfalls and Wallingford's was no exception to the rule, but if he possessed what Bunny Watts had sardonically designated a knack with the women, he was not without the necessary armaments to ensure his own protection—and theirs. He felt that the time was not far off when he'd have to slap little Veronica down—not hard, perhaps, but hard enough.

He felt Chris looking at him as they walked slowly along the empty street towards Donald's apartment on East Seventy-third, and knew that he could not evade the answer. "Is that all I've got against her, that she doesn't know her own mind? Yes. In all honesty I can't say that I have anything else."

Chris seemed suddenly beside himself. "I think she's in love with me. She's difficult, not like other women. Not like Miriam. But gifted. Her ideas . . . her mind. . . ."

Donald had reflected bleakly that that was how Clare had impressed *him*, and Chris was nowhere near as green as he'd been, twenty years ago! Maybe, he thought glumly, there's something to be said for marrying below one's intellectual level, whatever the hell that might mean, or for taking a page out of Bunny's book and not marrying at all. But he knew that he didn't want either alternative for his son as he would not in any honesty have wanted it for himself. And he'd consoled himself with the thought that perhaps Veronica's mother might have something constructive to offer on the problem . . . they had agreed to meet for lunch one day soon to talk about their children, and now as he sat waiting for her to emerge from the telephone booth, where she seemed to be taking an inordinately long time to complete her call, Wallingford had to smile—not without wryness—at himself. Their children . . . Delia's child, and his!

Well, that constituted a bond between them, a convenient point of departure for whatever might lie ahead, but it hardly accounted for the sudden heat in his groin as he remembered her face when he'd seen it out there on the cold street, the smile faint on her lips, her eyes filling like pools with an inexplicable relief when they met his.

CHAPTER

XXIV

IN THE telephone booth Delia felt the receiver grow clammy in her hand as she heard Dipper's voice: "Mis' Hight? Frances? She checked out."

"Are you sure?"

"Checked out five minutes ago."

"There may be a mistake. Would you mind ringing her room number, please?"

"No use ringing her room number when there's n'b'dy in't, isther?"

"Did she leave a forwarding address, can you tell me?"

"Dint leave nothin'."

"I'm her sister. Would you please see if there is a message for me from Mrs. Hight?"

"Mis' Hight dint leave no mesge."

"Thank you," Delia said, faintly.

She stood for a moment with waves of apprehension going through her, then she called her house, but Katie reported no message from Fran. Delia hung up but lingered in the booth, trying to control her agitation. It's an act, she tried to assure herself. An act. Fran knows what she can do to me by disappearing like this. She's done it before. She did it to Herbert. She knows she can make me suffer on her account, and she'll play it to the limit. Three years ago after a quarrel over a bill she disappeared and there was a silence that lasted six months. Then the long agony . . . the private detective agency, the missing persons bureau, the search through newspapers in shrinking expectation of a reported accident or suicide . . . the helpless friends called in to help! Fran has me at her mercy and she knows it and I know it. I'm going to be made to pay for that slap, for losing control of myself, for the unforgivable treason of letting her know that I see through her, and I've never gone as far as I went today, not in all these years . . .

Through the dusty window of the booth Delia could see Donald Wallingford at a table at the far end of the room. He seemed to be staring at her, wondering why she took so long, and asked herself whether she might perhaps ask his help. Then revulsion swept through her at the thought of confiding in a stranger, revealing all the details of this stupid, frightening affair. But one thing was certain: she couldn't just stand here doing nothing. In a desperate hope that the Leonard might have been mistaken and that another voice than Dipper's might answer this time, Delia dropped a dime into the slot and dialled the hotel.

Dipper answered: "Mis' Hight? Jess mint."

Delia caught her breath as she waited. Then his voice, sounding like an intestinal rumble, surged into her ear: "Mis' Hight you said? M'm lookin'. Num. Num Mis' Hight regstred."

"You're quite sure? It's very urgent. Please send someone up to look in her room, will you?"

"Mis' Hight checked ert."

"Did she leave a message?"

"No mesge."

"A forwarding address? She must have left a forwarding address. Would you mind looking to see . . ."

Dipper bawled suddenly: "Chri sake lady! M'tellin' you Mis' Hight left no fording dress nuttin'. Dun you unnerstan Glish for Chrisake?"

Delia left the booth and made her way to the table where

Wallingford was waiting for her. A waiter brought their drinks and as Donald rose and pulled out her chair she gave him an apologetic smile. "Sorry to have taken so long."

He helped her off with her coat and draped it over the back of her chair. "You seem upset. Is there anything I can do to help?"

"It's all right, thanks. And I don't mind saying this drink tastes wonderful."

"If it's Veronica you're worried about, she called me a few minutes before I left the office, something to do with her manuscript. She sounded in good health and spirits."

"It wasn't Veronica," Delia said, managing a smile, and to herself: If it isn't Veronica, it's Fran. One or the other . . . inevitably, one or the other.

"How is the manuscript coming along?" she asked Donald, for something to say. "Is there much work to be done on it?"

"A little. It's pretty much of a finished job though, as it stands."

"Veronica has always been a perfectionist in her way."

"I told her that the thing had what—to borrow from Blake —I'd describe as a fearful symmetry. She seemed pleased." He looked at her seriously. "You know, I'd like so much to talk to you about Veronica's novel, but I'm stuck with this pledge she exacted from me, not to discuss it outside the firm." He gave a slight, impatient laugh. "It's frustrating, and I believe needless. I would like to understand her better than I do—as much for Chris's sake as for any other."

Delia nodded. "I would like to understand her better for all our sakes!"

There was a brief silence. Donald thought: the ostensible reason for our being here today is to discuss our children's problems, but somehow they seem rather unimportant or at any rate, temporarily remote. Excitement was rising and falling in him like a tide. He was filled with uncertainty about himself—a feeling he did not recall having had for a long, long time. As for Delia, her thoughts were engaged in a tug-of-war—to give herself over to the simple pleasure of the moment, or to make some excuse to him for not being able to have lunch, and rush back to the Leonard in a final and desperate attempt to find out what had happened to Fran.

Donald said presently: "You realize, I think, that Chris is pretty deeply involved with your daughter. More so, I'm afraid, than she with him."

Delia gave him a quick look. "Is that your opinion? I don't know, really. You see, I'm not in Veronica's confidence . . . so I can only observe, and draw my own conclusions."

"She carries her uncommunicativeness rather far, doesn't she?" remarked Donald. "In a way I suppose we have no right to be talking about them. They're of age . . . and entitled to privacy." When Delia remained silent he went on with a touch of diffidence: "I've often asked myself at which point in our lives children cease to be children and parents cease to be parents. I can't say that I've found the answer. I worry about Chris's happiness as you must worry about Veronica's."

She nodded. "And there is so little we can do for either of them."

"So little they will let us do!"

"If only happiness were a teddybear one could give them on birthdays or Christmas, it would all be so simple, wouldn't it?"

They talked about their children, about Veronica's early promise as a writer, about Chris's, comparing their talents and their personalities. Veronica, Delia pointed out, had always been a driver. She never spared herself, even as a very young child. "Once she had an idea she stuck with it, never letting it go for a minute. Whether it was a book she was reading, some problem in her school lessons, a poem or a story she wanted to write—she had this capacity for losing herself in it, for making herself part of it to the exclusion of everything that went on around her." Delia sipped her cocktail and Donald watched her intently, trying to find something—some clue to the fancied spirit within her, some glancing insight, an echo. There was none. Occasionally when she spoke her daughter's name her lips trembled slightly as if at some remembered pain, and he felt an instant responsive spasm in the depths of his body, as though he watched, from a distance, some horror he was powerless to avert.

"It has always been essential to Veronica that she prove something," Delia said, with a little frown of which Mr. Ramond would not have approved. Silvia, Donald Wallingford recalled, had never frowned. "Silvia's beauty expert had warned her that it was unbecoming and never in Silvia's born days had Silvia taken a chance on doing anything which might prove unbecoming. . . ."

"If Veronica were not genuinely gifted, I'd say that she operated under some sort of compulsion which must be as bad for her art as for her health, and I am still not sure that it isn't bad, in a way."

"Bad for someone," Donald murmured, off guard, then quickly:

"Bad for Chris, perhaps, though he doesn't see it. Part of his involvement with Veronica springs from his terrific admiration of her literary abilities. At the same time I suspect him of being more than a little . . . shall I say envious?"

Delia nodded. "I've wondered about that, myself. I think I can understand it in a way. Not having any talents myself I have always envied those who had. In Chris's case it might be more painful, since he is talented."

"In a different way than Veronica, though. Chris is a dilettante —and that bothers me a bit. He has ambitions as a creative writer, but from what I've seen of his work it is too much on the critical level . . . too cool, too detached from that . . . well, from that central fire which I think I recognize in Veronica."

"And yet there is no real reason why they shouldn't be happy," Delia said in a low voice. "Both have so much to bring to life, to each other. And there *is* an attraction. You say he is involved with Nonny . . . there are times when I feel pretty sure that in her own undemonstrative way, she is with him."

And he to the extent of being willing to walk out on a very nice girl for Veronica's sake, and of Veronica's taking it quite for granted that he should."

"Miriam Werth," Delia murmured, frowning. She gave herself a curious little shake, almost a shudder.

He smiled drily. "Sexual attraction needs no excuse, and never has."

"Just the same, I find it hard to forgive highway robbery if it's only to amount to—well, to pilfering."

"How about grand larceny?"

She shrugged and he got a distinct impression that he was somehow on delicate ground. "Look, Mrs. Dalton," he said quickly, "there's very little you and I can do about these kids, at this point. It is a relief to be able to talk . . . to . . . you know, air the subject a bit with you. I have tried, perhaps mistakenly, to stand between Chris and anything I thought I recognized as having the makings of tragedy. At any rate until he was old enough and strong enough to be able to take it. I haven't wanted him to suffer, or what was worse, to develop a taste for suffering."

He looked at her gravely. "As I suspect your Veronica has. You don't mind my saying that, do you?"

"Of course not."

Donald thought he discerned some urgency in her gaze, as though she were on the verge of asking a question and couldn't quite bring herself to the point. When she said nothing he went on gently: "I have refused to allow a tragic view of life to shut off other views, as I know it can do to the young and sensitive. Even at the risk of having Chris grow up a bit lopsided, I preferred it to the cult of suffering of which I see too much. I hate suffering." He brought it out with a kind of violence. "I hate suffering, but I hate a pretence of it even more." He waited a moment, his face more serious and intense than she had seen it.

"Above all I haven't wanted Chris to suffer *artistically*. Blake tells us that a tear is an intellectual thing, and ever since I made the discovery that Chris was going to be an intellectual, I've dreaded his tears. Do I make myself clear?"

"I think so," Delia said slowly. Again Fran's face rose before her eyes, Fran's eyes unrelieved by tears, Fran's mouth a knot of revenge.

"What I haven't been willing to accept until recently is the truth that we can no more dictate the terms of our children's suffering than we can the terms of their happiness." He laid his hand on Delia's where it rested on the table between them. "When, out of their kind of suffering comes a book like Veronica's, I know I'm licked."

He spoke strangely, breathlessly, and then for a long time neither could think of anything to say, but sat with their empty glasses before them, each conscious of the feeling of the other's hand, of the imminence of something they had come to believe was forever excluded from their lives. Donald wanted to pick up her hand and kiss it, to ask her, at this most inconvenient moment and in this most public place, what the hell they were doing talking about their children when they ought to be talking about themselves. He wanted violently, with the sudden panic of a man who feels young but who knows he isn't, to tell her that he'd learned the lesson of a loneliness which makes you perceive for the first time in your not so lily-pure life that there is no happiness so complete, no privacy so urgent, as when you lead your beloved into a quiet room and lock the door on the whole world of children, strangers, relatives, enemies, friends. Clare had never been able to make him feel like this. Nor had any of the others.

The magic passed. He felt her hand turn leaden in his, and something told him that he was sitting next to a badly frightened woman.

She spoke presently with dry lips. "I shouldn't be here . . . like this . . . drinking . . . talking!" She made a half movement of rising to her feet, but he held her firmly. "Tell me, Delia. I've felt it since we came into this place. What's bothering you?"

And then, unable to resist the temptation of his sympathy, his ready strength—how long since she'd known anything like it?—Delia told him about Fran. Put in that nutshell it seemed pitiable indeed—her own jealous, mother-concern for Nick, Fran's drunk-enness, their quarrel at the Leonard Hotel not an hour ago, and now Fran's disappearance. Donald had a vague recollection of having heard about this sister—Chris must have mentioned her, and now he listened, holding Delia's hand and waiting for the trembling recital to come to an end. Then he signalled the waiter and ordered another drink for them both, and a menu. When the man had gone he turned, smiling, to Delia. "Here I've been sitting gabbing, while you . . . but let's have lunch, then I'll go back to the Leonard with you and we'll see what we can do."

CHAPTER

XXV

IT WAS snowing, flakes as large as feathers drifted on the city and melted dirtily into the asphalt. People carrying Christmas packages smiled sentimentally at the descending whiteness, some paused to drop coins in the Salvation Army tambourines outside Arnold Constable's, and the plastic angels above Saks sang *Star of Bethlehem*, bringing gleeful anticipation to the very young and nostalgia to the middle-aged, while far overhead in the broken featherbed sky a plane's engines throbbed towards Europe.

Veronica left Wallingford's office and walked slowly uptown, gazing at the store windows. She had just delivered the final revised version of her manuscript to Donald, and he'd said cheerfully: "Nothing more to worry about now except the proofs. After that—the reviews!"

"I don't intend to read the reviews."

He laughed. "Never knew a writer who didn't." Then, with a quick glance: "You don't need to worry . . . I don't."

She'd noticed that he'd nicked his chin when shaving and that the blood had dried on the tiny wound. She'd got into the habit of noticing everything about his appearance so there were moments when, alone, she could build him up cell by cell, and to the sound of his voice and the small, characteristic gestures of his hands. The way he filled his pipe and then seemed to forget to light it.

The way his expression changed when he was thoughtful. The way he smiled—when he meant it and when he didn't. He crowded out other people and there were occasions, like this afternoon, when she'd felt herself suddenly consumed with a despairing and violent desire. It had made her awkward during their brief conversation, horribly self-conscious yet at the same time more than half willing that he should see her trouble, that he should make some gesture—a word, even, of tenderness, of understanding.

But he did nothing of the sort.

"I'll read this over again in the next few days, and call you if there should be anything more we need to discuss. But I'm sure it will be all right. Have fun now, Veronica, and relax."

She hesitated, hoping that since it was the end of the day he would suggest that they go out and have a drink together. It was some time now since he'd suggested any such thing and she sensed a reserve that was new to their relationship—one that had not been there in the beginning, when he'd been all warmth and gaiety and friendly helpfulness. Flattering. Attentive. They'd talked about other writers he knew and their methods of work and their peculiarities, love affairs, marriages, and so forth. He'd appeared to have all the time in the world to take her out to lunch or to cocktails, and several times he'd walked part way home with her at the end of the day, for the exercise he said, and because he lived only a short distance from her own home. Now all of a sudden that was changed and he seemed always up to his ears in work. When they did meet he made a point of bringing the conversation around to the subject of Chris, or of confining it strictly to her book. He was always kind, courteous, but distrait. Veronica had a frightening sense of being about to lose something that had—almost overnight, so it seemed—become unimaginably necessary to her, and on a sudden reckless impulse to save it she now took the initiative and suggested that since it was almost Christmas he allow her to treat him to a martini at Longchamps while she drank a beer.

He shook his head, his smile the one he kept, she was sure, for

Mrs. Frankwood Honeywell and her dog. "I have an engagement this afternoon. But give me a raincheck, will you, Veronica?"

She'd felt herself flushing, hating herself for her own humiliation. "Sure. Another time. I ought to get busy with my shopping anyway."

He accompanied her to the door and opened it. "Pretty hat you're wearing. Something new?"

She got a meager satisfaction from being able to tell him that the bright knitted ski cap was a present from Chris.

"Very becoming," Donald said, and they stood for a moment in the open door of his office, in a clatter of typewriters from the rooms beyond, and the spraying, professional smiles of women secretaries. Donald said lightly: "Guess I'll have to ask Chris to choose my hats. He seems to have the know-how."

Veronica gave a perfunctory laugh and escaped into the elevator and out to the street. The stores were gay with colored lights, the air stirring with the spirit of festival and re-birth. She walked slowly, her face lovely and unsmiling under the blue woolen cap Chris had sent her from Boston. So Donald was pleased that Chris should have sent her a present, pleased that she apparently cared enough to wear it, pleased that Chris loved her . . .

The snow melted on her cheeks, still hot from the flush of shame which she'd felt when Donald refused her invitation to go out for a drink. She tried to rally herself, to snap out of it by reminding herself that he was after all a busy man with many calls on his time, but somehow it didn't work. Up till a couple of weeks ago he'd seemed to have time enough and to spare. True, they were still working over her manuscript, discussing it, going over it point by point, and now that that part of it was over there was really no imperative reason why he should have to see her just whenever *she* felt like it . . . But no, there was something else. He was different. Why try to fool herself that that difference hadn't first manifested itself three weeks ago, right after that party on Thanksgiving eve, when he'd asked Delia to lunch with him and

had not asked *her?* Of course you might say that it was mere politeness, that living as a bachelor, as he did, such a luncheon was the
only return he felt he could make for Delia's hospitality. But it
still didn't add up . . . why, why should he not have asked her,
Veronica, too? And had Delia gone to lunch with him anyway?
She'd said nothing about it, nor had he, and Veronica was
damned if she was going to ask the question of either of them.
There was something else queer, too. Delia was away from home
more often than she'd ever been in the past, and with no apparent
reason, for certainly the rummage shop which she ran for charity
with Nadine Bowers, could not claim so much of her time, nor
could the Red Cross. On two occasions recently, unable to con-
tain her feverish curiosity, Veronica had called both places to ask
for her mother, and on each occasion she'd received the answer
that Mrs. Dalton was not there. It was true that Delia had been
in a state about Fran's disappearance from the Leonard. There'd
been a spate of telephone calls, trying to track Fran down, and
finally a post card had come from somewhere on Long Island
to say that she was all right, that she'd found herself a job pro
tem. in a branch bank and that she would be writing at greater
length or coming into town one day soon, and would see them.
That was all. They heard nothing further, but even that bit of
news had seemed to calm Delia's first lunatic terrors on her sister's
account, and life had resumed its normal routine . . . more or less.

More or less. Rather less than more, Veronica reflected, and
tasted a bitterness like gall in her mouth. Catching her at the
telephone a few days back when she'd been trying to reach Delia
at the Bowers, Katie had stood in the door watching her with a
peculiar smile on her customarily impassive old face. "Your mother
went shopping," she volunteered when Veronica, flushing, had
hung up.

"Said she wouldn't be back for lunch and for me to fix you
anything you wanted."

"Big of her," Veronica had muttered, then tried to pull herself
together under the old woman's sardonic gaze. "I just wanted to

find out what she plans to give Nick for Christmas so I don't go and duplicate it."

Walking up Madison Avenue in the softly falling snow Veronica told herself that if there was one thing she was not obliged to do under law, it was to make a fool of herself. This expecting special attention, special favors from a man just because he was going to publish her book. And what was there so extraordinary about that? What was it Chris had said once. . . . . "Today's achievement is tomorrow's *remainder!*" and "In the age of obsolescence art has its appointed grave."

Better perhaps to listen to the son than to the father. The latter had an ax to grind. Why expect him to be more interested in her as an artist, as a person, than he was in her product as a source of profit? He probably laughed at her behind her back with other writers, the way he laughed about Mrs. Honeywell and her corgie.

She could imagine him over drinks at the Roosevelt for instance, talking with some blasé established writer like William Faulkner or Katherine Ann Porter or even perhaps some nonwriting friend like . . . well, like Delia. Why not?

"I have a hell of time with these young beginners! You wouldn't believe it but there are some who not only expect you to spend every working hour praising their damned novels, taking them out to meals, feeding them drinks, but take it for granted that you must want to go to bed with them afterwards!"

His father, Chris had said, was coony about women. Meaning that he was quick on the getaway, which in turn meant that he probably had to be. Although he hadn't given that impression the evening he'd spent with them, sitting with Delia on the sofa, hanging on every word she said as though it were some miracle of wit and learning, watching her as though he were committing her to memory like a piece of music or a line of poetry . . .

Silvia.

Could that be at the bottom of it? Having read her book, then meeting Delia, could he suddenly have started to have mixed feelings about the book . . . doubts . . . qualms? Could he? Falling for Delia the way people did, even hard-boiled people like Chris and Miriam, the Bowers . . . others too numerous to name . . . falling for the way her hair grew from her temples, lighter there than as it thickened towards the rest of her head, for the sweep of her brows and the way her eyes were set, and for her wide, full-cut mouth which seemed to shape the promise which her eyes withheld . . . falling for that, and for the notes of her voice that was her voice and no one else's, no one's . . . could Wallingford, suspecting she was meant to be Silvia, have recoiled at an imagined treachery—recoiled from *her*, Veronica? He hadn't said so. He hadn't even hinted such a thing. And how should he have? This was between herself and Delia and no one else except perhaps that little mound of dust back there in the graveyard behind the house in Connecticut, and *he* would never know now, whether all was always fair in love and war, but Delia would know, and what did it matter anyway what Donald Wallingford thought . . . *Let him,* she said aloud into the falling snow, to the surprise of a passerby. Let him think what he likes . . . let him!

The snow melted as it touched her face and she felt the dampness through her shoes. Everything in the city turned to filth and corruption, and you could blame it on the people . . . on these masses who imagined themselves happy because Christ had died for *them!*

O come let us adore Him!

Everyone betrayed everyone and it all started from the first betrayal . . . fittingly, in a garden. In a park with trees and a bridle path and the first peering faces of dandelions in the young grass. Everything turned to corruption. Love, aspiration, trust. So long as it sprang from the human heart it remained rotten at the core. It colored everything. The snow, whitely immaculate, coming to replenish the earth, turned at once to liquid soot. Rain, purest of elements, filled the gutters to become a watercourse for excreta. Plastic angels piped hymns to snare the attention of wayward customers, and tambourines sang for pennies to buy a turkey dinner for the rummies on Skid Row.

"Veronica!"

Veronica wheeled to see Miriam Werth crossing the street towards her. Miriam, too, carried parcels. Her nose was pink with cold and her eyes shone like a child's. "Talk about coincidence! Hold these while I find my handkerchief, will you?"

Veronica took her bundles while she found a handkerchief and blew her nose. "Thanks. Guess who I almost bumped into crossing Fifty-seventh Street?"

"The Archangel Gabriel."

"Donald Wallingford and your mother, getting into a cab."

They fell into step and Miriam asked: "Shopping? You don't seem to have gotten very far."

"I haven't." Veronica had a sudden, inexplicable beauty. "Nick wants a trout rod, but I've an idea they cost a mint."

"I just bought him a necktie at Saks. Want to see?"

Veronica admired the tie. "Did they see you? Mother, I mean, and Donald?"

"No. I yelled, but they seemed rather preoccupied."

She peered at Veronica through the floating snowflakes. "You look blooming, I must say. What news of the book?"

"It's all over but the shouting."

"Well, I feel pretty good myself. I *love* shopping. I love looking at all the pretty things and thinking of all the people I'd like to give them to. It's the one time I really wish I had skads, so I could blow it." She poked into a paper bag. "I got this for Delia. I thought that with her hair and eyes . . . nice, m'm?"

"Oh come let us adore Him!" choired the angels with devastating sweetness into the snow-flowering air. Veronica felt her heart blowing up inside her, like a balloon. She said abruptly: "You're coming to us for Christmas dinner, aren't you?"

Miriam tucked various unwieldy bundles under her arms and scuffed the wet snow with her overshoes. "Can't. I'm going to my cousins in Brooklyn."

"No, come to us. Chris will be there, and his father."

Miriam stared at the darkening street, alive with figures and striped with sharpening light from doors and windows. Everything had a wonderful artificiality, making her think of the stage when she was a child. "I promised my cousins I'd go to them. I see them very seldom, and this seemed like the right occasion."

"You'll miss Chris again."

"He'll be around, won't he? I mean, what does he get—two weeks?"

"We're going skiing to the White Mountains. Chris, Nick, and I. It was Chris's idea."

"Sounds like fun."

"Come with us, Mim."

Miriam laughed. "Me ski? I never *larnt*."

"Come anyway."

"Whenever I try anything strenuous, I strain something. Swimming's my gambit, and I save that for summer."

"In that case you'll probably miss Chris altogether."

"I guess he can take it," Miriam said lightly. She smiled. "Looks as if you were going to have a regular family gathering."

"If Fran comes. We don't know about her yet."

They came to a bus stop and Miriam said: "I've had all the walking I want for today. Come on back with me and I'll give you coffee and croissant. There's a good concert on WQXR, Casadesus playing."

"I guess I'd better spend what's left of the day picking up a few yuletide mementoes."

They waited in the cold, the snow turning to rain on their heads. Right and left the avenue glittered gold and black in the falling darkness and they saw the bus bearing down on them, crammed with people.

"Oh God!" Miriam cried. "Maybe I better take the subway. But that'll be jammed too. Where'd I get this Christmas spirit anyway? What's the percentage in being a Jew if you have to subscribe to other people's nonsense?"

Suddenly, Veronica did not want to be left alone. "Don't go, Mim! Come back to the house with me. We can hear the concert over my radio, and Katie'll fix us something to eat."

But the bus arrived, the doors sprang open, spewing out passengers, and Miriam, with a quick smile and a shake of the head, clambered aboard with her bundles and was borne out of sight.

Veronica continued slowly up the avenue. The thought of her mother and Wallingford together had a strange effect on her, almost as though she'd taken an aphrodisiac. Ashamed, at a loss, she tried to persuade herself that after all Miriam might have been mistaken . . . Then suspicions which she'd been trying to suppress for the past few weeks began to harden into certainty. As she'd passed her mother's bedroom door earlier this afternoon Delia had called after her: "I shan't be home for dinner tonight, Veronica, so why don't you call Miriam and ask her to drop in, and perhaps go to a movie?"

A whiff of perfume had blown across Veronica's face as she hesitated by the door, and she'd had a glimpse of her mother in a new dress, a darker honey than her hair . . . an impression of loveliness, of love, which had left the girl shaken with this unacknowledged sense of excitement, desolation, and despair. Donald Wallingford's voice sounded mockingly in her ears: "I have an engagement this afternoon, but give me a raincheck, will you, Veronica?"

A raincheck!

A shop window caught Veronica's eye and she stopped to look in it, an automatic reaction designed to bring her agitation under control. This was the shop where Charles was in the habit of buying his riding paraphernalia. She used often to come here with him, and one Christmas he'd brought her in to be fitted for riding breeches though she never did learn to ride properly, being secretly afraid of horses and going through her lessons simply because she didn't want to disappoint him.

Standing there in the cold, staring at the window, Veronica struggled to get her emotion in hand. Perhaps, she thought, they have fishing rods, and I might price one for Nick. She went in and the place smelled poignantly familiar with its combined odors of tweed and polished leather and a warm furriness that made her eyes burn with tears. A salesman told her that they did not carry fishing rods, and she thanked him and went out and stood before the window again, and noticed a riding vest in Tattersall and above it on a sort of stand, and giving a curious effect of a head with the face missing, a black velvet riding cap. Suddenly the window swam before her eyes and all its radiance rushed together in broken patterns of light and darkness which were recognizable objects moving towards each other, image imposed on image, and it was like that day when she'd received Wallingford's letter telling her he liked her novel and wanted to publish it, and she'd gone downstairs to Delia's desk and every familiar object on it had seemed to change character before her eyes, to become creations of her own mind, just as the contents of this window seemed to be doing now, and she heard herself whispering that something was wrong and that the Tattersall vest should be spattered with mud and bits of grass and early dandelions crushed under an arc of thrashing hooves and flying stirrups, and a strange voice was screaming in her ears:

"Look out for the child! Look out for the child!"

And Charles' eyes, blue as scillas, gazed up at her from the grass, and his voice whispered: "Delia. Fetch Delia."

And the strange voice nagged in her ears in huge and searching inquiry: "Who is Delia?"

Who, indeed? Who is Silvia, what is she, that all our swains commend her?

Turning abruptly from the window Veronica walked on, a rage of feeling drying her tears before they could fall.

CHAPTER

XXVI

In the elevator going up to his apartment with Delia, Donald put his arms round her and kissed her hair. "You poor darling, you're frozen!"

"I'm not, really. I'm thawed for the first time in weeks . . . months . . . years!"

"The first time?"

She put a gloved finger on the cut on his chin. "Not the first time, no. The first was that afternoon we lunched together and you went with me to the Leonard and tried to help me find Fran."

He said thoughtfully: "We were very circumspect that day, as I remember, though I had a hell of a time keeping my hands off you."

"And there was I trying to think up some suitable way in which to express my gratitude!"

"While I mulled over possible suggestions that wouldn't shock you unduly, seeing it was only the second time we'd met." He laughed. "God, what a waste of time."

He kissed her again, keeping his lips on hers as they slid past the third floor, towards the fourth where he lived. Delia gave a little gasp and held him off, and he demanded belligerently: "Why?"

"It might stop and people get in."

She leaned against the wall and studied him gravely. "What does this make, though—the sixth time or the seventh that I've ridden up here with you?"

"The seventh. Remember the first?"

"I do. And I remember thinking that it might be a bit like going to heaven—that rushing breathless sensation, half anticipation, half fright. I must say you were very nice. Not a bit forbidding as I rather fancy the custodian of the pearly gates might be:"

"I was being Sir Galahad, not Saint Peter."

He pressed the emergency stop button between floors and took her in his arms again and kissed her throat under the soft warm collar of her coat and she put her arms round him and abandoned herself to the embrace.

"We weren't very . . . leisurely," she murmured, out of breath. "We didn't . . . waste much time, did we?"

"Why the hell should we?"

They looked at each other in the harsh overlight of the elevator, locked together in space. Then he pressed the release button and they moved smoothly on to the fourth floor. The doors opened and let them into the passage. It was empty and the silence was touched faintly by the distant sound of traffic and the grumble of steam radiators. Wallingford found his keys and opened the door of his apartment and Delia went in before him and waited while he closed the door. Then he took her in his arms in the darkness, where a faint glimmer of light shone against the window at the far end of the room that smelled of him and of an intimacy which had already become indispensable to her. He took off her hat and threw it on a chair, then her coat, and reaching behind her shoulders unfastened the long zipper of her dress and drew it down, baring her shoulders, imprisoning her in her own dress, kissing her as though he would never stop.

Later, lying beside her in the big bed, he studied her profile and marvelled at the look of innocence which passionate fulfillment can bring to the human face. Delia's hair shone like water flooding the pillow, and she lay so still that in a queer spasm of alarm he bent and touched her closed lids with his fingers, and her eyes opened, gazing up at him.

"I was afraid you'd died," he murmured. "You lay so quiet."

She gave a little sigh, as though he had indeed brought her back from some unfathomed depth of contemplation, as though the tranquillizing experience through which both had passed had crystallized in her to a kind of stilled radiance, stirred by his touch to another, airier flame.

"Strange," she murmured, and reaching up her arm, drew his head down to her shoulder.

"What's so strange?"

"That it should always be strange."

"Don't know that I care for the always."

Gaiety moved her and he felt the ripple of it down the length of her body beside his.

"Well, it has been," she said, "with you."

"With you and me, you mean?"

"And hasn't it been with you—and anyone else?"

"No comment on that."

"Thank God," she said, "we're fifty!"

"I'm not prepared to thank God for that, not even at this holiday season. I'd much rather we were both twenty and that there never had been a Charles or a Clare."

She said nothing, and he went on: "I seem to have developed a morbid interest in your past life. Tell me about Charles."

"I've already told you about Charles."

"You neglected to mention whether you loved him."

"Don't be collegiate."

"Did you love him?"

"Of course. I was nineteen when we met, and he was handsome and had what the Irish call a *way* with him."

"I'm glad he's dead."

"And I'm glad Clare is married to a vegetarian."

"Tell me more about your life with Charles. Begin at the beginning."

"Well, as I say, I was nineteen and love was in the air. Papa and Mama were an ubiquitously devoted pair, Fran had just got herself engaged to Herbert Hight, and the atmosphere was what one might say—shot through with IT. So when Charles Dalton appeared on the scene—we were living in New Hampshire, near Lake Umbagog, that summer, and he was visiting mutual friends near by—I'd already been softened up for the kill."

"I can see you," Donald mused, gloomily. "Nineteen, a little rounder than you are now, with long sunburned legs in a bathing suit, and that look on your face like a little girl when she first hears Jingle Bells played by the Salvation Army."

"Charles wouldn't be flattered to hear *that*."

"He was vain, I bet."

"How could he help being vain? Everyone liked him. Men, women, and children. Dogs and cats. Even birds liked him."

"I know the type."

"He had charm, and he knew how to use it."

"And he used it on you? Tell me how—no, don't tell me."

She told him, and he was silent, angrily caressing her breasts.

"Odd," Delia went on after a pause. "I mean, odd that Charles should have been attracted to me. I was really quite uninspiring. People used to congratulate my parents on my *goodness*. The word, in my mind, became synonymous with plainness, dowdiness, crooked teeth, and a taste for arithmetic."

"Fran was the glamour girl, then, I take it?"

"Yes. Although we were twins, Fran had everything. She was what everyone described as the *positive* one of the two. You can see what that made me."

"War and Peace," he murmured. "Sense and Sensibility. Miss Jekyll and Miss Hyde."

"It never occurred to me that I could compare with Fran in any single thing, or that because she'd gotten herself a husband, I might too. I was pretty and I knew it, but my prettiness never seemed to get me anywhere. Then, the year after Fran and Herbert went to live in California, along came Charles. Fresh out of

Harvard, and bursting with enthusiasm about everything under the sun, but chiefly about himself. I found him irresistible and was foolish enough to hope that I was perhaps the only one who had found him so. I couldn't have been more mistaken."

"Let me see," Donald murmured, calculating. "That was the era of prohibition, bath tub gin, Scott Fitzgerald, and those chamber-pot hats for women. I'd just graduated from Bowdoin and had a job on a Portland newspaper, and was palpitatingly considering seducing a pretty waitress who served me breakfast at Liggett's drug store."

"Did you?"

"Go on about Charles. How come you were so innocent?"

"I wasn't innocent. Merely undiscerning."

"Comes to the same thing."

"Charles was most eligible. Good family, lots of money, and the first convertible that had been seen around town since the Model T. But his parents were conservative and insisted that he finish up at Harvard Law School before giving us their blessing, which meant our waiting four years. As it turned out we waited only two."

"That must have been tough enough."

"It was tough for me. I wouldn't answer for Charles."

"And you never slept with him all that time?"

She said after a moment, plaintively: "I've never understood why they call it *sleeping*."

"Did you?"

"If you must know, I did. I was afraid that if I didn't some other woman would, and of course some other woman did anyway."

"While he was engaged to you?"

"Then and afterwards. When we were married. All the time." Delia went on dispassionately: "Men like Charles are not cut out for matrimony, but it took me a long time to find that out. When I did it was pretty much too late."

"Too late for what?"

"Too late to do anything about it. Too late to go on loving him, trusting him . . . you know."

"You must have had some feeling left for him, hadn't you?"

"Yes, if you call habit feeling, or loyalty, or the instinct to shield and the reluctance to admit, and pride." She gave a short, impatient laugh. "I'd started by being so much in love, so hideously romantic, amazed and gratified that anyone as attractive and popular as Charles should love me, that it took time and a succession of shocks to waken me to the realization that I was after all just another woman in his life, one to whom he found himself unexplainably legally attached. But as for me, I *felt* married to him."

After a pause Donald said: "You've told me there were other guys in your life . . . I don't want to pry."

"No?"

"Well, I've told you about the other women in my life!"

"About one or two, yes."

"Who do you take me for, Casanova?"

Delia turned, pressing her lips to his ear. "I wouldn't care if you were Casanova. Or even if you were Charles Dalton. You see, I've never been quite as fond of a man as I am of you."

"Fond?"

"Fond."

There was a long silence, the room darkening round them, snow drifting against the windows, the excluded universe carolling faintly beyond their consciousness, or their care.

Wallingford said at last: "There was someone called Kingsley Bates whom you mentioned the other day. When exactly did he come on the scene?"

She replied readily enough: "Oh, some time after I'd been married to Charles. After Nick's birth, actually. Charles at the time was living with two other women, I believe, besides me."

"And you knew it?"

"Well, he had peculiar notions of what constitutes discretion and what doesn't. One of the ladies, I learned afterwards, didn't even know that he was married. She called on me after his death, with letters he'd written her, in which he'd made some rather rash promises. She wanted a cut of his estate, but Freddie Bowers took care of that." She laughed a little. "Poor Fred. He's had to take care of so much, where Charles was concerned."

"Don't try the broken wing technique with me," Donald warned her, grimly. "I'm out for the truth, so let's stick to Mr. Bates. Just how did you happen to get mixed up with him?"

"Through Charles."

Donald leaned on his elbow and stared down at her. "Through Charles?"

"It was one of those coincidences that E. M. Forster is so good at. Kingsley was the brother of one of Charles' mistresses, and he —Charles—brought Kingsley and the sister to the house one afternoon, for drinks. I believe Charles had some idea that Kingsley might serve as a red herring, and so he did—for about two weeks."

"And then?"

"Then he fell in love with me."

"The bastard."

She smiled apologetically. "And I with him."

"I suppose I asked for this."

"It was the most natural thing in the world. Inevitable, in fact. Kingsley was a sweet boy, and I had been in a state of emotional deprivation for years."

"Since the birth of Veronica, you mean?"

"Yes," Delia said slowly, and he recognized a curious, involuntary shift in tone whenever Veronica's name was mentioned. "Since the birth of Veronica."

Wallingford said with sudden fierceness: "I loathe these revelations, but I have this need to know everything about you. Everything!"

"Have you really? Charles never did."

"Not even about Kingsley?"

"I doubt that he had an inkling about Kingsley. I didn't have to be very clever about it, either. Charles was always so full of himself, I don't think it entered his head that his wife might entertain—extracurricular interests."

"How old was Nick when Kingsley showed up?"

"About five. Veronica was nine . . . going on ten. It was the year before Charles' death."

He hesitated, a prey to conflicting emotions of jealousy, appeased love, perverse amusement. "Are they both—Veronica and Nick—Charles' children?"

"They are both Charles' children." When he was silent, she asked: "Would it make any difference to you to think that perhaps they were not?"

"I don't know. It shouldn't. What the hell business is it of mine? Yet the truth is yes, in a way it would. I guess I'm the kind that prefers to keep his jealous eggs in one basket."

"To put it a little less airily—promiscuity is not in your line?" And before he could answer she added thoughtfully: "Nor in mine. Charles rather sickened me for that. Though I will say that life became definitely simpler when I no longer had any illusions about him."

"Didn't it occur to you that you could have got a divorce?"

"It did, but I couldn't bring myself to take the step." She moved, and he felt her hair warm and alive against his mouth.

"I suppose I am conventional by instinct. And then there were the children. I'd had a taste of what emotional insecurity could be, and I didn't want to wish it off on them." She was silent a moment, then went on: "There was something else. Fran was divorced, and I couldn't have borne for us both to be in the same boat."

"Has either of the children the remotest idea what kind of a man their father was?"

"Why should they have? Nick, I think, scarcely remembers him, and Veronica . . ." she shrugged. "Veronica remembers him too well, and in her own way."

"Wouldn't it have been healthier, fairer all round, for them to have shared something of your disillusionment?"

She stared into the warm shadows of the room and it was impossible for him to read the expression in her eyes. At last she said:

"Perhaps it would. I don't know. But by the time I'd got round to thinking about it, their little patterns were set, and I didn't have the nerve to try to break them." Then in a matter-of-fact voice she added: "There is something I haven't told you. You asked me the other day why I finally broke with Kingsley Bates, and I said I'd explain later."

"Don't if you'd rather not."

"I might as well. You see, Kingsley and I would probably have continued our affair after Charles' death if something hadn't occurred to shock us both . . . well, into cold reason. It happened the day that Charles was killed. One afternoon in spring. Katie had taken Nick for a walk, and Charles and Veronica had gone to the park, where he was to try out a horse he hadn't ridden before. Veronica was told to wait for him at a certain spot, and they were to return to the zoo for tea. This was an established thing with them, every Saturday. And it gave Kingsley and me a chance to be together for a little while. Well, that was the afternoon that Charles was thrown from his horse, and he died almost immediately, before Veronica's eyes."

Wallingford lay beside her, motionless, and Delia said: "It seems that just before he died, Charles asked that I be fetched. Veronica heard him and came running to find me. She had her own latch key and let herself into the house and rushed into the parlor, where she found me with Kingsley. In an extremely compromising situation."

He said nothing, and Delia put her hand on his head, holding it against her shoulder. "We had no time to pretend, and anyway it would have done no good, not with Veronica. She saw at once, and understood at once."

He exclaimed angrily: "How could she—a kid of ten!"

"A very unusual kid," Delia said quietly. "It was, for her, the culminating shock. For me, too."

She sighed, kneading his temple lightly with the tips of her fingers. "I don't know whether you will believe this or not, but that afternoon did something to me, so that there hasn't been another man since."

"Couldn't you have explained things to Veronica? Wouldn't it have helped?"

"What was there for me to explain that wasn't self-evident, there before her eyes?"

"But the reasons—the reasons!"

"The reasons for my infidelity? You must remember that Veronica adored Charles. He was the one human being she believed in, or has ever believed in. He was her god in a way. But I was unlucky with her from the beginning. Inexperienced as I was, jealous, hurt, insecure, I took my frustrations and misery out on her when she was no more than a baby, and defenseless. I've been trying to make up to her ever since, but I guess it's too late."

"Perhaps," he muttered, "if even now she were to know the truth about Charles?"

"What truth? That he was gay, debonair, generous, kind—and that he loved her? The truth that people loved *him*, and that it would seem, from what she'd observed with her own eyes, that I was the one person who didn't?"

"I still don't see why you should have to take the rap for Charles."

She was silent and he had a feeling that no matter what he said she would remain so. Lying together in the friendly darkness each faced an awareness of something unrevealed in the other, a darker darkness between them, and in sudden revulsion against this flaw in their perfection Donald gathered her naked body to him and buried his face in the moonlit mass of her hair. "The young love their suffering," he whispered, searching for her lips, finding them. "The innocent love their guilt. But you and I have no time for substitutes, my darling. And it's going to be you and me, from now on."

CHAPTER

XXVII

Chris, sprawled on the sofa in Miriam's apartment, watched while she untied the ribbons on the package which he'd brought her. A short-wave program from London filled the room with the voices of young boys singing carols. From a neighboring apartment more music built up the premature darkness with a blurred obbligato of sound, and Chris said restlessly: "Those kids' voices give me a hollow feeling inside. Not nostalgia exactly, but something like."

"Reminders of a lost innocence?" Miriam suggested. "Remembrance of things past?"

"Nothing nameable, or even describable, unless you could say it was of a stage vanished almost as soon as reached . . . a sexless purity which no woman's voice has ever matched."

A single voice detached itself from the others and soared poignantly in a suddenly arrested silence, then faded out and Miriam glanced at him. "Precarious, all right . . . a year or two more and they'll sound like ducks in a mill pond." She rolled a length of ribbon round her fingers and set it aside. "This looks expensive. Is it?"

"Very, but you're not supposed to open presents till tomorrow. No fair doing it on Christmas eve."

"I shan't see you to say thank you unless I do it now."

"You could come skiing with us."

She shook her head. "We've gone over that. While you and Veronica are breaking your necks on the icy slopes you can think of me embedded in the soft warm bosom of the Kramer family on Brooklyn Heights."

"Sissy."

She removed the cover of the pasteboard box and delved into a nest of tissue paper, drawing out a smaller box tied with tinsel cord. For a moment she hesitated, looking at it with an odd expression.

"Open it." He watched her steadily. She had removed her spectacles and her eyes were beautiful, deep and glowing like the eyes of a deer, their heavy lashes making twin half moons of shadow on her cheeks. She was wearing a close-fitting dark green dress with a high collar, and he noticed the shape of her breasts, and the way the dress clung to her shoulders and thighs, a dress seductive in its studied simplicity.

Miriam got the box untied and lifted out a string of amber beads on a gold chain. She looked at Chris. "Nice. Thanks a lot."

"Like it?"

"Of course."

She replaced the beads carefully in the box and went into the kitchen where the coffee pot was boiling over. "I mailed your present," she told him, raising her voice above the music of the radio.

"Not another cigarette lighter, I hope?"

"I'd thought of it, the way you leave them around." She sounded airy, distant. "No, this is a necktie. Highly original idea. It has that personal touch so indispensable at this season."

"Christmas is baloney," Chris said, moving his shoulders deeper into the cushions and watching her as she stood inside the kitchen door, her body silhouetted against the light. "Except for seeing the people one likes, it's a lot of horse."

"You'll be seeing all the people you like tomorrow, won't you?"

"Not all."

"Those you like best, anyway."

"Wish you were going to be there, Mim."

"You can spare me a thought, deep in the heart of Brooklyn."

She reached up on a shelf and brought down the cups marked HE and SHE and poured coffee in them and set them on a round tin Mexican tray with a plate of pastry and a jar of marmalade. "You haven't begun to tell me about Cambridge and everything. How's my brother Jerry?"

"Haven't seen much of him lately. He's being very exclusive."

"He thinks the same thing about you."

There was a brief, dangerous silence, then she asked lightly:

"Have you finished the piece you were doing for the Advocate, on Conrad?"

"I don't seem able to finish anything these days. Ideas come to me, then they sort of thin out and slip away." He frowned. "Don't seem to be able to—you know, concentrate as I used."

She came into the room carrying the tray. "That about Conrad sounded like a good idea. A comparative study of him and Melville. I'd set Conrad above Melville, just on the score of style."

"Yet Conrad's style I believe is the reason he has been treated cavalierly in certain quarters for so long. It's tended to obscure his profound psychological insights, many of which Melville seems to stumble upon by accident . . ."

Miriam set the tray on the table before him and smiled.

"Like old times, isn't it?"

"Like old times." Chris was trembling suddenly. "I see the old cups are still holding out."

"SHE lost her handle, but I glued it back."

Miriam sat down beside him on the sofa. "It was last Christmas you gave me these, remember? No reason why they shouldn't have held out this long."

She dropped two lumps of sugar in his cup, and added cream.

"Concrete things have a way of lasting when everything else gives out. People die, relationships go on the rocks, but a fragile thing like a china cup or a bit of glass can last forever."

She handed him his cup, not looking at him. "It's why some

of us have this bug about possessions, I guess. Something of ourselves to hand on, when we're through, or hang on to while we're
here. I never quite understood it before, but I think I do now."

They stirred their coffee. Then Miriam said: "Guess that's why
Veronica helped herself to the cigarette lighter you'd left with
me. She was pretty deft about it, too. Like a shoplifter."

"I'll get you another."

"Heavens, no!" She laughed. "I don't mind sharing it with
Veronica. I'm not that proud."

"You are proud. You're just about the proudest damned thing
I know."

The tension between them was like a wire about to snap.

"Tell me more about the Conrad article."

Chris forced himself to talk while she listened, sitting near
him, not touching him, their consciousness of each other almost
unbearable to both. Suddenly he had run out of ideas, and reaching
out a hand for the pastry, upset his cup and filled the tray with
spilled coffee.

"Damn," he muttered. "Too many drinks last night, I guess."

She ignored the mess. "Where were you last night?"

"My train was late and Dad and I spent the evening boozing."

Talking about his father made things a little easier.

"How's Donald?" Miriam asked. "I haven't set eyes on him
since that night at Delia's."

Chris smiled faintly. "I've never seen him in such good form.
I get a distinct impression there's a woman around."

Miriam glanced at him quickly. "Any ideas as to who it could
be?"

Chris hesitated. "An idea, no more than that."

Somewhat to his surprise Miriam said no more, and as the
silence between them threatened to stretch into eternity and
Eine Kleine Nacht Musik poured into the room it became an intolerable reminder to both of things which neither could forget,
nor bear to remember. Chris thought: My God! This time last
year we were lying together on this same sofa and the damned

telephone rang and rang and we let it ring and I thought that this
was the be-all and end-all of everything, and I loved her crazily,
for ever. Her fine breasts, her thick black hair falling over my face,
and neither of us giving a damn about Christmas, the telephone, the music, the universe! Now I can't even touch her or
look at her . . . my whole body's gone numb as though I'd been
shot with a hypodermic. And all because of Veronica. Because of
Veronica's voice, slurred and husky; Veronica's goddam eyes cool
and steady and stand-offish like a cat's, Veronica's *presence*, still
and explosive . . .

The afternoon it happened, six months ago . . . I was so sure of
myself and of Miriam and Veronica came walking into this room
wearing that old tweed skirt with the fringed pockets and a navy
sweater, and that straight shining hair of hers not even properly
brushed, and the way her mouth curled as she spoke and the implied criticism of everything, of everyone, repelling you, impressing
you because she didn't seem to give much of a damn even about
her own opinions. And at once that transfusion between her and
me, a great pulse pumping between us, frightening, exciting as
hell. And lying awake all that night at home trying to sort it out
in my mind and seeing both of them under my eyelids, the two
of them like two photographic images blurred together, and
Miriam's fading, fading, and my trying frantically not to let her
fade, not to let this thing happen, but it did happen, and now here
we are, Miriam and I, pretending, knowing the thing's ended and
finished, and once that's happened, boy, you're through . . . you're
through with the one you're through with in a way you wouldn't
believe possible, so what the hell's the use? What the hell's the
use?

He felt Miriam's eyes and forced himself to meet them. She
said quietly: "You didn't have to do this."

"Do what?"

"Come to see me, bring me a present, go to all the bother."

"I wanted to."

"You didn't, really. You haven't for a long time."

He was silent, staring at the cup marked HE and its huge, ridiculous saucer. He'd seen them in the window of a junk shop on Third Avenue and had bought them as a sort of joke for Miriam last Christmas, and she'd been delighted and used them whenever he came to see her, whenever anyone came.

"What is the use of pretending like this?" Miriam asked in the same quiet voice. "One shouldn't try to fool oneself, or the other person."

"I don't want to fool anyone." Did he say it, or just imagine that he'd said it? He felt queasy with guilt, and with the liquor he'd drunk the night before, trying to build himself up for this afternoon. And he hadn't been able to sleep, thinking about it, and now here it was.

"I didn't expect you to come tonight," Miriam said after a pause. She stirred the last of the coffee in her cup and drank it. "I didn't expect you, tonight or any night, ever again."

"Do we have to be tragic?" He tried to sound matter of fact but it didn't come off. She was a beautiful, passionate girl with a generous and exciting body, and he knew she loved him, and that he was not treating her very well. It wasn't even as though Veronica could compare with her—not that he could be entirely sure of that, or not yet anyway. Veronica had kept him at a distance with those hot-cold eyes of hers and that air she had, challenging, appealing, sure of herself at one moment, pitifully unsure the next. She could hurt him but he was not yet sure that he could hurt her. They were like a pair of panthers, drawing blood from each other even in play.

Miriam said slowly: "No, we don't have to be tragic. There's nothing you can do about it, nothing I can do. Nothing Veronica can do, either."

He said roughly: "You're worth a dozen Veronicas. Don't think I don't know it."

She shrugged. "You're literary, both of you. Intellectual rivals. Has it occurred to you that there is nothing more deadly?"

"Look, Miriam. You've just said that there is nothing any of us can do about it. I have no excuse. I feel as if I were sort of infected. As if I'd taken some sort of dope."

"You know that she's developed a crush on your father, don't you?" Before he could speak she went on: "Donald praised her book, and that was the beginning. But now she wants him for a different reason. She wants him because she sees that someone else wants him."

"Delia," Chris said, and felt sicker and sicker. "But what's the use of talking about it, Miriam? I think I know what's the matter with Veronica. She needs to be loved. More than anyone I know, she needs to be loved."

"More than anyone you know?"

"Oh Miriam!" He leaned across the sofa and seized her hand, pulling her down so her breast rested against his and their faces were close together. "Miriam, darling! I feel like a heel . . ."

She stared into his face and he watched the tears flood her eyes and felt them salt and warm on his lips.

"Chris," she whispered, and let her whole body sink upon his. "Chris. This time last year, do you remember?"

"I've been thinking about it."

"What's happened to us? Why, so suddenly, did something have to happen to end it?"

"I don't know. I don't even know whether it would do any good to know."

He stroked her hair, brought his hand to rest on the nape of her neck, and kissed her gently on the lips. But it was no use. It didn't stir him. He had to force himself to repeat the caress while his whole being suddenly throbbed with desire for Veronica.

"But to us, to us!" Miriam clasped him in her arms, straining against him. "It's crazy, it's wrong! It couldn't happen to us. Not after what we've had. Not after all the things we've done, planned, looked forward to! We're so close. We believe in the same things, share the same ideas, the same thoughts! We've never quarrelled or fought or even disagreed seriously. I've never competed with you, or even wanted to. It's been like being one person —you and I, one person!"

Yes, Chris thought, dully. And that's the whole trouble. We've been one person instead of two. Even in the act of love I've been able to forget you as I feel I could never forget Veronica. With her or away from her, I ache for her. I ache.

Miriam levered herself on her elbow, and her face, suspended thus above his, had great beauty and a terrible sort of exuberant suffering which thrilled him without moving him either to pity or desire. He felt that his passion for Veronica had aroused Miriam to a height of emotion she might never otherwise have reached, and he took a secret satisfaction in the thought, in its perversity and complication.

"Chris," she whispered, reading her failure in his face. "Oh Chris!"

Half an hour later he left her and walked quickly up the dark little street towards the subway. Windows stained the black asphalt with brilliant color and the air trembled with a sound of bells. The great city, always pushing forward, relentlessly straining away from the past, seemed to pause a moment to get its breath, to cast a look over its shoulder as if in search of something it had missed in passing.

Chris lifted his face to the winter cold and drew it into his body with a shudder of relief and anticipation. Every season is a beginning, every completed act the forerunner of one as yet undreamed. A sense of release, of a great weight fallen from his shoulders, made him feel that he was walking on air. How different from the way he'd felt earlier when he came this way to see Miriam, carrying his present for her in his pocket . . . but now that was over and done with. And she'd been fine, really. Fine, except for that moment on the sofa and the taste of her tears on his lips, and when he'd tried to take her in his arms she'd got abruptly on her feet, tossing her head back in a gesture that would have been stagey from another woman but not from her.

"Look," she said in a normal voice. "If I'm to get out to Brooklyn before supper . . ."

Miraculously composed after that moment of weakness, she had helped him on with his coat and given his shoulder a light pat at parting. "Goodbye, Chris, dear. Have fun."

"Miriam!"

She had put on her glasses and stood away from him, smiling. He said something very silly. "Miriam, you're not going to let this make any difference, are you? To us . . . to Veronica?" And she'd replied with an easy laugh: "It has made all the difference in the world. Goodbye, Chris. Merry Christmas. And don't come back."

A large woman carrying bundles bumped into him and he apologized though it was her fault. She gave him a big smile. "O.K. kid! Merry Christmas!"

Chris lifted his hat. "Merry Christmas . . . and don't come back."

He reached in his pocket for his gloves, and his fingers encountered something unexpected. Coming to a stop on the sidewalk he took out a small pasteboard box containing the amber beads he'd bought Miriam. For a moment he hesitated, conflicting feelings prompting him to toss the thing into the nearest trash basket. Then he thought better of it. There was no one to mark the gesture, and they'd cost quite a bit, and would come in useful at some future date. Putting the box back in his pocket he ran quickly down the dank maw of the subway entrance and caught the first train uptown.

CHAPTER

XXVIII

WHEN Charles was living the family used to spend Christmas in the house at Marbury in Connecticut, an old red-painted house which Charles bought when he married Delia, and where they regularly spent their summers before he died, though not so regularly afterwards. The house stood a little distance from the main highway to New York, in a copse of oak trees above a narrow dirt road bordered by elms. In summer the rooms were filled with the moving shadows of the branches and with the sound of leaves rustling in the wind. The harsh cries of blue jays came in through the open windows in the morning, with an occasional deep whistle from orioles which nested in the elms, and a hammering noise of woodpeckers at work in some worm-ridden old stump in the wild growth behind the house.

In winter there were no orioles but the jays still called from tree to tree, woodpeckers still hammered for grubs, and chickadees, shy in summer, emerged from hiding and came fearlessly to the feeding station which Delia had fixed for them years ago. Two days before Christmas Charles would drive down alone from New York to air the house and get the furnace going, and Christmas eve Delia arrived by train with the two children and

Charles met them at the station in the old Dodge touring car which he'd had for heaven knows how long and which nothing would induce him to junk, although it was expensive to run and almost impossible to keep in repair. He had strongly sentimental feelings about all his possessions and could never bring himself to part with them even when they'd long since outlived their usefulness.

Suitcases and Christmas packages would be stored on the back seat of the Dodge while Delia and the children rode in front with Charles. Delia always held Nick on her lap, and Veronica sat wedged happily next to her father, and they drove away from the station along snowy roads with the top down if the weather was clear, along icy or muddy ones with the top up if it were not. Veronica recalled very clearly the sound of a broken chain as it went clackety clack against the mudguard, and Charles roaring carols as he drove; she remembered Delia's nervous smile and the feeling of Delia's thigh braced against a possible skid, and Delia's arms making a protective cage round the little boy on her lap.

In the country as well as during holidays in town Charles liked to dress like an English squire, and he looked the part in his old hound's tooth jacket, whipcord breeches, and leather leggings dating from the First World War. He rarely wore a hat and his light, sun-bleached hair blew back from his face when he drove, and his blue eyes shone with enjoyment, making him look very young and gay.

In spite of an outward carelessness of dress Charles was extremely fastidious about his appearance. His clothes had a special elegance, and he was always very clean and smelled of the expensive French cologne which he bought at Brooks Brothers or Tripler's, in town. No matter how far he rode or how hard he worked round the house cutting trees or planting them or stacking wood, cleaning out the swimming pool in fall, mowing the grass and scything brush, Charles never lost that country squire appearance, that expensive aura which marked him as a man who did the things he did not from necessity but from choice.

After his death, whenever Veronica thought of him she thought of him thus—as a man who'd had the art of living as he liked, in a kind of primal innocence and health, a nobility of spirit which he spread around him and which were as peculiarly his own as his humor, his generosity, and his love for people and for life. Remembrance of that lost vitality made the thought of his death unbearable to her even now. She couldn't prevent herself imagining his strong, active body buried under the stifling earth of the little graveyard behind the Marbury house, in the pathetic company of its original long-departed owners, for he'd left instructions in his will that that was where he wished to be buried, never dreaming, of course, that he would die when he did, or indeed that he would ever die, death not being one of his preoccupations and the idea of it a mere romantic exercise like his love for riding horseback or tearing along country roads in that antediluvian Dodge.

Every winter from the time she learned to walk, Charles would take Veronica into the woods with him when he went to cut a fir for their Christmas tree. He was very fussy about its being the perfect height and size to fit the space between the east windows of the living room, and he would never permit the use of electric lights but insisted on candles in those little metal holders that clip on the ends of twigs, and on wonderful old-fashioned decorations that had been his when he was a boy and which had come from Germany years ago and for some extraordinary reason still survived. After his death Veronica came on the box with each of these precious objects carefully wrapped in tissue paper by Delia. There were balls of gold and silver in tinsel nets, fragile, iridescent birds with sapphire tails, stars which changed their color with the changing light, and whole carillons of silver bells. Unseen by anyone, Veronica had smashed the lot, pretending afterwards that it happened by accident.

When there was snow on the ground Charles took a sled and Veronica rode on it, her scarlet trousered legs stretched stiffly before her, her face pink with ecstasy and cold, thrilled to the core that she should always be chosen for his sole companion, since he never asked anyone else to go with him, not even Nick when Nick had grown old enough to walk and often yelled to be allowed to come too. Long after Charles' death Veronica would muse over the fact that he'd always wanted her and no one else. There was seldom any variety to those little expeditions from the house, across the frozen lawn and down an ancient cart track between the iron-colored trunks of oak and hickory, skirting stone walls built by men and women and oxen working together more than a hundred years ago, walls which ribbed the fields in perfect squares and rose into view when the leaves were gone and the earth thrust itself upward to meet the sky.

Reaching the fir growth beyond the hardwoods, out of sight and sound of the house, Charles would move in leisurely fashion from tree to tree, measuring them with his eye, frowning a little, talking as much to himself as to Veronica where she sat watching him from her perch on the sled, watching the gray squirrels and the chickadees as they made a lively pattern of movement among the last few, frozen leaves. Once she'd seen a fox come down the ridge from the direction of the graveyard, his coat gleaming red in the sun, his neat little tracks seeping up indigo shadow behind him, and she'd called to Charles to look, but the fox, startled by her voice, had turned and run swiftly back up the ridge and out of sight.

The tree selected, Charles removed his jacket and scarf and gave them to her to hold, then he took his ax from its leather sheath and spat once, lightly, on his palms. First he sliced off a few of the lowest branches of the tree, and a sharp resinous fragrance escaped from the wound and touched Veronica's face and became, for her, inextricably part of the song that Charles would be humming or whistling between blows of the ax while his face got redder and redder, his hair glistened in the sun which shone also on his strong white neck and on the hairs at the base of his throat. He took his time, and the sun sifted lower and lower towards the ridge where the hickory trees stood up like porcupine quills between Veronica and the graveyard of men and women who had raised the stone walls and perhaps planted the trees, whose axes had sounded hard and clear on long forgotten winter afternoons, sending the foxes scurrying to their dens, and whose bones had lain a long time lost to sight and memory under the heaped snow.

On winter evenings in New York, coming home late from a movie or from visiting friends, when the streets were emptying and a pause settled on the huge, restless scene, Veronica caught herself thinking of those past evenings, as darkness groped down between the gray branches of the oak trees and a blue jay going late to roost skimmed down the track before her eyes, and the sled runners crunched on the hardening snow to the strains of Charles' voice singing Tannenbaum, O Tannenbaum . . .

On the way home she usually walked because the tree took up all the room on the sled and it was important that none of its branches be broken or bent. Charles carried the ax on his shoulder and dragged the sled by its rope wound around his wrist, and one hand held Veronica's mittened paw while he matched his step to hers. He was never in any hurry, and his soaring gaiety made her think of a raft which bore her up through the falling darkness, in safety towards the golden windows of the house which waited for them at the end of the fast disappearing track.

That was how it used to be in winter, and more important to her than what came afterwards—more important than the parties and the friends who dropped in with last-minute packages and stayed to drink Tom and Jerries before the open fire, men and women who had a way of dividing up, one lot grouping itself round Charles and the other round Delia, and she'd become aware, as she grew older, of the special warmth and excitement they brought with them into the house, like invisible presents to be delivered secretly when no one was about . . .

There would be cake and ice cream for Nick and her, and paper snappers with mottoes, and everyone suddenly absurd in paper caps singing between great eruptions of laughter in which Charles' voice soared above them all. And there was the tree they had cut the day before standing transformed and aglow with something not native to it, heavy with strange and glittering fruit, with peacock colored birds shining and fading among the branches, and its wild fragrance the only reminder of the cold and the snow and of the red fox running, running like a flame through the falling dusk.

In summer everything was changed and the lawns ran smoothly into beds of day lilies bright against the woodlot. Blue jays sounded their clanking note in the oak trees, robins built unimaginatively in the little ironwood where a black snake found the nest every year and every year ate the eggs, and Nick ran naked over the grass with Delia crying after him: "Mind the poison ivy!" and Charles appearing with a great clatter of hooves up the driveway on his gray horse Pedro which he boarded with a farmer neighbor up the road, in a barn with the cows. "A horse needs cows to keep him warm in winter!" Charles would say, and Veronica tried hard to learn how to ride because Charles wanted her to, and she did after a fashion, though Pedro terrified her and every minute spent on his great heaving back was a bad dream which never betrayed itself in her bright, fixed smile.

Charles had built the swimming pool himself, piping water from a spring across the road, and when Veronica was about five years old he taught her how to swim. He was a fine swimmer and could stay under water a long time, and it used to make her breathless to watch him walking about on the blue floor of the pool, his hair standing on end like weeds and a succession of silvery bubbles rising to the surface above him. She did not fear water as she did horses, and he taught her how to dive and stay under and the principles of correct breathing and how to conserve her strength over a long stretch.

It was difficult for Veronica to recall exactly when she began to notice that when Charles had to be away on business or for one reason and another, the friends who came to visit them at Marbury

were usually quite different ones from those who came when he was there. It must, she decided, have been when she was about seven or eight that this fact dawned on her consciousness, though it was not until much later that she began to look upon it as being somehow a little strange. Fran for instance never showed up when Charles was present, nor did some of the young men and their wives, nor the young men who were frequently Delia's guests when she was alone in the house with her children and Katie or Fran. Little by little Veronica learned to distinguish between the temperaments and characteristics of all these people, and it seemed to her that those who came with Charles were a livelier crew, more like him in their tastes, greater favorites with herself and Nick than were those who came when he was away. These last seemed even to have a certain positive physical dissimilarity from the first in much the same fashion as the orioles who nested in the elm trees were dissimilar to the jays, though both are birds and both live in trees, and Veronica learned to think of this second group as being particularly Charles friends, in the intangible way in which Delia's friends were more or less exclusively hers.

One facet of the arrangement which puzzled Veronica was her Aunt Fran's place in it. Although Fran and her mother were twins, it had always appeared to her that the resemblance ended where it began—in their looks. In every other respect she would have expected Fran to have far more in common with Charles and his coterie than with Delia and hers, yet this apparently was not so. It was not until much later—not, in fact, until shortly before Charles' death, that it occurred to Veronica to wonder how it happened that Fran was never a visitor in the house at a time when Charles was home, and why her aunt's appearances seemed to coincide like clockwork with his periodic absences. For some reason she found it difficult to accept the explanation which Katie readily supplied in answer to her question. "They don't get along too well, your father and Mrs. Hight," adding by way of a dividend: "They never have." Even if this were true, Veronica felt pretty sure that it could not be due to the single obvious reason why anyone should have objected to sharing the same roof with Fran—her drinking. Charles liked his liquor, so did his friends, and she felt instinctively that it was not in his nature to carry any objection which he might have had on the score of Fran's overdoing to the extent of leaving his home on protracted business trips whenever she was due to arrive. What then, did keep him away, and what could be the reason of their not, as Katie had put it, getting along too well, or of having never got along? Veronica had the impulse, on several occasions, to put the question to Charles himself, but some childish qualm of tenderness, a fear perhaps of placing him, whom she loved above all human beings, in an embarrassing corner, always intervened and she said nothing. She could of course have appealed to her mother for enlightenment, but by the time her interest had reached the thermal point she had passed that of ever asking Delia anything. There remained Fran, and Veronica decided to tackle her aunt on the mystery the very next time she showed up. The opportunity presented itself during the summer preceding Charles' death, when he had to go away to some lawyers' convention at Atlantic City, and sure enough, this was the signal for Fran to come east for a visit with Delia and the children at the Marbury house.

Veronica had by this time worked herself into a state of secret resentment against her aunt for what she now firmly believed to be the reason for these separations—if Fran were not to come then Charles would not have to go, and she, Veronica, would not be continually faced by the prospect of that unendurable blight which descended upon her world the minute the door had closed behind him. She was never to forget that last summer without him, and looking back on it she told herself that it was in the nature of a preparation, an initiation into what she was to experience when he was dead. She felt the very air to be altered; an unnatural silence settled over everything, and she could not bring herself to go into the woods for walks even when Delia and Fran offered to go with her or went by themselves with Nick toddling between them, holding their hands. For Veronica there was nothing but emptiness, a hole delved in the center of the world, into which Charles had cruelly and inexcusably vanished, leaving her to shift for herself.

One night Fran, who had the adjoining room, heard her sobbing and came to her room and sat down on the edge of the bed.

"What's the matter, moppet?" Fran asked, and stroked her hair, lying dark as seaweed on the pillow.

Suddenly and with a concentration of bitterness she herself was not prepared for, Veronica cried out: "Why do you keep coming to us and driving Father away? Why do you, Fran? *Why . . . why?*"

There was a brief and astounded silence, then Fran gave a queer laugh. "Why you crazy kid! What's got into you?"

Veronica twisted violently over on her side and lay with her back to her aunt, her face leached in tears, her throat swollen so she could hardly breathe. Fran leaned over her and Veronica got the familiar, inevitable odor of whisky on her aunt's breath.

"Nonny, what is it? What's bothering you, honey? Tell me. Tell Fran."

But Veronica could say no more, and in a minute or two Fran got up and went to find Delia, leaving mother and daughter alone together. Delia put her hand on the child's shoulder and kept it there for a moment without speaking, then she said gently: "Is there anything worrying you, pet?"

Veronica got it out then, viciously, between sobs: "Why must Father go away every time Fran comes to see us? Why can't he stay? Why does she have to come to us the way she does?"

Delia replied calmly, her hand stroking the tense shoulder under the bedsheet. "You're not being very bright, my sweet. It's nobody's fault that Father has to be gone on business when Fran comes to visit. You've heard about coincidences. That's how it happens."

Veronica twisted back towards her, her wet face suddenly hard and unchildlike in the glow of the bedlight which Delia had turned on. "Is that so?" She stared at her mother. "Is that so?

Then why did Katie tell me that Father and Fran don't get along, and that they never have?"

"Katie only told you what is perfectly true. There's nothing very mysterious about it. Lots of people don't get along. But the reason why he goes away when he does is because his business takes him. Look, Nonny. Why don't you ask Father, yourself, when he gets home? Or if you like call him up at Atlantic City . . . I have the number of his hotel. Would it make you feel better to do that?"

Veronica lay silent, her eyes hard as agates. A strange thought was shaping itself in her anguished mind. Delia was being just a little bit too calm, too self-possessed to be convincing. She was acting like a trained nurse when one had measles, or like the doctor who came to take your pulse and whose hands were always sure and cool and steady, and who was never fazed . . . never, by anything no matter how sick people got, no matter even if they died.

By now the private and dangerous game which Veronica played with Delia had become a habit. It was a game which she'd labelled Cats and Mice, or Seeing without being Seen, and it consisted of her pretending to believe what she didn't believe, of permitting her mother to imagine that in any given argument, she'd been won over and convinced when the contrary was the truth. So now after waiting a few minutes, Delia bent and kissed her, put out the light, and went away. And when the door had closed on her mother Veronica sat up in bed and listened to the voices in the next room. Subdued voices, pitched just above a whisper, but she got some of it.

"You didn't say anything, did you, Fran?"

"Say anything? What would I say to upset her like that?"

"I don't know. She's got something on her mind. It worries me."

"Nonsense. She's missing Charles, that's all. You've told me she always goes into a tizzy when he leaves home."

"I know, but this trick she has of putting two and two together . . . and I hate to see her so upset."

Their voices fell into an indistinguishable murmur, then Fran laughed. "She's nuts about him, isn't she?" Another laugh. Then Delia's voice, murmuring something, and Fran, with a yawn: "Well, it's a wise child, I guess, that knows its own father. . . ." Veronica knew better than to go to Katie with that one, or go to anyone else for that matter. She put it away in the back of her mind for safe keeping, and the following winter, at school, the older sister of a classmate obliged her with an explanation of Fran's remark, which, if it did little to clear up the mystery, seemed nevertheless to have a definite place within it.

On fine days during Fran's visit they went swimming. Fran was a fine swimmer and would spend hours at the pool or sunning herself on a blanket on the grass with nothing on except her sunglasses, and Delia was worried for fear the neighbors might call and find her completely unclad. Fran would laugh and say: "So what?" and Veronica privately sided with her aunt, remembering that Charles occasionally made the same reply—"So what?"—when Delia protested about his reckless driving, or his walking nude around the house, or telling dirty stories.

Charles did not come back until the week after Fran had returned to San Francisco, and by that time Veronica had lost weight from not eating properly and her eyes had dark shadows from not sleeping, and one day she had heard Fran remark to Delia: "The child acts like a woman in love!" And Delia gave Veronica a quick glance, but said nothing.

That, Veronica calculated, was probably the same night when Fran and Delia had one of their violent quarrels over Fran's drinking.

"Please, Fran, no more tonight. Not with the children around."

"They're asleep."

"Please, Fran."

"Oh God, Delia! Can one more, more or less, make any difference?"

"You're crocked. You can hardly stand up straight."

"Well, I'll sober up by taking a dip before going to bed."

"You'll hurt yourself."

"And a lot you'd care if I did."

"Oh stop it, Fran . . . please stop it."

"Think what a lot it would let you out of if I were to drown or break my neck or die of D.T.'s!" And with a drunken laugh: "You with your secrets, I with mine! And Charles, poor dear Charles . . . such a boy at heart!"

A door had slammed and there'd been a dull fury of voices behind it, then after a while Fran had come weaving into Veronica's room.

"Awake, kiddo? Like to take a swim with me?"

They'd crept out of the house without Delia hearing them, and slipped into the dark pool where the stars broke in tiny explosions and it was cold and rather wonderful to be in the black starlit water at that hour, and Veronica had thought: "If only Father were here!"

Emboldened by the darkness, by Fran's tipsy friendliness, she asked suddenly: "Don't you wish Father was here now, Fran?"

Fran, floating stark naked and shining in the velvety water, laughed. "Wouldn't be proper, would it? Under the circumstances."

At that moment there was Delia standing at the edge of the pool, saying in a hard voice: "Veronica, come out at once. It's too late and too cold for you to be in the water."

Fran had protested angrily: "Leave the child alone for a change, Dele! She won't melt."

"Veronica, did you hear me?"

"It doesn't become you to act the heavy mama, Delia. Leave her alone. She likes being with me. Don't you, Non?"

Suddenly, amazingly, Delia had leaped into the pool in her nightgown and was pushing Veronica towards the ladder at one end. "Go on, Veronica. Hurry up and get out."

Fran was laughing and thrashing in the water behind them.

"Honest to God, Delia, the way you act one would think. . . ."

Delia followed Veronica up the ladder and took her by the hand, quite roughly, and led her back to the house and into her—Delia's—room. "You'll sleep in here tonight."

It was a voice Veronica could not remember having heard before. Delia got a towel and rubbed her down, then turned back the covers of Charles' bed, next to her own. "Get in there, Nonny, and go to sleep."

Veronica snuggled down into Charles' bed and glanced furtively at her mother. Delia was getting out of her wet nightgown and was shivering and there was a strange expression on her face, a desperate knotted look as though she were holding back some terrific explosion of wrath; she said no more but found another nightgown and got into her own bed and turned off the light. For a long time Veronica lay staring into the dark, hearing an owl hoot in the woods, hearing Fran come into the house and go to her own room and the door close after her, and then there was nothing except the sound of the wind stirring the oak leaves beyond the darkened windows, and she longed for Charles with such intensity that it seemed he must know it and come home, open the door and walk in and pick her up in his arms as he usually did after an absence, and push the hair back from her forehead and kiss her, and say: "How's my girl?" And she whispered to herself in the huddled warmth of the bedclothes: "He is my father, he *is*, and I'll die if he doesn't come back soon. I'll die."

She didn't die. Fran went away, and then Charles came home, and the following spring when she was ten years old he died, and for a long time after that she had not wanted to go back to the house in Marbury, nor ever to go near the swimming pool in which he'd taught her to swim, or go walking in the woods along the old cart track beside ancient stone walls. And she never had gone to see his grave in the tiny cemetery beyond the hickory trees, though Nick went often, and told her about it. She hated the house in Marbury and everything connected with it, though the violence of her feeling passed with time, and changed, and became something quite different, melancholy yet strangely exciting as she began to write about it with that special sense which a writer develops about certain places, people, things that he knows very well have always existed in and of themselves but which now take on a life new to them, and become the creatures of his imagination in a realm known only to him.

CHAPTER

XXIX

CHRIS took the Seventy-second Street entrance to the west side drive and as he came up into it he saw the long arc of the drive's lights falling away before his eyes, and the river striped with color from advertising signs on the Jersey side, and the great bridge ahead. The night was cold, clear, and the car's radio tuned to a Rock 'n' Roll program to which Nick was whistling an accompaniment from the back seat.

Chris slipped off his glove and reached for Veronica's hand. The bridge streamed through the darkness before them, ruby dots of color sliding across its length like beads on an abacus. Affected by the sight, by the proximity of the girl beside him, by a rich vista of days and nights freighted with a long-contained desire, Chris turned off the radio and began suddenly to recite, his voice clear and precise above the sound of the car:

> *"Under the shadow by the piers I waited;*
> *Only in darkness is thy shadow clear.*
> *The City's fiery parcels all undone,*
> *Already snow submerges an iron year . . .*
>
> *O Sleepless as the river under thee,*
> *Vaulting the sea, the prairies dreaming sod,*
> *Unto us lowliest sometimes sweep, descend*
> *And of thy curveship lend a myth to God."*

He finished and after a pause Veronica said: "Pity Crane had to die."

"He'd shot his bolt, hadn't he? I mean, like Rimbaud, he was through early."

"I can't help wondering what he might have written if he'd lived to read that sign: 'In event of enemy attack do not stop. Drive off the bridge.' "

> "O harp and altar of the fury fused,
> (How could mere toil align thy choiring strings!)
> Terrific threshold of the prophet's pledge,
> Prayer of pariah, and the lover's cry,—"

Nick sat in the back seat, listening to their voices. He was troubled by thoughts which he found difficult wholly to understand. This had been a strange Christmas, the strangest he could remember, and he hadn't enjoyed it much. In fact he told himself now that he hadn't enjoyed it at all, notwithstanding the presents, the gaiety, and the excitement of the occasion which had always delighted him in the past. Nothing had seemed in the least the way it used to be as recently as last year—as last Thanksgiving even, and he resented it bitterly and with a petulance which he hated in himself but which he could not restrain. At first he'd tried to pin the pervading air of strangeness down to Fran's unaccountable absence. It struck him as being plain crazy that she should have come all the way from California to be near her family, and then not come to them at least for Christmas Day. Delia had shown him the telegram which she'd received the day before, and which said simply: "Peace on earth, good will to men. Merry Christmas. Signed Fran."

There had also been a Christmas card for him, with a check from Fran, and one for Veronica, but it seemed that Fran herself would not be with them. "I don't understand," Nick said. "What's got into her all of a sudden?"

Delia shrugged and replied with unusual indifference that Fran apparently had other plans for the holiday. "I talked to her on the phone and she said she'd met some old friends of hers down there on the Island, and they'd begged her to spend Christmas day with them, and that she'd be coming in town right afterwards and would see us then."

"Old friends!" Nick repeated, sceptically. "Who in the hell old friends would she have found on Long Island, and why haven't we ever heard of them before?"

"Oh well," Delia said cheerfully. "If that's the way Fran wants it, we have no right to bother her, after all."

Nick let it go. He was actually not sure how much he really wanted to see his aunt after that last evening he'd spent with her in the Village at Thanksgiving. Memories of it had pursued him through the intervening weeks, and he couldn't help feeling that their relationship had undergone a peculiar and rather disturbing change. He found it hard to think of himself as a young nephew anymore, and of her as a somewhat unpredictable but still, well understood and well beloved aunt. She was unpredictable all right . . . he smiled a little grimly as he remembered the fight in the bar, and the scene in her room at the Leonard afterwards. Then he tried to persuade himself that perhaps if they were to meet again under normal circumstances, here at home, among familiar surroundings, everything would be as it was in the beginning before they went on that crazy binge . . .

At this point in his musing Nick's uneasiness took another turn and he shifted in his seat, staring at the lights of Riverdale as they streamed past his window. Was it possible, he asked himself, to take even one's mother's existence for granted? Something had happened there, too. He'd become aware of it the instant that he set foot in the house three days ago. A feeling indefinable but intense like one you get when you go to a place where a person has died or just been born—it was as if the air itself had taken on a new character with the unwelcome knowledge, shaking you to your depths, that everything and every one you have ever known and believed beyond the possibility of change were no longer what you thought they were. And it all came from the way that his mother had greeted him the afternoon he'd come home for the Christmas vacation. Ordinarily, whenever they met after such a separation Delia was gay and affectionate in an unobtrusive sort of way. He'd never been able to endure too close a contact with her, for their love was an indirect thing, freighted with mysteries each was content to let alone. But this Christmas when she'd come to the door to let him into the house Nick had sensed her emotion instantly, piercingly, a current of feeling sharper than any he'd ever detected in her—something that was not really intended for him.

She was happy. He frowned, thinking of it. Happy! For days he had carried the discovery round with him in a furtive sort of way as though it were something strange and rather indecent which he must try to understand in private. She was happy and she was different . . . Christmas morning when a florist's box arrived addressed to her he carried it up to her room and watched while she opened it, and then he understood why she was *different*. Lifting out the yellow roses that Wallingford had sent her she bent her face over them and smiled at Nick with an expression in her eyes—as though she were trying to tell him something for which she could not find the right words, but he'd left the room before she could speak, his heart raw within him.

Throughout the next few days he behaved abominably. During Christmas dinner, to which the Wallingfords came, and the Bowers, he insisted on drinking more wine with the meal than he was supposed to, smoked one cigarette after another, and loudly and continually deplored the absence of his Aunt Fran and Miriam Werth.

"Off with the old friends," he muttered in a tone intended especially for his mother's ear. "Off with the old friends, on with the new!" Then, aloud: "Why didn't Miriam come tonight? I bet she wasn't even invited." He stared at Veronica. "I thought she was supposed to be your friend. What's happened so suddenly that you didn't want to ask her?"

"Don't be a dope," Veronica retorted, coolly. For some reason she appeared less affected than the others by his odd behavior.

"Miriam was invited, so was Fran. They had other dates, that's all."

"Can't say that I blame them. No fun to be where you feel you're in the way."

He'd continued in that vein, noisy and insufferable, taking a savage pleasure in his mother's astonished silence, in Donald's and the Bowers' guarded good humor, and in the particular attention which he forced them to extend to him.

Later, in the kitchen, Katie had said to him reproachfully:

"Grow up, Nick."

"I feel more like throwing up."

She took the half finished glass of wine from his hand and emptied it in the sink. "Throw up, then. It would make more sense than anything else you've done all evening."

He felt weak, as though he really might be sick; he wanted to burst into tears, to fall on her neck, kick the furniture.

She looked at him discerningly out of her old, wisdom-ridden eyes. "Why don't you go get yourself a dame? Maybe that'd be the answer."

"The answer to what?" He didn't want to ask, he wanted nothing so much as a good rip-roaring fight, with her—with anyone. "The answer to what, old Know-it-all?"

"To whatever it is that's eating you."

"Me? I'm the only one with a good digestion in this whole goddam outfit."

He stamped out, ashamed of himself but unable to do anything about it. It didn't help when Wallingford singled him out for particular kindliness with talk about their projected visit to Todd's Harbor next summer, or for Delia to suggest that instead of his driving to New Hampshire with Chris and Veronica, he might like to stay home and go to the theater with her. "Or if you'd prefer, we might go out to the house at Marbury for the weekend."

He'd stared at her with hostile eyes. "Why should I want to go to Marbury this time of year? To feed the chickadees?"

"Darling, just as you like."

He'd felt her tenderness, her seeing through his act, but he was not grateful for the favor, aware now that he shared it with someone else, and detesting the thought.

That night when he'd gone to bed Veronica came to his room and curled up near his feet, and for some minutes neither spoke. She said at last: "That was a stupid way for you to act this evening."

"Thanks."

"Making an exhibition of yourself."

"Thanks." Then, vindictively: "I've seen you, at times."

She was silent, then: "Yes, you have. I'm not a very good example to you, I'm afraid."

An unusual admission from her, but he swallowed his surprise.

"It's not your job, and if it was you could stuff it."

She lighted a cigarette and tossed the package to him. "Who's job is it, then? Mother's?" And when he said nothing she gave him a faint smile. "Why should you care so much if they *are* having an affair?"

He laughed. "I care? What about you?"

"There's no point letting a thing like that hurt you. Stupid."

"So what?"

She looked at him steadily. "I hate to see you being hurt, and there isn't anything I can do about it except tell you it's stupid. I know what I'm talking about."

"Sure you know what you're talking about. You've written a book so you know everything."

She put her hand on the shape of his feet.

"Nick, listen. You can't do anything about it. You can't do anything about other people. But you can stop yourself from being hurt too much by just telling yourself over and over that you don't care."

"Is that what you've been telling yourself about Mr. Wallingford?"

He'd expected to get a rise out of her with that, but she surprised him again by her refusal to be moved. "If you want to know, yes. I like him. Why shouldn't I? But he likes Delia better, so that's that."

"And Chris?"

"Chris is all right." She hesitated. "Relationships aren't as simple as you seem to think. But you'll learn."

"Stuff it, will you, and let me go to sleep?"

"That was a silly act you put on tonight because you let everyone know what was happening to you. Everyone—even the Bowers, even Katie."

He smoked angrily, avoiding her eyes. She said in a gentler tone than he could remember ever hearing from her: "I hated to see it. Since Father died I've been fonder of you than of anyone. I still am. I hate to think of you being hurt." She gazed at him with a gathering intensity. "There may come a time . . . something might happen . . . to make you not like me, or at any rate, to be mad at me. When that time comes . . . if it comes, I want you to promise me something."

He looked at her suspiciously. "What?"

"That you won't just take things for granted, for what they may appear to be, but that you'll come and ask me. Promise you'll do that and I'll promise I'll be honest with you."

"I don't know what the hell you're talking about."

"Not now, but you might, some time. Promise?"

"If you promise to stuff it and let me go to sleep."

She rose and stood for a moment looking down at him. "Quit being hurt and mad. You can't marry Delia, you know."

In the front seat of the automobile, Chris's head and Veronica's were illumined briefly in the beam of an oncoming car, then he heard Chris quoting again:

> "A quatre heures du matin, l'été
> Le sommeil d'amour dure encore.
> Sous les bocages s'évapore
>   L'odeur du soir fété . . ."

"Give me a minute," Veronica said, consideringly. They were approaching the Merrit Parkway, a concrete channel opened before them, bordered by trees, the square eyes of houses peering behind flowerless shrubs in the winter dark.

"Rimbaud?" Veronica asked. "Sounds like him."

"Rimbaud. Only it isn't summer."

"Though it will soon be four o'clock in the morning!"

Nick watched their two heads close together, saw Veronica turn her face towards Chris and Chris bend down to kiss her. He looked away, feeling lonelier and older than he had ever felt in his life.

CHAPTER

XXX

THE evening after their children had left for New Hampshire, Donald drove Delia out to the house in Connecticut. On the Saw Mill River the willows looked like illustrations by Rackham in the yellow flare of the headlights, and it started to snow, large hesitant flakes drifting through the darkness, then disappearing.

Delia murmured uneasily: "Perhaps I should have used more persuasion on Nick and got him to come with us."

"He didn't know I was coming, did he?"

She laughed guiltily. "I didn't mention it, no. I thought I'd wait and see how things broke."

"I'm afraid he'd have resented my being along, but he's got to get used to the idea sooner or later." Donald glanced at her profile in the faint glow of the dashlight. "Don't you think we might as well let them into the secret, Delia? It isn't as if everyone didn't have a pretty good suspicion about us anyway."

She hesitated, leaning against his shoulder. "I'd more or less intended to break it to Nick if he'd come with us tonight." Then, after a pause: "I know you're getting restive, but darling—just a little while longer! It's been so long since I've enjoyed a—a situation in privacy."

"If that's your real reason!"

"It's the most important one. You know, orientals believe it is a mistake to disclose one's happiness and good fortune to the world. They say it's just asking for trouble."

"We've got to come to it some day. I certainly have no intention of keeping our *marriage* a secret, have you?"

"Of course not. But this . . . to be together as we are, seeing each other privately, the sense of owning our own lives." She sighed. "You've no idea how I dread the fuss, nice though it will be in a lot of ways."

"Why not in every way?" He put an arm round her, drew her against him. "Don't tell me you have any reservations, at this stage."

"None about us, no. Just about the children, and Fran."

"Listen, Delia. This is *our* weekend. No children, no Fran, no complications. I won't have it."

She was meekly silent, but the thought of Nick haunted her. That he was jealous and unhappy over her friendship for Donald, she knew very well, and it gave her a helpless feeling to realize that there was little she could do about it, that this was a storm which he must ride out alone—the first in his life! She tried to deflect her thoughts with more cheerful ones about Fran and Veronica. Fran had called up from East Hampton and had sounded sober and in good form. The job at the bank was holding up—didn't pay much but it gave her something to do and extra cash while she looked around for something better. She was seeing quite a bit of her friends the Pearsons with whom she was to spend the day. Delia didn't really mind, did she? They would be together right after Christmas and plan something really nice over New Year's, with the children . . . wonderful, wonderful to know that that hideous quarrel was a thing of the past, and Fran on her feet—for the time being at any rate. As for Veronica, the child seemed to have taken a round turn on herself and to be making a definite effort towards friendliness. She'd been gay and relaxed during Christmas, helpful with Nick, and her relations with Chris were apparently restored to their original happy basis, for Delia had come on them unexpectedly, in each other's arms in a corner of the hall, the dazed, lost look of lovers in their faces. The sight had thrilled her almost unbearably, sending her back to her own lover in a mood of such passionate abandonment that—constantly surprising as he was always to find her—Donald had asked in wonder what it was all about.

They were in Connecticut now and as they left the main highway and drove along a narrow road with a heavy growth of trees on either side Delia said: "It's not far now. But watch out for the deer."

She'd hardly spoken when one came bounding out from the darkness and across their path, its tail a white banner lost almost at once as it melted into the trees on the farther side. The headlights picked up a detail here and there, fragments of an old stone wall sparkling with mica, bracken still golden above a powdering of snow, and last summer's oriole's nest swaying empty from a skeletal branch.

Delia said: "It's lovely in the daytime. We'll take a walk after breakfast. There are cart tracks which must go back more than a hundred years."

The road streamed ahead, a dark channel in which a few drifting snowflakes melted as they fell. "That opening to our left leads through the woods to the cemetery where Charles is buried. The next turn is our driveway . . . there's the mail box."

It gave Wallingford a curious pang to see the name painted in worn capitals on the metal box: Charles Dalton, and perhaps guessing his thought Delia explained that it had never seemed worth while to change it.

They turned in at the driveway and drove cautiously up the weed-grown lane littered with fallen leaves, and then, abruptly, Donald stopped the car, leaving the motor idling softly. He peered into the heavy gloom of the oak copse where the russet leaves still clung, giving a richness to the branches until he switched off the lights.

"Ghosts," he said, and nodded.

Delia caught the glimmer of light in the farther density. It shifted, flickered, seemed to go out, then burst into brighter flame.

Delia said in a low voice: "Someone's got a fire going in the living room—the fireplace faces that window. And there's another light, in the kitchen."

Donald turned off the motor. "Well?" he asked. "What do we do now?"

Delia hesitated, at something of a loss. It was a lonely spot, her nearest neighbor a mile up the road and probably asleep, since it was long past midnight. As they watched, figures seemed to cross and recross before the light, and Delia fancied she heard voices inside the house.

"Tramps," Donald suggested. "Or some loving couple in search of a roof, like us." He reached into the glove compartment and found a flashlight. "You wait here while I go take a look."

"Oh no you don't. I'm coming with you."

They got out of the car and began to walk up the drive under cover of the trees, their snow-booted feet noiseless on the packed leaves. Delia thought uneasily: Suppose they turn out to be ugly customers, what should we do? Donald took her hand.

"Scared?"

"I hate the idea of trespassers, and they might set fire to the place."

"We'll reconnoiter from outside, to begin with."

They made their way with caution, then Delia spotted an automobile parked near the front door. "Couldn't be anyone I know," she whispered. "No friend would think of coming down without asking . . ."

Donald considered for a moment. "Let's try to get a peek at them through a window. If it looks bad we'll go find the sheriff."

The house stood dark and square against a rampart of trees, and as they aproached it they saw that there were lights in several windows and in the downstairs hall. In anticipation of possible winter visits, Delia never had the power shut off, and now the look of her house lighted up as though for a party seemed the last word in effrontery, and her nervousness evaporated in sudden, proprietary rage.

"Two years ago people broke in and stole the blankets! Last year they came again and left a frightful mess and burned a hole in the living room floor. Heaven knows why the house didn't go up in smoke. I could kill them!"

Donald motioned her to silence, and they stood for a moment, listening. There was no mistaking the sound of voices, muffled though they were by the intervening walls. A man's laugh was followed by the high-pitched scream of a woman, and more laughter. Hand in hand, like children playing hide and seek, Delia and Wallingford ran across the frozen lawn and came to a crouching halt among the azaleas under one of the living room windows. Here they waited, getting their breath and listening to the sounds from the room beyond. Presently they heard another, more disturbing noise—that of a fire crackling dangerously, and as if in corroboration of their fear a voice cried suddenly: "For God's sake, Luigi! No more kerosene. What do you want to do—burn down the joint?"

Delia caught her breath, and raising herself on her toes, peered into the room, Donald beside her. The parlor was more or less a shambles. Dust covers had been pulled off the furniture and thrown in corners, glasses, bottles and plates of food were scattered around among odds and ends of clothing, and a log fire was burning savagely in the fireplace, aided by copious applications of kerosene from a Cape Cod lighter beside the hearth.

On the floor before the fire a man sat warming his bare feet, and a young woman in red slacks and a black lace brassiere was pouring a drink from a bottle into one of Delia's favorite glasses. But Delia's attention was concentrated on the couple seated on the sofa at right angles to the window. One, a heavy-set man in a crumpled business suit and with the face of a depraved baby, the other—Fran.

As Wallingford gazed at the tableau vivant a curious premonition which had assailed him when he'd first got out of the car now made the whole scene somehow inevitable. At this remove Fran's resemblance to Delia was unmistakable and he felt a jarring within him, as though the missing part of a puzzle had somehow fallen into its rightful place.

While they watched, Fran rose and began to walk unsteadily across the room towards the fire. Her voice reached them where they stood outside the window. "Damn you, you wop! Didn't I tell you not to put more oil in that fire?"

The barefooted man was young and dark, and looked as if he might be dangerous. "Who you calling a wop?"

"Damp that fire down before we all burn up."

The man on the sofa called to them placatingly: "Cut out the rough talk. Come on back here, Franny girl. Fire's O.K. Luigi's no wop, he's a friend. Come on back and I'll mix you another drink."

Fran was swaying slightly, and she looked, Donald thought, impressive though drunk.

"Get up," she told Luigi, and gave him a shove with her foot. "Get up and get some water and put that thing out. I didn't invite you here to burn the house down."

It was now the turn of the woman in the red slacks. "Who was it invited us out here anyway? Think we'd of come if we hadn't been invited? You lousy old bag, now you call us names. Don't you take it from her, Lou. You don't have to. Nobody's got to take it from her. Can't pay her own debts then goes around calling people names."

"Nobody's going to call me names," Luigi said, and rose to his feet.

Delia whispered: "We better go in."

She unlocked the front door and they went in, across the

hall to the parlor, in time to see Luigi seize Fran by the hair and begin violently to shake her while the woman in the red slacks laughed and the man on the sofa besought everyone to quit trying to spoil a good party and to join him in another drink.

Donald crossed the room and caught Luigi by the arm. "All right," Donald said in a dispassionate voice. "I guess that'll be enough for now, Luigi."

Luigi released Fran and stared at the interloper. "Who you calling Luigi, and who asked you to come busting in here, big boy?"

Donald dropped his arm. "Calm down," he said, soothingly. "Calm . . ."

He never finished the sentence for Luigi's left hand slid into his pocket and flew up, catching him full in the face. He lost his balance, recovered it, and came charging back at the Italian, only to receive another blow that sent him reeling into a chair, blood from a set of brass knuckles leaking into his right eye. His jaw, too, seemed to have come loose and his mouth seemed suddenly to be filled with salt.

Delia went over to him, snatched the scarf from her head, and made it into a pad which she held against his face. Over her shoulder she addressed the suddenly silent group: "This is my house, and you'll please leave it—now, at once."

"Your house!" Luigi exclaimed. He looked at Fran. "What's this dame doing here anyway—and that guy? What's the idea, them busting in and trying to pick a fight with me?"

"You better all get out," Fran said, unsteadily. She turned away from Delia. "Go on home. The party's over."

She sat down on the nearest chair and began to do up her hair. The man on the sofa started to rise to his feet, then collapsed.

"What the hell?" he inquired, plaintively. "What's it all about? Friends of yours, Franny? Why'nt you tell us you were expecting company? Loss room, ah? Come on over here and tell me what'n the hell it's all 'bout."

The young woman in the red slacks had risen from the floor and was struggling into a thick cable-knit sweater through the neck of which her face presently popped forth, like a clown's. "Nobody got to ask me to leave," she declared, with hauteur. "But before I go I'm going to collect my dough, and Luigi's." She stared contemptuously down at Fran. "Couldn't pay your bill at the night club so we bailed you out. Hadn't been that you were Pearsy's doll we'd have told you to go you know what. And he should of known better to pick up with a character like you. *Lady,* he said. Lady my ass!"

She whirled on Delia. "Sisters, are you? Well, Fran here claimed she didn't have the price of a drink left when the time came we had to leave the Blue Rooster Inn, see? It was her idea we all drive out here in Pearsy's car and spend the night. Now we're told to get the hell out, and it's going on two in the morning. Nice way to repay friends what help you out on a rainy day!"

Luigi had found his shoes and socks and was putting them on. He slid an uneasy glance at Donald, who was beginning to come to but who looked deathly ill.

"Come on, Bella," said Luigi. "Let's get going. Ready, Pearsy?"

"Can't fine my nettie," Pearsy said mournfully. "Look und' the sofa, Lou, see if it's there. Makes me feel like I might woops if I bend. Don' like blood. Never have. Always makes me wan' woops."

"The hell with your necktie. Come on."

The girl called Bella shook her head. "I'm not leaving until Fran pays back the dough she borrowed from us. Sixteen bucks, and that don't include the tip we left for the waiter."

"Neb mine the dough," Pearsy besought them unhappily. "I'll take care of it. Fran's my guest. I'll take care everything do with Franny."

"Why the hell should you?" Bella shouted at him, emotionally. "Just bcause she took a roll with you in the back seat coming out here, you responsible for her debts? Besides I'm not collecting from you. I'm collecting from *her.*"

Delia opened her pocketbook and took out two ten dollar bills.

"Here," she said, handing the money to Bella. "That should take care of everything."

Fran watched the transaction, her face twitching. She was on the verge of a seizure and the sweat stood out on her skin like rain.

"Get out," she whispered. "Get out, all of you get out!"

Pearsy clambered to his feet, assisting himself by means of some invisible rope trick, and looked reproachfully at her. "You and me had a little agreement, remember? Back there'n the 'n. Little agreement. Now why'n hell all've a sudden . . ."

Luigi glared at Bella, who was pawing through her pocketbook, spilling lipstick, compacts, and loose cigarettes on the floor.

"What'd you think you're doing, Bella? You got the dough. Now come on for Christ sake!"

"I'm trying to find the change. It was sixteen bucks, and she give me twenty—that leaves four bucks I owe her."

"Please don't," Delia begged desperately. "Never mind the change. Please go. My friend here is very ill. Please."

"Nuts," Bella retorted, and thumbed through a lump of assorted currency at the bottom of her pocketbook. "Nuts to you, sister. I may be no lady according to your standards, but I don't go interfering in other folks' affairs neither. Nor I'm no short change artist. Sixteen dollars was what we paid out for your sister's share of the party, and that leaves four dollars change. We'll skip the tip."

She handed the money to Delia, then picked up her fallen impedimenta and snapped her purse shut with an air. "Sorry the boy friend got hurt, but Lou here is a boxing champion and how was he to know you weren't both just strangers walked in to hold us up?" She gave Fran a dirty look. "Bye bye, babe! Guess you know where to find Pearsy when you want him, but you can count us out on the next round."

Luigi dragged her out of the room and Pearsy trailed after them, casting dolorous glances over his shoulder at Fran as he went. The front door slammed after them, and the rasp of tires on the frosty ground faded into silence.

Delia bent over Wallingford. "I'm going to get you some ice to put on that."

"I'm all right," he muttered. "I'll come out with you."

He rose, steadying himself on her shoulder while Fran sat rigidly staring at them. Then suddenly, appallingly, she began to scream.

CHAPTER

XXXI

DONALD opened his eyes in a glare of sunlight and was immediately conscious of a dual impact of pain and cold. The bandage which Delia had made for him had slipped off during the night, and now, stretched on the sofa and swathed in blankets, he blinked at a window fused with light, then closed his eyes again as the pain stabbed him wider awake. After a moment he tried, experimentally, opening and shutting the injured eye. The lid felt stiff and twice its natural size, but the pain, as he gradually realized, was due not to damage in the eye itself—he could see with it—but to the savage cut which extended from brow to cheek and merged with the one on his lower jaw. Freeing a hand he gently touched his eyelid, which seemed to spit back at him like a hot iron. Luigi, he thought. Nice character, Luigi. Bella too. And Pearsy. All nice characters, including Fran.

He closed his eyes and the events of the night gambolled past his vision like a succession of red-hot demons to the accompaniment of a noise which must have been going on for a long time—from the beginning of time, in a sort of extended scream like machinery out of order, knife-sharp, slicing the blessed oblivion of sleep into bloody rags.

He opened his eyes with a convulsive start and through a web of pain saw a blue jay perched on a branch outside the window. The screaming stopped, and heaven, blue-roofed above the snow, flowed gently into the room. Somewhere under him a vigilant furnace turned itself on like a creature coming to life, and he turned his head cautiously to see Delia asleep in a chair beside him, her face as expressionless as a sculptured angel on a gravestone. But her hair had fallen loose over the cushions and it had the life and movement of water moving over stones, shadowy and vibrant, inviting his touch. He reached out a hand and took a strand of it gently between his fingers. It felt like warm silk and sent a reviving thrill through his aching nerves. I'm alive, he reminded himself, wonderingly. I'm alive and she's still lovely, but there's Fran in the next room, and our weekend without complications has verily gone the way of all foul . . . He mused: That I should have thought to play the hero only to be knocked silly by a pint-sized character out of nowhere! Eschewing the tragic view and regarding all forms of violence as the nadir, that I should find myself caught in the gears like any unwary five-year old in a bandsaw. It called for a laugh, except for his jaw, which seemed to rule out laughter for some time to come, except perhaps from his friends.

Beyond the window the blue jay shone resplendent as a rajah in the diamond light, a breeze probed the oak leaves, mining gold, and Donald had a sudden craving to be out in all that clarity, to be part of it and to have it become part of him.

He rose and made his way to the bathroom, and the first glimpse of himself in the mirror was scarcely restorative. His jaw was badly swollen and his eye the shape and color of a baked apple. The slightest movement made his head feel as if it were stuffed with marbles. He managed somehow to get himself shaved and bathed his eye in cold water, telling himself that all he needed to confirm the myth of the age was a black eye-shade and a well cut Viyella shirt. Moving with the minimum of effort he went to the kitchen and started the coffee. They'd brought supplies with them from town—bread and butter, eggs, milk, a roast chicken, fruit. He found these in the refrigerator and realized that Delia must have fetched them from the car sometime during the preceding night.

Around him as he drank the coffee and eased a soft-boiled egg tenderly into his mouth, the house stood silent, abnormally normal considering what it had to take the night before. As the coffee and food went about their business, Donald began to feel better and found himself able to review the recent past with something approaching his customary sardonic outlook. The screaming noise had stopped at last, run down in his head like a machine that has run out of fuel, though the somewhat amputated view remained and he supposed would remain until his eye had healed and restored vision brought totality into focus. As it was now, all he could see was a blurred chiaroscuro of Fran when she started tearing off her clothes and screaming obscenities at Delia. "Always interfering . . . always horning in! All right, so it is your house . . . so's everything yours . . . this guy too no doubt, and where'd you pick him up? Superior . . . pure . . . damned creeping female Jesus . . . but this time I'm through . . . I've had it . . ."

She'd said other things, and Donald catalogued them methodically as he spread butter on a piece of bread and ate it like an old man who'd forgotten to bring his dentures to the party. There'd been quite a lot of other things—drunk, Fran was nothing if not fluent. And he wondered what could have caused her to break off when she did, and after a moment's wild staring at Delia and at himself—the unwinking, dilated eyes of one on the border of insanity—she'd rushed out of the house with Delia after her.

Dazed, half blind with pain, Donald had followed, forgetting his flashlight. Outdoors the nightmare assumed a worse tangibility, the figures of the two women springing like spectres through the darkness and vanishing into it, their voices splintering the night like splintering glass. There had been for him the strangeness of the place and the strangeness of the situation. Unused to the peculiar humiliation which pain inflicts and to an emergency which he had managed with such adroitness to keep out of his life, he remembered telling himself that this was not war, nor was it magnificent, and he would have nothing to do with it. He stumbled over mole runs and felt like weeping from the agony in his eye. The cold was a tiger that took great bites out of his flesh, and his gathering rage growled in his ears. Never in his life having wished anyone dead, he told himself that if he ever met Luigi again he'd kill him. Dimly, he remembered hearing Delia say that there was an empty swimming pool somewhere around and he heard himself mumbling that he hoped Fran might fall in it and break her neck.

Then a shadow moved towards him, arms went round his neck, a body pressed against his, lips found his lips and before he knew it he'd clasped her to him, returning her kisses with his bruised lips in an onrush of desire compounded of a stinging pain and strangeness in the erotic dark. In a second he realized that the woman in his arms was not Delia but Fran, her laughter muffled against his beaten face. "Oh darling!" She clung to him with the terrible strength of urgency. "Darling . . . darling . . ."

He tried to hold her off, then Delia was there, her voice near, collected, cool: "Go on back to the house, Donald. I'll take care of her."

Ignominiously he obeyed, and stumbled back to the house and to a bathroom, and was sick. What had that deluded hero Pearsy called it? Woopsing. Well, he'd woopsed, then staggered back to the warm, lighted parlor with its clutter and cigarette smoke, its atavistic scent of burning logs, and poured himself a drink from the remains of a bottle forgotten by Fran's guests. He had no idea how long a time passed before Delia returned, supporting her sister in her arms. Donald went to help her and between them they got the unconscious woman into bed on the couch of what used to be Charles' study. Delia found a heating pad and put it to Fran's feet. She bathed Fran's face and warmed her hands, then tucked the blankets round her and put out the light and left her, turning at last to him.

Donald felt her dominion over the crisis as, more than once in the brief time that he had known her, he'd felt the imminence of some new discovery. She made him lie down on the sofa and put an ice pack on his eye and removed his shoes and brought blankets to cover him. He let her wait on him. Luigi's punishment seemed to have peeled several layers from his faculties, and as he lay with closed eyes, his head a cavern filled with darting lights, chimera, echoes, it was with a special clarity that he heard Delia's movements as she brought wood from the woodbox in the hall and rebuilt Luigi's pyre into a lucid flame. He listened as she went the rounds of the house to make sure that the windows were closed, the doors locked, the furnace in working order, the pulse of her house beating a steady and recognizable rhythm . . . the rhythm of love.

"If there was one thing that Silvia lacked without knowing she lacked it—how could she know? It can't be feigned, and if she'd had it she would not have been Silvia—the one thing she lacked was the capacity for tenderness. You felt the lack of it in her touch, you missed it in her china cold eyes, her practical smile."

As the demons pranced through the reddened cavern behind his closed lids and hissed in his ears Donald heard himself answering a voice that seemed more insistent than the rest: "You missed the bus, Veronica! You missed the bus."

Then its wheels were rushing towards him with flashing brass and crashing cymbals and he'd fallen under them and felt their abraded edges cutting into his mind as a knife cuts cardboard and another voice was screaming in his ears: "Darling . . . darling . . ." Fran's voice, then Veronica's voice, the voice of defrauded love turned cannibal, battening, devouring: "She coveted only to be coveted, never to give, never to belong. . . ."

"Give me a raincheck on that, will you, Veronica?"

With a wrench that made him groan Donald had opened his eyes and saw Delia moving round the room, picking up the debris, setting chairs in their place, bringing the fiends of chaos to heel.

"Darling . . . darling . . ."

"Yes?" She left what she was doing and came to the sofa where he lay. "Hasn't the aspirin helped, Donald?" Deftly, she moved the ice pack, easing the pressure on his eye. "I wish I had a sleeping pill to give you."

He took her hand, drawing her down to sit on the sofa at his side.

"We didn't think we were going to need sleeping pills, did we?" he whispered with a grotesque attempt at a smile. She said nothing for a moment, and he felt her touch like a moth against his aching jaw. Then she said gently: "Don't try to talk or to move. It'll be easier tomorrow."

"Will it, Delia? Will you tell me, tomorrow?"

Returning her gaze was like peering into the infinite complex pattern of goldstone or agate. She bent and kissed him, his brows, the side of his nose, the unhurt cheek in a way he did not remember having been kissed before, and half alive though he felt he'd dragged her down to lie beside him, and then he supposed he'd gone to sleep or perhaps just passed out, awakening at high noon to hear the sun banging its fist against the sky and the blue jays shouting in the woods.

His breakfast finished, Donald went to the living room door and looked in. Delia still slept and there was no sound from Fran's room. Noiselessly, he let himself out of the house and winced as the cold sun beat up against his face. But there was no wind, the sky was limpid, and a woodpecker busy somewhere round a corner of the house. Skirting the empty swimming pool he came on the beginnings of a rough path through a break in a low stone wall, and decided to follow it.

The light snow of last night lay everywhere, patterned with the freshly made slots of deer, and that most beautiful of all tracks— a fox's, running blue with shadow through the woods, over the ridge to the graveyard where Charles lay buried. His was the newest headstone and the young granite sparkled next to the lichened stones over Michael Biggs and Mary his wife, of William and Reuben their sons, and Michael's father Edward Henry Biggs, born June 6th 1740, died May 12th, 1832. "The Lord hath given and the Lord hath taken away, blessed be the name of the Lord."

Nicholas Charles Dalton, aetat forty-eight years and three months, lay with his feet towards the east and his head beside a fir balsam which must by now have rooted among his bones. As Donald stood among those few headstones, twisted and toppled by frost and flood, he thought of others like them near his home in Maine. He'd always rather fancied such places, which had none of the sanctified pretensions of the more fashionable abodes of rest. These small, half forgotten, half neglected islands of melancholy satisfied his need for fitness when the hulabaloo was over. The thought of death inspired no profound emotion—he held it to be too trite for that. Rather as he looked around him at the cracked urns, the crudely chiselled lettering, the discolored granite and weathered slate, Donald could feel only wonder that so much that goes into life—and into books—the love making and the funny stories, the boozing, the niggling spite; wounds healed and sickness overcome, subtlety, sensitivity, day-to-day cowardliness and moments of high courage, everything that is deeply, silently felt and occasionally worth expressing, should come to this in the end.

He lit his pipe and marvelled that tobacco should taste so good as the windless cold numbed the pain in his battered eye. Overhead a jet plane traced its course by a long trail of vapor, which, as he watched it, uncoiled like a snake shedding its skin. Deadly and beautiful it was as it thinned out on the invisible currents of air.

At last he turned and followed the fox track which had led him here, and which now led him away, out of the graveyard, down the ridge to the path, thence to a stand of fir and hemlock black against the hickory growth. Sticking up from the snowy ground were the stumps of young trees cut years before, and he could smell the sunlight drawing fragrance from the living boughs.

Here the fox had paused, circled a stump with investigative nose and left the brush marks of its tail in the snow before turning off the path. From where he stood, Donald could see the exquisitely precise ovals of its track disappearing among the trees. He stood quite still, remembering days in Maine when he used to hunt foxes, of the peculiar charm of a wild creature's trail leading you on and on towards deeper mystery, until you came at last on its dead and mangled body or lost it at the entrance of its den. His pipe had gone out and he relit it, striking a match on one of the stumps which Charles had left. As the frail blue tendril of smoke rose in the air Donald stood with his gaze fixed on the fox tracks, and an extraordinary idea occurred to him. Incredible, grotesque—but it made better sense than *Silvia* ever did! He gave a sudden laugh, then put his hand to his injured jaw. God!

Last night when he'd looked in the parlor window and had seen Fran for the first time he'd had a sensation as though part of a puzzle were falling into its rightful place and that he would undoubtedly come back to it later for a final appraisal. Now it seemed as if the puzzle were spread before him on the snowy ground, but although the piece he remembered from last night was there, all right, the rest of the picture was not what he had thought it was. It was, indeed, entirely different, though with a completeness all its own. He tried to restrain a rising excitement by reminding himself that if Veronica could be mistaken, so could he, and the question remained, who was to put either of them right?

Last night before he fell asleep he'd asked Delia to tell him something. What a fool to imagine that she would! She'd buried it deeper than Charles was buried up there on the ridge, and a thing so buried powders away, so when you come to dig it up there's nothing to find, and only a particular richness to the grass to testify that there had been something, once. No, Delia would tell him nothing, and he would not ask her. Time enough when Veronica's novel was out and they faced each other at last. But would Delia tell . . . even then? She'd shown what she could take . . . wouldn't she even take Silvia, and say nothing? Donald felt an overpowering admiration for her, suddenly—an emotion complete of itself, one he could not recall having felt with such intensity for any other being, and for this too he was glad, since it made what they had together a thing also complete of itself, a condition in which neither Charles nor Clare nor Fran nor the children had any share.

Delia greeted him at the kitchen door. She looked pale, but composed. "I was beginning to wonder what had happened to you! Where did you go?"

He told her.

"But how did you find the shortcut through the woods? It's very misleading when there's snow on the ground."

"I borrowed Veronica's guidebook," he said, unthinking. Then going to her he took her in his arms. "This morning when I woke up I wasn't sure that I was alive. Then I saw you, and knew I was."

"Your eye," she murmured, horrified. "Your face . . . it looks worse than it did last night!"

"Nothing serious, though I guess I'll stay away from the office until I look a little more civilized."

She said abruptly: "Fran's gone."

Donald released her and went to the stove and picked up the coffee pot. "Did she have anything to say for herself before she went?"

"I didn't wake up until just a little while ago, and found this note."

Fran had written on the back of an old envelope: "I'm going to the corner and ask Gibson to take me to the train. I'm sorry about last night. There's no point in my trying to say more now, except to tell you not to worry about me. I'll write you in a few days."

Donald poured a cup of coffee for himself and one for Delia.

"No use my pretending that I'm not relieved she's gone," he said, and set the cups on the kitchen table. They sat facing each other and sunlight made an island of warmth round them. "Not much fun for you, though, to have to start worrying about her all over again."

Delia shook her head. "No. That business last night fixed it. When that thug hit you . . ."

"And I folded up like an old paper bag that's been out in the rain!" He managed a laugh. "I don't mind saying though that there was a moment there when I'd gladly have killed Luigi."

"So would I," said Delia. He saw the skin round her nostrils whiten and a hard look come on her face. "I could have killed them all, every one of them, not excepting Pearsy."

He poured cream into his cup and stirred it without looking at her.

"It was habit, I suppose, that sent you out into the cold and dark to find Fran when she ran away?"

"She didn't run away. It was D.T.'s all right, but it was also part of the act. She'd have had the neighbors down on us if I hadn't gone out and brought her in." She added slowly: "It was rather worse than usual, though, last night."

He looked at her for a moment, then said: "I guess you saw what happened out there in the garden, with me?"

The color came painfully into Delia's face. "I didn't know, I wasn't sure." She glanced away. "Oh God."

Donald tossed a lump of sugar at her across the table. "It's O.K. kid." he said softly.

"It isn't O.K. and you know it isn't."

He waited a moment, then: "Does it usually take that form with her?"

"Often enough. Too often. Sometimes there's a fight, and she gets beaten up."

They drank their coffee and Donald said thoughtfully: "Well, Pearsy looked harmless enough. Be another story if it was Luigi."

Delia winced. "It doesn't make any difference to her who they are, or what they are. During the war she had a job in Washington and she'd pick up service men and take them to her apartment. The Bowers stopped in to see her once and found her unconscious and the place a shambles. They had to get a doctor for her."

Delia rose and went to the stove, coming back with the coffee pot.

"I don't know how she's survived some of the things she's been through. It isn't even as if sex meant anything to her, especially."

There was a moment's silence, then Donald said: "I thought at first that Veronica was your big problem. Now I see there's another."

She drew her breath in a long sigh. "You've been worried about Veronica and Chris," she said at last. "Wondering whether they could make a go of life together. Have you thought whether you and I can? Because there's always going to be Fran. It doesn't really matter how little I care what happens to her—and after what happened to you last night, I give you my word I don't care at all—she's never going to let me go."

He waited, and Delia continued: "I'm all she's got. In the beginning, when we were kids, I used to believe that she was all *I* had. I clung to her until she shook me off. Then the roles were reversed. It's been like that ever since her divorce."

"The audience and the mirror," he murmured, nodding. "You give back the reflection she wants to see—herself at the time of her youth and vigor and beauty. She can always look at you and see herself minus the hideous things she's done and become. And then, you're always there for audience."

Delia nodded. "And as time goes on and she gets older, it will get worse. I can take it. I've taken it all my life. But can I ask you to take it?"

He rose and knocked the ashes of his pipe into the waste basket. Last night out there in the darkness, listening to their voices crying like lost birds, he'd asked himself the same question: Could he take it? No use fooling himself that he hadn't hated it, and that the blows he'd had to take from Fran's pal Luigi hadn't cut deeper than the flesh, or that the kisses he'd taken—and given—out there in the dark hadn't stirred a peculiar turmoil in his veins. They had. And there was Veronica, and the weird ideas that had occurred to him this morning out in the woods. Such things as he had learned, and the things that he hadn't learned, yet, had their place in art, no doubt, but then the drama was intrinsic, related to itself, certainly not to him. He had known writers and poets who carried their ferment into their conscious lives, and he was sensitive to their needs and understood that for them such ferment was an indispensable part of the whole. It was why he could forgive Veronica. But Delia was not an artist, nor was he. They had the option of becoming victims, and the question he had asked himself last night, and which she asked him now, still waited his reply.

As he stood in the middle of the kitchen floor cleaning out his pipe with his penknife he looked up and met her eyes, filled with the resignation which experience had taught her. He smiled. "Remember that day you met me for lunch at Le Roi's? That first time after the party at your house? That was the second time we'd met. And I watched you come out of the telephone booth where you'd gone to call Fran, and when you walked towards me through the crowd I saw that in a certain light, in a certain mood, you were not really beautiful at all. I saw your face made plain by anxiety and fear, not young any more, not even proud."

Delia looked away, saying nothing. Donald finished scraping the pipe and tapped the black dust from it into his palm. "I saw a good deal that afternoon. Great unhappiness, which had become ingrained like a cicatrice. A gift for silence which had driven the natural gaiety underground like a stream of water after an earthquake. I saw the the struggle that never let up, and the struggle to conceal the struggle. I saw how you must hate it all, hate the things and the people who boxed you in, who always came between you and your human desire for love and enjoyment and peace of mind."

"Do you think it was quite fair to see so much?" Delia asked after a short silence, but he continued as though he hadn't heard:

"I saw murder on your face, a whole succession of murders, starting—I wouldn't be surprised, with Fran."

She didn't deny it and he put the pipe down on the table and dusted off his hands, and looked at her. "It wasn't even as if there were any grandeur in all this. Neurosis in people like Fran doesn't make for interest, nor even necessarily for pity. The truly wicked, the truly corrupt, are not the hardest people in the world to put up with. They don't touch our lives closely enough. It's these amateurs in vice, the partly respectable, the parasites, rotten in spots, that we have to watch out for."

Still she did not speak, and Donald sat down facing her and leaned his elbows on his knees and stared at the floor. "Years ago when Clare asked me for a divorce so she could marry McKennicot, I made up my mind that I was not going to let it hurt me. I was still, you see, fairly young, and what my decision really amounted to was that I was not prepared to admit that I had already been hurt. However, I persisted in my self-delusion and it carried me through. What I didn't understand at the time was that I'd been hurt long before our break-up. I'd been hurt when I let myself fall in love with a woman who hadn't the slightest feeling of tenderness for me and who married me because I was the only man who'd ever asked her. Since then, as I've told you, there have been other women and I've had a very good time, taking it all in all."

He straightened in his chair and stretching out one foot, slid it under hers, balancing her ankle on his. "What it boils down to is that you're the only woman for whom I have ever had complete feelings. Know what I mean by that?"

She smiled faintly. "Tell me."

"Well, we could call this thing off now. I'm frankly not in love with the situation you're in. I hate it. But when I think what my life would be without you I know there wouldn't be any life worth mentioning. Not even the makeshift life I more or less enjoyed before I began to love you. I suppose the truth of the matter is that I'm not really crazy about you at all. I'm saner about you than about anyone I've ever known."

They were silent, then Delia gave a little laugh. "Once," she said, "when Fran and I were quite young she came home with a black eye, a memento from her current boy friend. I was very upset, but she explained to me in some detail what I missed by not going in for these virile types. I was too unsophisticated, she said, and I believed her and was upset after that on my own account."

"Too bad I wasn't around," Donald said, and touched his bad eye with a gingerly finger. "I could have told you what you missed."

CHAPTER

XXXII

THE fog was drifting in from the east as Nick set the tiller over in an attempt to pick up what little air there was. For a minute or two the sail stiffened and the little boat began to move towards the shore. He could see the tops of spruce trees on the island and hear water breaking along the shingle, and knew that they must be approaching the little bay where he planned to anchor and go ashore. This was the first time he'd been allowed to take the boat out alone, and it was bad luck that the fog should close in to complicate things. He didn't want to spoil everything, run the boat up on a rock, for God's sake, or what in his eyes would seem almost as bad—be forced to admit that he didn't dare take a chance in this poor visibility, and so turn ignominiously around and go home.

He glanced at the girl crouched on the narrow deck beside him, half lost in the folds of his oilskin, from the collar of which her yellow head emerged like a buttercup, and her eyes like particles of the silver steel backdrop of the sea.

"O.K. Linda?" he asked. "Think we can make it?"

She smiled, showing childish teeth. "Should. There's Puppa's lobster buoys. Comes off deep here when the tide's sett'n. You drop anchor now, we kin row ashore."

Nick peered into the drifting vapor. A gull appeared, then

seeing them, veered away, crying. A red and black lobster buoy slid past their bows and the sound of water on the shingle was very clear.

"O.K." he said with sudden decision. "Here we go. If you'll just loose that sheet."

Clumsily, she unhitched the main sheet from its cleat and the sail came down in a hurry, burying her in its folds, part of it going over the side. Aghast, Nick tossed the anchor overboard and paid out the line till he figured he had enough scope. He felt the boat stand still and the sea murmur against its sides, then he ran back amidships and helped Linda extricate herself from the sail, and between them they got it furled neatly enough. He smiled at her. "That was my fault. Sorry."

"No harm. I just didn't calculate it'd come down that fast."

She was flushed and gay and excited. Older than Nick by two years, she looked younger. Her hair was clear yellow, her eyes took their color from the sea in its varying moods, and she moved with the soft litheness of a young cat. Nick could scarcely bring himself to look at her, for he was at that stage of love which resembles a fear of falling, a combination of terror and desire which left him in a state of almost continuous breathlessness. He had never been in love before. He'd thought about it, and had been amused and interested, tempted to emulation of some of his friends at school, most of whom had girls steady or otherwise. But although he had fooled around more or less he had never really been taken over as he found himself a few days after his arrival at Todd's. There were moments now when he felt a bit like one of those balloons which, released by its unwary owner, soars upward and away to heaven knows what unforeseeable destiny, and he only hoped that Linda would keep a tight grip of the string that held him down to earth—and to her.

He hauled in the dinghy and helped her into it and handed her the lunch basket that her mother had packed for them. Then he coiled the painter with a professional air, hoping that she missed none of these skills, painstakingly acquired during his stay with the Wallingfords at Todd's Harbor. Tossing the painter into the dinghy he lowered himself into it and picked up the oars. Linda sat in the stern seat with the lunch basket at her feet, and as he pulled away from the yacht Nick saw its slender mast and gay pennant dissolve in the fog, and then there was only Linda, her face shaped and colored like a rose in all that cool grayness, and their two voices cupped in the silence, with the creak of rowlocks and the sound of the sea groping among the stones on the little beach towards which he rowed.

Linda said conversationally: "Lots of fog this time of year." She pronounced it *fawg*. "Days it's so thick Puppa don't even go out tend his traps fear he won't never git back."

"I bet your father knows his way blindfolded," Nick said. Turning to glance over his shoulder he saw the island coming up behind him, spined with spruce, the beach a pale half-moon and its stones rubbed by the sea into sophisticated forms of sculpture, so it seemed to Nick as though some gigantic human hand must have been at work here, nature itself being to his mind erratic and imprecise. Veronica and Chris were forever picking up these odd-shaped pebbles and oh-ing and ah-ing over them and talking about Lipchitz and Brancusi and lugging them all the way home, only to forget about them once they'd got them there.

"I bet," Nick said, "you could put a paper bag over your father's head and he'd still know where every lobster trap was and could pick them up and find his way home without moving an inch off his course."

She laughed. "He'd like fine to hear you say it, but it ain't true. Puppa's had some awful narrer 'scapes. Sea's so high you wouldn't believe. Fawg, ingin trouble and like that. Puppa don't like the sea only to make a living. He ought to know."

Nick thought of her father, Paul Haskett, a slight brown man with gray eyes and a gradual smile, his face etched by the weather, his hands bandaged over the sores that were always forming on them from continual handling of the wet, salt lines.

"Not that Puppa ain't awful smart when it comes to fishin',"

Linda went on with pride. "He kin see the fawg-blossoms lyin' out to sea and tell you right off what the weather's got a mind to do without listenin' to no weather reports and like that. Why last night when they knew we was comin' out here Mumma put the radio on and it said the wind was north-west and a good day comin' up, and Puppa come in the house and told us he could smell the wind had shifted and we was due for fawg. Not bad, he said. But some."

Nick thought of Linda's mother, a large bundle of a woman in faded print dress and battered moccasins, her orbit the kitchen with its varnished walls and plastic curtains framing pink geraniums in tin cans, a proud new linoleum on the floor, so dazzling it hurt the eyes, a wood-burning stove dented with use, and everywhere a smell of clothes still warm from the iron, and a throat-catching reek from bait barrels seeping in through the open window.

He remembered the day he'd met Linda for the first time, the day after his arrival at Todd's. Sailing with Chris and Veronica among the islands off Frenchman's Bay, Mt. Desert hunched like the spinal column of some marine monster against a gossamer sky, they had sighted Paul Haskett's lobster boat rocking on the sea as Paul hauled his traps and this yellow-haired girl perched on the housing, swinging her blue-jeaned legs. Coming alongside, Chris hailed them—old friends of his, he'd explained to Veronica and Nick. Neighbors since he was born.

"Any luck, Paul?"

"Hi there, Chris." Paul glanced at them from under his stained khaki cap. "Fair."

It was, as Nick was to learn, never better than fair. These people were by habit monosyllabic. It saved time and breath.

Chris turned to the girl. "Hi, Linda. How's tricks?"

"Good." She pronounced it *goo-wud*.

"When you coming over to see us?" Chris asked. He was holding the little sailboat in the wind and the sail trembled like a restive horse. Linda's blue eyes drifted from Chris to Veronica, thence to Nick.

"Be over one of these days," she said casually.

Chris introduced his guests, then turned again to Paul. "Any chance of lobsters for supper tomorrow, Paul?"

"Wouldn't be surprised if there wuz. How many'd you want?"

"Two apiece would make ten, better put in two extra."

Paul, a freshly baited trap balanced on the gunwale before him, smiled faintly. "How's Don making out these days? Book publishin' goin' goo-wud?"

"Fair to middlin'," Chris replied, falling naturally into the idiom. He grinned at Veronica. "Here's one of Dad's authors, Paul. We'll see you get an autographed copy of her book when it's out."

"Better make it out for Mumma and me," Linda said with a laugh. Her eyes rested interestedly on Veronica, and then as though with a kind of inevitability, turned again to Nick. "Puppa don't have no time to read nothin' except the newspaper."

"Don't always get through that without I fall asleep in the middle of it," Paul said gravely. He flung the trap into the sea and turned to his daughter. "You goin' to peg them lobsters or aint you?"

Before Linda could answer he looked at Chris. "She comes out here a-purpose to help me peg lobsters and bait the traps, then all she does is set there in the sun gettin' herself a tan so she kin knock the boys' eyes out over to Trenton Saturday night!"

Chris laughed, his hand pushing the tiller to one side. "Coming about," he said, and Nick ducked as the boom swung towards him and then they were moving away from the Hasketts, the glittering water stretching between them, the sun white on their slender little boat and on the two figures which grew smaller and smaller as he stared back at them, at Linda's gleaming head, and it seemed to him that she stared back at their sail as it bent tight and clean on the homeward tack.

He thought a good deal about the Hasketts after that, and about the relationship between them and his own friends. It seemed to him to be exactly right in its understanding of equality. Accustomed to the wary exchange, the spurious good fellowship which characterizes relations between buyer and seller in the city and the suburbs, he felt instinctively that this was the right thing and that he would settle for it any day, and for an existence like that of the fisherman and his daughter in their white lobster boat with its home-made look, its simplicity, its absence of superfluity and waste. Next day when he'd gone to the village to do an errand for Delia he'd met Linda, and they paused awkwardly to talk. Nick invited her to have a soda with him at the drug store, and that was the forerunner of almost daily meetings since. Somewhat to his surprise, the situation had been accepted almost without comment by his mother and the others, but on thinking it over he decided that this must be due to the special charm which the atmosphere of Todd's seemed to exercise upon all of them.

The dinghy slid into shallow water and Nick jumped out, followed by the girl. Between them they dragged the dinghy up the beach out of reach of the tide. Then Nick suggested that they explore, taking the lunch basket so they would not have to come back for it when they got hungry. Side by side, they walked along the beach between windrows of driftwood inscribed in cuneiform characters by some abstruse insect brain, and felt the hard round shapes of the beach stones under their feet. Everywhere he looked Nick was conscious of a kind of richness offering itself to his gaze. Beach peas and a kind of sea myosotis grew just out of reach of the tide. Caught in the drying seaweed were the opalescent shells of mussels and spectral skeletons of crabs. Here and there some incongruous object arrested his attention—part of a kitchen stove, a sofa cushion, a lobster buoy with a remnant of frayed rope toggled on it.

"From ships wrecked at sea?" he wondered aloud, romantically, and Linda laughed. "No. Just dumped over the side so's to get rid of 'em, I guess."

Above the beach the land levelled off in an old sheep pasture and beyond that to a conglomerate of rock galleried by the sea into thin sheaves like the pages of some gigantic, improbable book, and in other places ravenous fangs among which ferns and hare-bells were unconcernedly growing. The place seemed quite deserted. There was not even the sound of a sheep bell, not a voice. The fog closed them in, shutting out the world, until suddenly Nick became aware of a kind of murmuring going on in an invisible cranny beyond the fang-like rocks far below his feet. Voices. Human voices, arguing softly like lovers. Pauses. Kisses. The sound of a laugh.

He felt a sudden surge of anger and disappointment. He hadn't wanted to share this spot with strangers—with anyone, least of all with lovers. He didn't want people horning in on his privacy, which had never seemed so precious, but his reaction was more complicated even than that. This was the first time in his life that he had been absolutely alone with a girl and he had chosen this particular little island as being, for him, the only place in the world to be so alone. Already in these few minutes since their setting foot on the shore, he had a possessive, intimate relation with it, as, much later, he was to have towards his own house, and the bed he would share with his wife. He did not understand this now, but as he stood hesitating, listening to the love-making and the argument going on down there out of sight, he had a sudden impulse to turn round and go away, taking Linda with him to some place where they could really be alone.

He turned to find her gazing at him with an odd little smile.

"Listen," she murmured, and put her hand on his arm. He started to say something, and then suddenly he understood what that sound was all about. It was the sea, pushing against the fissiparous rock, mouthing it, endlessly, insatiably feeding upon it, taking the island to pieces morsel by morsel, a syllable at a time.

Relieved, feeling something of a fool, Nick laughed. They moved on, climbing the height of land grown to spruce and layered with moss, and came out at last at its farthest end, the hidden sea before them and a bell buoy sounding its lonely note like an Alpine sheep lost among the clouds. Here they sat down with the trees at their back and the water a hundred feet below, and watched gulls come veering out of the fog to drop clams on the rocks, then to land and feast.

"Funny," Linda remarked, "how they seemed to know. Wonder when they first discovered that it'd work."

Nick gave it as his opinion that everything in nature was funny, and having said as much, again felt like a fool. He wanted to impress her. It was a new ambition for him, one of many to which he seemed recently to have become prone.

Linda however considered his remark in perfect seriousness, and to his relief agreed that he was probably right, and that everything in nature *was* funny. "Including," she added, not looking at him, "human nature."

They listened to the bell buoy and watched the gulls cracking clams on the ledge below.

"It's funny," Linda said—the word seemed to be a favorite with her—"about this place. I've been coming here ever since I can remember, with Puppa, when he hauls his traps. I don't guess there's a tree on this island, or a rock or a stone, that I don't know. Now here I am with you, and ten days ago I didn't even know there was such a person."

They were silent a moment, then Nick went on to say that he wished he had enough money to buy this island. "I'd put No Trespassing signs all over it, and only my friends would have the right to come here. Then when I heard the sea talking to itself like it does back there, I wouldn't get mad thinking there were a bunch of goons getting ready to cut down the trees or leave a lot of trash around."

She shook her head. "That's summer visitor stuff, that No Trespassing stuff. Folks don't go for it, not round here. They wouldn't pay no attention anyway, except maybe to take the sign down and light a fire with it."

Nick was afraid he must have sounded like a snob, and was instantly ashamed. "I guess you're right. I hadn't thought of it that way."

She said kindly: "You take Donald Wallingford now. Of course he aint strictly speaking summer visitor because his folks come from Todd's to begin with. His grandmother was a Todd. But Donald wouldn't no more think of putting up a No Trespassing sign than nothin' at all. He owns a lot of land, too. Not much good now, most of it, because it used to be pasture and there aint enough cows nor horses left to make it worth while payin' taxes on it. Land poor, Donald is. You know what his wife done when they first took to comin' down here after he was married and they had Chris? I don't remember it because I wasn't born till after. But she—Mrs. Wallingford, Clare her name was, had them No Trespassing signs, and No Huntin' No Fishin' signs stuck all over the place so to keep people out the woods they always walked in free and for nothin' long before she was dreamed up. And she went and had landscape people come all the way from Bar Harbor and set up a paling fence round their house, with a gate in it you had to open to git in the garden and it sure looked unreal after the way everybody in Todd's had always knowed it. Exclusive. Made you feel kind of unwelcome just to look at it. And I guess most people felt that way about Clare anyway. Then after they was divorced you wouldn't believe it, but Donald went around himself and took away all them No this and No that signs, and he pulled down the fence Clare'd put up at God knows what expense, and burned the lot." She laughed. "Nobody said nothin' about it— not to Donald that is. Guess they said plenty to each other. It was just like he'd been let out from behind the bars, was what Puppa said when he heard Clare's white-painted palin's had gone for kindlin' the livin' room fire."

Nick listened without comment. He had already heard quite a bit of gossip about Donald's wife Clare, and it had a peculiar interest for him. He wondered how the townspeople liked Delia, and what they were saying about her behind her back. Not that he cared, he assured himself, loftily—after all what the hell difference could it make to Delia? And yet he knew that he did care, and that she would care, too. In the brief time that they had been at Todd's she'd made no secret of her liking for the place, and of her desire to be on good terms with the people. Donald had laughed when she spoke of this, and said: "Take it easy. You're being given the once-over, and it takes time. They'll come round, don't you worry."

Linda went on breezily: "Until Donald married Clare there never used to be a lock on his house that ever worked. And nothin' never got took, neither. But Clare didn't approve of that. Way she saw things, it were safer not to trust nobody—not even her nearest neighbors."

She hesitated, looking at him lazily from under her gold lashes. "I've heard Mumma and Puppa say often enough that there really wasn't anything bad about Clare Wallingford. She was a good woman in the strict sense of the word, is what Puppa always said. Only she made him madder'n hell when she came in the house one fall and started in to tell him how she thought he'd ought to vote in the town election for first selectman! It were the kind of thing she was always doing, to everybody. Anyway she and Puppa had words and she clean lost her temper and said things Puppa never has been able to forget. Said we was all shiftless and not good for doing any single thing except haul lobsters." Linda laughed. "Know what Puppa said to that?"

"What did he say?"

"He stuck his head out the door as she was goin' away and said: 'You likes to eat lobsters, don't you, Mis' Wallingford?'—He never would call her Clare though nobody's ever called Donald anything but Donald. 'You like to eat lobsters,' bawls Puppa at her back as she goes off down the road—'an' what's more you aint so proud but what you say we'd ought to charge you wholesale 'stead of the reg'lar price so you kin save a nickel on the pound!' "

Linda laughed again, joyously. "Puppa's not the kind of man'd take any guff from women like Clare Wallingford. But it was tough on Donald. She was always doin' things like that. Sayin' things. Joined the Farm Bureau just so she could give the women advice on how to lead their lives. Told 'em they looked the way they did with their bad figures and everything because they lived on carbohydrates, and she made a lasting enemy out of my grandmother asking her why in the world she didn't spend some of her savin's on a set of false teeth 'stead of just beatin' her food to death with her bare gums like she done to the day of her death, and my grandmother was long past eighty when she died."

Nick frowned. "Queer," he murmured. "I mean, that Donald should have had a wife like that."

"He married her when he was awful young. And she must of been goodlookin' too. Mumma says she was. Puppa didn't think she was so hot. 'One of them heavy-duty blonds,' he called her. But then he couldn't abide the sight of her. She scared him. She scared most people round Todd's. Scared them and made 'em feel badly, you know? By tryin' to take away their self-respect."

Nick listened, bemused by the sound of her voice and her flat, overemphatic accent, his eyes fixed on her long blue-jeaned legs on the grass beside his.

"Funny," Linda went on after a pause. "Way things turn out. Best thing ever happened to Donald Wallingford was when Clare run off with that dietitian." She turned suddenly and gave him a direct look.

"Know what folks around here is wonderin'?" And without waiting for an answer: "They're wonderin' if Donald and your mother's aimin' to git married."

He was silent, feeling her gaze probing him.

"Are they?" she asked, a bubble of laughter in her voice. "You don't have to tell if you don't want. It'd be nice, though, if they did git married."

"I don't know," Nick said at last. "They haven't said anything."

"We like your mother," said Linda after a brief pause. "She sure aint one tiny bit like Clare! Don't preach and don't teach and don't condescend, nor she don't break her neck tryin' to be natural, either. Tell you something?"

He turned, glad for an excuse to look her in the face.

"There's not a person in Todd's that knows Donald Wallingford wouldn't like to see him happy, and there's quite a few thinks your mother's the woman could do it."

"How can they? They don't know her."

"Well, dopey! How'd you feel about it?"

Nick hesitated. How did he feel about it? Certainly not the way he'd felt a few months ago back in New York, when the heavens had seemed about to fall and crush him and his entire world seemed to be standing on its ear. And now suddenly he asked himself just when had that feeling left him—the jealousy, the frightening, incomprehensible pain, the besetting fear of loss? For it was gone . . . amazingly, inexplicably vanished, leaving him himself, whole, yet subtly changed.

"O.K." Linda murmured mockingly. "Not tellin', ah? I don't care."

He said abruptly: "I don't mind telling you, Linda. Honest, I don't. It's just that there isn't anything to tell. I don't know how I'd feel. Nothing much, I guess. I guess it would be their business."

She said nothing but threw herself back on the grass, clasping her hands behind her head. Nick could see the long straight lines of her body, her small breasts making two white tents under the boy's shirt she was wearing. Her hand, lying near him on the grass, was lightly tanned and well cared for, its nails varnished the color of checkerberries—the hand, as he recognized it, of a spoiled child, one who is certainly not going to give herself callouses pegging lobsters and stuffing the stinking herring-bait into bait bags for her old man—or for anyone else. He had a sudden crazy impulse to do what he'd once seen Donald Wallingford do with Delia's hand— carry it to his lips, but he restrained himself.

"Then there's Veronica and Chris," Linda murmured, her eyes closed. "Cosy, ah? But it would leave just you, wouldn't it?"

He gazed intently at a patch of open sea and a lobster buoy over which the fog was moving like steam. He was thinking that back there at Donald's house they had each other, his mother and Donald, Veronica and Chris. And he understood at last what had been happening to him all these past months and why his strange unhappiness and dissatisfaction should so suddenly have evaporated. In New York he had begun to feel increasingly as though he were being excluded from a felicity in which up until then he'd always had his share. It was not his mother's fault; it was not Veronica's, not Chris's, nor Donald's. It was not his own fault either. It was nobody's fault, but it had nevertheless poisoned the whole summer for him and had made him piercingly conscious of all the other poisons which seemed to be floating around the place and interfering even in the lives of people whom he supposed had every reason to be happy. He'd felt an intolerable pressure which he could not understand, a sense of undisclosed mysteries, tensions which had, amazingly, made him regret the day that school was finished and he was home for the long summer vacation with nothing to do but wonder what the hell it was all about . . . and then they'd come to Todd's, and it had been just as simple as leaving all your complications behind like so much forgotten baggage, and this too was in its way as puzzling as everything that had preceded it, but something that he was at least happy to accept. And he had Linda to thank for it. He caught his breath. Linda! And a whole week had gone by like lightning and he hadn't even kissed her.

"Penny," Linda offered, opening her eyes and smiling at him under her golden lashes, and at that he turned his head and looked at her, a grave-faced young man with hawk nose and heavy brows.

"I was wishing," he said, slowly, "that I might never have to leave this place ever again."

Her look became incredulous. "Don't you like it in New York and Connecticut?"

"Oh, I like it, all right. But I like this better. More than better. This island, I mean. Todd's Harbor." He wanted to add: And above everything else, you. And your father and mother and that shabby little house with the smell of warm laundry and the bait barrels . . . These things have become important to me through you. Because you are the first person I have chosen for myself without having the accident of relationship wished on me by fate. Everything that has happened to me since we got to Todd's has been like this. It's been . . . *goo-wud*. Life has been a free thing like the sweep of those gulls coming out of the *fawg*, like the sliding rush of a boat when the sail fills and she goes over on the port tack. I want to wake up every morning to the noise of lobster boats putting out to sea, the picture of them under my eyelids . . . long narrow boats low on the water and giving you the feeling which other machines don't give you on the land, because whatever has to do with the sea belongs to the sea. The sea is master, and I for one would like to settle for that.

Nick said none of these things. They were indeed unsayable, scarcely coherent, fragments of desire and image that would go to shape a lasting image of this day, of this girl whom he had not known existed until a week ago and whom he now believed he could not possibly live without . . . this girl whom he planned to marry and bring to this island every summer of their lives, to lie here in a heat and ecstasy of feeling which could never thin away to nothing, like the *fawg* . . .

Linda was gazing at him lazily, a smile on her lips, which matched the color of her nails. "You like it here, is that it?"

"Of course." He lowered himself cautiously on his elbow, so close that he caught the scent of her hair. "Of course I like it here. I'd like to spend the rest of my life here."

"I don't guess you would, if you really had to. You sound the way summer folks do because they come on vacations and can always go away if they want. But for us there's nothing to do. You can see. Nearest movie's all the way into Trenton. No stores. No nothing."

He wanted to say: "There's this!" For as long as it would last, and it had lasted a long time. A thousand years ago, perhaps, the sea had quarried the island away from the mainland, and in a thousand years to come this tuft of grass on which they lay would be down there in the gently waving kelp, and where he and she would be by then . . . who knew, who gave a damn?

"I like movies and stores. I like civilisation." Linda stretched out her hand and touched his lightly, with a teasing, conciliatory touch, and again he wanted to take her hand and kiss it, and again the thought of doing so paralysed him.

She went on coolly, conversationally, letting her hand linger on the grass next his: "Todd's is all right for a spell, the way Donald Wallingford and Chris use it, for rest and vacation. But don't forget that although Donald's folks came from here *they* chose to go some place else and make a life that isn't just blistering your hands on fish lines and going on relief when the price of lobsters drops out of sight." She frowned. "Know something? I never did like any single thing I ever heard about Clare Wallingford and the way she was forever beefin' and criticizin' Todd's Harbor folks for being shiftless and lazy and good for nothin', but there was somethin' to it just the same. It's why it hurt like it did, to hear it. People have never forgotten her nor forgiven her, not because she exaggerated or was lyin' in what she said—but because she was tellin' 'em the truth. Look at Puppa. He's stuck. So's a lot of 'em in Todd's Harbor stuck. Not because they can't help it, but because they want to be stuck."

"Well?" Nick said, feeling defensive about her father, and closer to her because of it. "There's worse things than wanting to be stuck in Todd's Harbor."

"Maybe there is, but I wouldn't know about it."

Over to the westward the bell buoy chanted with the rote of the sea and a gull came mewing out of the sky, so close they could see its yellow feet and its dark, seeking eye.

"That's all there is to Todd's," Linda said. She moved her shoulders on the grass and it brought her closer to him so he could see the tiny golden hairs on her lip. "Fawg warnin's and sea gulls and whether you kin expect to git thirty cents a pound for your catch." She pronounced it *ketch*. "Or whether it'd be better to go on strike an' use up what savings you got and try and force the price up to thirty-five."

Her eyes opened wide and he saw that in this light they were the color of slate, exactly like the sea.

"Not for me," Linda said, softly. "Not on your life . . . for me."

Putting up her hand she touched the tip of his nose and drew her finger down over his lip, letting it rest against his mouth.

"Dope," she murmured, and he saw the color rise along her throat to her brows, and her lips parted, showing her small white teeth.

"Who's a dope?" he whispered, wondering whether he were going to die before he could make it.

"You."

"I don't see why."

She slid her hand round the side of his face and hooked her fingers behind his neck, drawing him down towards her. "You don't?"

He could hear his own heart, and it sounded like the engine in her father's lobster boat. "No," he muttered. "No, I don't."

"Well then, what in heck you waitin' for?"

He sank against her, the uproar in his blood drowning out the sound of the bell buoy as her arms went round him, pulling his head down to hers.

CHAPTER

XXXIII

WALLINGFORD's house, built by his maternal grandfather a hundred years ago, stood in an open field which sloped towards the shore and a small, deep cove a mile or two from the village of Todd's Harbor. Behind the house spruce and hackmatack formed a windbreak against north-west storms, and the shore, reaching out in two spruce-covered arms, hugged the cove east and west, leaving the southern entrance open for navigation and to the vagaries of a fog-ridden southerly wind.

The house was simple, with small low-ceilinged rooms, open fireplaces and pine floors tilted and scarred by age. Donald's contributions towards modernization had originally consisted of book-cases and the installation of electricity, and it had been left to Clare to insist that they pension off the outdoors privy and replace it with a proper bathroom. Donald had resisted this innovation partly from an instinct to annoy her—her reasons were always so damned right that already after the first year of marriage they were beginning to get him down—and partly from a genuine conviction that one could carry the American passion for improvement a trifle too far. He had always rather liked going out to the pretty ivy-covered bower tucked discreetly out of sight among the trees, its interior gaily decorated with magazine covers and the initials of visiting firemen through the years. Donald had even installed a shelf to hold ashtrays and books, and there was an old lobster buoy, retrieved from the shore after a storm, on which one could rest one's feet. But Clare would have none of it. She thought it disgusting and primitive that everyone should know whither you were bound when they saw you sidling in purposeless fashion in the general direction of the hackmatacks. Besides, hornets had taken up residence under the eaves, and there were always mosquitoes. The denouement however came one morning when Donald heard cries of terror and ran out to find Clare boxed in and a skunk unconcernedly parading to and fro before the door. Skunks being what they are, notoriously immune to threats or blandishments, he'd been obliged to leave Clare where she was till the beast finally made up its mind to retire. He'd retired, too, and laughed his head off in the privacy of the house, but when half an hour later Clare showed up with battle flag flying he knew he'd lost the round, and a landmark held in honor by three generations was lugged off by old Willy Doane, who combined the profession of undertaker with that of junkman, and so Clare got her bathroom after all.

Grandmother Todd's garden had long since sunk into oblivion, though her lilacs survived, gnarled and knotted at each corner of the house. The lawn, such as it was, stretched from the sills to the rough stubble of the field between house and shore. Wild roses grew among the rocks and gullies, and as the land soured towards the sea it ran to blueberries and cranberries known to the people of Todd's Harbor from one generation to the next. Donald had always given his neighbors full and free access to this natural crop. He liked to watch them, men, women, and children, up-ended as they harvested the fruit in bags and baskets, and to hear their voices and an occasional burst of laughter come drifting in through his windows. Later he'd find a few jars of crimson jelly made from his own cranberries, or a bowl of blueberries in a garland of their own leaves, left on his kitchen table by way of thanks. But to this too, Clare had objected. She declared that she had nothing against the neighbors but that she liked privacy and saw no reason why it shouldn't be respected. As a rule, bored by argument and constantly balked on minor issues, Donald shrugged and let her have her way, but on this point he'd been adamant. Bad enough that she should have stuck those No Trespassing signs everywhere and placed that unfriendly paling around the lawn—he'd submitted to this only after a most unpleasant scene—but on the question of the berries she'd suddenly found him inflexible.

"Todd's people have picked berries here since my grandfather built the house, and before. They're going to be allowed to pick them as long as I live. Do I make myself clear?"

Well, he had won that round, but victory left a bitter taste; it affected his life-long feeling about the place, which had always meant to him something that Clare could not understand. It did not occur to him at the time that, possessive and domineering as she was, she might have been just a bit jealous of his love for the house and his affection for his neighbors and friends. All he did know was that she was forever trying to improve something by changing it, sticking her foot in the course of a continuity he valued, patronizing him before his friends, and while shutting herself off from whatever enjoyment the place might have had to offer—and it had a great deal—preening herself on her righteousness and zeal for bringing light into the lives of these aborigines.

That Donald's grandmother had been a Todd counted for much in his favor among the inquisitive, close-mouthed, in some cases cross-grained folk whose ancestors shared the cemetery with her on the hill overlooking the village and the sea. The present generation of Todd's had accepted the fact of his own desertion from their ranks as no more than proof of a communal superiority in which they shared. Donald Wallingford, they reminded each other, was no mere summer visitor like his wife. He was Matilda Todd's grandson and his own father had left Todd's to study medicine in Boston, and had done well. So in his chosen field had Donald. But any man in Todd's could have done as well if he'd had a mind to, and Donald would have been the last to deny the boast.

It was not easy for him to account, even to himself, for the deep attachment he felt for this place. Something homesick in him, something perpetually at odds with whatever is meaningless and ephemeral in the life of a city, drew him back here every summer and served as a touchstone for disquiet while he was gone. Clare had accused him of being hopelessly sentimental and he did not try to deny it, knowing that Clare herself had gone through life without daring to be spontaneous for fear of being considered naive by her friends. It was an era when a woman refrained from kissing her own child because it might be bad for him, and for her. Physical demonstrations were suspect: the calisthenics of the connubial couch were committed to memory out of Krafft-Ebing or Havelock Ellis, and there were times when Donald had found himself wondering whether he'd gone to bed with a drill instructor.

It was not in Clare's power, however, entirely to destroy the charm of Grandmother Todd's house, or of Todd's Harbor itself, and after their divorce Donald came back to it with an enormous sense of gratitude and relief, the more personal and intense because he sensed that Chris did not entirely share it—their associations were different, and so, as men, were they.

Discussing it one day with Delia he said: "Perhaps it means what it does to me because nothing really bad has ever happened here. There were accidents, yes. Paul Haskett's brother fell out of his mowing-machine and his leg was so badly mangled it had to be amputated. Ken Todd, a distant cousin, was hauling lobsters just off the point when he somehow or other lost his balance and fell overboard and was drowned. Aside from those two acts of God, if you care to call them that, there has been no evil and no wickedness in sight of these windows. And people have been decent to each other under this roof."

While Nick went sailing with Linda Haskett and Chris and Veronica explored the mountain trails at Mt. Desert, Donald took Delia on a round of his property and they talked over what might be done to bring the soil back to productivity, and what repairs were needed on the house.

"I haven't done much these past few years," Donald said, his arm around her as they strolled across the rough fields where sweetfern testified to the acidity of the land. "A month in summer and a couple of weeks in fall for the duck hunting is about all the time I can spend here, so I've let things more or less slide. Tell me what you think, what you'd like."

Delia hesitated. In the week that they'd been here she'd taken on color and her eyes had a serenity he'd not noticed in them before.

She said at last: "I can't think of anything that needs to be done, unless it's the sills on the north side. They look a bit wobbly . . ."

"You wouldn't like a garden?" he suggested. "There's lots of room for one, and the soil's all right round the house."

"Did Clare have a garden?" she asked tentatively, and he laughed.

"For a year or two. Very formal. Standard roses and shrubs that cost a mint. Then sheep got in one fall when we were away, and ate the whole place down to the ground." He added meditatively: "I always wondered about those sheep. They never bothered to come around before Clare planted her garden. It must have been the expensive diet that attracted them."

Delia murmured: "I'm so afraid of doing something Clare did, that you wouldn't like!"

He laughed. "I was afraid you might feel that way. But you do so many things that Clare wouldn't have been seen dead doing, and I like them all so much . . ."

The sea hissed against the rocks and they watched a sea-hawk hover, then plunge into the water and rise again with a fish glittering in its talons. Plover were calling from the salt marshes to the westward, and presently they saw Paul Haskett's boat passing the cove, with Paul alone at the tiller. He lifted a hand in greeting when he saw them, and they waved back. "No Linda today," Donald remarked as they walked on. "Not since you arrived, as a matter of fact. Paul must feel rather short-handed without her, not that she's much use in a boat. Too busy manicuring her nails or keeping the salt out of that pretty hair."

Delia said after a minute: "You know, I think Nick's got a case on that girl. Suppose it's all right?"

"Probably not."

"Do you mean that? Because I am concerned. He's so young."

"It seems to me that he's grown up rather suddenly these past few days."

Delia frowned. "I've noticed the change, too. I heard him ask Chris if he could borrow his razor the other morning!" She laughed, then said seriously: "Do you think I ought to speak to him, Donald?"

He broke off a piece of sweetfern, crushing it in his fingers, and the scent of it was strong on the air. "Speak to him about what—the facts of life?"

"Well, I never have. I've thought about it and wondered, but I figured he'd probably get it all at school. They're pretty advanced nowadays, in that line."

Donald said carelessly: "Wouldn't surprise me if Linda Haskett hadn't introduced him to a post-graduate course as of last week."

"But Donald, no! It could be serious, you know it could. He's a *baby*, and she must be at least two years older."

His arm around her shoulders, he led her on towards the mailbox at the entrance of their road. "Linda's seventeen. I wouldn't worry. She's bright. She took Chris on a year or two ago and I can't see that it did either of them any harm."

Delia looked unhappy. "I don't like it. Silly of me, but Nick's romantic and rather intense about things."

"What do you think you should do? Give him a lecture on the birds and the bees, and tell him he's too young for all that nonsense? When he's already proving to you—and to himself—that he isn't?"

"But not sixteen! And nothing can come of it. They can't even be engaged."

"Who's talking about an engagement? What's really bothering

you is that he's been slow getting around to things. There's not a boy around Todd's Harbor—and damned few anywhere else I can think of—that's Nick's age and still, shall we say, unaffected? Hell, leave him alone." He laughed rather shortly. "As a matter of fact you and I ought to be grateful to Linda Haskett. Nick was in bad shape when we first got here, and before that in New York. He resented me like the devil, and he couldn't hide it. If he's going to have a case on anyone, better that he have it on Linda, not on you. As you say, he's romantic and intense. For all I know he's planning to marry her and settle down here at Todd's and become a lobsterman like Paul. But I've an idea Linda has other plans for herself."

Delia said helplessly: "What does one do about these children?"

"One thing we don't have to do is generalize about them. Let Nick see that you trust him, and he'll trust you. If there's trouble he'll know where to come for advice, and if he's lucky he won't have to. . . ." After a pause he added: "Nick's not like Veronica. He's a giver. Don't try to make him miserly."

"That sounds all very well, but what if Linda should have a baby?"

He shook his head. "I'm telling you she's a bright girl. Now this may sound brutal, but the truth is Linda doesn't really give a whoop about Nick. She's out for something serious, and with a future. She wants a guy who can marry her and take her away from Todd's to the big city, and Nick can't do that. Not yet at any rate and by the time he gets so he can, they'll probably have forgotten all about one another."

"She could still have a baby," Delia insisted. "And she could pin it on Nick. I'm really worried."

Donald laughed. "Listen. I'll let you in on a confidence. Linda has a steady, but he's in the army, due to get out this fall. Actually they're engaged and going to be married as soon as he gets home."

"Somehow that doesn't help at all. Poor Nick!"

"Yes, poor Nick. But this is the first time, for him. There'll be others. It may never be the same, but he'll never be less romantic, less intense. Better make up your mind to it, my dear. The damned little fool is *always* going to be in love from now on!"

They were at the mail box and Donald took out a package of letters and the *New York Times* in a brown wrapper. They sat down on a broken rail fence and Delia read a letter from Katie saying that Fran had been in town and had spent the night at the house and that she seemed very well and was still holding her job in Long Island, and had not even asked for a drink. "She was real nice and like she can be when she has a mind to, and seemed glad to hear you were having such a good time with the children, and said that she was writing you herself, in a day or two. The painters have got through in the kitchen and it looks real smart and fresh, but now the water closet in the downstairs bathroom leaks and Finlay's says they can't do nothing about it until next week so I've had the water turned off in there but there's nothing for you to fret about and I like to think of you in the country at peace in your mind because God knows, you've had it coming a long time. . . ."

She smiled, thinking of Katie, relieved to get the news about Fran. The sisters had met briefly, twice, following the débâcle in Connecticut, but the subject had been mentioned by neither. Fran was obviously too far gone in shame and contrition even to venture an apology or to ask Delia any questions as to her relationship with Donald, and Delia had been thankful enough to leave it at that.

"Letter from Bunny." Donald skimmed through it, laughing. "He's having a hell of a time with Mrs. Honeywell. Seems her book's in page-proofs and now she wants to rewrite the whole last chapter describing the death of her dog. It isn't, she thinks, half poignant enough."

He put the letter back in its envelope and looked at Delia. "Bunny says he's sending down advance copies of Veronica's novel, and that others have gone out for review." A curious expression passed across his eyes. "You'll be able to read it very soon now."

Delia seemed scarcely to hear. They rose and continued their walk towards the house. "I know you think I'm being silly about

Nick," she said presently. "I'd like to feel that he was going to enjoy life and love with the least possible degree of misery."

Donald stuffed the letters into his pocket and took her in his arms. The smell of sweetfern was all round them, and the faint dry rustle of poplar leaves shivering in the warm breeze, and they could hear the fish-hawk's shrill cry where it hovered on its black wings above the sea.

CHAPTER

XXXIV

DONALD would have liked to tell Delia that in his opinion there had been altogether too much of this wishful thinking, this instinct to protect the young from the inevitable consequences of their growing up. That she was justified in her qualms about her son, he knew. But he knew also that there is a limit to what a parent can do—he'd found that out himself and had watched others find it out. And he could have told her that much of the unhappiness and complication of which she spoke was in no small measure her own fault. She'd gone overboard with Veronica and the results were not happy. It did not follow that because she had tried to leave Nick more or less to his own devices, or because her affection for him had been quite different to what she'd felt for Veronica, he'd been simpler to deal with, more rewarding, less of a responsibility and care. What did follow was that no matter what the technique she'd used in bringing him up, he was now about to slip his tether, emotionally, and her reaction to this was as much that of a jealous woman's as it was the natural anxiety of a mother.

Donald wished he could have felt free to speak of these matters with Delia, but he judged instinctively that the time was not ripe.

Unless he had completely missed his guess, a measure of enlightenment was already on its way to her and to her children, and that all three were probably going to be hurt by it he felt pretty sure, but, as he reminded himself, of the three Delia and Veronica, at any rate, had it coming. He could only hope that it wouldn't be too hard on Nick.

Again and again as the weeks passed, Donald had found himself reflecting on the strange notion which had occurred to him in the Connecticut woods the morning after he'd had his eye blacked and his jaw almost broken by Fran's friend Luigi. He'd meditated on it at some length and had been more than once tempted to tax Delia with the monstrous suspicion, but something invariably held him back. Perhaps because in the first place he knew her well enough, now, to be fairly certain that she would tell him nothing. He'd had an insight into her mind and realized the degree of loyalty of which she was capable. It was, perhaps something rather more complex than loyalty in the conventional sense of the word. Delia, he felt, could *become* the thing her conviction demanded of her; he would get nothing from her that was not herself or part of herself.

And perhaps after all he might be mistaken! Months ago, back there in the snowy woods he'd told himself that if Veronica could be mistaken in her assumptions, so could Donald Wallingford be mistaken in his. Which meant simply that no matter what Veronica had said in her story, or whom she'd held up to scorn or extolled as a martyr, Delia was still left with the choice of letting Nick see her as Silvia, or revealing Charles to both children for the heel he had always been. Left to Delia, that was where it might end. It is a wise child who knows his own father, and hers would have to be satisfied with being no wiser at the end than they had been at the beginning. It was grim, all right, whichever way one looked at it, and no alternative except one that, even if it should exist, Donald was convinced she would never take.

At this point in his reflections Donald was seized with fury at the remembrance of what Delia *had* had to take—of what she had taken all her life. He had not exaggerated when he confessed to her at Marbury that morning after the fight—if it could be called that—with Luigi, that he hated her situation. He did hate it. He hated the very thought of her sister Fran. There had been moments when he thought he hated Veronica, but that had passed. Veronica, as he now saw it, had planned her revenge and her own punishment in one and the same breath, and he could not help marvelling nowadays at the way in which she was evidently preparing herself—and subtly, with a kind of wistfulness, preparing *them*—for what was to come. It was as if, having made her decision, she was already savoring revenge *and* punishment, living through an experience not yet made flesh, trying to put behind her what still lay before, and making the most of whatever innocence there might be left her in these few remaining weeks. Innocence to love and to let herself be loved, to turn out her pockets for the last crumbs of childhood she had to offer Delia, and to accept Delia's hesitant response as her natural and unquestioned due.

Of the relationships which existed between all of them, nothing was said. It was tacitly understood that both couples should go their own way. As for Nick, he practically lived at the Hasketts.

This arrangement left Donald and Delia to themselves, and as the days passed he found himself less and less concerned with those complications and equivocations in her life that had so troubled him in New York. He could not dismiss them entirely from his mind, but when he thought of them it was fleetingly, with a sense of incredulity and lessening disquiet. Perhaps this was in part due to the charm of the place he'd always thought of as home, and of the spell which it laid on his spirit—a spell which Clare had sensed and which she'd tried to exorcise in her splay-footed fashion, but which somehow had managed to survive. In an occasional simple-minded mood of which he was a trifle ashamed, Donald liked to fancy that a benign genii roosted in the attic and spread its beneficence through his small domain. The presence of this spirit—could it have been his grandmother's?—had never seemed to him more in evidence than during the visit of Delia and her children. How else account for the lightness of heart, the silliness, the fun in which they—with secret wonder at themselves—passed their days?

Whatever the cause of this happy state of affairs, whether astral or otherwise, some lapse of etheric vigilance or perhaps the jealous intervention of a rival afreet put an end to it, temporarily at any rate, two days before the arrival of those advance copies of Veronica's novel—a date which Donald had privately set aside, with a sigh of resignation, as that for an inevitable settling of accounts all around.

It was Saturday, clear but with a swathe of fog hanging out to sea and a light breeze. Donald had driven Delia on a round of the neighboring villages, and on the return journey he suddenly turned off the highway and drove along a deserted stretch of road gullied and worn from lack of use, into a rough meadow where he shut off the motor. The top of his convertible roadster was down and the August heat cascaded on Delia's bare head. The air smelled of asters and sweetfern, an old horse cropping the grass near by lifted its head and gazed at them for a minute, as though about to ask a question, then went back to its grazing.

Donald took out his pipe and began to fill it while Delia stared at the scene spread before her eyes. The meadow in which they were parked was grown up to purple and white asters and sloped to damper ground, where a belt of loosestrife held the land in check against the sea. To the west the shore described a sharp curve like an elbow crooked to form the harbor where fishing boats glittered like paper toys, each nosing into the wind, each mirroring itself in the water, so that although there were not more than a dozen boats anchored there, each by doubling itself had become a twin, and the harbor had a crowded look.

A solitary fish pier marched with Japanese precision straight and taut from the village street into the sea. Gulls perched on its uprights or clamored above the gurry buckets, their droppings like thick white paint on the salt-scoured wood. Lobster traps were stacked on one side of the pier and these, too, had an almost exotic air, probably, as Delia thought, because human hands and not a machine had fashioned them. Against their laced and intricate patterns the lobster buoys and gasoline pumps made exuberant cones and pyramids of color—scarlet, orange, and black.

The village itself drifted with thinning density from the main street and its few stores to the houses scattered along a rise of land. One-dimensional, not unlike their owners; slab-sided and innocent of any recognizable architectural norm, since most of them had been put together by men who combined the rudiments of the joiner's skill and the aptitudes of garage mechanics, independent of a sterner preoccupation with their essential trade, the sea.

Here and there Delia discerned the makings of a garden—a bed of zinnias going to seed, a geranium taking the air in an invalidish way before its ignominious return to a tomato can in somebody's kitchen window. Radio aerials and television antennae clawed the sky, and the chrome of new automobiles semaphored the bruised skies of sunset with a message of marvelous irrelevance.

"That," Donald said, "is what I wanted you to see. My favorite view of Todd's. Not much changed since I was a kid. Perhaps a boat more or less, more cars certainly, and those damned antennae, though I must say that in a queer way they have come to belong to the rest of it. At first I resented them. Now they merely give the scene a hirsute air, like Paul Haskett's face before his Saturday shave."

Delia gazed at the little harbor with its boats, at the small friendly houses and the green land hemmed by the sea, and felt an unexpected stir of emotion. She sat where she could see the chimney of Donald's house sticking like a clam neck above the trees, and knew that when the sun set one would be able to see, from this spot, its light strike the windows, setting them afire.

She asked musingly: "Why do I have a feeling that John Marin may have painted it?"

"For all I know he did paint it. He lived not far away, and knew this countryside well."

She asked jealously: "Did you bring Clare here?"

"Once or twice. She didn't care for it especially."

Delia looked at the cobalt water and the boats blazing like things forged in the white heat of the sun. They could not have been whiter, or looked more as if they were about to burst into flame before her eyes. This light, she knew, would not last. Already the fog was moving towards them, the color of bloom on grapes.

She said after a moment: "I've been trying to think of what to say to you about this place, about our stay with you. It all sounds quite superfluous. I ask myself how much life here at Todd's has had to do with my reactions, with this sense of permanence in a shifting world, of values which remain intact."

He smiled faintly. "You've said it. Clare would undoubtedly have done better. She wouldn't have stopped until she'd found just the right words and peppered me with them." He smoked contentedly for a moment or two. "Clare always had the right vocabulary for music, painting, books, and she wasn't insincere really. Nor was she wrong. She had in fact a rather horrible way of being almost always right." He laughed. "You've helped take the taste of Clare out of my system and restored Todd's to me as it used to be before I knew her. You've given me back the old sense of irresponsible pleasure in a state of things which I know very well would stand improvement, but which I for one would rather have stay as they are."

A fish hawk, black and silver in the slanting light, towered above the harbor and hung on quivering wings, its telescopic eye marking a herring school which lay in the shadow of the pier.

"It's been a strange experience to have you here," Donald continued thoughtfully, "you've undone so much that Clare did, and you've been so right even though by all logical standards you've been all wrong." He took her hand. "Clare's peculiar lack of charity made it possible for her to see into people's motives and the murky cracks and crevices in which they try to hide their poor little secrets. She loved burrowing. She loved to drag out the shame which she knew exists in most lives, and to hang it, as she would have described it herself, out on the line—to air." Lightly, he kissed Delia's hand. "You haven't done that. Even with your own son you haven't done it. You've let him keep his little secrets, and don't think he'll ever get over being grateful to you."

Delia said in a low voice: "I don't think I like secrets very much. I couldn't do what you tell me Clare liked to do . . . burrow . . . but that doesn't mean that I think secrets are necessarily healthy things."

"We all have them."

"Have you?" She asked lightly.

"Sure. Haven't you?"

She said nothing, she seemed not to have heard his question, and they sat for some minutes silently watching the old horse as it cropped among the weeds nearby.

He continued after a slight pause: "For the intellectually un-initiated the emotional response is, I believe, the most honest of all. I'm always amused by literary critics who try to interpret painting or music in literary terms. They're caught in the trap of having to use the only symbols at their command in order to try to describe other symbols for which there is no literary counter-part. The more abstract the painting and the more abstruse the music the more fatuous the literary man's efforts to pin these down in symbols which make any kind of literary sense. And if they should somehow or other make that kind of sense, they certainly don't make painting sense, or musical sense. That was what Clare tried to do with Todd's Harbor. She disapproved of it so violently —of everything it stood for, its backwardness, its shiftlessness, its politics, its morals, its very physical appearance, that by the time she'd finished dissecting it, it wasn't Todd's Harbor. The people weren't the people I'd always known. They weren't even people."

He nodded at the scene before them. "So far as that's concerned, the change can be only in a certain direction. More plumbing. More radios. More television antennae. More automobiles, and in the end—more automatons. To be an individual nowadays a man must remain as poor as Job, or cultivate a mild form of lunacy as he would his garden."

She looked at him curiously. "You have more than a slight streak of pessimism, haven't you?"

"Perhaps because I find pessimism effective as an inoculation against despair. And you know how I feel about *that*."

Abruptly, he changed the subject. "Next year when we come back it will be for longer. I'll take most of the summer off."

"Next year! I remember when we were children next year sounded like the millenium."

"This is August. October we get married. Then Italy for a month. Then next July back here to Todd's."

She held his hand and they watched a sailboat tack into the harbor from the eastward. Like the lobster boats this had the look of a toy as it moved soundlessly over the water, the sun brilliant on its sails. There were four people in the boat and they recognized Nick and Linda, Veronica and Chris. They saw Nick go forward and stand beside the anchor while Chris brought the yacht up into the wind.

Delia said: "I hope they have sense to come home before the fog shuts down. It looks as if it might be coming in thick later."

"Guess they're just stopping to drop Linda." He looked at her inquiringly. "Any easier in your mind about that situation?"

She laughed. "I don't know why I should be. Just thanks to the generally demoralizing atmosphere of the place. But he does seem happy . . . sure of himself. I haven't the heart to spoil it."

They watched the sail come down in a shimmer of light and shadow and as Nick threw the anchor overboard Delia fancied she

could hear the splash. The light changed, took on depth and richness, and as if at a signal the restless gulls left their occupations
and flew high above the harbor and the little islands, taking the
fading light on their wings and carrying it out of sight.

CHAPTER

XXXV

Donald took his time driving back to the house. He wanted to show Delia the blueberry lands north of the harbor, and they drove for an hour over rough tracks, between outcroppings of rock and a few fire-blasted pines standing with a strange and spectral air high above the sea. In fall, Donald told her, the ground-cover turned a color known to artists as alizarin crimson, and it flowed for miles over this terrain, a blood-colored, eerie, strangely beautiful sight without a trace of life.

"It seems out of character with the rest of the country, as though part of another continent had been washed up here by the sea in some forgotten age, and stranded with all its characteristics intact . . . the hunting ground of gnomes and Martians."

They got out of the car and walked a little distance hand in hand. In his faded blue work shirt and dungarees, his face sunburned and his hair blowing in the wind, Donald seemed to her a changed man. This, she felt, was his true background, this was where he belonged. Without a definite sense of place herself, she knew that she could adapt to his, and for the first time in her life she found herself desiring the experience. "Whither thou goest I will go; and where thou lodgest, I will lodge: thy home shall be my home, thy people shall be my people . . . where thou diest, will I die, and there will I be buried. . . ."

340

"Fog's coming in," Donald said, and they watched it roll towards the land, a great bank of purple vapor flushed by the sinking sun.

"We better beat it," Donald said. "The kids should be home, and I could do with a drink."

The fog was thick as they drove up the dirt road towards the house, and it was with a gust of relief that Delia spotted the yacht safely moored in the cove, and Chris and her children rowing in to shore.

Donald parked the car and they got out. Chris hailed them, and they waited, watching the last of the sun touch the three young faces and run golden over their heads, giving them for a moment the improbable look of angels in blue jeans.

"Got the lobsters," Nick said, and swung a pailful of the creatures by its bailer. "Two apiece and a couple extra for growing boys."

"Why didn't you bring Linda?" Donald asked him casually. "There's lots of food."

"I asked her, but she said she had to write letters. Said she'd like to come tomorrow instead. That O.K.?" He looked with a touch of diffidence at Donald, then at his mother.

"Of course it's O.K. The understanding being of course that the youngest members of the party wash the dishes afterwards." They walked towards the house, Nick swinging the pail and shouting:

> *"Let's all go balmy*
> *And join the army*
> *And see a life we never saw!"*

He was in tearing spirits and the others smiled as they listened. Donald opened the front door and they trooped in, bringing a smell of fog with them, and a smell of the sea, and the cool freshness of the fading day, and in the parlor, seated in the chair which used to be Grandmother Todd's and smoking a cigarette, they found Fran.

Surprise and consternation washed them like a tide and went out to sea, baring the hard rock of certainty. Here she was, and it was no dream that she was here, but, rather as Donald was the first to perceive—grimly, instantly—the opening scene of a big act. So sure was he of this that of all the little group he was the least taken aback. The good genii in the attic had fallen asleep at the switch . . . but he was convinced that even the safety lock which Clare had put on the door would not have kept Fran out for long.

She rose as they entered, putting a book which she'd been reading on the table near her chair. "Hullo, everyone." Then to Donald with a faint smile. "We've met before, haven't we?"

"I believe we have." He gave her an ironic bow. "Welcome to Todd's Harbor. I hope you haven't had to wait too long without so much as a cup of tea . . ."

"Fran!" Nick cried explosively. He set the pail of lobsters on the floor and went to her, kissing her on both cheeks. "How in heck did you get here?"

"By plane from New York to Trenton, then by taxi to your door."

Nick kept his arm slung round her neck. He was in a state of euphoria, beyond reach of the tension which held the others in its grip. "I didn't know you'd met Donald! When did that happen?"

Before Fran could answer, Delia interposed in a cold voice: "Why didn't you let us know you were coming, Fran? We could have met you at the airport."

"I didn't know until the very last moment that I could get a seat on the plane, and anyhow it didn't really matter. I knew I'd find you—Katie told me you were still here. And since I'm not staying more than a very short time it didn't seem worth while to put anyone to unnecessary bother."

The sisters stared at each other. Donald felt the swift, searching terror in Delia's mind, and his moment of indecision hardened into a sudden resolve to let her go through with it—to let them both go through with it, all three of them, Veronica, Delia, Fran. Each in her way had asked for what he was positive, now, was in the making, but this time there was no Luigi to knock him out in the first round. He would have all his faculties about him to see Delia through this one, whether she wanted him to or whether she didn't. This was his house, she was his girl, and he felt his pulse quicken in the clash of that first measuring glance which passed between the sisters and which moved simultaneously to Veronica, who among the lot had had nothing to say—even Chris had joined in the chorus of exclamation at first sight of their visitor—but Veronica had walked to the window and now stood with her back to them, staring into the fog.

Nick was still incredibly unconcerned. "Lucky the plane made it into Trenton before the fog shut in. And what makes you think you can get back in a hurry? You'll have to spend the night. You can have my bed and I'll sleep on the boat. Did you see the boat, Fran? Out there in the cove?"

He looked from one unresponsive face to the other and Donald watched him with a growing tenderness. How was he going to take it, when it came? And he had to take it; better now, buoyed up as he was, than at some moment of ebbing joy, some adolescent down-beat that was sure to come.

"What about a drink?" Donald suggested briskly. "I can mix us a cocktail. There's lots of time before we have to put the lobsters on."

Delia shook her head. "I think perhaps Fran and I had better go somewhere else where we can talk. Isn't that what you want, Fran?"

"No," Fran said calmly. "It isn't. I'd prefer to say what I've come to say right here in front of everybody. I'm rather tired of these huddles, if you want to know."

They stood awkwardly, all except Donald, who went to the fireplace and got the fire burning with slivers of driftwood. He took his pipe from the mantelpiece and knocked it out on an andiron as Nick, suddenly aware that something was wrong, dropped his arm from Fran's neck and thrust his hands in his pockets. The frown began to delve into his face and his eyes hardened at this first threat to a paradise which he had begun to take for granted as having a permanent place in the scheme of things.

"I think," Delia said, looking at Fran, "that notwithstanding what you say, it would be better if we went upstairs, or into the next room. I doubt whether anyone else would be especially interested . . . I really do."

"You're wrong, dear. They're sure to be interested. Veronica especially. And I want Nick to stay, and Chris. Why not? It seems as if we were all in this thing together, after all."

She turned to Donald and he felt her antagonism like a bared knife. "As Veronica's publisher and a friend of the family. . . ." It was not precisely a sneer which curled the corner of her mouth, nor was it precisely anything else. "As a friend of the family I hardly think that Mr. Wallingford can evade responsibility for at least part of this situation."

"Let's sit down, shall we?" Donald suggested. "How about another stick for the fire, Nick? And the lobsters might as well go into the kitchen, don't you think?"

"Sure." The boy plunged out of the room, carrying the pail of lobsters, and came back with an armful of wood which he dropped noisily into the woodbin. Delia winced. "Nick, dear."

"Sorry." He brushed off his clothes and looked at her. "What goes on anyway? Wouldn't you rather the rest of us went for a walk, Mother?"

"I would rather you stayed," Fran said crisply. She'd turned suddenly quite red. "What I have to say concerns you just as much as it does the rest of us. Running away isn't going to help."

"Who's running away?" He looked at her belligerently. "But if Mother doesn't want us around . . ."

Delia interposed again. "This happens to be Donald's house, Fran. I think we owe him some consideration."

"We owe him nothing," Fran retorted, measuring the emphasis of her temper as if by a slide rule. It had to last to the very end, and that, as Donald could see quite plainly, was a long way off. "We owe Mr. Wallingford nothing, although I feel that he owes us at least a word or two of—shall I say explanation?"

"Say it," he invited her cordially, his own temper well in hand. "If it's the word you want, say it by all means."

Delia was trembling. "Fran, I have no idea what this is all about and why you've invited yourself down here . . . Just bear in mind, though, that you've made enough trouble for us all in the past. Is it asking too much to spare us whatever it is you have in mind, now?"

Chris put his hand through Veronica's arm. "Would you rather Dad and I took a walk, Nonny? This looks like a family party."

She turned and suddenly Donald couldn't take his eyes from her face. It was the face of someone very young, about to be shot.

She addressed herself to her aunt. "I see you brought my book."

All eyes turned then to the book which Fran had laid on the table, and which she now picked up and held as though it were the notes for a speech. The book had a glossy dust cover and there was a photograph of Veronica on the back.

"Who is Silvia?" Fran raised her eyebrows slightly. "It does seem as if you'd made up your mind who she is, and what's more— *what* she is!"

Nick said interestedly: "Nonny's book? Let's have a look, Fran."

But Fran was intent on her niece. "So this is what you've always thought of Delia." She turned to the others. "You'll be interested to learn that Veronica has done a neat job of crucifixion on her mother. It's something which all of us who appreciate art should be proud of."

Delia sank suddenly into a chair, as though her legs had given way. Donald resisted an impulse to go to her, to pick her up in his arms and carry her out of the room and out of reach of everything. But what would it prove? He'd be carrying her burden with her, just as she had carried it wherever she'd gone for the past twenty-odd years. And this was not Delia's act, it was not even

Veronica's . . . it was Fran's, and the sooner she got it over with the better for everyone.

Fran returned to Grandmother Todd's chair and sat down. "Could I have a cigarette?" she asked Chris. "I just finished my last."

He gave her one and held a light for her, and they waited. She blew a plume of smoke and began with an air of careful detachment:

"I was in town two days ago and called your friend Miriam Werth, who invited me to dinner at her apartment. She showed me Veronica's novel, which she'd been asked to review for her college magazine. Since she'd finished it I asked if I might borrow it. Naturally, I was excited." She glanced at Delia. "Maybe you'd like a synopsis, I mean aside from the blurb, which describes it as a distinguished work of prose in the great tradition of Proust and Henry James." Turning to Donald she asked with a smile: "Is that your opinion, if I might ask?"

"We have a department which takes care of the blurbs."

"I'm sure you must have."

"Donald thought: "I wish Bunny were here. She's the justification—if he needed one—of every unflattering idea he's ever cherished about her sex."

Fran turned the book over in her hand and looked at the title.

"Briefly, then, this is the story of a child who grows up in New York and Connecticut. A boy named Larry." Once more she looked at Veronica. "Why the disguise?"

Veronica replied dispassionately: "It's easier, sometimes, to put oneself in somebody else's skin. Gives one—you know—a different, a more oblique approach."

"I'll say it does!" Fran laughed. "But to go on. I'll make it short, since you're all going to read the thing for yourselves. Larry, then, is used as a kind of mirror to reflect the personality of his mother, Silvia. And Silvia is a nymphomaniac, beautiful, calculating, cold. Like most cold-blooded things she lives on blood, the life blood, preferably, of other human beings."

Fran opened the book as though to refresh her memory, then closed it. "None of these things is said, not a vice is named, hardly a fault. The child understands nothing. He merely registers whatever he sees and hears and carries his discoveries to his only friend and confidant, an old bum he's taken up with in Central Park, where he spends most of his time. The bum tells Larry about his own life, and each pities the other for his separate reasons. Through the sensibility of the poor old man we see the truth behind Larry's innocent disclosures. We see Silvia as she goes suavely about the business of deceiving her handsome, unsuspecting, upright and adoring husband, as she plays at motherhood in order to hoodwink possible critics among her friends, and we are given every opportunity to have a good look into what heart she has, a frightening experience, believe me. But Larry of course knows nothing of all this. Sensitive, easily hurt, he does realize in a dim sort of way that his mother has no more love for him than she has for his father, but no one can explain to him why this should be. The bum, angered by what he can discern of the child's tragedy, tries to comfort him. "You're lucky to have a father," he tells the boy on one occasion. "That's better than nothing." And he adds mysteriously, as though to himself: "If it should so happen that he *is* your father, and you might as well take her word for it, because it's all you're ever going to get!"

Fran tilted her head a little, showing her fine profile to the others as she gazed silently at her niece. Far out to sea the bell buoy tolled restlessly, a lonely and lovely sound reaching them through the fog.

Fran went on: "One afternoon in spring when the grass is turning green Larry's father goes horseback riding in the park and his horse throws him, and he is killed before Larry's eyes. Just before he dies he looks up at the little boy and manages to whisper: 'Fetch Silvia.' A murmur goes round the group of strangers who've rushed to the spot, among them the old bum who turns to Larry and asks: "Silvia? Who is Silvia?"

Delia stirred, her shoulders rigid, and again Donald wanted to go to her, and again he held back. His unlit pipe between his teeth, he was watching Fran. How far would she go? How far would she carry it . . . as far as Veronica had already done, or farther? How far *could* she carry it?

Nick turned suddenly to his sister. "What was the idea, Nonny, dragging Father's accident into the story? Couldn't you have bumped the guy off some other way?"

Chris laughed—a brief, quickly stifled explosion which brought the ghost of a smile to Veronica's lips. Fran took Nick up at once:

"No, she couldn't have done it any other way. It had to be done the way it happened. Delia had to have her nose rubbed in it, and just to make sure that there should be no mistake in *her* mind when she read the book, or in mine, who knew something of the truth, Larry is shown to us as he rushes home with the dreadful news, thinking only to fling himself into his mother's arms, and finds her in the arms of a strange young man."

Delia raised her head and looked steadily at Veronica. "Is this true, Nonny? Is that what you've said?"

Before Veronica could speak Fran broke in: "You can see for yourself, Delia. It's all down so you can't miss it. The description of Charles, the description of yourself. Every detail. The fiendish little touches, the turns of speech, little tricks of expression and manner, all diabolically observed and ruthlessly exposed."

"But what's the idea?" demanded Nick. "What the hell is it all about, Veronica?"

Veronica gave a curious little sigh. "Fran talks as if we were the only people in the world who are going to read the book. But there'll be others, perhaps many others who don't know anything about any of us, who've never heard of—of Delia, and who'll get something quite different out of it, who won't at all see what Fran sees."

Fran turned on her with passion. "Do you think it matters about the others, as you call them? Doesn't it occur to you that what does matter is that I should have read it, that Delia will,

Nick, and our friends, and that none of us can be fooled for a single instant as to whom you intended Silvia to be?"

Veronica replied slowly: "Whatever there is in it . . . of Delia, then . . . is between her and me. It's nobody else's business, nobody's."

Fran's eyes were blazing. Anger made her look ten years younger, made her queerly beautiful, and Donald closed his own eyes for a moment, hating to see that radiant likeness to Delia, that blurring of personalities which brought to mind suddenly, incongruously at this moment, a picture of how they must have looked twenty years ago in the full loveliness of youth . . . The vision induced another, of himself this time, dazed and half blind with pain, stumbling through the garden behind Delia's house, and in that shrouding darkness a pair of arms going round him and lips pressing upon his and a voice crying darling, and he knew now that he could understand Charles at last . . . understand him very well indeed.

Donald forced himself to look at Fran and to listen to her voice: "So it's nobody's business that you've painted Delia as a woman incapable of fidelity to man, woman, or child?—nobody's business but yours and Delia's? But I happen to be Delia's sister, and where do I come in—and where does Delia's son come in? Or aren't we supposed to count as having the least interest in Delia—or in you?"

Nick gazed wildly at his mother. "I hate this," he muttered. "I don't get it and I don't want to get it."

Delia held out her hand to him in a gesture of appeal. "It can be explained, Nick. I think it's up to Veronica to explain. After all, it's her book."

Nick leaned sullenly against the wall, his fists clenched in his pockets. "How could any one mistake Silvia, whoever the hell she is, for Mother? After all, Donald read the book. He didn't make that mistake. Did you, Donald?"

Donald smiled at the boy. "I read the book and I admired it. Then I met Delia." He paused, feeling their sudden concentration upon him, feeling their anxiety, the full weight of Delia's fear, Veronica's mounting guilt, and the boy's bewilderment; feeling with a savage satisfaction, his power to drive Fran out into the open and to put her through her paces as no one had ever dared to do.

"Then I met Delia and whatever private reservations I might have had about the book went by the board. You see," he addressed himself deliberately, exclusively, to Nick: "Nothing made any difference to me after I'd met Delia. I fell in love with her. I asked her to marry me."

He reached on the mantel behind him and found a box of matches.

"Your mother didn't want this mentioned just yet. She felt that Veronica should be allowed to enjoy her own triumph to the full, without any rivalry from us. But I think it's silly to go on keeping secrets at this point. One of these days before very long, Delia and I are going to be married. That, I believe, should make it clear enough how much I think Delia resembles Silvia—or how much she resembles anyone else."

He finished, and felt a tingle in his flesh as Fran's hatred reached out to him like a high voltage current. So she hadn't forgotten that little incident in the garden at Marbury, either! He didn't think she had. He wondered briefly how much she might have discerned of herself in the portrait Veronica had drawn with such deadly accuracy while going so wide of the mark where Delia was concerned, hitting the truth, as it were, by ricochet . . .

Fran rose violently from her chair. "I congratulate you and Delia both, of course . . . but that still doesn't explain . . . it certainly doesn't excuse your letting Veronica get away with the things she's said in her novel!"

Donald shrugged. "Naturally, when I read it, I wondered a bit. As a publisher, I wonder about most books that pass through my hands. There's almost inevitably some degree of truth, some personal element, biographical, autobiographical, in every sincere piece of work. And yes, when I met Delia for the first time, and even afterwards, I recognized certain things which I could trace back to the story. I certainly didn't think it in especially good taste from that standpoint. In one of his novels, Somerset Maugham makes the comment that a writer cannot afford to be a gentleman, and I am sure that my partner Mr. Watts would give it as his opinion that a lady can afford even less to be a writer. For which reason I find myself in agreement with Veronica—that whatever of a dubiously ethical nature there is in her book, it remains something between her mother and herself."

"And knowing the nature of that something you accepted it, and have published it! How could you?"

"Because I thought it first rate. I still do."

"And that opinion obviates any first-rate ethics which might be involved?"

"What would you rather I had done?"

"Destroyed it!"

He laughed. "Those are your ethics, not mine."

Nick kicked at the floor with his shoe. "I still don't see why Veronica felt she had to write that kind of a book. Why did you, Veronica?"

She answered him directly: "Because it was the kind of a book I wanted to write."

"But a bunch of lies like that!"

"It isn't lies. At any rate not in the ordinary sense that you mean."

Delia looked from one to the other of their young faces. "Veronica, tell me something. Do you believe that Charles was not your father?"

Veronica hesitated, and suddenly Donald didn't want to look at any of them. He suffered from a heartache new to him, and recognized it as the price of his involvement, without which he would be a lonely man.

"Do you believe that, Veronica?" Delia repeated, and her voice was filled with wonder.

"I do believe it," Veronica said at last, with extraordinary firmness. "I've always known he wasn't my father."

"You're nuts!" Nick shouted in a fury. "You're off your rocker . . . you ought to be beaten up!"

Delia motioned him with her hand. "Just a minute, Nick." She looked at Veronica. "You loved Charles. You loved him more than anyone in the world. I always knew that. How could you have felt such a love for him if you believed . . . whatever it is you did believe?"

Something like a sob escaped Veronica. It was a strange sound, coming from her. But she spoke steadily enough: "I knew that Charles loved me because he believed I was his child. I knew he couldn't have known what I knew, that he loved me out of ignorance, and that if he had known I wasn't his, he couldn't have helped but hate me. Or at any rate, that he couldn't have gone on feeling about me as he always had."

Delia was silent. And so, strange to say, was Fran. Donald thought, here we are. This is it. They've come to the end, so far as it is the end, so far as Delia and Fran are resolved that it shall be the end. Veronica has had her say, and that leaves it up to Delia, and there she is faced with Nick and his new, young, terrible doubts of her, and why, somewhere along the way, didn't it occur to her that something of the sort was bound to happen one day, and she be bound to make her choice between the two children—between the hurt she would be compelled to inflict on Veronica, and the pain she might have to administer to her son?

Fran started to say something when Nick broke in: "It stinks. Why don't you tell her it stinks, Mother? That she's all wrong about Father and about you? . . . Why don't you tell her?"

"Because I don't think she'd believe me," Delia said, and her voice seemed to sink back into her body as though the will that had held her up were suddenly breaking in two. "And anyway, I think this scene has gone far enough. It can't have been much fun for everyone else."

Nick's face had a drawn look and he was trembling, as Donald saw, with a very grown-up rage. "Well, I'll believe you," he declared, his voice just a shade off key. "You can tell me, can't you? I'm in this too, aren't I? If Nonny's going around getting off all that stuff about you and Father, I've got to know whether it's true or whether it isn't."

Delia raised her head and met Donald's gaze. Cornered, she was turning to him, and again he felt their combined attention, as if they, too, had felt Delia's desperate need and acknowledged it as being theirs also—the need to call it a day, to have done with the hideous embarrassment of it all. A word from him—something reasonable and reassuring would be enough to restore the balance of things the way each would have it, for how else could they have it? Say something, Delia seemed to beg of him. For God's sake, Donald, say something . . . if you really love me . . . if you really want to help me, protect me!

He lit his pipe and flicked the match back into the fireplace behind him. "I think Nick deserves an honest answer," he said. "I think it's up to you to tell him, Delia."

The fire made soft fluttering movements in the fireplace, as the driftwood sent out tiny flags of color—purple, crimson, rose, and they heard the bell buoy, now clear, now faint, and the fog moved up and pressed against the panes like some great beast leaning there for warmth.

Delia gave him a strange look and he thought: She sees through my game, she knows that I know, and that I am not going to come to her rescue, or to Fran's, or to Veronica's, or to Nick's. And she knows why not, that it would be no rescue at all but simply another connivance which will leave us all exactly where we were before.

"Well," Delia said at last. "What am I supposed to say? Defend myself to my own children?" She flushed. "This is all quite outrageous, really."

Nick said roughly: "Tell me about Charles."

"Tell you what—that Veronica is wrong, that Charles *was* her father, and yours? Well, it's true. He was."

"It's your word against mine," said Veronica, suddenly very white. "That's all there is, isn't there? Your word against mine."

Delia gave a sad little laugh. "Yes, that's all there is. And don't you think we might as well leave it at that?"

Nick took a turn round the room. "But that business about Veronica . . . or whoever it was in the book . . . coming back and finding you . . ." He broke off, horrified by his own words, and the silence seemed bottomless. Delia said at last: "Do you think it's fair to tax me like this before I've even had a chance to read the book? I shall be in a better position to answer your questions, Nick, when I have read it. In the meantime I'm afraid you're just going to have to take my word for it that Charles Dalton was your father and Veronica's. That's all I have to say for the moment."

She rose and turned to Donald. "I'm sorry about this. It's the second time you've been exposed to unpleasantness on my account. I promise it will be the last."

She was composed and steady and he had a sudden clear recollection of her as he'd seen her that night in Connecticut when he lay sick and helpless and watched her bringing order into the confused and disordered room.

She went on: "I'm sure you and Chris have had enough of us, so if Nick will get the car Veronica and I will pack and I think fog or no fog, we had better start for New York tonight."

So it was a dead-end after all and he had been wrong, and there was nothing for him to do except take her in his arms there before the lot of them, and say the hell with it, you're not going, and none of this matters—a tempest in a teapot, to be ignored and forgotten as the days pass and the truth of our own making takes over where all the lies leave off.

"Darling," he said, and at the word he sensed rather than saw a movement from Fran, a swift, involuntary gesture, one which he was later to define as springing from some savage impulse of denial, as though she would have snatched the endearment for herself.

She had been silent for some minutes, now she turned and spoke to Veronica. "You'd like to leave things at that, wouldn't you, my dear? Your word against Delia's, hers against yours, and no one, not even you, any wiser as to the facts?"

"Fran!" Delia said, sharply.

Fran ignored her. "It took your novel to bring home to me once and for all what a really lousy set-up this has been for the past twenty years. It took your book to prove to me how lousy art can be, and artists, when they build on lies from beginning to end."

"Fran," Delia repeated.

Some instinct of malice and experimentation made Donald put his arm around her and he saw at once that this gesture was not lost on Fran. She flushed and her eyes seemed to hesitate as though not quite sure where to look.

She said with a harsh laugh, "Veronica is sure she has all the answers. She's been sure of that, since she could walk. Busily building up her case against Delia like the—what is that seashell, the many-chambered something or other. Quietly, in secret. Feeding on this and that lie, a half-truth here, a careless word dropped there."

"You dropped quite a few yourself," Veronica shot at her suddenly. "When you were drunk. And even when you weren't. And why pretend that you're so concerned over Delia's suffering . . . over the fact that she might possibly have been misunderstood? You've always been jealous of her. You've always hated being her twin. You know you have."

"Oh God," murmured Delia in despair. "Must we have this . . . must we? Must we?"

Donald held her close. He felt an enormous excitement springing in his nerves as he realized that the struggle was not now between Delia and Fran or Veronica and Delia, but between aunt and niece. Veronica, he saw, was not going to give in meekly. How alike they were, he thought, Fran and Veronica, and he could have cried out with the sense of triumph.

Fran was smiling unpleasantly. "You've misunderstood so much," she said, with a shrug. "You've misread so much, it's hardly to be expected that loyalty, responsibility . . . and gratitude, would be in your catalog as things worth feeling, worth writing about."

Delia made a move to free herself of Donald's clasp, and Fran gave her a quick glance. "You might as well relax, Delia. This is something I've wanted to get off my chest for a long time. You've always managed to prevent it . . . to head me off . . . but I've had enough . . . and I'm tired of playing the weakling, the souse, while you. . . ."

"You've no business!" Delia cried passionately. "You have no right!"

"Well, you deprived me of the right some time ago!" She stared at Veronica. "For twenty years I've allowed Delia to take the rap for me. It's been one long continuous fake, and this is what it's led to. Where you've been imagining that Charles Dalton, that poor long-suffering man, was deceived all his life, that he was *not* your father—perhaps not even Nick's father—that Delia was *Silvia*, meretricious, shallow, vile——"

Delia interrupted: "Fran, just remember one thing. You and I made a most solemn promise to one another and we've kept it in spite of everything. I hold you to that promise, Fran. I hold you."

Fran shook her head. "You seem to forget—you've made such a point of forgetting it, that I do believe you've become totally deluded on the subject . . . but this does happen to be as much my business as it ever was yours."

"It is not your business. You surrendered your right in the case years ago."

"Veronica has made it my business."

"I won't have it! Let's go into the next room. We'll talk about it there."

"On condition that Veronica and Nick come with us."

"This is no concern of the children, Fran. For heaven's sake!"

"It's every concern of theirs. How can you deny it, Delia?"

Nick caught his breath. "Do we have to go on digging? Spill it, Fran, for God's sake."

Donald said in a low voice to Delia: "You've had it coming, Delia. You've tried to play fair, but it doesn't work to try to play fair for other people."

She gave him a frantic glance. "You don't even know what you're saying. This is between Fran and me. It's our affair, and I will not have the children in on it."

Fran shrugged and addressed herself once more to Veronica. "Delia has become so accustomed to the role of martyr that she doesn't realize what that makes the rest of us. She acts as though there were something unnatural in my reactions to your book . . . in my feelings of outrage on her account." And with a laugh full of bitterness: "It seems I'm not even allowed the normal feelings of loyalty . . . remorse."

"Remorse?" Donald gave her a faint smile.

His voice, his smile, seemed to dispel in a flash whatever lingering hesitation she might have felt, for she whirled on Veronica.

"You've always been wrong about Charles. He was your father. And you've always been wrong about Delia. She is not your mother."

In the silence which deepened round them Donald could feel Delia's heart stirring like a captive thing, too long captive.

Veronica's gaze was fixed on her aunt. "Having gone so far," she said slowly, "you might as well let us have the rest."

"Yes, I might as well." Her voice, firm till this moment, wavered ever so slightly. "I'm your mother, Veronica."

Donald dropped his arm from Delia's waist and meeting Chris's glance, moved with him towards the door. In passing he paused by Nick who stood looking from one face to the other, his own incredulous. Donald touched his arm. "We'll leave the ladies to their wine and cigars," he said softly. "Come on out to the kitchen and have a beer with Chris and me."

The boy hesitated, gave him an uncertain smile. "All right," he said, and they left the room together.

CHAPTER

XXXVI

For several minutes the three women sat listening to the sound of the bell buoy, and it seemed to swing their thoughts, their emotions in its uncertain rhythm, harnessing their attention as to the one coherent note in all this chaos. Her bolt shot at last, Fran looked as if the ordeal had drained the last drop of her vitality and left her an old woman. After reaching the peak of emotion there seemed nothing left but to turn and come back. As the awareness of this dawned upon her, her glance moved nervously round the room in search of something, anything upon which it might rest with comfort. It encountered the far-off gaze of Grandmother Todd in her walnut frame, but like so many eyes which had met hers, there was, in these, nothing for her. She'd given up the secret around which she, like Veronica, had built her many-chambered nautilus, and what did it amount to after all? A few words which a few years from now would have left nothing worth remembering. Nothing from nothing leaves nothing . . .

Delia was gazing at Veronica. "Nonny, dear," she said. "Is there anything we can say to you, or do for you?"

Veronica remained silent and Delia rose impulsively and went to her, drawing her down to the sofa at her side. "Oh Veronica, it all seems so silly now, so unimportant. I wish I could make you see it that way."

Veronica's face had lost its brilliance, but she seemed composed and gave Delia the ghost of a smile. "I suppose there are proofs of all this . . . I mean, I suppose there are?"

"Yes, my dear, there are proofs."

"One has to get used to things, doesn't one?" Veronica murmured. She looked at Fran. "I still don't understand, quite. How, when you were married to Herbert and Mother married to Charles . . ."

Fran seemed oddly grateful for the question and the release it gave the lingering tension in her nerves. She sat down and rather shakily lighted a cigarette. "If you can take any more . . . if Delia can . . ."

Delia shrugged and Fran said after a pause: "I've told you, I think . . . often enough . . . ad nauseum in fact, that after my divorce from Herbert I came to New York and stayed with Charles and Delia in their house on Sixty-eighth street. I was shot to pieces and didn't want to be alone. Actually I guess I was having some sort of a breakdown, though that's no excuse for the way I behaved and I'm not trying to make it an excuse. Anyway, I stayed with them for a month."

Veronica watched her steadily. Always, in the past, Fran's recital of her history had come to an abrupt conclusion at this point. Even in her most drunken moments it had not progressed beyond it. Queer, now, to be listening to a continuation of the story, almost as queer as all the other feelings that were coursing through her, feelings she'd never had before, churning her to the depths.

Fran was saying: "I didn't get any better, or any easier to live with. The drink had really got me . . . not that that's any excuse but I was beside myself with loneliness." She stared broodingly at the window, a gray void against the fog. "It had all been my own doing, but that only made it worse to think about. I had never dreamed that after living with a man for eight years, life could be so completely empty and meaningless. I'd never dreamed

how much I cared about Herbert. Anyway . . ." she pulled herself together with a shudder.

"Anyway, I behaved abominably to everyone. And then I had a
quarrel with Delia, and said that I was going to leave her house.
I think perhaps I hoped she'd protest, try to stop me, beg me to
stay. But she'd had enough, I guess. Anyway I packed my suitcase and Charles drove me to a hotel in a taxi."

She glanced away from their faces. "Charles had a few drinks
himself, and we ordered more to be sent up to my room. I swear
I don't think he had an idea in his head about me . . . I didn't
about him, anyway not then." She reddened, staring at the floor.

"It was twenty years ago and in spite of all the things that had
happened to me—my boozing, wasting my time, and then the
divorce—I was very good-looking. Delia and I were terrifically
alike in those days and Charles used to make jokes about it. Not in
very good taste."

A smile trembled on her lips and died there. "I'm not trying
to say that he got so drunk that he mistook me for Delia or anything of the sort. He just felt damned sorry for me and when I
went to pieces he tried to comfort me. He stayed longer than he
should have. And not for the last time."

She rose abruptly. "God, how it must sound to you now! I
wouldn't have believed it could sound so horrible . . ."

She made an effort to control herself and went on: "I came to
my senses eventually and realized what a beast I was making of
myself, what between us Charles and I we were doing to Delia. But
contrition was a bit late, and I discovered that I was pregnant."

She looked at Veronica. "Are you going to hate me for this?
There's no reason why you shouldn't."

Veronica shook her head.

"Well, I told Charles, of course. I had to. He was in a
state, because although he was no saint, this was going pretty far
and he felt terribly guilty about Delia. So did I. He would come
to see me in the hotel and we drank a lot of whisky and wallowed

in our guilt and I guess that was one way of trying to face it. We were having our cake and eating it too. And of course it appealed to my sense of drama. We decided that the only honest, decent thing left to do was to confess everything to Delia and throw ourselves on her mercy."

She stopped and they could hear voices from the kitchen—the sound of pots and pans, Chris's easy laugh. Fran went on:

"Well, we told Delia, and that's something I can't go into now . . . it's something I've always tried to forget, but I never will. Delia was not an actress and she was in love with Charles and she hadn't been able to have a baby herself, and now here was this situation. Well, to make a long story short, she came across. I was in a panic. Suicidal even. And Delia said that she and Charles would take the baby, adopt it legally, and bring it up as theirs. I was to go away and stay away for a few years, and then when we'd all calmed down I could see the child, on condition, of course, that I kept to our agreement never to speak of the facts to anyone. This was not for my sake or for Delia's or for Charles's—it was for the child's sake."

She raised miserable eyes to Veronica. "For your sake, Veronica."

There was silence for a minute, then Fran said: "Delia and Charles kept their end of the bargain faithfully. But as time went by I couldn't control my curiosity and my morbid concern with the situation. Delia had told me that if I was ever indiscreet and irresponsible enough to reveal any of this, she would shut her doors to me forever. I knew I couldn't bear that . . . she was all I had." She smiled faintly at Veronica. "I was not then . . . I am not now, the maternal type. I didn't want you, Veronica, or to stake any claim in you. I swear that. You were in good hands. The best. And Charles was crazy about you. I wouldn't be surprised if he found it quite easy to fool himself into the belief that he hadn't really done anything so very wrong . . . or even that you were Delia's child after all!" She laughed. "He had the most elastic conscience of any human being I ever knew. This is not said to poison your mind against him. There was no reason in the world why you shouldn't have loved him as you did. He died when you were too young to understand the type of person he was. It's not for me to talk to you about Charles . . . but you can't blame me for feeling almost crazy with shame and indignation when I read your book and saw how utterly you'd got the picture crossed up. That you should have blamed Delia . . . tried to revenge yourself, and Charles, on *her* . . . I couldn't bear it. Not after what I'd done to her, I couldn't."

There was a long silence, then Veronica said in a low voice: "I'm thinking about Nick."

Delia took her hand. "Darling, Nick will be all right."

Fran looked at them with tragic eyes. "Yes, he's got you. I doubt whether he'll have much use for his Aunt Fran after this."

It was part of her punishment—the hardest, perhaps, that they did not move to deny the possibility or to offer the trivial consolations which her heart craved. She waited a moment, then went to the door. There she turned, the actress in her putting up a brave front. "There wouldn't be a chance, would there, that I might be able to make myself of some use helping with dinner?"

Without waiting for an answer she left them, closing the door after her. Veronica drew her breath as though it hurt her to do so. She said with a queer laugh: "If I feel like anything, it's like the worst kind of a fool."

"You don't need to. You're not a fool."

"But the book . . ." her voice broke. "I shall ask Donald if there is some way to stop distribution at once."

Delia shook her head. "Then you *would* be acting like a fool." She put her arm round the girl's shoulders. "Don't let's have any more melodrama. I couldn't bear it."

Veronica waited a moment or two then she said:

"In the beginning, I did want to hurt you. I had been hurt and as soon as I grew old enough to feel that it was in my power to hurt you I began to work out ways and means of doing it. Because I loved Charles. Because loving him yet believing that he was not my father, I had this idea that it must be wrong for me to love him. And I hated you for being, as I thought, the reason of it all. And then I hated you more because I wondered whether he could possibly have loved me, as he did, if he'd known that he was not my father. Wouldn't he have hated me then, as I hated you?"

Veronica continued more steadily: "I suppose I wanted to love you too, but something always interfered. A feeling. Even now, even after I'd worked it all out in the book, I can't quite explain or describe that feeling. I was afraid of you, I guess."

"You had some reason. I was not very kind to you in those early days."

Veronica stared at the fire, faint now as the driftwood burned to ash, a single purple flame quivering in its center.

"There used to be a look on your face sometimes which made me wonder whether perhaps you might be wishing me dead. Sometimes when I must have been very young and you were giving me my bath I'd feel the strength of your hands and knew that you could very easily have killed me, if you'd really wanted. And always it somehow came back to that thing about Charles. I strung it all together like beads on a chain." She touched the ones at her throat, gold and amber beads which Chris had given her the day they came to Todd's Harbor. "And Fran may have made a vow of silence but she didn't always keep it inviolate. She'd drop hints . . . a word here or there. Or perhaps I imagined it. Perhaps being ready to believe what I'd made up my mind to believe, I read meaning into everything that happened around me. My meaning. I don't know. But I knew better than to ask. I didn't want to put people on their guard against me. I didn't want to miss anything."

Delia smiled rather queerly. "You little demon!"

"Yes, I guess I was, just that. But what I really wanted to find out was why you didn't love me. That was at the bottom of it."

Delia nodded. "I can see, now, how it would be."

"I kept a diary," Veronica went on. "And it was out of that

that the book began to grow and take shape. You remember how I was always so keen about writing, and about books? I sometimes asked myself what might have happened, what sort of a person I would have become if I'd had different tastes, and been more like Nick. But I knew I had a taste for writing . . . I think I must have discovered it very early. It was wonderful to know that I could do something no one else could—no one that I knew, anyway. It—it made me feel better about things. Especially after Charles died and I felt I had nothing left."

She looked quickly at Delia. "I'm not trying to sound sentimental. I don't want you to think I'm asking for pity . . . even for forgiveness. I'm just trying . . . you know, to clear things up as much as I can."

"I understand," Delia said. She studied the profile beside her. It seemed pitifully youthful.

"I don't quite know when I got the idea that I would make a book out of all the things that had happened to me, or that I believed had happened. When I was about sixteen or seventeen, I guess. And the more I thought about it, and when I'd written a few short things and they'd been praised . . . suddenly I *felt* the book. There it was. I had to write it, no matter what happened."

"But the secrecy," Delia murmured after a moment. "You were so quiet about it. Even to the last minute . . . till today when Fran dropped her bombshell. You must have known what was going to happen when we read it, Veronica."

"Yes, I did know. And for a long time I thought it was all right because I could always change my mind and burn it up if—if my conscience got the upper hand. It almost did, once. Then something happened. Something very slight. I found—I mean I had a suspicion, an idea, that I might perhaps lose Chris. That he might turn away from me to someone else. I couldn't bear the thought. It wasn't even that I was so crazy about him myself, but the thought of losing him seemed in a strange way to revive all sorts

of sleeping horrors in me . . . loneliness . . . fear . . . humiliation . . ."

Her lashes moved slowly, shrouding her gaze. "I begin to see
how much I've always resembled Fran psychologically. They say
acquired characteristics are not inherited, but I wonder whether
they cannot be sometimes unconsciously imitated? She has always
been a devouring woman. I guess she's the sort of person who can
never have enough . . . of anything. Without even loving it. Just
wanting it."

Delia said with a sigh: "Somehow I find it very hard to bear
that you should have known so much, felt so much, Veronica!"

"Well, that was because I was . . . I!" She smiled faintly.
"Anyway, the moment I had this sudden fear that Chris might be
slipping away from me I decided I'd send the book to his father—
that I'd take the step, and the risk, because if it worked . . .
if it was accepted and I got myself published, I would have
scored . . . off him . . . proved something . . . triumphed. And of
course once it was out of my hands I still knew I could get it back
if not at the last moment, then almost at the last."

"But you didn't try to get it back, did you?" Delia said gently.
"You went through with it. I can understand how you would.
Even without being any kind of a creative person, myself, I can
understand that."

The color deepened in Veronica's cheeks. "My decision became final after Donald read it and praised it. I might as well be
honest about it now. It went to my head—to hear him say the
things he said. I guess I didn't have an idea how greatly I needed
that kind of reassurance . . . that I was some good. That someone
believed I was worth something."

She seemed to be nerving herself for a final disclosure, and
it came at last in barely audible tones: "But it still wasn't enough
to be admired and praised by someone whose opinion you respected, and whom you respected as a—as a person." Awkwardly,
with a shy desperate gesture, she put her hand on Delia's
knee. "I fell for Donald because he was nice to me. But for

another reason too. I wanted to dominate him . . . it sounds fantastic. But I did. I felt that if he admired me as a writer . . . how much more he would admire me if he were to fall in love with me? I'm telling you this because it makes me sick, now, to think about it and I don't want you to have any idea . . . if you have had any . . . that there is anything of that feeling left in me. I was horribly jealous and miserable when I saw he liked you. It seemed to me to sum up all my feelings and suspicions about you. That you took everything away from me."

Gently, Delia stroked the bright, shining hair on that averted head. "Perhaps you should hear a little of my side of things now. I'm going to tell you that in the first place I, too, loved Charles. I was very young when I married him, and very naive. When Fran was divorced and came to stay with us, I was at the height of my feeling for him, and of course I trusted him. Perhaps under it all I didn't really . . . one can fool oneself about such things. But I didn't fool myself about loving him. You can imagine what it did to me when they came to me one day and told me that they'd been sleeping together, and that Fran was going to have a baby."

She felt Veronica's body tense against hers.

"I won't go into my feelings, except to explain that I had been bothered for some time because I hadn't been able to have a child. There had been two miscarriages, but the doctors assured me there was nothing seriously wrong, that it would be all right eventually. It turned out later that they were right, and I had Nick. But at the height of my love for Charles and my private worry about what I was beginning to look upon as my sterile condition, I was suddenly brought face to face with the situation between your father and Fran."

She hesitated, her hand resting lightly on the girl's hair.

"I could see no way out of the problem. Fran had been divorced long enough so that there was no question of Herbert's responsibility—and anyway there was her confession to me, and Charles's. I was in a state of shock and one sometimes does queer things under certain circumstances. My pride was a shambles . . ."

Veronica turned to look at her, saying nothing.

"What I did then will not be chalked up strictly in my favor on Judgment Day. When Fran asked me hysterically what in God's name she was going to do, I said that I would take the child. There was a hideous exaltation in the thought of my own magnanimity, in the knowledge that I could, after all, rise above my pain and humiliation, my sense of betrayal, rise above Charles, above Fran, the two people closest to me on earth, whom I had most admired. So it was all taken care of with the greatest decorum and discretion. Freddie Bowers helped. He's a lawyer, and he has always been our friend."

"Freddie Bowers," Veronica murmured, wincing. "So *they* know!"

"We needed advice, and we knew we could trust Freddie. Fran was confined in New York, after which she went back to San Francisco, and Charles and I brought you home to Sixty-eighth Street."

Veronica was silent, and Delia went on: "The decision to adopt you was not difficult. I was buoyed up with the excitement, by the dreadful strangeness of the situation. I had the feeling that I'd performed some terrific feat of courage and endurance, and in a sense of course I had. It did something to retrieve the humiliation and pain of Charles' faithlessness, and Fran's. Like you with Chris . . . I wanted to *score* off them, and I did, up to a point." She frowned.

"And I had normal maternal feelings which hadn't had much chance to function. I told myself that it would be the most natural thing in the world to love you and treat you exactly as though you were mine. I did, at first. But I hadn't bargained for the depth and extent of my own hurt, or faced up to the implications of my own decision . . . that it was for keeps. As you began to grow I saw Charles in you—and I saw Fran. My own husband, my own sister. I tried hard to overcome my feelings. You were a child, totally innocent, and I wanted to go on loving you and do everything for you as if you'd been mine. But the past was too much in the present and I was too young, inexperienced, disillusioned. And there you were, a living and continuous reminder of what, try as I might, I couldn't forget. I'm afraid that in a hundred little ways, some perhaps not so little, I made you suffer for it."

She rested her head for a moment against Veronica's. "I woke up finally to the enormity of what I was doing, and realized that I simply had to pull myself together and be the heroine I had till then merely fancied myself as being. I had to forget the past. I had to forgive. I had somehow to make myself accept the consequences not only of Charles' and Fran's action, but of my own. I'd taken you on, and I was falling down on my job. I can't tell you when, or at what point in the next few years I finally reached a stage when I found myself really loving you and wanting you. I think perhaps it must have been about the time that Nick was born, and I realized at last that I was a mother, not just some sort of foster-parent or glorified nurse. I buried the past, then. It was never mentioned by Charles or Fran or me or by anyone. Words have a way of giving life and substance to things, and by keeping silent I felt that I had buried the truth about your parentage as far as Fran was concerned. But by that time I'd made too many mistakes . . . mistakes of hysteria, jealousy, resentment, pain, and they bore fruit in your feelings for me. I realized then that I had asked for it, and that there was nothing for me to do except grin and bear it as best I could."

Veronica said hesitatingly: "There is something . . . don't tell me if you'd rather not. But I've often wondered. Lots of people liked you who didn't seem to care especially for Charles, and there was a man called Kingsley Bates. The man I found you with that afternoon when Charles was killed and I came home unexpectedly. He loved you, didn't he?"

"For a little while, yes. We had an affair. It was after Nick's birth and I'd come to the end of any illusions I might have had about Charles and myself. I felt the need of distraction. Perhaps in a way it was my method of avenging myself for what Charles had done to me."

"And since then?" Veronica asked her with a shamed little smile.

"Since then has there been anyone else? No. It's been something of a desert, if you want to know. Until Donald showed up." She laughed on a sudden, unexpected note of gaiety. "Poor Donald. . . ."

Then, quickly: "Nonny, tell me, what difference is this going to make in your relations with Fran?"

"I don't know. I haven't come to that, yet. I've always been fond of her, sorry for her. And I can't see why it should make much difference." She added breathlessly: "I've always thought of you as my mother."

She rose. "Shouldn't we go and see what's going on in the kitchen? Might make it less embarrassing for them . . ."

Delia walked with her to the door, then held her back. "Nonny, one thing. What about Chris?"

"He wants to marry me."

"And you, do you want to marry him?"

"I don't know. What do you think?"

"Oh my dear, it's for you to say!"

Veronica shook her head. "I don't know. I would like . . . I mean I don't want to end like Fran . . . I want to love."

Without warning she was in Delia's arms, thickly, hopelessly sobbing, and for a long time Delia held her, waiting for the paroxysm to pass. Then she said: "Things are never going to be easy for you, Veronica. Your life will always be at the mercy of your imagination. But I wish it could be happy."

Then, freed suddenly from the matrix of deadened hopes, she cried:

"I would do anything—anything, to help you be happy!"

Veronica found a handkerchief and blew her nose. "Yes," she whispered. "Yes, I know you would."

CHAPTER

XXXVII

In one way and another, none of which they were to remember very clearly afterwards, they got through the remainder of that evening, and even succeeded in imparting to it something of the form, if not the spirit, of a normality which had existed before the arrival of Fran. But to be maintained, such tension must exert an equal strain between its points, and the point centered in Fran had, a few minutes after dinner, snapped with an almost audible sound of breakage. Scattering a few disjointed words of apology, she took herself upstairs to the room which Nick surrendered to her for the night, his own plan being to sleep aboard the yacht.

"Isn't it too thick outdoors for that?" Delia asked, but Donald reassured her. The boat was no great distance off and they would make sure of Nick's being snug aboard before turning in themselves. He had sensed in the boy what he felt himself—this instinctive desire to retreat from an over-extended participation, into solitude and the dark.

"I'll give you a hand with the dinghy," Chris said. "Coming, Veronica?"

Delia stood in the doorway with Donald and they listened to the voices on the shore below, and to the click of rowlocks as Nick pulled towards the yacht, the powerful beam of Chris's flashlight pursuing him into the fog.

Then Delia said: "I've decided not to wait over, Donald. I couldn't, with Fran, and since flights will probably be cancelled because of the weather, I think I'll start driving back with her in the morning."

He kissed her. "Just as you like."

"I haven't the heart to rob the children of their last few days here with you. May they stay, and you can put them on a plane or train later?"

"Need you ask?"

They were silent, listening to the receding creak of rowlocks. Then they heard the dinghy bump against the yacht and Nick's voice:

"All a-board!"

Donald turned back to the house, drawing Delia with him. She said with a slight laugh: "You know, I have an urge to do something horribly prosaic, like washing the dishes!"

"So have I. Let's do."

*   *   *

It was long after midnight when Fran finished the whisky which she had brought with her from New York, and, still dressed, opened the door of her room and made her way cautiously downstairs to the hall. A light was burning in the parlor and the door was ajar. She peered in and saw two figures curled on the rug before the fire —Chris and Veronica. The latter was asleep, her head resting on the boy's lap, but Chris was awake and stared at Fran as she appeared in the door.

"Feel like a swim," she told him in a hoarse whisper. "Go out to the boat and surprise Nick. Want to come?"

He shook his head, never dreaming that she meant it, and after a slight hesitation, swaying a little on her feet, she put her finger to her lips in a drunken gesture of connivance, and went out. In the hall she waited a moment, wondering whether she ought to waken Delia and suggest that they take a walk instead. But no.

Delia wouldn't want to do that. She'd lost Delia. She had at long last lost Delia. It was the price one paid for setting someone else free, Fran reminded herself with a feeling of enormous wisdom. Ye shall know the truth and the truth shall make you free . . .

Well, Delia had Donald Wallingford and Veronica had Chris and no doubt in time Nick too would find somebody and they would all be happy and life would settle down to its nice dull middle-class routine. Only she would be left out. As usual . . . she would be left out . . .

She yearned poetically for the smell and the feel of the fog and the fresh darkness of night. Carrying the half-filled glass of whisky she'd brought downstairs with her, she let herself out of the front door, closing it carefully behind her, testing the rough ground outside with cunning feet. The fog moved before her and seemed to lure her like a promise of extended arms. The house vanished, swallowed in the great toothless maw of night. She could smell the wild roses and knew they must be somewhere, their little pink faces like children's, playing hide and seek. Like herself and Delia when they were little, growing up near Lake Umbagog and gathering the wild roses and flags that grew near their home. Delia in a blue dress, she in a pink one, and their hair done differently because although identical twins they were not supposed to look so much alike for fear of psychological complications . . . rivalries, frustrations. There must, their father had always insisted, be individuality or there was nothing.

Flowers! The scent of summer flowers and of childhood and the sound of forgotten voices. Love. Security. God. The strong arm of the night holding you to its breast, its lips on yours . . . at last. And out there in the cove Nick rocked in his cradling boat, wrapped in a caul of innocence. Nick! The one person who, like her, was alone. Nick who had always been kind to her, understanding despite his youth, chivalrous and sweet. In all this fog-bound jail of life Nick's youth shone like a star and she had a sudden yearning for its light.

Halfway between her stumbling progress from the house to the shore she stopped to take a drink from her glass, then dropped it, and after groping for some minutes in the darkness, gave up and staggered down to the sea which she could hear muttering among the rocks. Fog flowed upon her and she embraced it with rapture, feeling herself purified, reborn. No regrets now about what had taken place this afternoon, back there in the house. No regrets. She had been sober and thoughtful and in full control. And Wallingford had scorned her with his eyes and his smile . . . preferring Delia, of course. Damn him . . . She tripped and almost fell, then recovered herself. Well, truth long suppressed and vitiated by neglect had breathed the open air at last, and he had her to thank for that, not Delia! The truth had made them free . . . all of them. It had made Nick free . . . kissing her goodnight earlier in the evening he'd whispered in her ear:

"Let's go on another binge in New York when we get back!"

He'd said it to comfort her, to cheer her up, to let her know that nothing really mattered, that he still loved her and trusted her when all the others . . .

She was among rocks now, great slippery weed-covered rocks, and there was the water hissing and murmuring in the darkness and she felt it pouring into her shoes. She hesitated, swaying, and stared into the density. The riding lights of the yacht moored a hundred yards off in the cove glimmered a moment. "Nick!" Fran called, and her voice was caught and thrust back into her throat by the gray, furred paw of the fog. "Nick!"

She would swim out to the boat and see him. It was no distance. She'd noticed it when she came in the taxi this afternoon. And she loved to swim. The cleanness of it, the harsh purity of salt water against your flesh, scouring you to the bone, to the marrow. Clean and absolved, she could face life again. Why not? Nothing was finished until you were dead. And the sea would bring her a new life.

Fran waded out and felt the water wash against her knees, cold, cold, yet casting its spell of purity upon her being, her spirit. After a few strokes in that bitter stream she came to herself and peered through the darkness for a glimpse of the boat and its light. There was nothing—nothing except fog. Turning, she started back towards the shore, her body paralyzed with cold. The shore receded as the boat had done and the swelling tide cast her back and broke over her head and she sank a moment, her feet searching for an expected firmness of rock, but there was none. She struck out again, and again the sea flung her back and now she could no longer feel her own body. It was lost—gone, leaving her destitute indeed. A cry burst from her as she made one last lunge towards the shore.

"I can't make it," she announced then, suddenly, and without surprise. It was the first moment of clarity she'd had in a long time, and it was to be the last; then the fog and the sea closed over her for keeps.

On the boat, Nick tried to concentrate on Veronica's novel, which he'd spirited away without anyone's noticing. He'd helped himself to a can of beer from the little icebox in the galley, and now lay stretched comfortably in his bunk, smoking a cigarette. Thoughts of Linda kept intruding on his efforts to stick with the book, and when he stopped reading for a minute and reflected on the events of the past evening, there was Linda again—the smell of her hair, the color of her eyes, the sound of her laugh. He would see her tomorrow. They would spend the whole day together . . . that was all he could think of, all that mattered.

It was very late and the beer made him sleepy, but he wanted to stay awake and think of Linda. Veronica's book slipped off the edge of the bunk and fell to the floor, and at last he reached up a hand and put out the light in its gimbal above his head. He lay with the feeling of the sea under him, languid and friendly, and with the smell of the sea and the fog seeping in through the partially open hatch. Linda came very close to him in the darkness and he murmured aloud: "She must be thinking about me. Right now, at this moment, she must be thinking about me."

A luminous moment held them fast, then he slept.